THE PERFECT GAME SERIES

samantha christy

Books Publishing Group

Saint Augustine, FL 32092

Cover designed by Letitia Hasser | RBA Designs

Cover model photo by WANDER AGUIAR

Cover model – Christoph L.

ISBN-13: 978-1986756105
ISBN-10: 1986756106

For Jeannie.
You were the first person to ever lay eyes on my books.
Thank you for giving me the courage to go forth.

Samantha Christy

Benching

BRADY

THE PERFECT GAME SERIES

Samantha Christy

Part One

Brady

Samantha Christy

Chapter One

Don't think about it.

Do. Not. Think. About. It.

Fuck.

The funny thing about trying not to think about something is that it inevitably becomes the one thing you *do* think about.

I step off the mound and look at Caden, who is my catcher behind the plate. He nods at me. He gets it. He's one of the few people who does. He's also the only person I'll let talk to me when there is even the slightest possibility of a no-hitter, let alone a perfect game. Of course he's the only person. He's my catcher. We might as well be married with as much time as we spend together – on the field and off. And, both on the field and off, he's the only person who can talk me down or pick me up, depending on the need.

I glance up at the scoreboard. Seventh inning. This is when the absolute improbability of either a no-hitter or a perfect game starts turning into a remote possibility.

I pitched a no-hitter two years ago, and that alone is incredible. But a perfect game – a game in which there are no runs, hits, walks or errors – that is the Holy Fucking Grail of baseball. Only a handful of major league pitchers have ever thrown one.

I look back at my catcher who is raising a scolding brow at me from under his facemask. I don't need to see it to know he's doing it. I know it's there. And in all fairness, he *should* be raising a brow at me. I'm going to completely screw this up if I overthink the game.

Don't think. Just throw. Caden gives me a good target every time. Just play catch with the catcher. Don't even think about the batter. Get your sign and do your job.

I glance around at the crowd. Forty-thousand strong today. Saturdays always draw the best attendance. There are a few girls holding up signs behind the dugout declaring their love for me.

It doesn't help. They are only saying that because I'm a bad-ass pitcher. It does nothing to get my head out of the game. Why can't one of them hold up a sign with a joke on it or something?

I close my eyes and count backwards from five. I clear my head as best I can. I step back on the mound and look at Caden for the sign. Breaking ball. It's his go-to call when things are getting hairy.

I wind up for the pitch and release it down the left side, watching the way it curves across the midline and ends up on the inside right corner of the plate. That's why batters hate lefty pitchers – we practically graze the hair on their sacs with our curve balls.

The ump pulls his right arm across his body, and in a short, sharp motion, makes a fist next to his head as he calls the guy out.

The fans go crazy as we go back to the dugout.

I get a few pats on the back. But no one speaks to me. No one but Caden. My other teammates barely even look at me. It's bad juju and nobody wants to jinx it.

"Murphy wanted me to invite you for dinner. She's making pot roast."

I laugh. That's what I like about Caden, he reads me like a damn book and always knows what to say.

"Your fiancée's pot roast is amazing. So, hell yes." I put my jacket on to keep my arm warm on this cool fall day.

Caden puts on his batting helmet and heads out of the dugout. It's then that I notice there is a larger buffer around me than usual. In the dugout, we all seem to have our assigned spaces. Baseball is a game with a lot of superstition. We sit in the same spot every time. But today that is not the case. I've been given a wide berth like a force field is around me that people are afraid to penetrate. And when I get up to stand at the railing to watch Caden at bat, it's like the parting of the Red Sea. I shake my head and laugh quietly.

I watch as Caden's hit brings in Conner, adding yet another RBI to his growing number. But then they double-up on Spencer, getting him out at first and Caden out at second, ending the first half of the eighth inning.

Spencer comes back into the dugout, throwing his helmet against the far wall. Caden offers him a few words of encouragement while putting on his catcher's gear. Then Caden turns his focus to me as I remove my jacket and loosen up my arm.

"Let's do this," he says, giving me a chin up.

It's what we say to each other every time we take the field together. Nothing is different about this game and it's his way of telling me that.

I make my way to the mound, careful not to step on the foul line.

I throw my warm-up pitches and I can tell the crowd is feeling the excitement. They all want it. They want a perfect game. And I want to give it to them more than anything I've ever wanted in my life.

Well, almost anything. I frown and shake the bad thoughts away.

With each strike I throw, the crowd gets increasingly boisterous. They are all on their feet and the stadium has come alive.

The second batter of the inning comes up. I clear my head and step up to throw a fastball that gets fouled into left field. Conner runs over and catches it, getting the batter out to the collective cheers of the stadium. The fans want this to happen as much as I do.

Who am I kidding? *Nobody* wants this as much as I do.

I start counting them – four batters left. Twelve more strikes to glory.

Stop it!

Again, I step off the mound and take a breath. Caden walks toward me with a shit-eating grin on his face.

"We leave for Chicago tomorrow," he says.

"Yeah," I say, wondering why the hell he called time to come tell me the obvious.

"Tanya's in Chicago, isn't she?"

I can't help it when the sides of my mouth curve up into a smug smile.

"What's your record with her?" he asks.

"Five."

"Damn, Brady, even I haven't been able to give a woman five orgasms in one night." He holds out his glove for me to tap with mine. Then he turns and walks back behind the plate, never having said one thing baseball related.

I shake my head at his unconventional ways. And I think about all the things I can do to break that record tomorrow night as I strike out the third batter of the inning.

Caden smiles at me as we walk back to the dugout. He knows Tanya doesn't mean anything to me. None of them do. Not really. They are just something fun to take my mind off things when I visit each city. It took me a while, but I finally did it. I finally have one girl in each city where we play ball. Well, except New York and Tampa where I spend most of my time. It's not like I have thirty girlfriends or anything. They all know the score. I've told all of them not to expect my loyalty, my sincerity, and most definitely not my heart. All those things died five years ago.

We take our seats in the usual places as Sawyer gets ready to go to bat.

"Put one out there, Mills," I say.

He pats his chest right over his heart. "For you, dude."

All eyes turn to Sawyer, mouths agape that someone other than Caden would speak to me at such a critical time. But what the hell do they expect when I spoke to him first?

"Fuck you," Sawyer says to all of them before leaving the dugout.

A few empty cups and a can of chew get thrown at him before he makes his escape, and we all hear him mumble, "Prima donna pitchers and their stupid rules."

I laugh. Sawyer Mills is one of my best friends, along with Caden, and he's the least likely to put up with my shit. But the thing is, he's as superstitious as the rest of us, and I really think he only spoke to me out of respect. *Damn* – did I just put a hex on the whole thing?

I step to the railing and watch him do exactly what I told him to, putting one deep into the left-field stands. I turn to watch

5

Caden cringe, something he's done ever since he hit a fan with a home run ball. The fan who is now his fiancée. But when he sees on the JumboTron that nobody was hit and the man who caught the ball gave it to a kid, he lets out a relieved sigh and high-fives some teammates.

When Sawyer comes back into the dugout, he doesn't say anything to me, he just points at me and smiles. We look at each other like we both know what I did, what he did. I walk over and pat him on the back. "Nice job. It's all on me."

He nods. Good. I need him to know that if I fuck this up, it has nothing to do with him responding to my comment.

I sit on the bench and try to zone out for the rest of the inning. I think of Murphy and her award-winning pot roast. She's pretty much the only female friend I have who I'm not sleeping with. And Caden would have my balls on a platter if I even looked at her the wrong way. But frankly, I no longer think of her like that. She's become more like the sister I never had.

I know she feels sorry for me. She's one of the few people who knows about my past. And even she doesn't know the whole story. After she got engaged to Caden, I think she took me on as a project. A charity case. But she's so damned nice and sincere, I don't have the heart to tell her I don't want anyone's sympathy. So I take it begrudgingly and over the past year, she's become one of my closest friends.

Murphy thinks she's going to fix me. But I'm broken beyond repair. Baseball is my life now. It's my one and only love. The one thing I can't live without.

Someone touches my shoulder. "We're up," Caden says. "Let's do this."

I take in a deep breath. Deeper than any other breath I've ever taken. I count backwards from five as I blow it out. I throw my jacket on the bench and grab my glove. I nod at Caden as we part on the field, him going one way and me going the other.

It's the ninth inning and I'm nervous as hell. Caden has already had to come out to calm me down after I struck out the first batter. I've done everything I can to stop thinking. I'm tapped out.

Two more batters. Six strikes. I'll go down in history.

Shut. The Fuck. Up.

I try to calm myself, but damn it if Jay Jarrison — the biggest, baddest, most intimidating son-of-a-bitch to ever walk up to the plate — isn't sauntering out onto the field like he knows he's going to break me.

I dig deep. I think of Tanya. I think of Crystal and Abby and Jenn and Holly. Hell, I think of me *with* Tanya, Crystal, Abby, Jenn, and Holly — at the same time. Anything to shut up the shitstorm in my head.

Strike one.

I'm shaking. Literally shaking. I can't pitch like this.

Caden gives me the sign for a fastball. He studies the hitters. He knows where their weaknesses lie. He watches hours upon hours of tape before we play each series. I trust him.

Strike two.

I step off the mound because my hand is shaking too hard to pitch. I look into the stands hoping someone, anyone will do something to distract me, but all I see are people on their feet. They want to witness history in the making. I look back at Caden. He points to me. I know what he's saying. *Let's do this.*

I shake my head at him. I know he sees me trying to hold it together. He can't keep calling time to baby me. I have to do this myself. I look up to the sky and think of the one thing I never think of when I play ball.

I think of Natalie and Keeton.

By the time I count backwards from five, I'm calmer. Caden gives me the sign for a breaking ball. He wants to end this and get the guy out. He wants to wipe the smug smile off his big hairy face. I wind up, release the pitch and watch it all the way to the plate. This is it, this is the one.

But then I hear a crack – the distinct sound of wooden bat on ball – and before I can even comprehend what has happened, I hear another crack – right before I hit the ground, pain searing through my arm from my elbow to my fingertips as I see the baseball slowly roll away from me.

Damn it, it burns. My elbow feels like I hit my funny bone times a thousand. And along with the excruciating pain, numbness is working its way down my forearm, right to my fingers.

I look up to see the end of the play. Caden must have run up and gotten the ball before throwing it to first base, narrowly missing the runner as the guy steps on the bag, beating the throw. The stadium erupts in audible displeasure. Then Caden helps me up and off the field as Cole comes out to relieve me.

Caden shakes his head as we walk off the field to where the athletic trainers and team physician are waiting to examine me. "Nothing you could do about that one, man. It was the perfect pitch, Brady. No way is that ball getting hit more than one in a hundred times. It's not your fault."

I look over at him, pissed at myself for letting Jarrison get the best of me. Pissed at myself for not getting out of the damn way. Pissed at myself for thinking of *them*. It *is* my fault. It's *always* been my fault.

I stare down at my left arm – my pitching arm – as I hold it in my right hand, knowing that not only did I lose my perfect game, I might have just lost my whole fucking career.

8

Chapter Two

Her hand feels so soft in mine. It fits perfectly. I give her a squeeze. My eyelids are heavy, but it doesn't matter. I don't need to see her. Just knowing she's here with me, touching me – is everything. God, I've missed this.

I hear myself moan in pain. "It's okay, Brady," she says, lovingly. "Everything is going to be fine."

Brady? Natalie always calls me *babe*. I try to open my eyes, but I can't. My arm hurts and I'm confused.

"Nat?" I say, squeezing her hand again as I feel myself falling into a haze.

Natalie comes up behind me, jumping onto my back, wrapping her long athletic legs around me.

"Today is the day, babe!" she squeals excitedly. "The final game in the College World Series. You made it all the way. One more game and you'll be a champion."

I crank my head around so I can see her. "I'm not a champion yet?" I tease.

"You've always been a champion to me, but now the world will see you as one, too." She punctuates her words with a kiss on my cheek.

"If we win," I remind her.

"Oh, please. You'll win. The University of Nebraska has the best baseball team and everyone knows it. I'm just so glad the World Series is in Omaha and we don't have to travel with Keet."

She slides down my back and puts her feet on the floor just as our three-year-old son comes running through the apartment swinging a plastic bat. My instinct is always to tell him not to do that. But I'm a ball player, so it would be kind of hypocritical of me. Plus, I'm hoping he'll follow in his old man's footsteps.

"Are you sure your sister is okay with keeping him for the entire day? If we win, there will be all kinds of celebrations."

"When you win, babe." She grabs Keeton's bat before he swings it into the television. "And Katie loves watching Keeton. All she has to do today is study for her summer class. She can call me if she needs me and I can be home in forty-five minutes. You could ride the bus back if you had to."

I laugh when Keeton pouts for a second at the loss of the bat, but then he runs in the other room to grab his tiny glove and kid-friendly baseball.

"I'm glad Katie decided to enroll here," I say. "She's been a huge help."

"She has." Natalie swats my behind. "Now get your stuff, you have to be at the bus in thirty minutes. We'll walk you out. I have to pick up some snacks at the store for Keeton. I'll drive up in a few hours and be there in plenty of time for the first pitch. And don't showboat too much, it messes up your fastball. I know all the scouts will be there, but you have nothing to prove. By this time next week, I guarantee you'll have gone in the first round of the draft."

I can only dare to dream she's right. "You're a little biased, don't you think?" I pull her into my arms, leaning down to savor one last kiss before we walk out. Then I ruffle Keet's hair. "Don't drive Mommy crazy, champ. And have fun with Aunt Katie."

"Yay!" he screams, throwing his ball in the air and then catching it in his glove. That's my boy.

Nat grabs her purse and picks up Keeton. She heads out to the car to put him in his seat. "Don't forget the shirt," she says to me from the sidewalk.

"Never." I head out the door, grabbing my bag with my lucky shirt already tucked inside. I'm smiling from ear-to-ear as I shut the door. The next time I walk through this door, everything will be different.

"Love you, babe!" Natalie calls out to me.

"Love you more!" I yell back, walking in the other direction.

We live in married student housing right on campus, which luckily is only a ten-minute walk to the stadium since we only have one car between us. We've lived here ever since the little white stick foretold our future and we went to the courthouse in downtown Lincoln. Having Keeton may have moved things up a few years, but we knew when we were sixteen that we'd always be together. I find I'm practically skipping the entire way to the bus. This is it. I graduated last week. And next week, we'll find out where we're going. I don't even care who picks me. I just want to play ball and have Nat and Keet by my side.

I trip on the sidewalk and fall down, pain searing through my arm as a haze comes over me.

"Brady, are you in pain?" Natalie asks.

Again with the *Brady*. I open my eyes successfully this time to see the ceiling lined with fluorescent lights. I'm disoriented as I turn my head and look around the large room. There are many beds, machines making noises, and a lot of people in green scrubs moving about. I look at Natalie, confused because it's not Natalie.

Then it hits me and I relive it all over again in the span of five seconds.

Natalie's gone. Keeton's gone. My elbow is broken and my season, if not my career, is over.

Murphy looks at me with sympathetic eyes. She always looks at me this way, but I might have called her Natalie just now, so she looks even more pained than usual over my tragic past. She has an inkling of what happened but has never been told the details. Nobody has.

I sigh, wishing I could go back into the dream. Back to the day that was supposed to be the most perfect day of my life but turned out to be the worst imaginable. Fate has a way of fucking you over when you least expect it. And the fact that I helped it along is just another nail in their coffins.

The nurse raises the head of my bed and offers me a sip of water. "The doctor will be by to check on you soon."

I take a small drink that makes my sore throat feel a hundred times better. "Thanks," I tell her.

"Shit," I say to Murphy when the nurse walks away. "I forgot what happened for a little while." I look down at my arm that is immobilized. My elbow hurts, but what really bothers me is that I can still feel a burning, numbing sensation down around my fingers.

"They told me you'd be out of it when you started to come around."

"How's the game going?" I ask, needing to change the subject away from all the questions lurking in her head. I'm sure she knows exactly what the score is as my team, the New York Nighthawks, plays the Chicago Cubs. In fact, I'll bet she was watching it on her phone while she was sitting by my bed waiting for me to wake up.

"Four to three, bottom of the fourth."

I nod, pleased that my team is winning. "Caden score?"

She smiles. "Had a double down the third base line. Sawyer drove him in and then stole his way around the bases."

"Nice. He steal home?"

"Yup."

"Sweet."

Sawyer is our shortstop who also holds the league record for stolen bases for two years running. He's smaller than Caden and me, but he's freaking scrappy. He gets to the ball fast, and he runs like the wind.

"How are we doing, Mr. Taylor?" Dr. Sorenson asks, coming to stand next to me.

He's the orthopedic surgeon who works on a lot of athletes not only from the Nighthawks, but also from all the professional sports teams in the New York area.

"My fingers are numb and they burn."

He nods, squeezing one of my fingers at the nail between a few of his. "The hope is, once the swelling from your injury subsides, you will regain the feeling in your fingers. But I have to be honest with you and reiterate that based on your symptoms prior to surgery, I feel you have significant nerve damage. With that comes intense pain and numbness down the thumb side of your forearm and into the first two or three digits."

My head falls back against the pillow as I listen to the worst news an MLB pitcher will ever hear.

The doctor picks up my chart and looks it over. "The surgery on your elbow went well. We put in one pin and I would expect a full recovery where that is concerned. But as I said yesterday, your nerve was damaged from the contact of the fast-moving ball and there is just no telling when or if you will regain complete function. If you haven't made a lot of progress in three months or so, we can consider nerve transposition surgery, but let's not get ahead of ourselves. Nerve issues have been known to correct themselves over the period of a few weeks or months."

"Or never," I add, sullenly.

13

He looks at me with an empathetic smile. "It's a wait-and-see game, Brady. Don't go jumping to conclusions."

I close my eyes and absorb his words again. I heard them yesterday. Those and more. I know the drill. I'll be put on the disabled list and most likely sent to our spring training complex for intense rehab.

"But you're not very optimistic, are you?" I ask. "You've seen these types of injuries before with all the athletes you work on. Give it to me straight. What are the chances I'll pitch again? I need to know."

"Pitch, or pitch at the level you were two days ago?"

"Come on, doc. You know anything less than how I was would be catastrophic for me."

Dr. Sorenson mulls over my chart again. I feel like he's stalling. I glance at Murphy and I can tell she's thinking the same thing because she widens her eyes and moves them quickly in his direction and back.

He sighs and I feel like I've been stabbed in the chest. "Best guess — twenty percent chance. Maybe thirty. But I'm always conservative in my prognosis predictions, so please keep that in mind. I'd rather have you singing my praises than signing my death warrant." He laughs at his attempt at a joke.

"I appreciate your honesty," I tell him before he walks away.

I'm trying to hold it together when Murphy reaches over to take my hand. "How many kids grow up to be major league pitchers?"

I look sideways at her random question.

"How many?" she asks again.

I shrug and then scold myself when pain shoots down my left arm. "I don't know, like point one of one percent?"

She shakes her head. "Less," she says. "There are what, thirty MLB teams? And each team carries approximately five starting pitchers. That's one hundred and fifty major league pitchers. And how many males are in the United States?"

She takes out her phone and Googles it. "About a hundred and fifty million." Then she taps on the calculator. "That means of all the men in the country, and we're not even including all the foreigners who come and play, the typical male has a 0.000001 chance of becoming a major league pitcher. That is one in a million, or a millionth of a percent, right?"

I laugh at her not quite genius-level math skills.

"Shut up," she says. "You know what I mean. What I'm trying to say is that you accomplished something that a million other people couldn't do, and you're going to let Dr. Sorenson giving you a twenty-to-thirty percent chance bring you down? If little boys were told they had those kinds of odds of becoming a starting pitcher for the New York Nighthawks, they'd be over the moon."

I can't help the smile that overtakes my face. "Caden is always telling me you're a glass-half-full girl. I think I like that about you, Murphy." She is the most optimistic person I've ever met. It has me thinking about something. "I've been meaning to ask you, when's the trial?"

Murphy was wronged in a major way by her ex-boyfriend. And now both Murphy and Caden have to testify to put the guy behind bars. He's been charged with something like four felonies and five thousand misdemeanors. *Five thousand.* The guy should get far more time than he's looking at, which is two to five years based on what the prosecutor says.

"The scumbag's lawyer has already gotten two postponements, something about his client being too sick for trial.

Tony is scamming him like he scams everyone. But his day will come and Karma will eat him alive."

"I can't wait to see it happen," I tell her.

An orderly comes by to take me back to my room.

"Go home, Murphy. I really appreciate you being here for me when the guys are gone. Go watch the rest of the game. I'm probably going to sleep all evening anyway."

She puts her bag over her shoulder. "Okay, but I'm coming back tomorrow to take you home. And then I'm going to help you pack for Tampa."

"It's not like I don't pack for Tampa every spring, you know."

She motions to my arm. "Not one-handed you don't."

"Shit."

I'm not used to being so fucking useless.

She walks over and puts her hand on my shoulder. She looks down at me with a motherly expression, although I'm a good three years older than she is. "Take it from another person who thought her life was destroyed by a baseball – things will get better. Who knows what the future will hold, Brady."

I nod. I don't bother saying this is different. I don't bother saying her injury wasn't as critical as mine. I don't say it because that would make me an asshole. But I think it. Because I'm an asshole.

She turns to head out. "They said you'll probably be released around 2:00 PM. I'll see you then. Take it easy, okay?"

"Will do. Thanks, Murphy."

They wheel me back to my room and I immediately turn on the TV and find the game. I watch it, of course, but what I really want to do is go back to sleep and be with Natalie and Keeton.

Chapter Three

I walk through the training complex – something I've done numerous times before – and mourn the fact that I'm not here to play ball.

Normally, when we come here, it's after a three-month hiatus. When we walk through the front gate, elation washes over us at the thought of getting back into the game. But now, I just shake my head and hope that come next spring, I'll be one of the players making this walk.

Five months. I have five months to regain the use of my arm and hand. I guess I was lucky to get injured late in the season instead of early on. *Lucky.* Yeah, not a word I'd use to describe my life in the least.

I hear some commotion beyond the fence to my left and go over to peek through one of the slats. The Hawks' single-A minor league team is practicing on the complex field. My heart hurts – actually hurts – knowing I can't be out there. And even if my elbow and nerve damage heal, who knows if I'll ever be able to pitch like I did before. I've seen plenty of guys with injuries less severe than mine come back from rehab only to be different players. A lot of them end up being released from the team.

I'm not worried about that yet, however. They can't release an injured player.

I back away from the fence to stop torturing myself and continue my walk through the complex. I get stopped by a few people. Most of the organization knows me by sight. I paste on a smile as they wish me well.

I open one of the double doors that leads to the physical therapy building and curse loudly when it touches my injured elbow. I can't even open a fucking door properly.

"Can I help you?" a woman calls out from a desk in the corner, clearly perturbed at my choice of words.

I shrug an apology with my right shoulder as I make my approach. "I'm Brady Taylor. I have an appointment."

She looks at her computer. "Yes, of course. We already have all your information. Please have a seat over there and Rylee will be with you shortly."

I walk over to the drab brown couch and sit down carefully so as not to jostle my arm. I look around. It's not as if I've never been here before. I've been here for five years in a row, ever since I was drafted by the Hawks and quickly moved up through the ranks. We all go through some sort of rehab during spring training so I'm no stranger to this place.

Rylee. I try to think of who he or she is. I've met most of the athletic training and PT staff, but the name is not familiar.

A door opens and a petite brunette walks through. "Mr. Taylor, I'm Rylee Kennedy, your physical therapist."

She offers me her hand as I stand up. I shake it, noting how small it is and I wonder how this tiny person is going to work on a big athlete such as myself. "Uh, nice to meet you, Rylee."

She sees me assessing her and laughs. "Don't let my size fool you, Mr. Taylor, I may not be able to carry your weight, but I sure as hell can help get you back in tip-top shape."

I like her already. She's spunky. And direct.

"It's Brady," I tell her. "And I'm not sure anyone can get me back in tip-top shape."

She motions toward the door and I hold it open for her as we walk through.

"I've read your file. I'm aware of your injuries. And I've worked on a lot of players with nerve damage before. Don't worry, I've got your back." She smiles at me reassuringly. "Let's go into the room on the right for your evaluation."

As she goes through my chart and tells me what to expect over the next few weeks and months, I realize Rylee is stunning. Petite and athletic looking, I wouldn't be surprised if she had been a cheerleader or a gymnast back in college. Although her hair is in a ponytail, I can see that it's very long with loose waves at the ends. For a second, I allow myself to imagine pulling the hair tie out and letting her long locks flow over my naked body as she tugs on my dick.

Then the reality of why I'm here hits me once again and I realize that nobody is going to be tugging on my dick except me for quite a while. I won't even be able to fuck properly with only one arm.

"Are you getting all this, Brady?" she asks with a scolding furrow of her brow.

Damn, she caught me daydreaming. Why do I get the feeling this woman is going to put me through my paces?

"Yeah, uh … start small and easy with the fingers and wrist. No elbow work for two weeks."

She tries to suppress her smile. "So you *were* listening?"

19

I laugh at her calling me out. "I'm a fantastic multi-tasker, Rylee."

She rolls her eyes at me before asking about my pain level. Then she positions my uninjured arm several different ways and takes measurements. Then she tests the strength of both my hands by having me squeeze her hands.

She stares me down. "Don't hold back on me, Brady," she says, nodding to my right hand. "I can take it. I need to have a good baseline on both your hands and arms, not just your injured one."

I squeeze harder with my good hand, but I still hold back a bit. She's just so small.

"If you underestimate me, it will only hurt your recovery."

I give her all I've got, squeezing hard with my right hand and not being able to squeeze much at all with my left.

"That-a-boy," she says, finally accepting that I tried my best. But I don't miss how she has to shake her hand out and flex it a bit and it makes me feel bad.

My eyes automatically drift to the ring finger of her left hand, noticing how it's free of matrimonial hardware. Not that it matters much, but it reduces the likelihood of hassles. I hate hassles.

She must follow the movement of my eyes because she quickly uses the hand to close her laptop before she gets up and opens the door. "Let's get started then."

She leads me out into the main PT room that looks somewhat like a weight room. One of the walls is lined with training tables for patients to lie on. In the middle of the room, there are all kinds of machines including treadmills, stair climbers, and shoulder presses. There are weights and rubber balls of all sizes. There is a wall with carabiners attached to bands of different colors. There are pulleys and levers and switches. You name it, if it exists in the world of rehab, they have it in this state-of-the-art facility. It's why they send us here.

We do have a rehab facility back home with most of this stuff, but it's smaller and is for minor injury rehab and day-to-day stuff. As pitchers, we basically rehab every day that we play. But here, they rehab all four Hawks teams, from the single-A team that is based here in Tampa, to the double-and-triple-A teams in Tucson and Las Vegas. Basically, if you've been sent here for rehab, it's mission critical. If you've been sent here, all bets are off.

If you've been sent here, the odds of getting back in the game are reduced dramatically.

And everyone knows it.

Including Rylee Kennedy.

She directs me to sit in a chair and she pulls up a rolling stool next to me. I look around the room and see a few other people. A guy who looks familiar from when I was here for spring training is working on someone. And a young woman, probably a PT intern or an athletic trainer, is observing them.

Rylee hands me a squishy stress ball and asks me to squeeze it, watching me closely as I wince when I do.

"Does that hurt your elbow or your hand?"

"Both, but mostly my hand."

"Your elbow pain will decrease a lot this week and next. And while some nerve pain could be present until it regenerates, it will subside – although numbness, tingling and a burning sensation will persist."

"Wonderful," I say, squeezing the ball with less intensity than a goddamn baby.

She hands me a resistance hand grip – a device that looks like an oversized clothespin. "Try this."

As a pitcher, I'm no stranger to this exercise. Some guys will sit around and squeeze these to strengthen their hands whenever they watch television. I take it knowing I won't even be able to get it to budge.

She covers my injured hand with hers when she takes it back from me. "It's okay. You'll get there. This is only day one. I don't expect you to be able to do all these things."

She has me flex and extend my wrist which are both very hard to do to any degree. Then after a few more failed attempts at other exercises, she hooks me up to a TENS unit. I'm no stranger to this, either, and she doesn't have to explain that its purpose is to deliver electrical stimulation above and below the injury to help reduce my pain.

"We'll do ten minutes today," she says, opening her laptop to record some notes as the intensity of the stimulation increases to a certain point and then works back down before starting again.

"Are you writing in there that I grip like a girl?"

She laughs. "Don't flatter yourself, Brady."

I laugh with her, enjoying her smart-assery while at the same time trying to hide the true depth of my emotional pain.

"I know we didn't do much today. It will be like that for a few days, but if you want manual therapy, we can do that after the TENS."

I raise an eyebrow at her suggestively. *Manual therapy* – it just sounds so filthy.

She rolls her eyes, obviously reading my dirty mind. "*Massage*, Taylor."

I don't let my eyebrows fall.

"Oh, my God, do you want a damn shoulder rub or not?" she asks.

I laugh again. "Yes, Rylee Kennedy, I'd love a shoulder rub."

Chapter Four

The hotel I'm staying in is only a few miles from the training complex. It's the same one we use when we come in the spring. I'm in a suite with a small kitchen since I'll be here for Lord knows how long, but at least six to eight weeks. Maybe longer.

I'm the only one from my team who is here now. While that is a good thing for the team – it's not so good for me. Dylan Buckley, one of our outfielders, was down here for a few months recently after breaking his arm running into the wall while trying to catch a fly ball. Shattered his forearm in three places. He just got back to New York two weeks ago. He seems good to go and he played well last week, but in all honesty, the throwing arm of an outfielder is not as finely tuned as the pitching arm of a starting pitcher.

There are a few other players from the double-and-triple-A teams here in rehab, and of course the entire single-A team pretty much lives here. I'm sure I could find a few of them to hang out with, but it won't be the same.

I pull on a pair of sweats and very carefully remove my arm from the sling and slip it through the arm of a t-shirt. I guess the best part of being in Florida in October is that it's pretty nice down here. It's still beach weather and it never gets too cold, even in the winter. And with nothing to do most hours of the day, I plan on hitting the beach for some bikini-watching.

Tampa is the one place we visit where I don't have a girl. This was intentional as we are here for long periods of time each spring and I didn't want the hassle of dealing with the same girl for that long. I like it better when we're in and out of a city in a few days and then we may not go back for months. No hassles. And it's not enough time for one of them to get attached to me. The last thing I need is for someone to fall for me and to think there is a chance in hell I could ever return those sorts of feelings.

My phone pings, alerting me that my ride is here. Normally I'd run to the complex to get in some exercise, but I'm not allowed to jar the arm for a while, let alone the fact that it hurts like a bitch when it gets bounced around.

I make my way down the elevator and through the lobby. When I get in the car, the driver's eyes go wide. "You're Brady Taylor," he says.

"It appears so."

He looks at my sling. "Ah, man – tough break. How long will you be out?"

I shrug. "Few months maybe."

We've been told not to discuss our injuries outside of the organization. Jason, the team owner, would kick my ass if I said anything to anyone that would lead them to believe I have anything more than a simple break.

"Damn, the rest of the season? That sucks. I'm a huge Hawks fan. I know I should be a Rays fan and all since I live here, but my cousins Stu and Sammy, they still live in Jersey, where I'm from, and they send me stuff all the time to keep me a Hawks fan." He pounds his heart. "For life, man. My name's Lenny."

"Nice to meet you, Lenny."

I get out my phone and mess with it so the driver won't try to make more conversation. But it doesn't take long to get where we're going. Although the ride is paid for, I tip him anyway. I've never been one to be tight with my money like some – okay, one – of my teammates. Caden is always saving for a rainy day. He thinks that one day he could wake up and this will all be over. I look down at my arm before I get out of the car.

Shit. Maybe he's right.

I have two years left on a five-year contract. So even if I never make it back, they still have to pay me. But what happens then?

The driver hands me his card. "I'd be glad to drive you wherever you need to go while you're here, Mr. Taylor. The fewer people who see you injured the better. Especially the bookies." He laughs. "My uncle is a bookie. But he doesn't live in Jersey, he lives in Vegas with his new squeeze, Gemma. He dumped Stu and Sammy's momma a few years ago. It's okay though, she's better off without him."

Lenny talks too much, but he has a point. I take his card. The fewer people I have to deal with, the better. If it got out that I have extensive nerve damage, it could hurt the organization. Hell, I probably shouldn't even talk to the other guys in rehab about it. They are still wet behind the ears. They don't understand what it takes and how things work at the elite level. Damn – this could be a very lonely few months.

I walk through the complex, this time not stopping to peek through the fence. I'll be here for a long time. No need to torture myself unnecessarily.

"Mr. Taylor," the receptionist greets me when I walk in. "Nice to see you again. I'll buzz Rylee and let her know you are here."

"Thank you, uh …"

"Margaret."

"Thanks, Margaret."

"My pleasure."

Ten minutes later, Rylee opens the door and lets through a guy who is wearing a leg brace and using crutches. He raises his chin at me in greeting. I silently greet him as well and then watch Rylee follow him to the main doors to help him out.

"Sorry," she says, coming back to where I'm sitting. "I was helping him get his brace back on and it was giving us trouble."

"It's no bother. It's not like I have anything better to do."

I get up and we go back to the large room where she directs me to sit on a training bed. "You'll be able to do more and more each day. And Tampa is a beautiful place. But of course, you know that since you come here every spring."

I laugh. "I know all the best drinking holes if that's what you mean."

"Seriously? You've been down here for five straight years and all you do is bar hop? Surely you've been to the aquarium, or the bay front, or Pier 60."

"Spring training isn't spring break, Rylee. We work our asses off during the day and then we let loose a little after."

She winces. "I didn't mean—"

"I know you didn't." I sigh. "Shit. I didn't mean to bite your head off." I nod to my arm. "I guess this is affecting me more than just physically."

"Injuries tend to do that to anyone, but especially athletes." She examines my fingers. "How's the pain level today?"

Man, I feel like a douchebag for snapping at her like that. Now she's all business.

"My elbow feels a bit better. I didn't have to take a pain pill this morning – just ibuprofen. The lower arm and fingers still hurt

26

and tingle like a mother, but I'm not about to get hooked on Oxy to manage it."

"That's smart. But if you really need one occasionally, it's okay not to be so tough, big guy." She smiles at me and I feel like maybe she's forgiven me for my asshole comment. "Can I send you back to the hotel with a portable TENS unit so you can use it to help manage the pain?"

"Already have one. I'm a pitcher, in case it doesn't say so in my file there."

She rolls her eyes at me. "Good. Use it as much as you need to in thirty-minute increments. You can ice the elbow if the pain is bad, but not too much, we need your blood circulating to help with healing." She carefully removes my sling. "The bruising looks good, it's fading quickly. And the swelling has gone down noticeably since yesterday."

"Yeah, I noticed that too when I was in the shower this morning."

She looks horrified. "You're taking showers?"

"Uh … yeah. Unless you want my ripe ass to reek to high heaven."

"Of course you should be bathing," she says. "But you should take baths so you can lay your arm on the side of the tub and there is no risk of a fall."

I try to imagine myself fitting in the bathtub at the hotel. I guess it's bigger than most tubs, but still. I'm 6'5" and my feet would likely stick out one end. "Believe me, Rylee, you don't want to see me try to get in a bathtub."

Her eyes go to my feet and work their way up my long body. I know she isn't doing it with any sexual intention, but seeing her eyes on me like this, especially when we're talking about bathing and shit, it's hot.

"You could take sponge baths," she says. Then she laughs at herself. "Okay, fine. Just be careful, alright? We don't need you falling and breaking your other arm."

"Yes, Mom."

She puts me through my paces, getting out squeeze balls of various density and rubber bands I'm supposed to try and stretch between my fingers. I'm disappointed that I can't seem to do squat.

After a half hour or so, she tells me, "Okay that's enough work for today. I know you can't see it, but I can – you are making small improvements, Brady. And in about a week, you'll be making larger ones, at least with the elbow anyway."

The familiar-looking guy from yesterday comes over and Rylee introduces him. "Brady Taylor, this is my boss, Alex Burke. He's the one you're not going to tell about any screw-ups I make," she jokes.

I shake his hand. "I remember you from spring training."

"Good to see you again," he says. Then he nods to my elbow. "I wish it were under different circumstances."

"You and me both."

He whispers something in Rylee's ear, making her look irritated. She shakes her head at him and then smiles at me, embarrassed.

Alex walks back across the room, but then he stares at us. At her. I don't like the way he looks at her.

She wheels over a machine and gels a small wand. "We're going to use the ultrasound today to help bring blood to the elbow and promote healing. Don't worry, I'll be careful."

"I have no doubt."

I watch as she gingerly rubs the small wand methodically in circles, taking care not to touch the area around my bandage. "Are you getting your stitches out later this week?"

I nod. "I see the facility orthopedic on Friday."

"Good. I'll be interested to see his report. Hopefully he'll give the green light to start range-of-motion exercises in about a week. Your elbow will improve rapidly after that. In fact, let's get you on the schedule next Monday to see Matt, the strength and conditioning coach. He'll want to get you started on a daily workout and conditioning routine."

"Sounds good. I'll be happy to get back to it."

There are a few awkward moments of silence. Physical therapy is normally a lot like social hour. Maybe not so much here, where I'm one of the only guys in the room during the time the A-team is practicing, but back home, after practice and games and even on the off days, you might have ten guys in the rehab room who will all be talking and joking.

But Alex has left the room and the athletic trainer from yesterday is nowhere to be found. Right now, it's just Rylee and me.

And the growing silence between us.

I look up at the television in the corner. It's tuned to ESPN, of course.

"Do you want me to turn up the volume?" she asks.

She doesn't look uncomfortable at all. Maybe she doesn't even want to talk. She does this day after day so I suppose she's used to it.

"Only if you want to. I'm fine with conversation." I shrug my right shoulder. "Or not."

She smiles brightly. Maybe she was waiting to see if *I* wanted to talk.

"So, why number three?" she asks, wanting to know why I wear that particular number on the back of my uniform.

"Because number one and two were taken," I snap at her quickly.

She laughs, but I can tell she doesn't mean it. It's like she can see through me and my lame answer. But I've practiced it enough. Nobody needs to know the real reason I chose number three when I came to play for the Nighthawks.

"I've heard about you, you know," she says, looking at me out of the corner of her eye as she watches the ultrasound wand. "Your reputation with the ladies precedes you. You're what, twenty-seven? Do you think you will ever settle down?"

"Are you always this direct?" I ask.

She shrugs. "We'll be spending a lot of time together over the next few months. Might as well get the obvious stuff out of the way."

I might not like the questions she's asking me, but I do like her style.

"I'm sick of talking about that crap, you know? People ask me all the time about my personal life. What do you say we stick to other subjects and skip the usual bullshit?"

"I get that," she says, sympathetically. "It must be hard to be in the limelight day in and day out. But if we're doing it this way, that goes for me, too. No personal details."

"Deal," I say happily.

She goes back to her task, studying my arm as she works the wand around. She chews her lip like she's thinking hard. After a few minutes of this, we lock eyes and start laughing at the growing awkwardness of our silence.

"Um ... what are we supposed to talk about then? We're going to be together every day for months."

"We can talk about plenty of things." I look around the room. "The weather?" I say, jokingly.

She laughs again and I realize how much I like hearing that sound. Rylee is a very pleasant person to be around. She's soft-spoken yet gets her point across. She's easy on the eyes. And I get the impression she'll take a backseat to no one.

"No, really. We can talk about lots of stuff. Baseball, for one. You work for the Hawks, same as me, so right there we have a lot to talk about. Like, you're pretty young to have been hired by such a premier organization. How'd you score such a great job? And how old are you?"

Her eyes scold me. "Oh, like *that's* not a personal question, asking me my age."

"Nope – that's a fair one since you already know mine."

She quietly chuckles as she wipes the remaining gel from my arm before hooking me up to the TENS.

"Fine, I'll give you that. I'm twenty-six."

"You're younger than I thought. I pegged you for twenty-seven like me. That makes your job even more impressive."

"Well, my dad was a pretty well-known orthopedic surgeon. Wait, is that too personal?"

I shake my head. "It's circumstantial so it's fine."

She smiles at my 'rules.'

"Okay, so he was a top surgeon in New York City with a lot of ties to sports organizations. I think he started talking me up to everyone he knew when I started PT school. So when the opportunity arose with the Nighthawks, even though he was gone, I took the chance and applied. I guess my last name and his legacy got me in."

She keeps referring to him in past tense and I want so badly to ask her about him, but I can't break my own rules after only five minutes.

"And you wanted to live in Florida? New York too cold for you?"

"Actually, I want to live back in New York. I have, um … ties there. But I couldn't turn down this opportunity."

She has ties back there? What ties? Friends? A boyfriend? I can't possibly ask her, but damn it if I don't want to know. I berate myself for being so fucking stupid and obtuse.

"Talented *and* smart," I say. "Good call. It's a great organization. You'll probably work here until you retire."

"That's the plan," she says. "But only if they bring me back to New York one day."

"I'm sure they will if you're as good as you told me you are yesterday."

She cocks her head. "I never told you I was good. I mean, yes, I'm good at what I do, but I don't recall bragging about it like *some* people I know tend to do whenever they are interviewed."

"Hey, I *am* good. Why not flaunt it?" I look down at my arm. "Or at least I was."

She puts a supportive hand on my shoulder. "You will be again. You have to trust in that. I am. And I wasn't bragging, Brady, I was being reassuring."

"To-may-toe, to-mah-toe," I say.

"You're impossible," she tells me.

"That's what all the women say," I tease.

"I don't doubt it." She unhooks me from the TENS. "Now, do you want manual, uh … massage, er … a shoulder rub?"

She stumbles over the words as she blushes. Yeah, she's thinking about giving me manual therapy all right. I've been thinking of nothing else for the past twenty-four hours.

I laugh. "You bet I do. Why else do you think I come to this popsicle stand?"

Chapter Five

"Class, please welcome our new student, Natalie Maddux," Mr. Sears says. "Natalie's family just moved here from Indiana. Let's be sure to make her feel welcome."

I look up from my mindless doodles to see who has the same last name as my favorite baseball player. I see what must be the sweetest-looking sixteen-year-old girl I've ever laid eyes on. She looks around the room, confident yet nervous at the same time. I will her eyes to catch mine. Look at me.

She does — only for a second — but I'm sure it's a second longer than she held anyone else's gaze.

And I know for a fact that Algebra II just got a lot more interesting.

Natalie takes an empty seat in the front of the room. I sit in the back. I always sit in the back. And it gives me forty-five whole minutes to stare at her and think of how I'm going to play this.

When the bell rings, I quickly gather my things so I can catch her on the way out. Surely she needs to be shown where her next class is. But before I reach her, Lisa Matheny corners her just outside the door.

I stand back and lean against a row of lockers, watching her as she talks to Lisa. She notices me staring and her cheeks pink up. Her eyes dance *between Lisa and me, and when Lisa says something that makes her laugh, the soft melodic harmony of the giggle makes my dick twitch.*

I take in her innocent, girl-next-door appearance. She has dirty-blonde hair that can't decide if it wants to be straight or curly. She tucks a strand of it nervously behind her ear at my perusal. Her skin is creamy and pale, outing her as a brand-new SoCal girl. I'm not close enough to see the color of her eyes yet. But I'm sure whatever shade they are will be my new favorite color.

She's gorgeous.

Indiana must be heaven, because I could swear she's an angel.

Finally, Lisa leaves and I don't miss a beat before walking up to Natalie.

"Hi," I say, holding out my hand. "I'm Brady Taylor, future MLB star and a huge fan of Indiana. And anyone with the name Maddux is destined to be a friend of mine."

She makes that glorious giggling sound again as she shakes my hand, not pulling it away after the requisite two-seconds. We both look down at our hands, then up at each other. And we just know. Before she even speaks a word to me – we know.

"I'm Natalie Taylor," she says, starting to float up into the air. "And I am an angel, Brady, don't you know that? I'm your guardian angel."

I awake with a start, cursing myself when I roll onto my left side and pain reminds me of my new reality.

I roll back over and grab the pillow next to me, pulling it tight, wishing it were Nat. Wishing Keeton was going to bound through the door at any second and work his way between us, begging us to turn on the TV so we can all watch SpongeBob SquarePants.

The day we met was one of the best days of my life. Natalie and I became inseparable after that. And when I got offered a scholarship to the University of Nebraska, she applied as well. It was going to be us against the world. No matter what.

My phone rings, giving me a welcome distraction.

I reach over and pluck it off the nightstand to see another beautiful face.

"Hi, Murphy," I say, still groggy from sleep.

"Oh, shoot. Did I wake you? Wait, it's almost ten o'clock."

"No, it's fine. I was just getting up anyway. And there's nothing better to do here. Might as well catch up on my sleep."

"You've been there for almost two weeks now, haven't you found a routine yet?" she asks, knowing most ball players are creatures of habit.

"I have. It consists of sleeping, PT, and sometimes the beach. I have to say, I'm rocking quite the tan. But it's boring as hell."

"Caden told me you aren't going out much. Why not? That doesn't sound like you. Are you depressed? It's okay if you are – understandable even, but keeping yourself holed up in your hotel room most of the day isn't going to make things better. You need to get out and have some fun."

"I'm not depressed."

Silence.

"Okay, so maybe I am a little bit. But it's no big deal, Murphy. I just miss the game. I'm fine."

"Promise me you'll try to go have a little fun. I can't stand the thought of you down there by yourself doing nothing."

"I'm not doing nothing. I'm almost caught up on *Game of Thrones.*"

She laughs. Then I hear her sigh. "Brady, please."

I roll my eyes. "Fine. I'll go out. Are you happy? How many women do you want me to go out with?"

She huffs into the phone. "I'm not asking you to bed every woman in Tampa. Just find a friend. Another guy in rehab maybe. Someone from the A-team. Anyone."

When I think of her request, why is it that Rylee's face is the first to pop into my head? We've become friends, haven't we? I mean, I've talked to her for more than an hour a day for the last two weeks. And it's amazing how much stuff there is to talk about while still not getting too personal.

She's hot, yeah. And she makes my dick jump sometimes when I get a massage, but that's nothing I have any control over.

She's always talking about fun things to do in the city. The aquarium, the trolley, the pier. Things the guys and I haven't done before because they just seem too juvenile for a bunch of grown men to do. Maybe if I promise to keep my hands off her, she'll show me some of them. I know what she thinks of me. She made it clear on that first day. And Rylee Kennedy is not anyone's Friday night gal – I could see that from the moment I met her. But just maybe she would agree to be my Friday night *friend*.

"Brady, are you still there?"

"Yeah. Sorry."

"How's the PT going?"

"Okay, I think. I still can't feel some of my fingers for shit though. But we're going to start working on my elbow rehab today."

"That's good. Any idea how long you'll have to stay?"

"I'm not sure, but at least another six weeks or so."

"You know the team will be down in a few weeks, right?"

"Can't come fast enough if you ask me."

"At least you'll have a few days with them." She pauses. "Will it bother you to see them? Are you going to go to the games? I'm sure it must be hard to watch them play."

I nod even though she can't see me. "I'm not gonna lie. It totally blows watching other guys play ball. But, yeah, I think I'll go hang out in the dugout when they are here. It certainly can't make things worse. Plus, who knows how many more opportunities I'll have to sit in there with them."

"Oh, Brady," she says in that sympathetic motherly tone.

"It's fine. Anyway, enough about me. Tell me what's going on with you."

"Sooooo ..."

I can tell she has news and I feel like a dick not asking about her sooner.

"What is it, Murphy?"

"I'm going to try my hand at modeling again."

"No shit? That's fantastic. Tell me more."

"Well, Mason, Griffin and Gavin have been working with some local designers to brand a clothing line for the gym and they've asked me to be the model."

The guys she speaks of are the owners of the gym she helps manage. Caden got her a job there when they first met because he's friends with Mason, who plays for the Giants. I'm really pleased to know she wants to try modeling again. It was her passion when she moved to New York. One that got crushed by a baseball – just like mine did.

"Knowing Mason, he doesn't do anything small and you'll be on the cover of every fitness magazine in the world."

She laughs. "I don't know about that, but I think it will be fun. Especially since Griffin will do all the photo shoots."

"Well, congratulations, girl. I'm so happy for you."

"There's more," she says.

"More?"

"Yeah. And I know you are going to have a knee-jerk reaction to this, but just hear me out. The season will be over soon, so it's perfect timing. And you'll still be rehabbing when you come back.

It'll give you something to do, maybe even something to feel good about, and the bonus is, you'll get to hang out with me."

"What are you talking about, Murphy?"

"Oh, right. Well, the guys aren't only designing clothes for women, they're designing them for men, too. So, they'll need a male model and …"

"Fuck, no."

"See – I knew you'd have that reaction."

"I'm a ball player, not a model."

"Plenty of athletes are models. Look at all the guys who model jeans and tightie-whities."

"No."

"Come on, Brady. Just think about it. We all know you don't need the money, but that's just an added bonus. And think of who you'd be working with. Griffin is one of the most awarded photographers in the world. And he's so nice – not like a lot of other photographers who are pushy and demanding. And you'll get to hang out with Mason, too, since football season will be over – well, unless they go to the Super Bowl. And there's me – I want to spend time with you. Caden gets you three-quarters of the year, this is my chance. Please? Just give it some thought."

I close my eyes and shake my head. Murphy Cavenaugh is damn hard to say no to. But a model?

I wonder if she's just asking me because she thinks I'm done in baseball. Maybe she's trying to give me a back-up profession like Caden helped give her.

"I don't know."

She squeals into the phone. "I'll take it. *I don't know* is better than *no*. And it's definitely better than *fuck no.*"

I breathe out a sigh. "*I don't know* means I don't know, Murphy. Don't read too much into it."

"Fine. They don't need an answer right now. Like I said, it will be a few months before things will start moving forward. You have plenty of time to think about it."

"Yeah, we'll see."

I can almost hear her smile through the phone. I can see why she has Caden wrapped around her little finger. Murphy is one of the most caring, empathetic, trustworthy women I've ever met. She, and the angel I woke up with this morning.

I check the time. "Hey, I have to go. I've got to be at PT in an hour."

"Okay, good luck with your elbow today. I miss you, Brady."

"Miss you too, girl."

After we hang up, I fish Lenny's card out of my wallet and tell him I won't be needing a ride today. Today, I get to walk to PT. Rylee said it was okay to start doing that now since my elbow has healed enough to be jostled around more. And right now, Rylee owns me. She controls almost everything I do. What she says goes. She's the boss.

And I find myself getting turned on just thinking about it.

Samantha Christy

Chapter Six

"I've been offered a job," I tell Rylee.

She stops moving the ultrasound wand and looks me in the eyes. "You *have* a job."

I look down at my arm that is sore as hell after today's PT. "We don't know that yet, do we? My forearm still burns. My fingers are numb and I still can't grasp anything worth a shit."

"It's been two weeks, Brady. You have to give yourself time to heal. A hundred-mile-an-hour ball hitting your arm does a lot of damage. You're expecting too much. You are progressing at an acceptable level. You should be happy with that."

"Acceptable?" I say, deplorably. "I'll never pitch again if I'm just *acceptable*. I need to be *exceptional*, Ry."

She raises a brow at me. "Ry? We're using nicknames now?"

I shrug and she giggles.

"I have every reason to believe you will be exceptional again, Bray."

I give her crazy eyes and we fall into a fit of laughter.

"Yeah, it doesn't quite work on you, does it?"

"No, it doesn't. But my driver calls me BrayTay," I tell her.

"Your *driver?*"

"The guy who drove me to and from here for the past two weeks. Lenny."

"You hired a private car?"

I can tell she disapproves.

"No. He was one of my first Uber drivers when I got down here. The guy kind of grew on me and I figured it would be easier than getting a rental and driving with one arm. So I got his card and have been using him ever since."

"Wow. He must feel like he hit the jackpot."

I laugh. "Yeah. I'm a good tipper."

"So you're stuck at the hotel without a car unless you call Lenny."

"Pretty much. But it's only a two-minute walk to the beach."

She scolds me with her eyes.

"I was careful," I say. "Plus, those restrictions are lifted now, right? When can I start running?"

"Let's give that another week or so, shall we? You're going to need all your strength to keep up with my PT."

"I don't doubt it. Has anyone ever told you you're the Queen of Pain?"

Her face breaks into a beautiful smile. "All the time."

"Can I ask you a question, Ry?"

"As long as it's not a personal one." She winks at me.

"It's not. The doc in New York gave me a twenty-to-thirty percent chance at a full recovery, yet you tell me I'll be exceptional again. Why?"

"Brady, I couldn't very well do my job if I didn't believe what I do will help people. It's true, there are some people who will never completely recover, but I have to believe in myself in order to believe in you. And you shouldn't want anyone working on you who thinks differently."

"Damn, girl."

"What?" She cocks her head to the side.

"You'd get along great with my friend, Murphy."

She puts away the ultrasound wand. "I'm not looking for a setup."

"Murphy is a woman, Rylee."

"Oh, well in that case, I'd love to meet her."

"She lives in New York. She's engaged to my best friend, Caden."

"Kessler?"

"The one and only."

She gets a sweet, dreamy look on her face. "Oh, my gosh. Is she the home run girl?"

I laugh at the nickname the sports community dubbed Murphy after she was hit by his ball.

"Yeah."

"Well then, I have to meet her. Will she be coming with Caden when you guys play the Rays?"

"I don't think so. She doesn't travel with him much. She has a great job."

She hooks me up to the TENS unit and then starts typing away in my chart. Then she looks up as if she just remembered something. "Speaking of jobs – what was the offer you got?"

I nod. "That involves Murphy, too. She wants me to be a friggin' model, can you believe that? The gym she works for is the largest in the city and the owners are developing their own brand of workout clothing. They've asked her to be the female model and me to be her male counterpart."

"Oh, wow. Is that the gym Mason Lawrence owns?"

"Yes. How'd you know?"

"You said it was the biggest. When I was in PT school, people would talk about that place all the time. Did you know they have an athletic trainer and a PT on staff?"

"I did know that. Mason is a friend. I also work out there in the off-season, so I've used all of their services."

"So it sounds like you could do the modeling in addition to your day job, no?"

"I suppose."

"Why not do it then?"

I shrug.

"Oh, you think you're too big for it. Is that why?"

"No," I pout.

"You think a big-time MLB pitcher is too good to pose in workout clothes for his friend's gym, don't you? A friend who could very well profit greatly by having you do so. And his gym will prosper, possibly creating more jobs for people and surely resulting in increases in pay for those who already work there. Do you not want Mason Lawrence to be your boss or something? Are you one of those guys who is all alpha-male and can't stand having other people tell them what to do and how to do it?"

"*You're* pretty bossy and I don't seem to have a problem with that," I tease.

"Maybe not when your livelihood depends on it," she quips.

"I don't think I'm too good to do it," I argue.

"Then do it. What do you have to lose? It will give you something to do until you are one hundred percent."

"I'll think about it."

"Good. Keeping busy is good for the mind and it actually helps injured players deal with life better."

"I'll take that into consideration."

She goes back to her typing, but talks to me as she does it. "In fact, maybe you should think about getting that rental car. Sitting around all day is not going to help your recovery. You need to get out there. See the city. Have some fun."

"Or *you* could pick me up on Friday and show me the town."

She stops typing and looks at me abhorrently. "I'm not dating an athlete, Brady. Not to mention it violates my contract to date a player."

"Ha! You can thank Sawyer Mills for that. They even amended the wording to include family members of employees after not one, but two daughters of team coaches complained about him last year. But rest assured, I'm not asking you out, Rylee. I'm just asking a friend to show me the town."

"I don't know. And you've seen the town, Brady. Lots of times."

"I've seen the inside of bars, Rylee. I've never seen Tampa through the eyes of someone who lives here. You said yourself there are lots of places to see. So show me." I narrow my eyes at her. "And, hey, what's so bad about dating an athlete?"

"Sorry," she says, looking slightly guilty to have said it the way she did. "It's just that when you work day in and day out with them, you hear a lot of stuff and you get jaded."

I try to gauge the honesty of her statement. I mean, the way she said she wouldn't date an athlete, it wasn't like she was just making an excuse not to date me specifically, it seemed more like she'd had a bad experience with one or something.

But I can't ask her. That would be too personal.

I'm beginning to regret my rules. I wonder if she'd let me re-write them to just exclude *my* personal life.

"Come on, Ry."

She chews on the inside of her cheek for a minute. "I'd have to move some things around."

"What things?" I ask.

She closes her laptop and glares at me. "What happened to no personal questions?"

Damn. Now I really want to change the rules.

"Fine," I say petulantly, wondering just what plans she needs to move around. Does she have a boyfriend here? Or is he one of those 'ties' she mentioned leaving behind in New York? "So what do you say? Assuming you can change your other plans."

She picks up her pen and points it at me. "No flirting. No kissing. No accidentally brushing against my boobs and then claiming it was because you had one too many drinks. In fact – no drinking."

I stare her down, trying not to laugh at the fact that in all my time in the majors, not once have I had a woman say words like that to me. And I have to say, it's fucking refreshing.

I laugh. "Okay, I concede to all those things. You'll do it then?"

Her lips pucker as she considers it. "Under one condition."

I raise a brow at her. "As if there aren't any already?"

She rolls her eyes. "No throwing your money around. No first-class anything. No going to the head of the line because of who you are. Just a normal night for two normal people."

"That's *three* conditions, Rylee."

"Do you want to do this or not?"

I smile at her moodiness. "You drive a hard bargain, but yes."

"No violating the rules, Brady. Don't forget that within these four walls, I own you. I'm the Queen of Pain, remember?"

I try not to laugh again because she looks damn cute when she's so demanding.

And suddenly. I can't wait for it to be Friday.

Samantha Christy

Chapter Seven

Rylee pulls up in front of the hotel driving a fairly new mid-sized SUV. As far as twenty-six-year-olds go, she's probably making more money than most. I've heard other physical therapists talk about PT school and apparently it's a bitch, so she's paid her dues and earned her way to where she is, even if her father's name helped her get here.

I reach out to open the passenger door and then curse myself when I can't get a grip on it. Being left-handed, it's instinctual to try to do everything with that hand, especially since I got rid of the sling yesterday.

Rylee sees my actions and when I finally slip into the passenger seat, she turns to me. "You know, keeping the sling on a while longer might be a good idea. It'll keep you from doing those sorts of things with your primary arm."

"You told me I was okay to go without it," I remind her.

"I said we were getting to that point, Brady, but that you'd have to be sure to be super careful in how you use it. Your elbow recovery is going well. I don't want to see you have any setbacks."

"I hate that fucking sling," I tell her.

She just stares at me like I'm five and she's my schoolteacher.

"I'll be careful. Jeez."

She looks placated for now and puts the car in gear. As we pull away from the hotel, I notice what I didn't before. She's got her hair down. She always wears it up at work. And I can see why. It's very long. Her chocolate-brown hair is thick and wavy and I could swear it smells like fruit. It falls far down her back, well below her bra line, but not quite reaching the waistband of her jeans.

Rylee is stunning.

She catches me staring and raises a questioning brow.

"Where are we going and why did you have to pick me up so early?" I ask.

"Because our first stop closes at five. We'll have to make it quick, we'll be pressed for time as it is."

"Do you plan on telling me where we're going, or are you going to make me play twenty questions?"

She giggles. "I'm taking you to the Florida Aquarium. I can't believe you've never been. It's amazing."

"Fish? You're taking me to see fish?"

"Not just fish. Rays and sharks and all kinds of sea creatures you didn't even know existed. It's quite fascinating. It's on the TECO line, but I figure you've done that to death with all your bar-hopping."

"The TECO line? Oh, you mean the streetcar things? No, we don't bar-hop that way, we usually hire limos."

She shakes her head. "Of course you do. What was I thinking?" She shifts lanes rather erratically and makes a sharp turn as if she just realized that was where she needed to go.

"Rylee, do you always drive this badly? I mean, maybe I should take the wheel."

"Shut up. Last minute change of plans." She pulls into a parking lot and we get out and walk to an electronic ticket booth that has prices for the TECO line. She selects two unlimited day passes and before I know it, she's swiping her debit card.

"Seriously?" I ask, scolding her.

"It's ten bucks, Brady. I think I can handle it."

"You're not doing that again," I tell her.

"This isn't a date."

"You are doing me a favor, Ry. I'm paying tonight."

She grabs the two passes from the dispenser and hands me one without acknowledging my declaration. "Come on, the aquarium closes in an hour, we'd better hurry."

We hop on a car just before it pulls away. I can't help my smile as we make our way to our destination. She's right. Seeing the city this way is different. It kind of makes me feel like a kid.

There are plenty of kids on the streetcar. I try not to look too closely at the younger ones. Because every time I do that, I end up seeing one who has Keeton's nose that turns up slightly at the end, or one with dirty-blonde hair with a cowlick over his right eyebrow.

But when I look at Rylee, I see her eyes bounce from one kid to the next, the smile on her face telling me way more than I want to know. She obviously wants kids. One more reason I never get involved with women.

"Oh, look," she says, pointing out to the right. "There's a cruise ship in port today. I've always wanted to take a cruise. Sometimes I come down here with, uh … sometimes I come down here and sit on a bench up the bay a bit and watch them go out. It's fun to wave to them and know they are going to have the vacation of a lifetime."

"Why don't you take one?" I ask, but what I really want to ask is who's the guy she comes down here with. "I'm pretty sure you can afford it."

She glares at me. "Just because I have a good job doesn't mean I should spend all my earnings. I'm saving for the future. And blowing that on a frivolous vacation is not in my plan. I can go to the beach whenever I want – that's my vacation. Plus, I go back to New York every time I get a few days off."

I study her for a second, again, wondering who's in New York. "You're very, um … responsible, aren't you, Ry?"

She laughs. "Is that a nice way of calling me a tight-wad?"

"Tight-wad, penny-pincher, cheapskate – take your pick," I say with a wink.

"Yeah, well, if I'm a tight-wad, you're a squanderer."

"I guess we balance each other out then, don't we?" I say, rubbing my shoulder against hers.

She puckers her lips at me. "Not a date, Taylor. No touching."

"Oh, come on. I touch my teammates more than that."

She bites her lip and raises a suggestive brow at me.

"Get your head out of the gutter, Ry. I'm one-hundred-percent hetero male, and I'll prove it if I have to."

"Pul-ease," she says rolling her eyes.

"And it's not like you and I don't ever touch," I tell her. "You've given me how many massages in the last few weeks?"

"That's totally different and you know it." The streetcar stops and Rylee stands up. "This is us."

I step down from the car and offer her my hand. "I'm still allowed to be polite, aren't I?"

She takes my hand and shakes her head at herself. "I guess there are exceptions to every rule, aren't there?"

I'm counting on it.

We walk a few blocks to get to the aquarium. I make sure to have my wallet out and ready as we approach the entrance. No way is she paying for anything else.

"We're going to have to hurry our way through more than I would like, but I think you'll still enjoy it."

She looks like a kid going into a candy store.

As the ramp we're following goes higher and higher, the exhibits get more interesting and I find a few that I really do want to find out about. And whenever I stop our progress, Rylee can recite almost everything that is on the exhibit information plaque.

"Just how many times have you been here, Ry?"

She shrugs. "Let's just say I could be a tour guide for the aquarium."

"So marine biology was your back-up plan?" I tease.

"Excuse me," a woman says. "Would you mind taking our picture?"

She holds out a camera to neither of us distinctly and Rylee grabs it. "Of course."

The mother and her two young sons pose in front of some stingrays that are swimming behind a thick wall of glass. The older of the boys keeps trying to get his mother's attention while she's trying to get him to smile for the camera.

After Rylee snaps a few photos, the woman thanks her and they walk away. The kid, who must be ten or eleven, is still trying to talk to his mom. Then a minute later, the lady turns around and, looking embarrassed, she says, "I'm sorry. My son is surely mistaken, but he believes you are a baseball player for the New York Nighthawks."

I look at the kid who is about to burst out of his skin.

"He's right, I am." I walk toward the boy, holding out my hand. "Brady Taylor, and you are?"

His eyes get so wide I think they'll leave the sockets. He shakes my hand but doesn't say anything.

His mother laughs. "His name is Cameron. And that's his younger brother, Christopher. I'm Wanda. It's a pleasure to meet you and ..." She looks at Rylee.

"Oh, sorry. This is my friend, Rylee."

"Nice to meet you, too," Wanda says.

"Can I have your autograph?" Cameron asks, finally finding his voice.

"You bet. What would you like me to sign?"

He looks at his mom. "Uh, I don't know. I don't have anything."

She shoves their aquarium brochure at me. "Here, how about this?"

Rylee fishes a pen out of her purse and hands it to me tentatively. I stare at it. *Shit.* I can barely grip a pen let alone sign an autograph.

"You're a big Hawks fan, huh, Cameron?" I say, biding time as I figure out what to do.

"Oh, yes. We're from Albany. My uncle took me to a game last year. You were great. You always are."

"Thanks, partner."

Rylee leans close and whispers, "Just scribble something with your right hand, they won't know the difference."

Then she takes the brochure and holds it for me while I try to write something that in some way, shape or form resembles my name. It looks like chicken scratch. But when Rylee hands it to Cameron, he looks at it like he just got Willie Wonka's golden ticket.

"Wow! Thank you," he says, jubilantly.

Cameron's mom takes a few pictures of me standing between her sons, then she grabs the youngest boy's hand. "We won't keep you. You've made Cameron's day. His *year*. Good luck, Mr. Taylor."

"My pleasure. Have a nice day."

As she walks away, Cameron reluctantly follows her, looking back at me until they turn the corner.

I turn to Rylee. "Well that was an epic failure." I look down at my left hand and shake my head.

"Not for Cameron. You heard his mom. He'll never forget what just happened."

"I can't even hold a fucking pen well enough to sign my goddamn name, Rylee."

She puts her hand on my defective one. "It will happen, Brady. I have faith that it will. One day – maybe not next week or next month – but one day you'll be carrying on and won't even notice when it happens. On that day, you'll do something ordinary like open a jar of pickles without thinking about it. And when that happens, you'll know you've made it back. You'll know you can be a pitcher again." She looks up at me with those deep-green eyes. "When it happens, if it doesn't happen here, I hope you'll let me know when it does. Because it will be quite a moment."

"When?" I ask, wary of her optimism.

"Yes. When." She tugs on my shirt. "Now come on, we don't have much time to finish. There's so much more I want you to see."

We just make it through the entire place before closing time. And when we exit through the front doors, Rylee makes me jump when she squeals, "Oh, look! A ship is leaving. Come on, let's run down there and watch."

She runs ahead of me and then looks back, beckoning me to follow her. I stare at her for a moment before conceding to her wish. This woman, when we're in my therapy sessions, she's so focused and professional. But here, she's like a kid. Wild and free. Curious and inquisitive. She's so much fun. She's …

I stop myself right there. I've no intention of thinking of Rylee Kennedy as anything other than a friend, a physical therapist, or a sexual conquest. Hell, she'll be all three if I have my way. But she can't be more. She could never be more.

No one can.

Chapter Eight

I think back on Friday night as I walk the few miles to the training complex to meet with the strength and conditioning coach before my PT appointment. After the aquarium, we took a streetcar to one of Rylee's favorite historical parks and then we finished up the night by eating at a mom-and-pop sandwich shop – some out-of-the-way place tourists don't know about that delivered one of the best Reubens I've ever had.

I was home by eight thirty.

It was the best non-date I've ever had.

My weekend was spent partly at the beach and partly on the phone being badgered by Murphy to accept the modeling contract.

I'm really looking forward to Sunday, when my team flies in for a three-game series. I've tried hanging out with some of the guys here, but the incessant questions about playing for the Hawks gets old and sometimes I feel like they are just using me to get a leg up with the organization.

I open the doors to the weight room and find the person I'm looking for sitting at a desk in the corner. "Hi, Matt. Nice to see you again."

He stands up and walks over to shake my hand. "Brady, it's great seeing you, too, although I wish it were under different circumstances."

"You and me both."

He directs me to the desk. "Come, sit. We're just going to talk about things today and make a plan for the rest of your stay. How's the arm?"

"The elbow's good. Rylee and the doctor both say it's healing nicely." I make as good a fist as I can and pump it. "It's the hand that's really bothering me. It doesn't work for shit."

"We'll leave that to Rylee and your doctors. Here we're going to make sure your shoulders, legs and core stay strong for when you get back into the game."

Matt's a good guy. We all work with him and his staff during spring training. But I like him even more now that he uses words like *when* and not *if*.

We talk for half an hour and he puts together a schedule for me. He wants to get me in the pool as soon as my elbow can take it. He says that will work my shoulders and keep them loose. I look over the printout of exercises and the time he wants me to dedicate to strength training every day and I consider stripping Rylee of her title and transferring it to Matt.

Then again, what the hell better things do I have to do?

"You can do a lot of this on your own," he says. "But some of the more difficult sets that require use of the arm, I'd rather you do here where the staff can keep an eye on you. Go ahead and start with the leg and core exercises this afternoon. The rest, we'll wait for the go-ahead from Rylee."

I nod. "I'll come in the mornings before my PT and do what I need to here, then I can use the gym at the hotel for some of the other stuff."

"Sounds like a plan. Just shout out whenever you need me. Otherwise, we'll meet up once a week to keep tabs on your progress."

We shake hands again and then I leave the weight room, walking across the courtyard to the PT building. When I walk in, I don't see Margaret, but I do see a note taped to the window next to where she normally sits. It says she's out sick today and to go ahead and walk into the back.

I look at my phone and see I'm early. But I walk through the propped-open door anyway because it's boring sitting out here alone. I figure I can sit and talk to Brad as Rylee finishes up with him. Brad is here from Vegas. He tweaked his knee pretty badly when he had a collision with another player and now he's out for the season as well.

But when I look around the rehab room, it's empty. No Brad. No Rylee. No Alex or the athletic trainer who sometimes hangs out waiting for the A-team's practice to end – that's when things really get busy around here. And it's why they schedule rehab for guys from any of the other three teams earlier in the day.

I hear a voice and walk in its direction. As I get closer, I realize it's a woman speaking, but it's not Rylee. I peek through the open door to one of the offices and see Rylee's back. Her hand comes up to touch her laptop screen and she runs her finger lovingly along the edges of an older woman's face.

"When you get home from school, we have to talk about that nasty boy down the street," the woman on the screen says. "He bothers me with all his hanging around."

"Mom, we don't live on Flagstone Road anymore, remember? You live in the memory care facility and I'm down in Tampa for now."

The woman is her mother? And she's in a memory care facility? *Damn.*

I feel like a dick standing here and eavesdropping. But we don't talk about personal stuff. And for some reason, I want to know all the things she's not able to tell me. Things like maybe her mom is one of those ties she still has in New York. I wonder if she's the only tie, or if there are others.

"Tampa?" her mother says, putting her hand over her heart. "What are you doing in Tampa? It's so far away. Does your father know about this? He won't be happy. No, he won't be happy at all. Did you ask his permission?"

Rylee's shoulders slump as she sighs. "Mom, Dad has been gone for almost four years now. Remember?"

"Four years? Goodness, where did he go?"

I listen to Rylee and her mom talk for the next five minutes. Rylee sometimes plays along with what her mother is saying, and other times, she tries to remind her mother what reality is.

Her mother is a lot older than we are for sure, but she looks way too young to be having dementia or whatever.

Another woman comes into view on the screen. "Rylee, your mom is getting tired. Joe is going to take her back to her room while I chat with you."

Rylee and her mother say goodbye and then the woman replaces Rylee's mom in the chair she was sitting in.

Rylee's shoulders start to shake and I realize she's crying. "I'm losing her more and more each day, Barbara. It's killing me that I can't be there with her."

"We are taking good care of her, Rylee. You can rest assured."

"Mu-maybe I should m-move her down here after all," Rylee says, stuttering through her tears.

"Come on now. We've gone over this a thousand times. Your father wanted her here because we are the best. And you keep saying you'll move back eventually. So what if you move her down there, upheaving her life and her routines, just to put her in some sub-standard facility only for you to end up getting that transfer back to New York?"

Rylee sighs again. "You're right, Barbara. I know you're right. I just miss her, that's all. I'm all she's got."

"You're wrong, Rylee. She has me. She has us. We love her like our own mothers. I promise you she's getting the best care possible."

Rylee nods her head and then picks up her phone to check the time. "Barbara, I've got to go, I have a patient coming soon."

I finally back away from the office and head back to the door that leads to reception. Alex comes through a side door and looks around the room, having caught me walking towards reception and not away from it.

He looks back at the office Rylee is occupying. "Is there something I can help you with?"

He eyes me up and down. He doesn't like me. But that's okay, I don't like him either. I don't like the way he looks at Rylee.

"Uh, the sign said to come on back, but I saw Rylee on the phone, so I thought I'd just wait out front."

"Yeah, that's probably a good idea," he says.

He stares me down, waiting for me to walk away and go through the door. But I'm not backing down first. He needs to know he can't manipulate me. He finally shakes his head and retreats across the room.

Before I go through the door, I see Rylee come out of the office, wiping tears from under her eyes. I pretend that I've just now come in.

"Hi," I say, innocently, as if I haven't just eavesdropped on something I had no right to know about.

"Oh, hi." She tries to compose herself.

"Something wrong?" I ask, like I don't know she's dying inside.

"Eyelash in my eye," she says. "But I think I got it. Thanks."

I look around the room. "Where's Brad?"

"At the orthopedic. I had to work him in later this afternoon."

"I'm a bit early. Do you want me to wait out front?"

She shakes her head. "No. Just have a seat over by that training table and I'll get my laptop and pull up your chart."

While she gets ready for me, I pull out my phone and Google her dad. Surely there can't be too many orthopedic surgeons named Kennedy who worked with professional sports teams in New York.

It doesn't take me long to find him. Gerald Kennedy. He actually has a Wikipedia page. He married his second wife, Georgia, and had his one-and-only child, Rylee when he was fifty years old. Tragically, he died of a massive stroke at the age of seventy-two, leaving his wife, who was in a memory care facility with early-onset-Alzheimer's, and a daughter who was in her first year of PT school.

I look at Rylee as she logs onto her laptop, feeling sorry for a twenty-two-year old who had to deal with such massive amounts of tragedy. *Twenty-two*. She was twenty-two when it happened. Same age as I was.

I leave Gerald Kennedy's Wikipedia page to Google my own. I do that every once in a while to make sure it doesn't say anything about Natalie and Keeton.

When I was drafted by the Hawks, the story of their deaths hit the papers. I mean, how could it not? I wasn't even available to take the highly-anticipated phone call because I was burying my wife and child. Thankfully, however, the story died quickly and nobody cared much about a player who was starting out on the single-A team.

With my first few paychecks, I hired a service to scrub any existence of Natalie and Keeton Taylor on the net. I didn't need to be reminded of what happened and I sure as hell didn't need strangers or new friends asking questions.

Luckily, most baseball players are self-centered and even among the single-A team who knew my past, my story was quickly forgotten and replaced by tales of women, drinking, and successes in baseball.

As the years went by, I became known as the perpetual bachelor of the Hawks. The guy who would never settle down. The playboy of baseball. And if anyone in the media or the Nighthawks organization knows about my past, they don't ever say anything and for that, I'm grateful.

"Ready?" Rylee asks, coming to stand next to me.

I put my phone away. "Give me all you got."

She smiles.

I'm glad I made her smile after how sad she looked a minute ago.

"I'm going to push you more than I normally do today," she says.

"Do it. I'm ready."

"Good. Let's get started."

An hour and one mother-fucking-sore arm later, she's finishing up putting the TENS unit away as I quickly hop onto the training table. I love all of Rylee's massages, but I think my favorite is the intense neck massage she gives me when I'm lying on my back. She really gets in there and when her strong fingers push up and extend my neck, I can feel all the stress leaving my body.

She laughs. "Eager for a massage, are we?"

"I think I deserve a longer one after that workout," I say, stretching my neck and shoulders to relieve the tension. "You definitely earned your name as the Queen of Pain today."

"Well, as luck would have it we got started early, so I might just have a few extra minutes."

She doesn't talk much during my massage. I think she gets that I prefer to lie quietly and get lost in my thoughts and her hands.

Her hands. It amazes me that such a small person has the strength to manipulate large muscles such as mine. Surely she's the one who needs a massage after working on all the athletes that she does.

Suddenly, I find myself fantasizing about our roles being reversed. About Rylee being on this table. About her long locks being pulled from the hair tie and splaying over the table, the rich brown waves cascading over the edges. About my hands kneading and plying the tension from her neck, her shoulders … and how my hands wander lower, searching for the unexplored territory that lies beneath her Hawks-colored polo shirt.

Her hands fall away from my neck, causing me to open my eyes. She retrieves a towel from the cabinet and throws it over the growing problem in my sweat pants.

"You'll scare the children with that thing," she jokes, trying to hide her embarrassment.

I wink at her before closing my eyes to enjoy the rest of my massage.

I wonder what she thinks about it. Does it happen often? I can honestly say that in all the years I've been getting massages from female PTs, this is the first time I've gotten anything more than a semi.

I imagine her hands on me now, her very strong and capable hands going down on me and reaching under the waistband of my pants to stroke me.

Fuck. I know when I get back to the hotel, I'll be doing a lot more than just squeezing the stress ball.

I think I let out a groan or a growl and then her hands fall away. For good this time.

"Okay, I think you're good to go," she says, walking to her laptop to do some typing.

I sit up, keeping the towel over my lap.

"What would you say to a repeat of last Friday? Not the aquarium again, but something different. More Tampa culture."

She looks up from her laptop. "I'm not so sure about that, Brady."

"Why not? You had a good time, didn't you?"

"Yes, but ..." she looks at the towel that is hiding my waning erection.

"Oh, come on, Ry. Surely as a medical professional, you understand I have no control over that."

She sighs, thinking about it.

"You said yourself that getting out and being active is good for me. Would you rather I sit alone in my hotel room, crying in my beer over my bleak future?"

"Your future is anything but bleak. You are making great progress with your elbow. The rest will come. Trust me."

"Is that a yes?" I ask.

"That wasn't an *anything*," she says.

"You know you want to, Kennedy. We had a blast."

"I don't know, *Taylor*. It might not be a good idea."

Her eyes flit back to my lap, making me wonder if she thinks it's a bad idea because she *doesn't* want me, or because she *does*.

"I'll have to see. I'm not sure I could move things around again."

"You have quite the social calendar, don't you?" I tease.

"Yeah, that's me," she says, rolling her eyes. "Just call me Wild Child."

I hop off the table, tossing the towel to her. "See you tomorrow, Miss Child."

"I'll be here."

Before I've even left the building, I pull out my phone and make a call to Jason, the team owner, to see if there is anything he can do to facilitate Rylee getting back to her mom.

Then I jog back to my hotel, my balls bluer than the Atlantic, knowing I've got a date with my right hand.

Chapter Nine

I manage to scribble a few autographs with my right hand out in front of the hotel while I wait for Rylee. Word has gotten out that I'm staying here and it's become increasingly hard to come and go without being spotted. But when the familiar silver SUV pulls up under the hotel awning, I find myself racing through the fans to get to the one person who doesn't seem to care in the least that I am one of the top starting pitchers in the league.

Or was.

One bystander gets out her phone to snap a picture as I get in the car. I hold up my hand. "Please don't."

The last thing Rylee or I need is for her face to be plastered across the tabloids with rumors of us hooking up.

I quickly slip inside the passenger door. "Next time, why don't you park in the lot and I'll walk out? Or even better, I'll Uber to your place."

"Next time?" She raises her brow.

"Yeah. I think this should be our thing. Friday nights on the town. We'll call them *Friend Fridays* if it makes you feel any better."

She laughs. "Strangely, it does. But you don't need to come to my place. I'll be happy to meet you in the parking lot."

She pulls away from the curb and I give her a look. "I'm not going to stalk you if you give me your address, Ry. Plus, I'm pretty sure I could get it with one phone call."

"I don't doubt you could. You seem to be able to get anything you want, Brady. You lead a charmed life, don't you?"

My eyes close briefly. "You have no idea how untrue that statement is, Rylee."

"Oh, you poor thing," she says, sarcastically. "I mean, your injury aside, you've got it made. You make more money in one year than most people make in a lifetime. You're not exactly bad looking. You have a lot of friends – well except down here. And from what I can tell, you've got a woman on your arm everywhere you go. A different woman. It's almost like you have one in every city."

I sit in silence.

"Oh, my God! You have one in every city, don't you?"

"Not *every* city. I don't have one back home and I don't have one here."

"Why not here?" She thinks about her own question and then she answers it. "You are here for six weeks every spring. No attachments, right? See – case in point, you're living the dream."

"Things aren't always what they seem, Rylee."

Shit. Why did I even say that?

She studies me when we're stopped at a traffic light. "You're right, Brady. They aren't. I'm sorry I made assumptions."

I shake my head. "It's fine. You're right, I'm charmed," I say unconvincingly.

"Can you forget I said anything? I'm a terrible person to have said it."

"Sure," I say. "But I won't forget what you said about me being hot."

Her jaw drops as we pass by the familiar TECO line parking lot. "I did not say you were hot."

"Yes, you did," I argue.

"I said you were not exactly bad looking. Big difference, Taylor."

I laugh. "Whatever, Kennedy. So, where are you taking me?" I ask in slight disappointment. "We just passed the parking lot for the streetcar."

She smiles. "You like those, don't you? Me, too. Don't worry, tonight's plans include streetcars. But first I'm taking you somewhere else."

"I'm intrigued," I say, looking at the clock that hasn't even turned 3:00 yet. "You're not a late-night person, are you? And how do you manage to get every Friday afternoon off?"

"I put in a lot of ten-hour days, so I only work until noon on Fridays."

"So I'm your last appointment?"

"Yeah, why?"

I shrug. "I don't know. Just good to know, I guess."

We fall into comfortable conversation as we drive through the streets of Tampa. When we turn in to our destination, I chuckle. "You have a thing for animals, don't you, Ry?"

She laughs. "Don't flatter yourself."

I cover my mouth in feigned abhorrence. "Are you calling me an animal?"

"If the shoe, or hoof, fits."

"Watch out or you'll bruise my ego."

She rolls her eyes. "As if."

We exit the car and I stare at the large sign that reads 'Big Cat Rescue.' As we approach the entrance, I see a poster that says reservations are required and must be purchased in advance. "Uh, Rylee, I think we're screwed," I say, pointing to it.

She reaches into her purse and pulls out a piece of paper that shows paid reservations for two at thirty-seven bucks each. I reach for my wallet but she reads my intentions and stops me, putting her hand over mine. "Just, no."

"Rylee."

"Listen, you can pay for everything else tonight, deal? As long as it's not over the top like we agreed."

"Right, the rules. What are they again?"

"No touching. No kissing. No drinking. No frivolous spending."

"No fun," I interject.

She laughs. "I thought you said you had fun last Friday."

"I did."

"Well, there you go."

We spend the next few hours seeing over seventy exotic cats. Tigers, cougars, bobcats and more, all who have been abused, neglected or abandoned.

"I love this place," she declares, when we are finishing the tour. "Most people are afraid of these animals, but it makes you see that with TLC, even beasts can be tamed."

I look at her, wondering if she's talking about the cats or about me.

Before we leave, our tour guide asks for donations, stating this whole facility is run on them. I can see how much this place means to Rylee, so I get out my credit card. I show it to her and ask, "Do you consider a donation frivolous spending?"

She gives me a genuine smile. "Absolutely not."

I see her jaw fall open when I tell the tour guide how much to put on the card.

As we walk back to the car, she touches my arm. "A hundred bucks would have sufficed, you know."

"Go big or go home," I say.

"Why do I get the impression you always go big?"

I shrug and then she tosses me the keys.

"You trust me with your baby?" I ask.

"It'll be good therapy for your arm and fingers. Try to grip the wheel. Open and close the windows. That sort of thing."

My face breaks into a smile as I open the passenger door for her and then walk to the other side of the car. She laughs when I have to put the seat all the way down and back before I can get in.

"Where to?" I ask.

"Where else? The TECO line."

As we drive back through the city, Rylee gets a text, laughing at it as she taps out her reply. I wonder if it's from Alex.

"So, Alex seems to have a thing for you."

In my periphery I can see her head snap in my direction. "One: he doesn't. He's my boss and that would be against the rules, wouldn't it? And two: that's getting kind of personal, don't you think?" She holds up her phone, shaking it at me before she puts it away. "It wasn't Alex."

I don't miss, however, that she doesn't offer who it was. And when her phone pings again and she pulls it out to answer, I sure as hell don't miss her devious smile.

She likes this game. But damned if I'm going to let her know how much I don't.

I find a parking place and buy our passes for the streetcar. "Where to now?" I ask after we hop on.

"Ybor City," she says. "I'm assuming you've been?"

"Of course. They have some good bars there."

"We're not going bar-hopping, Brady."

"Then why bother?"

"You wanted Tampa culture, I'm giving it to you. Tonight you get to see it through *my* eyes."

I cock my head to the side and stare at her, looking into those green eyes that are gazing intently into mine. I swear there is something behind them. Something that says she wants me.

She lowers her eyes to the floor as she tucks a stray piece of hair behind her ear after a gust of wind flows through the streetcar. She's fighting it. I just can't decide if that's a good thing or a bad thing. I can't say how many times over the past month I've jacked off to thoughts of her intense green eyes. Her gorgeous hair. Her stimulating touch. But she's not like the others. She's different. Smart. Refined. Sophisticated. Fun.

She's also a woman you don't have a one-night-stand with. And anything else is off the table.

"Okay then, why do they call it Ybor City?" I ask, trying to change the subject in my head.

"It was founded as an independent town in the late 1800's by a group of cigar manufacturers led by some guy named Ybor."

"Hmm. Now that you mention it, I do recall seeing a lot of cigar shops there. My dad is a huge fan, maybe we could stop in a few places. His birthday is next month. Or, would that be throwing around my money?"

She laughs. "No, buying a gift for your dad is nice. We should do it. I've never been in a cigar shop before."

"You're missing out then."

"Ewww. I don't smoke, Brady. And as an athlete, surely you know it's horrible for you."

"I don't smoke, either, Ry. Doesn't mean I don't enjoy an occasional stogie."

She wrinkles her nose in disgust, making me chuckle.

"Brady Taylor?" someone asks from across the streetcar.

All eyes turn my way and I look at Rylee as she digs around in her purse, fishing out a pen.

I talk to several guys in the man's group, and when one asks for an autograph, I stupidly try to do it with my left hand. As I scribble out my name, the pen falls out of my grip and onto the floor of the car, then it rolls backwards and tumbles down the stairs. As I watch it fall onto the street and get crushed by a passing car, I wonder if it's some kind of twisted symbolism.

Some of the guys look at me as if they know I'm damaged goods. A nearby lady offers me a new pen and I finish the autograph with my right hand before signing a few more.

We get to our stop and the group of guys leaves the car. Rylee pulls me down next to her. "We'll stay on until the next one."

I'm relieved that she gets it. She gets that I don't need to be fawned over and prodded with questions. Not until I make it back. *If* I make it back.

"Hey." She rubs my shoulder with hers. "It was good that you tried. Maybe next time you'll be able to do it."

"Next time could be in ten minutes," I say.

She giggles. "Oh, right. Maybe next Friday you'll be able to do it."

My eyes snap to hers. "Are you saying you'll do this again?"

She shrugs.

"You don't think you'll run out of animal places to take me?" I ask with a wink.

"Have you ever been to Dinosaur World?"

I laugh out loud. "You really are just a big kid, aren't you?"

"Come on, let's get off here."

She stands up and offers me her hand. I take it, realizing it's the second time she's touched me tonight.

So much for the no touching rule.

Rylee leads me on a walk through Ybor Square, being the perfect tour guide. I get stopped by another fan and Rylee takes our picture. Then we make our way down the main strip, window shopping and people-watching as we decide which place to go.

The street is bustling at this hour as more and more people get out of streetcars, crowding the sidewalks of this popular Friday-night destination.

"That one looks good," she says, pointing to a cigar shop across the street that looks less crowded than most.

The bell above the door jingles as we enter, and the proprietor greets us in both Spanish and English. "Come. I have place for you," he says, leading us to the counter as a few people scoot over to make room.

Then he grabs two small glasses, much smaller than shot glasses, and proceeds to fill them with a splash of brown liquor. I glance at the bottle and then look at the makeshift sign behind the counter that reads 'Bourbon tasting' with today's date below it.

I look at Rylee and then at the tiny glass. I push it back to him. "No, I'm sorry."

The man looks saddened.

Rylee picks up the glass and hands it to me. "When in Rome," she says. Then she picks up her own and taps it to mine before downing the small gulp of liquor.

I throw my head back, laughing, before I do the same.

So much for no drinking.

We spend the next thirty minutes sampling bourbon and smelling cigars and by the time we leave, I've gotten a combination of the two that will definitely put a smile on my old man's face.

As we descend the steps back onto the street, my stomach growls, reminding me of the time. "Know of any decent restaurants here?"

"Sure, there are a few. What are you in the mood for?"

"Let's go for something fancier than sandwiches this time."

She stares me down.

"I didn't say Shula's Steakhouse, Rylee. Any old place I can get a steak will do."

We walk a few blocks over and stroll into a restaurant to find there is an hour wait. We check three more places only to find the same. Rylee throws up her hands in defeat when we exit the last one. I reach for my wallet. "There are ways to get seated, you know."

She rolls her eyes. "What? As in you either throw your name around or glad-hand the hostess?"

"Are you hungry or not? Because I'm starving."

"I'm not hungry enough to have you buy our way to a table or showboat your celebrity."

"Then what do you suggest?" I ask.

"I'll just eat at home," she says, walking back towards the main strip and the streetcars.

I grab her elbow and stop her progress. "You have to be kidding me, Ry. If you think I'm letting you go home hungry, you're crazy."

I get out my phone and send a text.

"What are you doing?" she asks.

"There is a good restaurant in the lobby of my hotel."

"Your hotel?"

My phone pings with a reply. "Yes, and Lenny will pick us up in fifteen minutes in front of Ybor Square."

"What? Why?"

"Because the streetcars take too long and we've been drinking. You should be sober enough to drive after dinner and then you can Uber back to your car."

She thinks about it as my stomach makes a loud noise. She laughs. "Fine. That's very thoughtful of you, Brady. Thank you." Then she gets on her tip toes and plants a quick kiss on my cheek.

My cheek burns where her hot breath flowed over it. Her soft lips have branded me like cattle and my pants get tight thinking of what else those lips could do to me.

So much for no kissing.

I tuck the cigars and bourbon under my arm and lead the way back to Ybor Square wondering how long I'll last before my assholery has me putting the moves on Rylee Kennedy.

Chapter Ten

"Table for two?" Natasha asks when we walk up to the hostess stand.

"Somewhere out of the way, please, if you don't mind, Natasha."

She smiles shyly. "I told you it's just Nat."

I don't think so.

I raise my chin at her, but I won't say it. I'll never say it.

"Right this way," she says.

Rylee eyes Natasha from head to toe as she guides us to our table in the corner of the room.

I hold out a chair for Rylee before taking my own. Then I thank Natasha as she bats her eyelashes at me.

"So, you and Nat," Rylee declares. Then she holds up a hand to keep me from speaking. "Sorry – don't say anything, I shouldn't have asked."

"It's fine. And I'm not sleeping with Natasha. I'm not sleeping with anyone."

She looks at me sideways. "But you've been here for almost a month."

I laugh. But before I can say another word, our server, Miguel, comes over and puts a bottle of wine on the table.

"Your usual, Mr. Taylor," he says. "Shall I pour you a glass?"

"Not today. Thanks."

"Mind if I have one?" Rylee asks.

I look back at Miguel and motion to her glass. "I guess we'll both have one then."

He pours our drinks and then hands us the menus. "I'll give you a minute," he says before retreating.

Rylee takes a sip of her wine and looks at me from over the rim of her glass. "Your usual?" she asks, when she sets it down. "As in you drink a bottle of wine at dinner every night?"

"Wow. If I could only be inside your head right now," I say. "You think I'm sleeping and drinking my way through Tampa, don't you?"

She shrugs an accusing shoulder.

"I ordered the same glass of wine every night I ate here the first week, so now they just bring me a bottle. They save what I don't drink and bring it out the next time I dine. I guess it's more economical that way or something. Whatever."

"At least *someone* is trying to be responsible with your money."

"I'm responsible," I say.

"How many cars do you have?" she asks.

"Three."

"You have three cars in New York City?" She shakes her head in disapproval. "I wouldn't be surprised if you pay more for parking than I pay for my monthly rent. I bet you don't even drive them much, do you?"

I shake my head. "I usually ride my bike. Easier to get around."

"You ride a bicycle?" she asks.

"I ride a motorcycle."

"Of course you do." She rolls her eyes. "And what floor is your apartment on?"

"Twenty-four."

"And how many floors are in your building?"

I sigh. "Twenty-four."

"The penthouse," she says. "Yeah, you are totally responsible with your money."

"What would you have me do, live in a fourth-floor walk-up in Harlem?"

"First off, I hear Harlem's not that bad these days. And second, I would expect a twenty-seven-year-old athlete who may be at the peak of his career to think about the future."

I call her out. "You mean a twenty-seven-year-old athlete who may never play again. That's what you really meant to say, isn't it? You think I need to save every penny I have in case I lose my job."

"I think we *all* need to be practical. Because you never know what can happen. And no, that is not what I meant, Brady. I'm still confident your nerve will regenerate."

I laugh disingenuously. "Tell me that again when you have to cut my steak for me."

She looks at me like she feels sorry for me. "I'll be happy to cut your steak, but not because I think you're helpless, Brady."

Miguel comes back and asks for our order. I nod to Rylee.

"I'll have the French Dip," she says.

"Would you like fries or onion rings with that?" Miguel asks.

"Fries, please."

Miguel looks at me. "I'll have the same, but rings for me. And a beer. I can't drink red wine with a sandwich."

"As you wish, Mr. Taylor. Ma'am?"

"What the heck," Rylee says. "Bud Light if you have it."

79

Miguel gathers our menus and leaves.

Rylee stares me down.

"What?" I ask.

"I had to badger you into going to the sandwich shop with me last week. You said you hate sandwiches."

"And look how that turned out, it was the best one I'd ever had. Plus, the French Dip is the cheapest thing on the menu. I'm sure that's why you ordered it. I'm just showing you that I'm not as irresponsible with my money as you think."

She fingers the bottle of wine on the table. "Mmmhmm, and how much is this bottle of wine?"

"I honestly have no idea, but it was probably the best one on the menu."

"You mean the most expensive."

I shrug. "Is there a difference?"

She laughs. "Just because it's the most expensive, doesn't mean it's always the best. But I'm proud of you. I guess baby steps are better than nothing. Just think of all the money you saved tonight. Your dinner bill will be half of what it normally is. And if you order a sandwich instead of a steak some of the time, and maybe house wine instead of that expensive wine cellar stuff, you'd save thousands of dollars every year. That's either good padding for your savings account or a lot of food for Simba and his friends at the Big Cat Rescue."

Our beers get placed on the table in frosty glasses. Rylee takes a drink and savors the taste. "Give me a three-dollar beer over a fifteen-dollar glass of wine any day."

"So, yeah. About this no drinking rule," I say.

She bites her lip. "I felt like we had to drink the bourbon. Did you see that guy's face when you said you didn't want any? After that, I figured the damage was done. So, what the heck?"

"Damage?"

"Yeah, you know, like if you were going to hit on me because I'd been drinking, you would have done it already."

"I don't hit on women, Rylee."

"No?" She studies me. "Then what is it? What do girls find so attractive about you that has them lining up to be invited into your bed?" Her eyes trace a path from my face down my arms. "I mean other than your muscles and your bank account."

"And the fact that I'm – what was it you called me – *not bad looking?*"

"Yeah, other than that," she says, trying not to laugh.

"It must be my natural charm."

She raises an eyebrow. "If you're so charming, how come *I'm* not falling at your feet?"

"Because you're smarter than most of the girls I hang around. Except for Murphy, but she doesn't count."

"Are you saying a woman has to be stupid to sleep with you?"

"It's not a requirement," I tell her. "But it helps."

She looks at me with serious eyes. "Brady, do you think you're somehow not worthy of a strong, intelligent woman? Surely your self-esteem isn't anything less than gargantuan."

I chuckle at her comment. "My self-esteem is fine, Ry. And smart women wouldn't put up with my rules."

"Rules?" She chews her lip as she looks at me. "Oh, you mean *don't call me, I'll call you* and stuff like that?"

"Pretty much. I know that makes me sound like a dick, but in my defense, they all know the score. I tell them all before we, uh … you know, that I'm not looking for a girlfriend."

Her look scolds me. "Surely you must know that some of them think they will be the one to change your mind."

I shrug an innocent shoulder. "I suppose some do, but it's not like they hadn't been warned. They're all adults and they make their own choices."

"I guess I can't fault you for that. I'm the same way, I suppose. I'm very focused on my career and my, uh … stuff. I don't have the time or energy for much else."

Stuff? Her mom? The guy she watches cruise ships with?

"But you have time for this," I say, waving my hand at our surroundings.

"That's only because I've decided you're fun. I can always make time for fun."

Miguel brings our meal and I look at it in a whole new light. I look at it through Rylee's eyes. And I think I *will* get as much enjoyment out of this as the most expensive steak on the menu.

"Miguel, can I please see the wine list?"

"Right away." He scurries off to fetch it for me.

"Have you learned nothing tonight?" Rylee asks.

Miguel returns with the menu and I hand it to Ry. "Pick a red and a white. Sensible ones. And I promise I'll drink nothing more expensive than what you select for the rest of my stay."

She smiles. She likes this game.

She peruses the entire list and then hands me the menu, pointing to her selections.

I'm impressed. She's obviously ordered her share of wine in the past. And she didn't even choose the house wines. The ones she chose are modest, but not cheap. Tasteful without being, what does she say, *frivolous.*

I eye her over the menu.

"What?" she asks. "I didn't say you shouldn't compromise."

She picks up a fry and swirls it in the au jus. "Okay, you have the length of the meal to lay it on me. Don't hold back, Taylor, I want to see your so-called *natural charm* that has all the ladies in a tizzy. I'll grade you on your performance later."

"Starting now?" I ask.

"Yes," she says, taking a bite.

I hold her stare and watch her thoughtfully, rimming my beer glass with my finger. Then I reach over and steal one of her fries and try to eat it suggestively.

She covers her mouth to laugh. "Oh, my God," she says around her food. "Does that really work?"

I laugh with her. "Shit. I don't know. I don't normally have to think about it. I just do it. You kind of put me on the spot here."

"Well you need to relax, Casanova. Because that was just bad flirting."

"Whatever. You see if you can do it better."

"*Anyone* can do it better," she says, laughing.

She takes a sip of beer, but some spills out of the side of her glass right into her cleavage. "Oops," she says. Then she takes her napkin and places it deep down the V-neck of her shirt and very carefully dabs the fallen droplets from between her breasts.

Fuuuuck me.

When I stop looking at her breasts, I realize I was probably staring far too long. I catch her eyes and she raises a brow.

I pick up her napkin from where she put it on the table. "You forgot this," I say, as I reach over and place it on her lap, grazing the inside of her thigh as my hand retreats back.

I swear I can hear her breath hitch when I touch her.

I smile as I take a few bites of my dinner.

We fall into comfortable conversation, each of us occasionally trying to one-up the other with our flirtatious gestures, words, or barely-there touches.

I'm drawn to her as she eats. I like to watch Rylee eat. It's very sensuous. A drip of au jus trickles down her chin and I reach over and catch it on my thumb. Then I stick my thumb in my mouth and suck on it.

At that moment, Miguel comes by the table to ask if we need anything.

"I'd love another beer, Miguel," Rylee says.

"Make it two."

As he walks away, Rylee fans herself and pushes her thick hair behind her shoulders. "Is it hot in here?"

I have to bite my tongue and agree with her. "Yeah, it gets that way in here sometimes."

She takes in a deep cleansing breath and I realize that all this flirting, real or not, is getting to her the same way it's getting to me. Hell, I've been sitting here with a boner for ten minutes now.

When Miguel delivers our beers, we reach for them simultaneously and each take a few long gulps.

"You must be excited for the team to be coming in on Sunday," she says. "You'll be able to hang out with your friends for a few days."

"You have no idea."

"Will you go to the games?"

"Hell, yes, I'll go. I'll sit in the dugout and cheer them on."

"No matter how much it hurts?" she asks in complete understanding.

"Yeah."

She takes one more bite and then declares she's too full to eat any more. Then she stretches her arms over her head, her t-shirt riding up her stomach to reveal a small tattoo peeking out from the low waistband of her jeans.

Shit. I have to know what that tattoo looks like up close.

84

She looks at me, knowing exactly what she's doing to me.

I drink the rest of my beer in one long swallow. She drains more of her own.

Miguel sees my empty glass. "Another round, Mr. Taylor?"

I look at Rylee. She thinks about it for half a second before looking at the time on her phone. She bites her lip in contemplation. "Okay, but it will be the last one," she says, lifting her glass as Miguel goes to fetch two more.

I look at my own phone. It's not even nine-thirty. "Yeah, last one. It's getting late, isn't it? Boy, I'm tired." I mimic her and reach my arms to the sky in a yawn and stretch that has my own shirt riding halfway up my torso.

I watch her as she looks at my abs. *Yeah, Kennedy, two can play at this game.*

She doesn't even pretend not to gawk at me. And it's damn sexy. *She's* sexy. But she's more than that. She's smart. She's funny. And she's not just hot, she's got a classic beauty about her.

Miguel puts our beers down in front of us, and before he walks away, I ask him to put the tab on my room as usual because we're leaving.

Rylee looks at our untouched beers. "Oh, we're leaving?"

"For the past half hour, I've been watching you flirt with me, Ry. But it's more than that, if I'm being honest. It's more than just tonight. You're damn sexy even without all this shit we're doing. I know we're just playing and it's all in fun, but if I have to sit here with this boner you've given me and watch you entice me for another fucking minute knowing I can't touch you, I'm going to explode. So, yes, I'm calling you an Uber and we're getting the hell out of here."

I chug my beer and start walking out through the restaurant. When I realize she isn't following me, I look back to see her studying her beer before she takes one last sip and leaves the table.

I pull out my phone to summon Lenny when Rylee's arm comes up to stop me. "I'm not ready to go home yet," she says, biting that bottom lip.

I shake my head. "You don't know what you're saying, Ry."

She pulls me aside, into a small hallway by the elevators. "You think you're the only one who's been affected by this?" She points a finger between us. "I'm a big girl, Brady. I can make big girl choices."

I pull her closer to me, close enough to smell her fruit-scented hair. "Are you sure? Because if you let me touch you, I'm not stopping until I make you scream my name."

She shifts around, pheromones escaping from her every pore. "What's your room number?" she asks, grabbing my hand and pulling me to the elevator.

We walk in and just before another couple joins us, she declares, "What makes you think I won't have you screaming mine?"

Holy mother of God.

Chapter Eleven

Before the door to my suite even shuts completely, I've got her against the wall. I cage her between my arms and stare down at her, gauging her willingness to participate in what we're about to do.

I think back on how much liquor she had. Some tastes of bourbon. A few sips of wine and a little more than two beers. Would that make her drunk? Surely she's a lightweight.

"Last chance," I say, my mouth hovering over hers, just inches from fulfilling my month-long fantasy.

She answers me by jumping up onto me and putting her hands around my shoulders. I grab her behind and support her with my right arm. But before I kiss her, she wriggles out of my hold and puts her feet back on the ground.

"I'm so sorry," she says, looking at my left arm. "I shouldn't have done that."

"If you think I can't hold you with one arm, Rylee, you don't know professional athletes very well."

"Right. Sorry. Let's try that again."

She jumps back into my arms and before she can even look at me to make sure I'm okay, my lips crash into hers. I start slow. Exploring. Teasing. And even before my tongue requests the parting of her lips, a groan escapes her.

I push her against the wall and sink my tongue into her mouth. We savor each other, each wanting to go deeper and get more. When I've exhausted my breath, I break our seal and trail my lips down around her jaw and neck. I flit my tongue at the lobe of her ear, earning me more throaty noises.

She's clawing at my back and neck. I can't pull her tightly enough against me. I don't want to wait another second to explore what's beneath her clothing. I back us away from the wall and walk towards the bedroom, only to trip over something and lose my footing.

"Your arm!" she squeals as we topple backwards.

In a split second, I'm able to spin us around so we fall onto my back and not hers, at the same time, protecting my arm that I wouldn't have even thought about if she hadn't warned me. It's only instinctual to try and brace yourself with your primary arm.

She comes to rest on top of me. "Are you okay?" she asks.

"You just saved my arm, Rylee."

"You just saved *me,*" she says.

I close my eyes. "I'm not usually such a klutz. Damn."

She burrows her face in my chest. "It's my fault. I wiggled out of my shoes and flung them off. They must have fallen in front of your feet."

I start laughing and Rylee's head bounces up and down as my chest rises and falls. Then she sits up, smiling as she straddles me. Her gaze falls to my chest as her hands find the bottom of my shirt. I'm no stranger to Rylee's hands on my body, and for that reason alone, the anticipation of what she could do with them has me reeling.

She slips them under my shirt and slowly works them up my abs. "Wow," she says. "Kudos to your personal trainer."

"I'm glad you approve." I lace my fingers behind my head and watch as she explores my chest, pushing my shirt up to my chin as she traces every ridge and ripple. I reach back and pull my shirt over my head, giving her full access to whatever she needs.

When she reaches my neck, I pull her towards me for another kiss.

"Mmmm," she mumbles into my mouth. "Beer and au jus."

I chuckle as my hands run up and down her spine, feeling everything from the ribs of her back down to the dip just below the waistband of her jeans. I reach a finger in and caress the spot just above her butt crack. She arches her back into me and moans.

The noises that come from her are enough to bring any man to his knees. I need more. I need to see her skin. Touch her flesh. I take the hem of her shirt into my hands and move it slowly up her back, waiting for her to give me the green light to remove it.

She sits up, holding her arms up high. After I peel her top off, I stare at what I've revealed. Breasts that are supported perfectly in a black satin bra, the ample fleshy globes pushing out over the top. Jesus. I knew they'd be spectacular, but I didn't expect this.

I've never been one to be particular about the size of a woman's breasts. Big, small – they all have redeeming qualities. But these breasts, I think they are the perfect size. I place my hands on them, gauging how they fit beneath. It's like two pieces of a puzzle that have come together. I find myself making my own throaty noises as I manipulate her through the bra.

She reaches behind her and unclasps it and it falls to my chest. Without the material between us, I can squeeze and ply and explore them even better.

"I'll take this over the stress ball any day," I say, giving her a squeeze with my left hand.

She laughs. "Let's see what you got, Taylor," she says, looking down at my hand as it caresses her.

I squeeze as hard as the hand will allow.

"Impressive," she says, smiling.

"Oh, you haven't seen anything yet." I scoot us over so I can lean against the end of the couch. She's still straddling me when I take one of her breasts into my mouth, sucking and teasing her puckered nipple as I gently twist the other one with my hand. My left hand.

I momentarily pull away and declare, "This is the best therapy yet. Think Alex would mind if I did this at every appointment?"

She throws her head back and bellows out a throaty laugh. I'm relieved. I didn't know if bringing up the guy who is pining for her would be a sore spot or not. At least now I know where he stands. And it's not nearly as close to her as I'm about to get.

After giving her chest ample attention, I focus my gaze on her stomach. I tug the waistband of her jeans down just a bit so I get a clear view of her tattoo. It's in the shape of a crooked heart with its two sides not quite connecting. I trace it with my index finger, making her shudder.

"I got it to try and hide the scar from having my appendix out," she tells me.

"It's nice," I say. "I like it." I abruptly change position, and move her onto the floor next to me so I can work my way down her body. "In fact, I want to taste it."

She mewls when my lips touch the tattoo. I smile and work my tongue around it as my fingers trace a line just below her waistband.

My dick is straining so hard against my fly, I'm afraid my zipper might burst open. I'm painfully hard and in need of release. I'm closer than I've ever been with anyone who hasn't been actively stroking my cock. I guess going this long without female companionship makes the beast needy. I moan to myself as I touch her silky soft skin.

Rylee props herself up on her elbows and guffaws. "Wait. Did you just say you needed to feed the beast?"

I look up at her with crazy eyes. *Did I really say that out loud?* "Uh, no."

"You did," she says laughing. "You said you needed to feed the beast. Is that what you call your penis?"

I look down at my pants and then back up at her. "Uh, no."

She scolds me with her stare and then motions to my pants. "I'm going to need to see it," she declares.

"Well that was the plan," I say with a wink.

"Drop 'em, Taylor."

"Like right now? Are you going to make me turn my head and cough?"

"Well, I *am* a medical practitioner." She giggles and instantly I know I'll do it. Hell, I'll do anything for this girl.

I realize what thought just went through my head and quickly squelch it. I don't have time for any touchy-feely emotions. I'll never have time for them. But right now, I'm in my element. She wants me to showboat. I'm the king of showboating. I snap up to my feet and in one fell swoop, bring my jeans and boxer briefs down to my ankles so I'm standing gloriously naked in front of her.

She cocks her head to the side and appraises my dick. It jumps under her perusal. She cocks her head to the other side, narrowing her eyes as she squints at it, like she's looking at a piece of abstract art trying to decide what to make of it.

"What the hell, Rylee?"

It's never taken a girl more than two-point-five seconds to grab my dick when it's been put on display in front of her.

"Hmmm," she ponders. "Beast? No. I'd say it's more of a barracuda."

I laugh as I take a step towards her before remembering my pants are around my ankles.

"Arm!" she yells as I fall towards her on the floor.

I put out my right arm to keep me from colliding with her.

I roll onto my back and remove my pants and shoes. "Damn, woman. You did it again."

"Maybe we should move someplace safer," she says.

I nod to the bedroom and she smiles.

I pick her up with my right arm. She gets a strong hold around my neck as I pull her up with me. "You know, the last time I checked, my legs do work," she says with a sarcastic grin.

It's not lost on me, however, that she makes no effort to extricate herself from my arms.

My bedroom is dark, only the light from the living room illuminating it. I walk her to the end of the bed and sit her down on it. Then she slips off and falls onto the floor with an "Oof."

"Shit, Ry. I'm sorry. I guess I'm not as accurate with my right arm."

She laughs, getting up and sliding back onto the bed until she lies back on my pillow. "It's fine, but are you getting the idea that the universe doesn't want us to do this?"

"Fuck that," I say, climbing on top of her. "I don't care what the stars or the signs or the magic eight ball says, we're doing this. There is no way in hell we're not doing this."

I start to unbutton her jeans, and then I pause when I think about how bad that might have sounded. I look up at her. "Rylee — we are doing this, aren't we? I didn't mean—"

"Brady, if we don't do this, I think I might spontaneously combust."

I smile and then proceed to remove her jeans and panties almost as fast as I removed my own. When I crawl back up her body, I take my time at every curve. Her knee – I kiss it. Her thigh – I caress it. The curve of her stomach – I lick it. She squirms under me as I dip a finger between her legs and spread the wetness up and over her clit.

"Move closer," she asks, breathlessly, holding out her hand. "I can't reach you."

"Anything you say." I switch sides and lean on my right elbow next to her. I use my left hand to tease her sex. I move my fingers in and out of her and circle my thumb on her pulsating clit.

"Oh, God," she says, reaching out to wrap her hand around me. "Best therapy session ever."

My laughter quickly turns to intense carnal need when I feel her soft hand stroking me. She runs her hand up and down methodically, stopping to collect the bead of moisture that seeps out of the tip. She reaches down to cup my balls.

"Jesus, Ry. I'm not going to last long."

I pull myself away from her so I don't blow my wad like an adolescent on prom night. I work my way down her body again, taking extra time to outline her tattoo with my tongue. Then I spread her folds and put my mouth on her. She moans and arches her body into me. Her hands grab my head and she threads her fingers through my hair.

My fingers work inside her, searching for the spot that will drive her insane. When I find it, she yells, "Brady, oh God!" Then she tugs on my hair, pulling me away from her. "I need you inside me. Now."

"Now?" I look up at her. She's so close. Just another few seconds.

"Please. It's been so long," she begs.

How long? I wonder. But now is not the time to ask. And it's too personal.

I hastily crawl over to the nightstand and fish around until I grab a condom from the box. I roll it on and situate myself over her, putting all my weight on my right arm. I enter her slowly, letting her small body adjust to me. But she grabs my ass and pulls me hard against her. She's as hungry for this as I am.

She's so tight. Her walls wrap around me and squeeze me as her arms explore my shoulders, my back, the crack above my ass.

"Jesus, Ry."

I'm so close I'm afraid I might go before she does. I reach my left hand between us and rub circles on her clit until her insides pulsate around me as she calls out my name.

Fuck. My name has never sounded so good. That's all I needed. My name coming off her lips like that sends me spiraling down into my own powerful orgasm as I add to her vocal exaltations.

I bury my head in her shoulder as I find recovery. Her arms fall away from me and onto the bed as if she's lost all her strength.

My body starts shaking as I laugh silently. Hers does the same, and as I roll off her and lie on my back, we dissolve into a fit of laughter, each feeding off the other. We're unable to stop.

"Stop it," she says, swatting me. "I can't stop unless *you* stop. And my abs are killing me."

"You're welcome," I say.

That makes her laugh harder.

We finally stop and catch our breath. "So that was …" I search for the right word, because there are so many to describe what I just experienced. I settle on the safest one. "… fun."

"It was." Then she throws her arm over her head. "Oh, my God, did we really just do that?"

I run a finger along her thigh. "Does it feel like we just did that?"

She quivers at my touch.

"So, how did I score?"

"Score?" she asks.

"Down at the restaurant, you said you were going to grade me on my moves. Well now that you've seen them, what's my score?"

She bites her lip in contemplation. "I'm thinking B-minus."

"What?" I ask, incredulously. "Why not an A?"

She smiles deviously. "Because I only had one orgasm."

I lift up onto my elbow. "Woman, you *told* me to stop. You were *right there*."

She's laughing again.

I roll over and shut her up with my lips. Then I spend the next hour earning an A-fucking-plus.

~ ~ ~

Rylee getting out of bed wakes me. I must have dozed off for a minute after our marathon session.

I get up myself and throw on a pair of sweats.

She walks silently into the bathroom to clean up and then I watch her walk out to the living room to get dressed. This Rylee is different from the one I had in my bed five minutes ago.

She sits down and slips on her shoes. Then she looks up at me. "That shouldn't have happened, Brady."

I take the seat across from her. "You don't have to worry," I say. "I promise nobody will know and your job will be safe. You have my word."

She nods. "I believe you mean that. But with who you are, there is always a chance you're being watched."

"Going to the zoo with my physical therapist isn't breaking any rules, Rylee." I motion to the bedroom. "Nobody has to know about what we do behind closed doors."

"Still, it's unprofessional. This can't happen again. You're good with that, right? I mean, you are used to one-night-stands."

"Of course I'm good with it, Ry. If that's what you want, but it doesn't have to be a one-time thing, you know."

"As in you'll make me your *Tampa girl?*" She raises an accusing brow.

In all the years I've been doing this. I've never felt bad about it. So why does that one statement make me feel about an inch tall? "It's all I'm capable of offering, Rylee. I'm sorry."

She shakes her head. "Don't be sorry, Brady. I know you. I knew what this was. And like you, I'm not looking for a relationship. But I'm not looking for a good-time guy either. I have responsibilities. I can't have distractions. I need to toe the line so I can get back to New York." She stands up and grabs her purse. "You can understand that, right?"

"Yeah." I pull out my phone to summon Lenny for her.

"So … are we good?" she asks.

"We're good," I say opening the door for her. "And Rylee?"

She turns around to look at me.

"That was a lot of fun. Thanks."

The edges of her mouth raise into a small smile. "I thought so too. So, see you Monday?"

"See you Monday."

I close the door and go pour myself a strong drink. I stare at myself in the mirror behind the mini-bar as I try to think if that has ever happened before. We had more fun than I can remember having since … well, in a long time. And she walked out. Done. Over. *She*'s the one who doesn't want a repeat.

I look at my reflection thinking it looks like a guy who just got dumped. And is sad about it.

"Fuck you, you pussy," I say to him, right before I down the rest of my drink and head to bed.

Chapter Twelve

I stumble across my bedroom, out to the living room to try to get my phone before the incoming call rolls to voicemail. I miss it but look to see it was Murphy calling. I check the time. It's almost noon. I grab the remote control and turn on the game. She probably wanted to talk to me before it started.

We talk a lot lately when the Hawks are traveling. She probably likes having someone else to talk to when Caden is away. And Murphy is great for keeping my mind off my issues. I look down at my left hand and reach over to grab the stress ball on the coffee table. I knead it obsessively – something I've been doing for the past few weeks. I've been told this won't necessarily change my prognosis, but it's something to do while I wait to see if I will ever play ball again.

Murphy must be especially lonely this week. Caden has been gone since last weekend and because they come to Tampa tomorrow, they won't be back in New York until Thursday. It's not often we have away stretches that long, where we bounce from city to city for three or four days each, but it happens once or twice a season.

I tap her number to return the call.

"Who is she, Brady? Spill."

"Well, hello to you too, Murphy. And what do you mean?"

"The girl you were eating dinner with in the photo. It's all over the internet."

"Hold on."

I pull out my iPad and Google my name, worried that someone took a compromising picture of us at dinner last night. My mind flashes back to all the flirting we did and I realize there were probably a lot of opportunities for someone to get such a photo. It takes me a minute to weed through the recent pictures on the tabloid sites. "I'm not seeing anything yet. How in the hell did you see something from last night? Are you stalking me?" I tease.

"I follow you and Caden and Sawyer so I get notifications whenever your names pop up in a story."

"Kind of dangerous, don't you think?" I ask. "I know how people can misconstrue things. I don't want you to get hurt unnecessarily when a photo of Caden and some girl shows up."

She laughs. "That happens so often, it doesn't even bother me anymore. I know Caden is committed to me."

"You've got him wrapped around your finger, Murphy. I've never met anyone who has to worry about cheating less than you. Oh, wait, here it is."

I stare at the picture of Rylee and me at dinner. The picture of her is blurry because she has her head thrown back and is laughing. It makes me smile, because this picture is the epitome of what our night was like. And before I realize what I'm doing, I screenshot the photo and save it to my phone.

"Who is she?" Murphy asks again. "Who's the bimbo?"

"She's not a bimbo," I bite back at her.

There is a pause. "Oh my God, Brady. You like her. I mean, you *like her*, like her."

"I do not."

"You do too."

"You don't know anything," I say petulantly.

"Humph," she pouts. "I've never seen you look at a woman like that before. What did you say to have her laughing like that?"

"We were playing a game," I tell her.

"Oh, reeeeally," she says, curiously. "What kind of game?"

"She wanted to see my moves."

"You were on a date with her," she says. "Why would she even have to ask?"

"Because it wasn't a date. We're just friends. And she couldn't believe women throw themselves at me so she said I must have moves. Then she told me my moves sucked and we made it a competition to see who was better at it."

Murphy laughs. "Sounds like a risky game if you ask me."

"You have no idea."

"Just friends, huh? Even after last night?"

I sigh. "I think so. But I'm not sure. I guess I'll find out at my PT appointment on Monday."

She snorts loudly into the phone. "You slept with your physical therapist?"

I lower my head. "I didn't intend to. I mean, I wanted to, but I never thought she would because she's so smart and responsible and then things just got out of hand with the flirting and the falling and the laughing."

"Wait. What falling? You didn't hurt your arm again, did you?"

"Thanks to Rylee, I didn't. But I fell twice and then I dropped her on the floor."

"Were you drunk?"

"No. Slightly buzzed maybe, but not drunk."

"Sounds horrible," she says. "Maybe she won't care if you don't want a repeat."

"It wasn't horrible, Murphy. It was fun. Like, really fun. And I don't have to worry about a repeat. She told me it's not happening again."

Laughter dances through the other end of the phone. "Oh, Brady. Maybe you've finally met your match."

"Mmm," I mumble.

"Oh, I see."

I roll my eyes. "What is it you think you see?"

"You *do* like her. And what you thought would be a roll in the hay has turned into something else. It's okay to have feelings for someone, Brady. It's good even. You can't go your whole life without opening yourself up to someone else."

"Quit shrinking me, Murphy. You don't know a thing about it."

"That's right, I don't. But someone should. You can't keep it all bottled up inside. It's not going to help you."

"I don't need help. Listen, is there another point to this phone call?"

"No. Not really. I just wanted to say hi and tell you to go easy on Caden and the boys. They've been on the road for a while."

I nod, remembering how taxing it could be on long trips. But I miss the hell out of it. I'd go on long trips every damn week if I could just play again.

The game is about to start and the camera pans the visitors' dugout. I think I see something and use the remote to rewind it so I can look again. "Oh, man," I say.

"What is it?" Murphy asks.

"They just showed the dugout. All the players were there, but nobody was sitting in the seat I always sit in."

"Yeah. Caden told me that's how it's been. They love you, Brady. They miss you. You hold that team together like glue and everyone knows it."

"But what if I—"

"You'll be back. I know it and they know it."

I look down at my hand, endlessly squeezing the stress ball. "I hope you're right."

"How much longer do you have there?" she asks.

"Five or six weeks."

"Are you getting out at all? I mean, with the exception of last night?"

"Not really. I tried hanging out with a few guys from the A-team, but it's just not the same."

"Well, your friends will be able to entertain you for the next few nights, so that's something. And you never know what else could happen."

"What does that mean?"

"Nothing. Just that you never know. Hey, the game's starting. I'll talk to you later."

"Okay, thanks for calling."

"I'm here for you anytime you need to talk. About anything, Brady, I mean that."

"Bye, Murphy."

I order room service then put down my phone and turn up the volume on the TV. Then I retrieve a bottle from the mini-bar and proceed to drain it while I watch my friends play the only game I've ever loved.

Three hours and a half-bottle of Jack later, I stumble my way back to my bedroom and into the shower. Then I walk to my closet and look for a t-shirt to wear when I eye something on the shelf.

I'm not even sure why I brought it with me. It's not like I ever wear it when I'm not pitching. It's my lucky shirt from Bumbershoot. The one I've worn under my jersey in every game since I was eighteen years old. It's old and faded and has been sewn up more times than I can count.

I take it with me to the bed and lay it on the pillow next to mine. Then I lie down beside it, wet towel and all, and I pass out.

"Best senior trip ever!" someone shouts over the crowd while a group of us are watching a band on one of the smaller stages.

Nat grabs my hand. "It really has been," she says. "I still can't believe my parents let me come. Four whole days away from them with only a few chaperones for the entire senior class. Who'd have thought?"

"Well they better get used to it, because when we go to Nebraska next year, they won't be able to tell you what to do any longer."

She looks up at me with that wrinkle in her nose that tells me she knows something I don't.

"What is it, Nat? You are still going to Nebraska with me, aren't you?"

"Of course I am. It's just that my dad said that if I get into UNL and move there with you, he might open up an office in Lincoln or Omaha."

I step back from her to gauge her seriousness. "You have to be fucking kidding me."

She shakes her head. "I'm not kidding, you know how protective he is."

"Shit. I'm not sure I could take four more years of Dennis Maddux. No offense."

"It'll be fine. He loves SoCal. He's been happier the past two years that we've been there than I've ever seen him. So he'd probably only show up in Nebraska occasionally to check on things."

"By check on things, I assume you mean check on me, *and how I'm treating his daughter."*

She wraps her arms around my neck. "You treat his daughter better than she deserves."

"Not even close," I say, picking her up so she can wrap her legs around me. "You deserve more than this. More than me. You deserve the world, Nat."

"You are *my world, babe. I love you."*

"I'm going to marry you one day, Natalie Maddux. You know that, don't you?"

"Know that?" she asks. "I'm counting on it. I'm going to be the wife of the best major league pitcher who ever lived. We're going to have a perfect life."

A guy walks by selling t-shirts. I whistle at him to get his attention then I point to myself. He looks through his shirts, finding one large enough to fit me and then he holds it up. It reads 'Bumbershoot 2009.' I dig a twenty out of my wallet and exchange it for the shirt. "You want one, too?" I ask Nat.

She shakes her head. "I'd rather just wear yours from time to time."

I thank the guy and throw the shirt over my shoulder. Natalie pats it and says, "Now you'll always remember this day, being part of the greatest arts festival in Seattle."

"With the greatest girl in the universe," I add. "Maybe it'll be my lucky shirt."

She smiles. "As if you need any luck. But I'll bet you'd look damn sexy if you wore it under your jersey."

"How would I look sexy if you couldn't even see it?"

"You're always sexy, babe. But knowing you're wearing it would be like a tribute to me, us, our love. And you'd be sure to score — with me anyway."

I laugh as she reaches around my neck and pulls me into a kiss.

"I'll never wear anything else under my jersey," I tell her when we break apart.

Samantha Christy

Chapter Thirteen

I smile from ear-to-ear when I hear a knock on my door. I hop off the couch and stride across my hotel room in three seconds flat. When I open the door, I see the hall is jammed with my teammates. Everyone yells their greetings. It's a boisterous hello resulting in a few doors opening down the way to see what the ruckus is all about.

I invite everyone inside, but most of my teammates shake my hand, offer a few quick words, and then retreat to their own rooms. All but Caden and Sawyer.

"They are a bunch of pussies," Sawyer says, coming in and making a bee-line to my mini-bar.

"It's been a long week," Caden offers. "You can't blame them."

"You don't have to babysit me, you know. We have three more nights to hang out."

Caden pats me on the back. "We're happy to be here, man. I know it must be hard being away from your family."

He doesn't mean Nat and Keeton. He doesn't mean my parents. He means him – them – my team. They are my family.

"I'm fine."

Caden eyes me with one raised, questioning brow.

I shake my head. "You and your fiancée talk too much."

He laughs. "You say that like it's a bad thing."

Sawyer picks up the stress ball I was incessantly squeezing and throws it at me. Instinctively, I put my left hand up to catch it. I'm able to catch it and grip it just enough so it doesn't fall out of my hand.

"You look fine to me, bro," he says.

"What do *you* know?" I throw the ball back at him. Then I realize something. That was the first time I've thrown something, anything, since my injury. It felt good. It felt damn good. But lobbing a toy across the room and throwing a one-hundred-mile-per-hour fastball are two very different things.

"How's it really going?" Caden asks, motioning to my arm.

I shrug. "Slow as shit. My elbow's healing fine, but some of my fingers are still numb. Everything's still up in the air at this point."

"So, what's on the agenda?" Sawyer asks, finishing his drink.

"I'm not going bar-hopping with you, Mills," Caden says. "Some of us actually need sleep."

Sawyer looks at his phone. "But it's not even nine o'clock."

"Doesn't it ever get old?" Caden asks.

"Only if you let it, bro," Sawyer says.

"I'm up for whatever," I tell them.

Sawyer looks at Caden, his eyes begging him to give in.

"Fine," Caden says. "But just a few drinks, and I'm not going any further than the hotel bar."

Sawyer hops off the couch. "Even better. Quick access to our hotel rooms, right, Taylor?" He nudges me and offers a wink on the way by.

Sawyer Mills and I are often grouped into the same category. The man-whore category. But we are completely different. While I tend to like knowing what I'm in for, thus having the same girl in every city, he never touches a girl more than once.

It's not to say I don't casually have one-nighters. I do. Especially at home and in Tampa, but I tend to be a creature of habit in all the other places. It simplifies things. No choices to make, no feelings, no emotions, no hassles.

Sawyer, on the other hand, is a bit of an enigma. Clearly he's gone on dates with women he likes. Women who would be good for him. Soul-mate types. I've witnessed it first hand as we double a lot. And I've been with him on more than one occasion where he's had to dump a girl after one date when he was obviously drawn to her and felt bad about cutting bait.

Either he's going for the record in women bedded like he's going for the record in stolen bases, or the guy is really fucked up.

Then again, aren't we all? I glance at Caden – well those of us who don't lead charmed lives.

Caden heads for the door. "Can we get this dog and pony show started then? I turn into a pumpkin at eleven."

We go down to the lobby and walk up to the hostess stand. "We're just going in to sit at the bar, Natasha."

She waves us by. "Go right ahead boys. And let me know if you need anything."

Sawyer raises his eyebrows at me when we sit down. "She's new. You done that yet?"

He knows she's new because this is the team hotel. Some guys rent a house during spring training camp, but those of us who don't, usually stay here. It's nice. It's convenient to both the beach and the training complex, and it has a great restaurant that tends to hire very attractive hostesses.

"Nah, you go ahead."

He narrows his eyes at me. "You've been here four fucking weeks and you haven't seen her naked? What is wrong with you?"

I brush off his comment and order a beer. Caden and Sawyer order one too.

"You're coming to the games, right?" Caden asks.

I nod my head. "Wouldn't miss 'em."

"It's going to be hard for you."

"Yeah. I know."

He pats my shoulder. "You'll get back there."

"So everyone keeps telling me."

"What have you been doing to keep busy?" he asks.

"You mean when Rylee and Matt aren't busting my balls?" I shrug. "I've been to the beach. I run, now that I'm off restriction. I'm all caught up on *Game of Thrones*. And I've seen a lot of the local wildlife."

He looks at me sideways.

"Don't ask."

Caden lifts his drink. "To getting the team back together again."

Sawyer taps his bottle to each of ours. "Can't happen soon enough."

"From your mouth to God's ears," I say, before taking a drink.

I see a woman walk through the bar with a scarf over her bald head, reminding me of something. "Hey, I haven't heard any news lately, how is Bobby's wife?"

Bobby Goodrich is one of our team's batting coaches. He's a good guy who we all call a friend. He used to go out with us often until his wife got sick last year.

Sawyer shakes his head. "It's not good. They found more cancer in her brain. It's all over her body now. She's thirty-three years old and might only have a few more weeks to live."

I close my eyes knowing Bobby is in for a world of pain. But he has his kids. And he knows it's coming. He can prepare. "At least they can say goodbye."

I chug the rest of my beer and ask for another.

Caden looks at me with sympathy. "Don't," I say.

"Speaking of doing things in your spare time," Caden says, wisely changing the subject. "What are you going to do about the job offer from the gym?"

"She told you about that, huh?"

"Of course she did. She's excited to get back into modeling. I don't think she'll give up her day job at the gym, I mean she practically runs the place now, but I've always thought she felt something was missing. She never got to prove herself. This is her chance. I'm proud as shit."

"I don't know, it just seems …"

"Beneath you?" Sawyer asks, popping some peanuts into his mouth.

Caden scolds him with a biting stare. "Athletes model all the time, you tool."

"It's not that," I say.

"You think if you do it, you're admitting you might be out of the game," Sawyer says.

He hit the nail on the fucking head. But I don't tell him that. I just take another drink.

"You can do both, you know," Caden says. "Nobody will think you're giving up just because you do some photo shoots for the gym."

"You sure are pushing for this, Kessler. Do you really want me to put on scant clothing and touch your fiancée? Because you know sex sells, right?"

He laughs. "Well, why the hell do you think I want *you?* Better you than some random nobody who thinks he has a shot with her."

I can see his logic. Murphy has been taken advantage of enough to last a lifetime. And Caden doesn't know it yet, but he just helped me make my decision.

Four attractive women walk up to the bar and order some drinks. They are clearly here for us. It's no secret the team is here.

Sawyer immediately starts talking to them and their incessant giggles echo throughout the room.

Natasha comes over. "Is everything okay gentlemen?"

Hotel workers have been told to keep an eye on things and call security if fans are getting out of hand.

"We're fine here," I tell her.

She eyes the women skeptically and looks back at me. "If you need anything, I'm right over there, just give me a signal or something."

"Will do. Thank you."

Natasha stares at me before walking away. No wonder Rylee thought I had slept with her. She's looking at me like I'm a mouth-watering piece of candy.

I look over at the table where Rylee and I dined the other night. I can almost see her throwing her head back and laughing like in the picture. Damn that was fun.

"Dude?"

I look at Sawyer who is trying to get my attention.

"Kylie asked you a question."

"Oh, sorry," I say, looking over at the women. "Which one of you is Kylie?"

The redhead holds up her hand.

"What were you asking me?"

"I heard you were going to be in town for a while and I was wondering if you needed a tour guide. You know, someone to show you all the best sights." She runs a finger from her throat down to her well-exposed cleavage.

I glance over at the table again and then look back at Kylie. I shake my head. "Thanks for the offer, I think I'm pretty well covered."

Sawyer leans over to me. "Is your fucking dick broken, too? What the hell, man?"

Caden looks at me for a second, then he turns to Sawyer. "Cut him some slack, Mills."

Kylie walks around behind Caden. "What about you?" she asks him. "Do you see anything here you like?"

He smiles politely. "I'm covered, too," he says. "I'm very happily engaged."

The girl scoffs and walks back over to take her seat.

I whisper to Caden, "What the hell does that mean, *'you're covered, too'?* What do you think I meant when I said that?"

He shrugs. "I don't know. Murphy told me some stuff. I guess I just thought—"

"Well, don't think," I interrupt. "Whatever she told you is something out of her overactive imagination. The woman reads too many romance novels."

"Maybe so," he says, finishing his beer. "Listen, speaking of Murphy, I think I'm going to head up and give her a call. I'm more tired than I thought."

He stands up and throws some money on the bar. I follow suit. "I'll go up with you."

Sawyer sees our intentions and narrows his eyes at me. "What's wrong with you?" he asks.

I lean in and pat him on the back as I whisper, "Looks like you'll have your pick of the litter. Have fun, my friend."

That perks him up a bit. "You mean I can only pick one?"

Caden and I laugh as we walk out of the restaurant.

He studies me as we ride up the elevator together.

"What?" I bite at him.

He holds up his hands in surrender. "Nothing. Jeez."

"Quit thinking about me," I say as we arrive at our floor and the doors open. "Go have dirty phone sex with your fiancée."

That puts a smile on his face. "I just might do that. But don't tell Murphy I said that, she'd be mortified."

"Later," I say, reaching my door.

I walk into my suite and stare at the wall I had Rylee pressed against Friday night. I start to get hard just thinking about it. Then I stare at the floor where she was straddling me, my dick begging for release as I picture her that way. I unbutton my pants, taking myself into my hand as I walk into the bedroom. Then I see the t-shirt still on my bed.

Fuck.

My dick goes flaccid as I fold up the shirt and put it back in the closet. And then I take a shower, washing all thoughts of my past, and any future, down the drain.

Chapter Fourteen

Rylee opens the door to the PT room. "I'm ready for you."

I study her face as I walk by. I don't want this to be awkward. She smiles at me letting me know we're good.

I see Alex in the room working on another player. He stops what he's doing and looks up at me. He's been jealous of me from day one. Rylee and I have gotten along well from that very first appointment. That's nothing new. I've even had the same experience with other PTs who are men. Well, not *exactly* the same experience. But sometimes you get stuck with someone who you can barely hold a conversation with because you just don't click.

"Did you have a nice weekend, Rylee?" I ask with a raised brow just to mess with Alex.

"I did. It was fun."

"I'm glad to hear it. What did you do?"

She widens her eyes as if to scold me.

She thinks about my question for a beat. "Saw some wild animals." Then she shrugs nonchalantly. "Even fed one of them."

I can't control my outburst of laughter because I know damn well we weren't allowed to feed anything at the Big Cat Rescue.

Alex walks by, eyeing what he thinks is his competition as Rylee sets me up to work with the bands attached to the wall. When he takes his patient into the other room, Rylee says, "Stop it."

"Stop what?"

"Oh, come on. You know what you're doing."

"In case you haven't noticed, Ry, that guy wants you."

"Doesn't matter. It's against the rules."

I raise a brow at her.

She rolls her eyes. "It was a one-time thing, Brady," she whispers. "It's not going to happen again."

"You had fun feeding the animals, didn't you? Especially the barracuda."

She looks around the room to make sure nobody has walked back in. "It was a lot of fun, but you and I both know it shouldn't have happened. We each have things we need to accomplish – *important* things – to keep our careers on track."

She directs me to try the stronger band since this one has gotten too easy for me.

"All work and no play will make Rylee a sad girl," I tell her when she settles back in at her laptop.

"I can play later. After I've accomplished my goals."

I blow out an acquiescing breath. "Fine. No more feeding the beast. So what would you suggest we do on Friday instead?"

She looks up from her laptop. "No way. No more Friday nights."

I smile. "You don't trust yourself with me, do you?"

"It's not that," she says. Then she shakes her head. "Well, maybe it's a little that. I just think we should keep things professional, that's all."

"I think I'm going to have to change your mind."

"You can try. But ask anyone, I'm pretty stubborn."

"Nobody likes a challenge more than I do," I say with a wink.

"Not happening, Taylor. In fact, the only way I would hang out with you again is if we had a chaperone."

I laugh. *Yeah, she wants me baaaaad.* "We'll see, Kennedy."

"Did you get to see your teammates yet?" she asks, changing the subject.

"They flew in last night. I had drinks with Caden and Sawyer. Hey, you should go to the game tonight."

"Have you not listened to anything I just said, Brady? I'm not going out with you."

"Not with *me*. I'll be sitting in the dugout."

"Oh, right. Sorry."

"Surely you have someone you can enjoy the game with."

Her face lights up. "Actually, I do."

Suddenly, I'm sorry I said anything about it. I was thinking she could go with a friend. A *girl* friend. But that look on her face has something gnawing at my gut.

I shut up about it for the rest of my session. When I know we're winding down for the day, I tell her what's been on my mind since last night. "I want to start throwing."

"Brady." She looks at me like my mom used to when I'd ask for a second slice of cake.

"Come on, Ry. I know my hand sucks. But I need to start throwing."

"It's barely been four weeks since your surgery."

"Exactly," I say. "You need to push me, Rylee. You need to push me harder than you push anyone else. I can take it."

She takes a minute and looks at some data on her laptop. "I'll tell you what," she says, hooking me up to the TENS. "You impress me this week and then we'll see about it next Monday."

117

"I thought I already impressed you on Friday."

She blushes.

"Don't get cocky," she says.

"I did that with you on Friday, too."

She laughs.

I love her laugh.

"You're incorrigible," she says.

Alex finishes with his client and sits at a nearby desk. "So, the team's in town," he says to me.

"Yeah. Thank God. I've been bored as shit."

"I'll bet," he says, eyeing me skeptically. He thinks I'm a douchebag. I've heard him make more than a few comments to Rylee about my extra-curricular activities when he didn't think I could hear him. Or maybe he did. I get it though, he's trying to protect her. Or fuck her.

Then he turns to Ry. "Maybe we should go. You know, show some support. How about it?"

Holy shit. The asshole is asking her out right in front of me.

Rylee looks more than a little uncomfortable. "Thanks, Alex. It's a good idea, but I already have plans."

"Plans with Stryker?"

I tense up. Rylee tenses up. It's as awkward a moment as we've had together.

"No, uh, can we not talk about that?" Rylee says, shooting Alex a punishing stare. "I like to keep my personal life out of the therapy room."

"Of course," Alex says, having the decency to look like he feels bad for being so unprofessional. "I'm sorry." He picks up his laptop and takes it into one of the offices.

Rylee looks anywhere but at me. I'm not sure if I should be pissed or impressed. I mean, who says guys are the only ones who can play around? Maybe Murphy was right. Maybe I've met my match. I just wonder how many more Strykers are out there. And does she take all of *them* to see the fish and the big cats and the streetcars?

And really - his name couldn't be Bob or Jim? Fucking Stryker. He's got a baseball name. Maybe he's a player. Maybe he's on the single-A team. Maybe she dates players after all. Maybe Rylee Kennedy has a boyfriend. *Shit*.

"I assume you want a massage today?" she asks, seeming to be in a better mood now that Alex has left the room.

Stupidest. Question. Ever.

"Haven't turned one down yet, have I?"

"Climb on up," she says, motioning to the training table behind me.

I lie on my back, watching her open the jar to get the greasy stuff that makes her hands glide effortlessly over my neck and shoulders. The anticipation is almost painful. I'm getting hard before she even touches me.

She starts working on my neck, but then stops abruptly. Five seconds later, she tosses a hand towel onto my tented sweatpants. "Maybe you should think about wearing jeans next time."

I chuckle, arranging the towel over my growing erection. I extend my neck and look up at her. "I can't help it, Ry. I know what your hands feel like on me. I know what they feel like on every part of me."

She uses her fingers to force my head back into position so that I'm not looking at her. Then she proceeds to give me a massage unlike any other. She may claim she doesn't want to see me again, but her hands tell me a much different story than her words.

~ ~ ~

Being back in the dugout is bittersweet. All the guys are trying their best to make me feel welcome. But it's still uncomfortable as shit knowing I'm not going out on that field. Knowing I have to stay in the dugout – useless and damaged.

I look down at my arm and run my right hand along a line from my elbow to my thumb. Sometimes it burns or tingles when I do it, but I don't mind, at least I'm feeling *something* there. I know it's only been a month, but I expected to get the feeling back in my fingers. I thought maybe the doctors were wrong, or that once my elbow started to heal, my nerve would heal right along with it. I'm trying to stay positive. I keep telling myself these things take time. And I'm reminded around noon every Monday through Friday that I *am* making progress even though it may not seem like it.

Still, I see the way the guys look at me. They all know it's more than just a simple bone break. They know I won't be back for the playoffs, something I might have managed if I were dealing with simply a fracture.

I pull the stress ball out of my pocket. It goes with me everywhere. When I'm not squeezing it, I'm stretching rubber bands between my fingers, or I'm using the hand grip.

I watch Caden give the signs to Cole, the pitcher he's been paired with the most in my absence, and it feels like I'm the other-fucking-woman. They work perfectly together, just like we used to. And when Caden calls time to approach the mound, they even laugh. Just like we used to.

After the inning, Caden removes his gear and sits next to me. "Cole's good. One of the best," he says to me privately. "But he's not you." He pats me on the back and then gets up to find his batting helmet.

I stand up and go to the railing, resting my elbows on it as I peer into the stands. I miss this so badly it hurts. I miss the fans. I miss the field. I miss the camaraderie we have as a team. I miss the good times with my best friends.

But despite all that, I find myself looking around at the crowd, wondering if Rylee is out there. And for the first time, I realize that when I leave here in a month, there is something else I might miss, too.

Chapter Fifteen

I come in through the front doors of the hotel, drenched in sweat from my afternoon run. I ran two extra miles today after my PT session. Might as well. It's not like I have to get ready for a night out. *No more Fridays*, she told me. I thought Rylee would give in as the week wore on, but she stuck to her guns.

As I make my way to the elevator, I think I see a familiar face and do a double take.

"Murphy?" I walk over to a sitting area by the reception desk to see my best friend's girl parked on a couch reading a book. She has a small suitcase by her side.

She looks up at me, smiling. "Surprise!"

I look around to see if Caden is here. I know he couldn't be because they went home to New York for three days and today they start a series in Kansas City. "What are you doing here?"

"Can't a girl fly in for the weekend to see one of her best friends?"

My heart soars to hear her say that. I've never had a chick as a best friend before, but Murphy has a way of working herself into your life whether you want her to or not. And at first, I didn't want her to. She was nice and sophisticated and … freaking hot. She was also engaged to one of my closest friends. I know myself. It was only a matter of time before I fucked up and made a move.

But miraculously, that never happened and now they are planning their wedding and she's become more like a sister to me than anything else.

"Yes. But why?"

She just smiles at me and gathers her things.

I shake my head. "What the hell did Caden tell you? It's not like I'm wallowing in self-pity down here, Murphy. I'm fine."

"He said no such thing. I just miss you and I needed a vacation."

I look at her small suitcase. "Just how long do you plan on staying?"

"I fly out Sunday night. I thought you could take me to the beach tomorrow so I could work on my tan."

I raise my eyebrows at her. "You're not going to watch the game?"

"I don't watch every game, you know."

I stare her down.

She gives me an eyeroll. "Okay, so we can stream it on my iPad."

I laugh. I'm pretty sure she never misses a game, even if she has to record them. When she's not working at the gym, she lives, eats, and breathes baseball just like we do. She'll make the perfect baseball wife – she has her own responsibilities separate from Caden, yet she's as passionate about the game as any woman I've ever seen. What a change from when Caden first met her and she knew nothing about the sport.

I pick up her suitcase. "You didn't get a room, did you? I have a suite. You can take the bed and I'll sleep on the couch. It'll save you a few bucks."

Murphy backs up and studies me. "I'm sorry, I was looking for Brady Taylor, the guy who couldn't care less who spends money and on what."

I laugh. "It'll be fun. Don't girls love sleepovers? Well, unless you think Caden will have an issue with it."

"There was a time when Caden didn't want you to look at me, let alone share a suite with me. All you ever did was look at my boobs back then."

I shrug. "Can't help it. It's an unconscious habit."

She cocks her head sideways. "You don't do it anymore." I'm amused that she says it almost as if she's upset about it.

"That's because you're like my sister, Murphy, and that would be gross. Plus, Caden would kick my ass."

"I'm not sure about that," she says. "I'm thinking it might be a draw."

"Come on. Let's head on up so I can shower and give you a proper hug."

~ ~ ~

I throw on some clothes and towel-dry my hair before joining Murphy out in the living room.

"What do you want to do tonight?" I ask.

"Maybe I should ask *you* that," she says. "I mean, I did kind of crash your party here. Did you have any plans?"

I raise my arms out to my side. "My dance card appears to be empty. I'm all yours."

"What about the physical therapist?"

125

I shake my head. "I told you. We're just friends. It was a one-time thing anyway."

She chews on her lower lip as she studies me. "But you didn't want it to be."

"Whatever. It is what it is," I say, pouring myself a drink. "On to the next one."

I slam down the decanter a little too hard, spilling liquid out the top.

Murphy walks over and uses a napkin to clean up my mess. "Maybe she would like to join us."

I laugh. "Not a chance. She said she wouldn't go out with me unless . . . Wait, you're brilliant."

I pull out my phone and type out a text to Rylee. Normally I don't care to have the numbers of the girls I date. But Ry is more than that. She's my physical therapist. And I think she just might be my friend.

Me: I think I have just the thing to change your mind about going out.

It takes her a few minutes to reply. All the while I stare at my phone, wondering what she could be doing late on a Friday afternoon if she's not with me.

Rylee: I doubt that.

Me: Remember how you said we'd need a chaperone?

Rylee: I was kidding, Brady. What, did you enlist Lenny or one of the A-team guys to be a third-wheel or something?

Me: No. But what if I told you the chaperone was the home run girl?

Rylee: Caden Kessler's fiancée is in town?

Me: The one and only.

Rylee: I'm not going on a double date, Brady.

Me: Caden is in Kansas City. If you were a good team therapist, you'd know that.

Rylee: I do know that. I guess I just assumed they'd be here together. I mean, what is Murphy doing in Tampa without Caden? Wait, did you set this up just because I said I'd like to meet her?

Me: She just showed up at the hotel. I knew nothing about it. Scout's honor.

Rylee: Why do I get the idea you were never a Boy Scout?

Me: Very funny. You've got me there. But seriously, I did not have a hand in this. Murphy was asking what we should do tonight and I just thought of you. Like I told you weeks ago, I think you two will get along great. And you DID say you wanted to meet her. I'm trying to be nice here, Ry.

Rylee: Okay, fine. But I still can't go out tonight.

Me: Why not?

Rylee: I just can't. Just leave it at that.

I find myself having an emotion that I never have. Ever. I see red. I see some goddamned guy named Stryker. And I try to push it to the back of my mind.

Rylee: But I might be able to meet up with you guys tomorrow night if she's still in town.

Me: Tomorrow would be fine. Can you be here at six? I'll take you both out for dinner and drinks.

Rylee: I think I can manage that.

Me: Great. See you then.

I put my phone away and turn to see that Murphy was watching over my shoulder. She gives me a smug smile.
"What?" I ask.
"I saw that," she says.

"Saw what?"

"I saw your jaw tighten when she said she couldn't go out tonight."

"You're seeing things. I think planning your wedding has turned you into some love-crazed woman."

"Or maybe it has fine-tuned my senses. Come on, Brady. Admit that you like the girl."

I throw my hands up. "I like the girl," I say. "I like a *lot* of girls, Murphy."

"Yeah, but you like her *more*. Don't you?"

"Are we in seventh grade?"

She smirks at me before she walks over to pull her suitcase into the bedroom. "I'm going to shower the travel grime off, then you're showing me the town."

"It's not like you've never been here," I call out after her. "You came down for a whole week during spring training this year."

She peeks her head out of the bathroom. "You're right, I did. And I barely left the hotel room."

I laugh thinking of how giddy Caden was the week of her visit. "That's my boy."

"No, that's *my* boy," she says, closing the door.

I listen to her sing shamelessly in the shower. It's unnatural for two people to be as fucking happy as they are.

I walk in the bedroom and put her suitcase on the bed for her. I stare at the bed and think about what Rylee and I were doing on it just a week ago. Then I glance over to the closet where my Bumbershoot shirt sits, folded neatly on a shelf.

Some people are just not meant to be happy.

Chapter Sixteen

I open the passenger door to let Murphy in. She laughs at me. "There is no way you are fitting in the back seat of this car. But thanks for the gesture."

She slips into the back of Rylee's SUV as I take my place in the front, but before I put on my seatbelt, I forge an introduction. "Rylee Kennedy, meet Murphy Cavenaugh."

Rylee turns around in her seat and shakes Murphy's hand. "I'm so happy to meet you." She holds up her arm, displaying a #MurphyStrong wristband. "I'm a big fan."

"It's nice to meet you, too," Murphy says. "I haven't seen one of those in a while."

After Murphy rose to fame as the girl who got hit by Caden Kessler's ball and then stole his heart, she was publicly humiliated by her ex who had been trying to extort money from Caden. After she bravely showed her face, refusing to let the ex get the best of her, fans printed t-shirts, hats, and wristbands in her honor.

I turn to Rylee. "So you'll show your support for Murphy, but not the team you work for?" I tease.

"What are you talking about? I love the Hawks."

"Then how come you don't wear t-shirts or hats?"

"Brady, I wear a polo shirt with the Hawks logo every day at work."

"Only because you're required to. When is the last time you've been to a game?"

"I might have caught one just last week," she says.

"You did?" I say, surprised. "Why didn't you say anything?" She shrugs.

Because she went with Stryker, that's fucking why.

"So where are we going?" she asks.

When I tell her what restaurant we're going to in Clearwater, she scolds me with her stare. "That's an expensive place, Brady."

"The rules don't apply tonight."

"Rules?" Murphy asks from the back seat.

"Rylee has a rule that I'm not allowed to spend money frivolously. She's all about being responsible and saving for the future."

Murphy laughs. "Oh, so that's why."

"That's why what?" I ask.

"Rylee, you'll be happy to know you are rubbing off on Brady. He wouldn't let me waste money on a hotel room when he has a suite."

"Oh," Rylee says, studying Murphy in the rearview mirror.

For a split second, I think she looks at Murphy the way I look at Alex, but then she forces a smile.

Murphy covers her mouth. "Oh my gosh, that didn't come out right. We didn't … he didn't … I mean, Brady slept on the couch."

"It's fine," Rylee says curtly, eyes laser focused on the road in front of her.

"I'm very happily engaged, Rylee," Murphy says. "I don't want you to think … I guess I should have kept my big mouth shut."

Murphy apologizes to me with her eyes. But she doesn't need to. I'm amused by Ry's reaction. She's jealous. But what's even more surprising is that I like it.

"Brady helped get Caden and me together," Murphy says. "Did he ever tell you that? He and Caden flew out to Iowa when I fled New York, and Brady made a very convincing argument for me to come back."

"Why do I find that hard to believe?" Ry says, looking at me out of the corner of her eye.

"It's true," Murphy says. "Beneath that rough and roguish exterior, Brady Taylor is actually quite charming. But he only brings it out for those he truly cares about."

I give Murphy a cease and desist look, but she ignores me.

"I happened to see a picture of the two of you at dinner last week," Murphy continues. "And he looked like he was being *very* charming."

I'm beginning to get the feeling that Murphy has ulterior motives here. She's playing matchmaker. Maybe she thinks Ry can fix me or something. But she's wrong. There is a lot more than my arm that's broken. And not even the best physical therapist in the world can help me.

"There was a picture of us?" Rylee asks.

"Someone must have snapped it at the restaurant," I say. "Don't worry, no one could tell it was you."

She looks relieved and I wonder if she's worried about her job, or worried about someone seeing her with me. Someone named Stryker.

We pull up to valet parking and exit the car. Onlookers watch us enter the restaurant and I think of how lucky I am to be escorting these two lovely ladies.

We get seated along the windows in the back overlooking the pier.

Rylee looks out the window longingly. "I love Pier 60."

I momentarily wonder why she loves it. Does she walk the pier with other men? Then I remind myself that I don't care. That I *can't* care.

"My dad taught me how to fish when I was young," she says. "We had the best times together. So, now when I want to feel close to him, I go fishing. Pier 60 is really long – good for fishing."

"I'm sorry," Murphy says. "Did you lose your father?"

Rylee nods. "About four years ago."

"I lost mine when I was twelve. But sometimes, it feels like it was yesterday. Every kid deserves to grow up with a father, you know?"

Rylee sighs and looks down at the table. She must really miss him.

The waiter comes over and I order a bottle of wine. I don't miss Rylee's smile. She knows I didn't order the most expensive bottle.

"What looks good?" I ask them as I peruse the menu. I glance up at Rylee. "And don't say the sandwiches. You are not allowed to order one tonight."

"I was thinking about a burger," she says.

"That's a sandwich," I admonish.

"It is not," she says.

"What do you think, Murphy," I ask. "Is a hamburger a sandwich?"

She looks at the menu. "Well, it's not listed that way. It's under *handhelds*."

"Right. You eat it with your hands," I say. "Like a sandwich."

"You also eat chicken wings and corn on the cob with your hands," Rylee adds. "Do you consider those sandwiches?"

Murphy laughs. "I think you'd better concede this one, Brady."

"One of these days, I'm going to get you to order the prime rib. Or the chateaubriand," I say to Rylee.

"That'll be the day," she says.

"When's your birthday? Surely you'd order it then."

"January 21st," she says.

I frown thinking it's well after I go home. "Maybe we can celebrate it late, when I come back for spring training."

The waiter comes to take our order before she can answer. But I get the feeling I might not have gotten one anyway. Rylee is so unlike the other girls I date. She never wonders when she's going to see me next. Never asks questions about the future. Of course, this isn't a date. She's only here because of Murphy.

"Speaking of spring training," Murphy asks, nodding to my arm. "Not that I think you won't be recovered by then, but what happens if a player is injured during that time? Do they stay home?"

I laugh. "Hardly. Nobody gets out of spring training. And remember, this is the best rehab facility around. That's why I'm here." I rub my left arm from elbow to wrist as I've done so often lately. "It's almost four months away, so who knows what will happen."

Rylee gives me a sympathetic stare. "Even if you aren't ready by then, I have confidence it will happen. These things can be slow, but that doesn't mean you won't make a full recovery and come back even stronger."

"If anyone can do it, Brady can," Murphy adds.

"I believe that's true." Rylee raises her wine glass. "To a better, stronger future."

Murphy and I tap our glasses to hers. "Hell, yeah," I say.

"Have you cut your hair?" Murphy asks after taking a drink.

I run my hands through it. "No. Why?"

She shrugs. "It just looks nice. Don't you think so, Rylee? I love Brady's hair. He always looks like he's just rolled out of bed, yet perfectly put together. I shudder to think what he looks like after a roll in the hay. Swoon-worthy, I'm sure."

Rylee's cheeks pink up and she sips her wine.

"And his face." Murphy reaches over and swipes a finger across my jaw. "Don't you think it belongs on the cover of a magazine? All these sharp angles."

"Uh, I suppose," Rylee says, gulping down another swig.

"You're not going to team up on me, are you?" I ask. "I haven't agreed to it yet, Murphy."

"I know. But you'd be doing the world a disservice if you didn't." She turns to Rylee. "You should see this guy without a shirt on, Rylee." She fans herself. "Can you imagine all the sportswear he could sell for the gym? I mean, those rock-hard abs. Go on, show her, Brady."

What the hell is Murphy doing? She knows Rylee and I slept together. Rylee shifts around in her seat.

I can't tell if she's really uncomfortable or just really turned on.

"I'm not sure this is the place, Murphy."

She laughs. "Oh, right."

"So, Murphy, how do you manage with Caden gone so often?" Rylee asks.

"Well, I have a job that takes up most of my time. Keeping busy helps. I miss him, of course, but with all my responsibilities and all my friends, it helps me manage being alone." Murphy looks around and then leans in closer to whisper to us. "And I'm not normally one to kiss and tell, but ... wow ... when Caden travels and then comes home again, sometimes we barely make it past the front door. I mean absence really does make the heart grow fonder. Last week, when I ripped his shirt off—"

Rylee's chair scrapes on the floor as she backs it away from the table. "Excuse me," she says. "I need to hit the bathroom before dinner comes."

Murphy and I watch her as she rushes through the restaurant.

I turn back to Murphy. "I know what you're doing."

"What?" She tries to look all innocent.

I shake my head and laugh. "If you'll excuse me as well, I'm going to see if she's okay."

"Yeah – you better. It looked like she was about to blow."

I walk to the back hallway and see a woman exiting the bathroom. "Ma'am, can you tell me how many other people are in there? My sister was upset and I need to go in and talk to her."

"You mean the girl splashing water on her face? I think she's the only one in there now."

"Thank you."

I go through the bathroom door and lock it behind me.

When Rylee sees me behind her in the mirror, she looks around the bathroom quickly. "What are you doing in here?" She looks under the two stalls. "And ... did you really just *lock* the door?"

"Rylee," I say, standing right in front of her. "I want you."

137

"I, uh …"

"If you can stand here and tell me you don't want me, I'll leave right now. If you can tell me that, even though I know it's a lie, I'll leave you alone." I put a hand around her and caress her neck. Her eyes close briefly and she takes a shaky breath. "But look at how your body reacts to me. I'm the same way. Just thinking about being with you makes me hard."

She opens her eyes and looks down at the bulge in my pants. And when her eyes meet mine again, I know what her answer is.

My lips crash down on hers and in an instant, we're tearing at each other's clothing. My hands go up her shirt and cup her breasts as she heaves them into me. Her fingers waste no time undoing my pants and I moan when she takes me into her hands.

My hand travels beneath her skirt to find her panties soaking wet. "Jesus, Ry." I lift her up onto the edge of the counter and I move the drenched cotton aside and slip in a finger. Then two.

She throws her head back. "Yes!"

She pushes my jeans down just enough to expose me completely. Then she pulls me to her. Just as my cock touches her entrance, I pull back. "Shit. Condom." I fish one out of my wallet. I put it on in record time and in seconds, I'm buried deep inside her.

Her legs spread wide giving me full access to her clit and I take no prisoners as I rub and circle and pinch it, sending her into a quick orgasm. She starts to scream and I cover her mouth with my hand. Then I lean forward and bite my hand so I don't yell out with my own release.

I rest my forehead on hers. Then her body shakes as she giggles. "You can move your hand now," her muffled words tell me.

I remove my hand from her mouth. "Shit, Ry. That was—"

"Fast?" She laughs, making me join in.

I step back and remove the condom, tossing it into the trashcan. I help her down and then hold her eyes in the mirror as I wash my hands.

She starts to look upset with herself. "I give myself an F," she says, pulling her skirt back down.

"What? No way, that was great."

"Maybe. But now I'm one of your stupid chicks." She shakes her head.

I nod to the counter. "Nothing about that was stupid, Rylee."

"It was irresponsible though."

I grab a paper towel and dry my hands. "You know, you keep saying things like responsible and professional and career. But it's bullshit, Ry. You can be those things. You can have those things and have this, too. There is nothing wrong with what we're doing. We're both adults here and we both need to let off steam once in a while. That's why you just did what you did, right?"

She nods. "Yeah. It's been a tough week I guess."

"We can do this if you want. You and me – four more weeks."

"You mean you want me to be your *Tampa girl?*"

I sigh and lean against the wall. "Yes. No. To be honest, I hadn't even thought about you like that. You're not like the others, but that doesn't mean I … I mean I can't …"

She puts a hand on me. "It's okay, Brady. I can't either."

"So, you see, it's perfect then. You're all about your career and getting back to New York. I'm all about getting back in the game. Neither of us is looking for anything more than good fun sex. We're a match made in heaven."

"Or maybe hell," she adds with a giggle.

"Come on, you have to admit we have a lot of fun together, don't we?"

She nods. "We do."

"So, what do you say, Kennedy? Four weeks, loads of fun, no strings and all the public bathroom sex you can handle."

She laughs out loud. "Well when you put it *that* way."

I pick her up and twirl her around. "Yes!"

Then I look at the time. "Murphy is probably wondering if we fell in. We've been gone for almost ten minutes."

"Wow – we brought new meaning to the word *quickie*," she says. "You go. I'll come out in a minute."

"Yeah, because *that* will make it seem like this didn't just happen," I tease.

She covers her face with her hands. "Oh my God, I'm going to be mortified."

I laugh as I unlock the door. "Don't be. Murphy orchestrated this whole encounter. You can bet on it."

Murphy appraises me as I walk back into the room and take a seat across from her.

"I was going to ask if everything was okay," she says. "But based on the look on your face, I don't believe I need to."

I can feel myself smile from ear to ear. "No, you definitely don't need to."

"I like her," she says.

I turn and watch Rylee make her way to the table, her face still flushed from our bathroom encounter. "What's not to like?"

I can see Murphy's triumphant smile out of the corner of my eye, making me realize I just said that out loud. "Don't read too much into that, Murphy."

She holds her hands up in surrender. "I wouldn't dare."

Chapter Seventeen

Physical therapy with Rylee has a whole new meaning now. We share secret glances, heated gazes and private jokes. If it wasn't already the highlight of my days, it sure as hell is now.

We've succeeded in pissing off Alex more than once with our laughter. He shoots me a dirty look every time our eyes meet. There is something about him that just rubs me the wrong way. What kind of boss asks his subordinate out in front of a patient? What kind of boss asks his subordinate out *at all?*

Then again, he could say the same thing about me.

Maybe we're both assholes.

"Stand up," Rylee says before she hooks me up to the TENS. "I want to measure your progress."

She has me flex and extend my elbow as she takes measurements and records the numbers in her laptop. "Squeeze," she says, holding her hands out to me. "Don't be a wimp about it."

I squeeze her hands as hard as I can. Well, maybe not with my right hand, because I don't want to crush her delicate fingers. But I try my hardest with my left.

"Good," she says, making some notes. "Despite what you think you *are* making progress." She picks up the stress ball on the table and hands it to me. Then she walks ten feet away. "Throw it to me."

I roll my eyes at her. "You're kidding, right? I'm used to throwing hundred-mile-an-hour fastballs to a guy who is sixty feet away from me."

"You have to start somewhere," she says. "Come on, just an easy overhand toss. We don't want to stress the elbow too badly, or the shoulder."

I toss her the ball.

She catches it and smiles.

"Did I pass the test?" I ask.

"It didn't fall out of your hand, so, yes."

"It's a stress ball, Ry, not a baseball. Big difference. I need to throw a baseball. I need to throw it at something. At someone. I'm dying here."

It's been five weeks since I've pitched. That's four weeks longer than I've ever gone in my life. I strained my arm badly a few years ago and had to lay off for eight days, but other than that, it's only a day or two of rest between games I start in. Even in the offseason you can find me at the pitching facility every day.

If I'm not throwing a damn baseball, who the hell am I?

I need to pitch. I need it like I need food. Like I need water. Like I need air.

I need it or I'll die – just like I told her.

Rylee is looking at my arm, lost in contemplative thought.

"What is it?" I ask her.

"Just a thought," she says. "A way to give you what you want and have a little fun, too."

I raise my eyebrows suggestively. "Give me what I want?"

She looks around to make sure nobody is listening. "Not *that*, you animal."

"I thought you liked my animal, Ry."

She shakes her head at my witty banter, but she's smiling, so I know she likes it.

She pulls out her phone and it looks like she's sending a text. A minute later, it seems she gets a reply. Then she looks up at me. "What are you doing tomorrow night?"

"A Tuesday? Wow, Rylee, you want me so badly you can't even wait until Friday."

"Are you free or not?" she asks, pretending to be annoyed.

I stare at her and wonder why she had to send the text. Was she moving around plans again? Making excuses not to see the boyfriend perhaps?

"I suppose I could be. What do you have in mind?"

"I'll pick you up at six."

I give her a cheeky grin. "You aren't going to tell me?"

"It's a surprise."

"I like surprises," I say with a wink.

Wait. No I don't. I hate surprises. I always like to be in control and know what, where, and when. Surprises suck.

Unless, apparently, they come from Rylee Kennedy.

~ ~ ~

"What happened to letting me drive sometimes?" I ask when she picks me up on Tuesday.

"You can drive home," she says. "This way I don't have to tell you where we're going. You'll see it when you see it."

"Are you taking me to see more animals, Ry?"

"Hmmm. There might be some animals there, but that's not what we're going for."

"Are we going to the circus?"

She laughs. "Not exactly."

I watch her as we drive out of the city. She loves playing games with me. And damn it if her games don't turn me on. Her face is lit with youth and exuberance. She's excited to be going wherever we're going. Or maybe she's just excited that she's going with *me*.

She turns to see me staring. "What is it?"

"Nothing. It's just that you're always taking us on these adventures. I really think you're just a big kid."

She laughs. "I guess I am."

"I like big kids."

Her smile falls and she stares straight ahead. "Just don't like me too much, Brady."

Never in all my years as a player have I had a woman say those words to me. I suspect there is more to Rylee Kennedy than I know. More than the mother in the memory care facility. More than the boyfriend or fuck-buddy named Stryker. More than her desire to get back to New York.

Something is preventing her from wanting me too much. From needing me for more than just sex. And for the life of me, I can't figure out why I want to know what it is.

"You're preaching to the choir, Rylee," I gaze out my window. "You're preaching to the choir."

Ten minutes later, something comes into view and I laugh. "Are you taking me to the fair?"

I see a tall, lighted Ferris wheel in the distance along the country road we're driving on. I think about what she said yesterday about giving me what I want and then I realize what they have at county fairs.

"Oh, hell yeah! They have baseball target games here, don't they?"

"Calm down. We may not work up to those." She pulls into the parking lot and we're directed down a dirt lane to another guy with an orange vest on who shows us where to park. She turns off her car and looks me in the eye. "I'm your physical therapist, Brady. You have to listen to me and trust me with your rehabilitation. They have lots of things here that we can use. Ring toss, dart games, and yes, ball throws. These things will not only help your elbow, but the dexterity in your fingers. But you have to only go as far as I say. I can't have you hurting yourself and impeding your progress. Agreed?"

I smile at her. I smile big. I feel like a kid on Christmas. I'm practically bouncing with excitement as we approach the ticket booth. I buy the book with the most game tickets and Rylee laughs at me.

She leans close and says, "You're not afraid of heights, are you?" I follow her eyes to the Ferris wheel.

"And two tickets for the Ferris wheel," I tell the guy behind the glass.

Rylee nudges me with her elbow.

"Better make it four," I say to him.

"I hope you're hungry," Rylee says as we enter the fair. "You can pretty much buy any food you can think of and they will put it on a stick and fry it."

"Salad?" I say, poking her in the ribs.

"Smartass."

I laugh. "Games first. Food later."

145

"How about one or two games first, then food, then if your arm can take it, more games?"

"Are you always this demanding?"

She starts to protest, but I cut her off and lean in close. "I like it, Ry. I like you bossing me around. Maybe when we're done here, you can boss me around back at the hotel."

The Cheshire-cat smile that takes over her face makes me want to scrap this whole plan and get right back in her car. I love how she tries to be all professional with me at work, but here, she's just herself. No boss in the other room. No appearances to uphold. And by the look in her eyes, I can see I'm in for one hell of a ride – and I don't mean on the Ferris wheel.

We take our time walking around and assessing all the booths. She finally settles on the ring toss. I hand the guy some tickets and Rylee picks up the rings. "These are lightweight, but they're small and you might have a hard time gripping them."

"Hand them over," I say, motioning for them. I toss one and my wrist goes limp and the damn ring barely makes it over the first bottle. "Fuck." I look around hoping no kids heard me.

Rylee takes a ring from me. "Try using your whole arm instead of your wrist. You still don't have great flexion and extension in your wrist, but if you make this an elbow exercise …"

I watch her demonstrate how she wants me to do it, still pissed that I can't even flick a four-ounce ring over the top of a bunch of soda bottles. She lands a ring on a bottle and wins a small stuffed prize.

"Is that beginner's luck, or do you bring all your patients here?" I tease.

The guy tries to give her a yellow duck, but she points to something else instead. "You want the hawk?" the guy asks, plucking another stuffed toy off the wall. "This ugly thing?"

"Yes, please," she says. She holds it up. "How apropos is this? And to answer your question, you are the only patient I've ever brought here. You're the only patient I've ever brought *anywhere*."

Why that makes me feel like pounding my chest, I don't know. I shouldn't care what she does when she's not with me.

"Now you try it," she says.

I toss the ring just like she said and, just like she said, it goes much farther when I use my elbow instead of my wrist. But I still don't ring the neck of a bottle. Not even after a dozen tries.

"Okay?" she asks, nodding at my arm.

"Bring it on," I tell her. "What's next?"

The booth next to this one has milk bottle pyramids that people are trying to knock down with softballs. I look at Rylee. "Not a chance," she says. "You know they weight down the bottom row with lead, don't you? You'd probably have to throw your fastball to get them down."

"I could probably do it with my right arm," I tell her.

"I don't doubt it. But you're not here to show off, are you?"

I look at the game. "I guess not."

"Good. Because the only two people here that matter are the two people who know how good you are."

"Were," I correct her.

"And will be again," she says. She pulls on my good arm. "Come on, let's do this one over here."

I hand over more tickets and the woman gives us each three bean bags. You have to throw them through the clown's mouth to win a prize.

"Ever played Cornhole?" Rylee asks.

"Not even when I was drunk," I say laughing.

"Well, you're missing out. This is kind of like it. I'll show you."

147

She proceeds to make all three. "Underhand?" I say. "You throw like a girl."

"Do you want to try for a larger prize?" the woman asks her, holding out a small plastic whistle.

Rylee appraises it. "No thanks." Then she whispers to me, "This is what you get for spending three dollars on the game?"

I crank my arm back to throw, but Rylee stops my motion. "No, Brady. Underhand."

"You have to be kidding."

She scolds me with the raise of her brow and I feel my pants getting tighter.

"Damn, woman, you really are bossy. Maybe we should make a stop on the way home and get you a whip and some leather."

"Throw the stupid bean bag, Taylor. And use your shoulder and your elbow. Not your wrist."

I make two out of three. "Better luck next time," the woman behind the booth says.

"I get nothing for making two?"

She shrugs and points to the rules.

"Well, that's a stupid rule."

Rylee hands me the small plastic bag with her whistle in it. "Here, you can have mine."

"Gee, thanks."

"Let's do that one now." She points to the balloon dart throw.

I get my three darts, attempting to throw one, and it all but falls out of my weak grip. Rylee arranges my fingers so I'm holding the dart between my thumb and my ring finger instead of my thumb and my first finger.

"I know it feels strange to hold it like this," she says. "But your ring finger is unaffected, so it may allow you to squeeze the dart better if you do it this way. And don't flick the wrist."

My thumb is still weak and numb, but using her strategy, I'm able to pop one of the balloons. And it's an overhand throw, so it feels damn good.

"Nice!" she squeals when I pop all three on my second try.

The bearded guy who runs the game hands me a rubber snake. I look at it and then fake an attack on Rylee's hawk. "Who do you think would win?" I ask.

"The hawk. Definitely the hawk." I don't miss how she's looking right at me when she says it. She clears her throat. "Let's get something to eat and then see how your arm feels."

We settle on a funnel cake and some kind of meat on a stick. We find a bench and do some people-watching while we eat. When we're done, I notice the line for the Ferris wheel isn't long at all.

"What do you say?" I ask, motioning over to it.

"Sure, why not?"

While waiting in line, some teenage boys notice me.

"Aren't you Brady Taylor?" one of them asks.

"I am."

"I told you," he says, punching one of his friends in the arm. "Can I get a picture with you? Nobody's going to believe it."

"Sure. You follow the Nighthawks?" I ask, as Rylee grabs his phone and snaps a picture of me with all three boys and then individually with each of them.

"Well, I like the Rays because I live here, but the Hawks are cool, too," he says, looking guilty.

"It's cool," I tell him. "You should root for your home team."

"You're on the DL, right? I saw footage of that ball hitting you. It looked painful."

"It was. But I hope to be off the disabled list soon. I'm improving every day." We're called up to the ride. "Nice to meet you guys. Enjoy the fair."

We sit in the chair and the worker pulls a bar down over us. Rylee looks scared. She shoves the hawk into my hands and holds onto the safety bar for dear life.

As our chair rises, she starts squealing – and not in a good way.

"Uh, Rylee, are *you* afraid of heights?"

She closes her eyes. "Terrified."

"Then why in the hell are we on this thing?"

"I thought it would be fun." She peeks out of one eye and then grabs onto my arm. "Oh, my God. This is horrible. Do you think the guy would stop it and bring us back down?"

I laugh. "Oh, we'll go back down all right, after we go up and over the top."

"Oh, God. Oh, God. Oh, God."

I scoot closer and wrap my arm around her, pulling her tightly against me. "Is that better?"

"Marginally. But, as strong as you may be, you couldn't save both of us if this thing tips over. What was I thinking?"

I laugh quietly. "The ride isn't going to tip over. But I promise you if it did, I'd save you."

She takes a hand off the bar momentarily to squeeze my hand.

The ride stops when we're at the very top. She tenses even more. "What the fuck!" she yells.

This time I can't help my boisterous laugh. "Why, Rylee, you do have a dirty mouth after all. I've wondered."

"This isn't a time for jokes, Brady. What if it doesn't start back up? What if we get stuck up here?"

"They are probably just letting a special needs person on the ride – that can take longer." I scoot to the edge to look over.

"Brady!" she squeals, her eyes still closed tightly as one of her arms tries to grab me. "Don't rock us."

I reposition myself next to her and put my hand on her thigh. "I wish you would open your eyes and see how beautiful it is. You can see the coastline from here. The way the lights line the shore is fascinating. I think I might even be able to see Pier 60."

That does it. She opens her eyes into a squint. "Don't look down. Don't look down," she mumbles to herself.

I rub my hand along the inner seam of her jeans.

"What are you doing?" she asks.

"I'm trying to help you relax. Is it working?"

She shrugs. "Maybe a little. And you lie – you can't see the pier from here."

"You can't?" I squint my eyes like I'm looking to find it.

"No. But it is beautiful. And worth seeing."

"I agree," I tell her, enjoying a totally different view.

She turns to find me staring at her.

My hand has traveled higher and higher and is dangerously close to being publicly indecent. "You know, I think it's tradition that if you get stuck on top of a Ferris wheel you have to kiss."

"Oh, it's a tradition huh?"

"Actually, it's bad luck if you don't. And you know how superstitious baseball players can be."

She smiles. "Well, I'm not about to be your bad juju."

I lean closer and twist my body a little before my lips find hers. Kissing her is something I've wanted to do all night. I thought I'd have to wait until we made it back to the hotel. Maybe I should tip the ride operator.

"Don't rock the car," she mumbles into my mouth.

We laugh into each other and then I deepen the kiss, hoping to make her forget her worries.

A minute later, the ride starts again and we reluctantly pull apart. "Tell me about your superstitions," she says. "Anything to keep my mind off this."

"Mine are pretty tame compared to some others I know. Did you know that Caden plays with Murphy's engagement ring in his back pocket?"

"I think that's romantic."

"If you're into that shit."

"Tell me about yours," she says.

"Mine are boring. I eat carrots."

"Carrots?"

"Yeah, they are supposed to be good for eyesight, so I eat a small bag of those miniature carrots every day I pitch."

"What else?"

"I never step on the foul line when I take or leave the field."

"I've heard of that one before," she says. "Anything else?"

I sigh. "I wear the same t-shirt under my uniform."

"Every game?"

I nod.

"It must be atrocious."

I nod again.

"What t-shirt is it?"

Why did I say anything? "Just some old thing I got when I was in high school."

"Oh. Well, it must mean a lot to you."

"It does."

We reach the bottom and the guy is asking people if they want to stay on or get off. I look at Rylee in amusement as she does everything she can to get the guy's attention. We step off the ride and I start dragging her back in the direction of the throwing games when a group of girls stops our progress.

"Are you Scott Eastwood?" one asks.

I look at Rylee who is doing her best to hold in a laugh.

"The actor? No."

"But those boys took pictures with you. You must be famous," another girl says.

"I play baseball," I tell them.

"Baseball?" The girls look at each other. "Are you sure?"

"Am I sure I play baseball, or am I sure I'm not Scott Eastwood?" I joke.

"Can we get a picture with you just in case?" one of them asks.

"Just in case I'm Scott Eastwood?" I laugh and look at Rylee who happily takes one of the girls' phones to snap a few pictures.

The girls giggle as they walk away.

I pull a laughing Rylee in the direction of the games until I see something and stop. Rylee bumps into my back and it's now that I realize I've been holding her hand. I look down at them just as I pull mine away from hers.

I don't hold hands.

I look at the game booth and then at Rylee.

"No way," she says.

We stand there and watch a guy pitch baseballs to a life-sized cutout of a catcher with a hole where his glove is. I can't take my eyes off it. I want to walk up there and pick up every ball. I want to hold one in my hand and feel the intricate stitching with my fingertips. I want to feel the glory of releasing the perfect pitch knowing it will be a strike even before the batter does.

"Fuck," I say, turning my back on the game.

A woman walking by with a young boy gives me a dirty look.

"Sorry, ma'am. Wait – here." I hold out all the stuff in my hands. "Does your boy want these?"

Rylee quickly plucks the hawk from among the other prizes we accumulated. "Not this one," she says.

I didn't think I could smile after what just happened, but damned if I don't.

I hand the boy the rubber snake and the packaged whistle and then I give his mom two tickets. "For the Ferris wheel," I say. "With my apologies."

"Thank you," she says as they walk away.

I eye the small dime-store stuffed animal Rylee is holding and question her with my brow.

"What? I wanted something to remember tonight. It's been fun." She looks hesitantly over at the Ferris wheel. "Well, mostly."

I laugh and grab her hand, pulling her away from the baseball toss and towards the parking lot. "Come back to the hotel with me," I say. "I'll give you something to remember tonight."

She looks up at me and swallows. "I thought you'd never ask."

Chapter Eighteen

There are two things I never do: watch the MLB draft, and go to funerals.

Not since that day – the day both happened at once.

I never got to hear my name being called live in the draft. I never got the phone call college players dream about getting. I never got to hold up a Hawks jersey in front of the cameras that would have been camped out at my apartment. I didn't do any of that – my agent handled it all in my absence. The names I did get to hear called, however, were Natalie and Keeton Taylor as they were lowered into the ground the same time I was making history. Because damn it if Nat wasn't right – I did go in the first round.

But today, I made the only exception I've made in five and a half years. I flew in last night to help bury a friend's wife.

I look over at Bobby Goodrich in the front pew of the church. He and his two young sons are clinging to each other. I'm gutted for him. For them. Because I know what they are going through. But at least they have each other. I know they don't see it that way and I'm not about to tell them things could be worse. But they can be. They have been. I'm living proof.

I often wonder what would have happened if one of them had survived. Would Nat and I have tried for another child? Would Keeton and I have been best friends?

Murphy grabs my hand. I'm sandwiched between her and Sawyer, with Caden on her other side. I'm not sure what I look like on the outside, but I'm dying on the inside. Having to re-live that day is not something I ever wanted to do. But Murphy convinced me to come. She said I can't avoid funerals my whole life and that I'd hate myself if I weren't there for my friend.

When the service is over, Caden and the other pallbearers walk up to the front to do their job. I never thought I'd be grateful to have this injury, but here I sit, thanking God that I don't have to carry her body out of the church. No way could I have done it, but it would have meant turning down a friend.

I turn to Sawyer and lift my left arm. "I have an excuse. Why aren't *you* up there?"

"This whole thing is fucked up," he says. "I can't be here."

I'm not even sure he heard my question. He's staring at Bobby's two sons. One is ten and the other is only four. I watch Sawyer stare at the older one like he's living a nightmare. He's shaking. He starts to hyperventilate and I shove his head between his legs.

"Dude, breathe. Are you okay?"

"I'm gonna be sick."

I pull on his arm, dragging him out the other side of the pew as we find the bathroom at the front of the church. I give him some space and guard the door. But I can hear him hurling into the toilet. *What the fuck?*

When I hear the faucet come on, I go back in. "Are you sick?"

He shakes his head at me in the mirror as he rinses his mouth out with water.

Maybe he just hates funerals as much as I do.

I pat him on the back. "You okay, man?"

"Do we have to go to the cemetery?" he asks.

I shrug. "It's customary. But if you can't handle it, don't go. I had the same thought myself. I don't think anyone will hold it against you."

He leans back against the wall of one of the stalls and runs his hands through his hair. "I should go. I want to be there to support Bobby. But – fuck, I didn't know it would be like this."

I stare at him. Sawyer's as much of a closed book as I am. And I feel like I'm looking in a goddamned mirror right now. *Who did he lose?* I wonder. What I am sure of is that it has something to do with the tattoo he refuses to discuss.

"You want to talk about it?" I ask, awkwardly, knowing that's what people say.

He snorts air out of his nose and gives me a knowing stare. "Do *you?*"

I step over to the door and open it, knowing neither of us wants to talk about our demons. "Come on, let's get through this and then we'll get shit-faced."

Sawyer's shoulders are slumped as he walks through the door. And it makes me feel like a prick that in this moment, I'm grateful for his pain, because I realize that by taking care of him and his memories, whatever they may be, I don't have to deal so much with mine.

~ ~ ~

"To Faleena," Murphy says, after the waitress finishes dolling out a dozen shots.

"To Faleena!" the rest of us shout before throwing them back.

Some of us headed over to a favorite team hangout after leaving the reception at Bobby's apartment. He's got both his family and Faleena's there to help him and the kids. He didn't need us hanging around longer than necessary.

I remember how I just wanted everyone to get the hell out. My team at Nebraska organized the reception. I know they were trying to be nice, but what they didn't know, what they couldn't know, is that I never wanted to see any of them again. Seeing them reminded me of Natalie and Keet. The only thing I wanted to do was leave everything and everyone behind.

So that's exactly what I did. I walked right out of the reception and packed a bag. I was supposed to report to Tampa a week later anyway to join the single-A team that was already well into their season. I just arrived early, that's all. And I *did* leave everything behind, everything but my clothes, some baseball stuff, and a few small pictures of my family that was no more. I didn't even clean out the apartment, I had Nat's parents take care of that.

I left behind myself as well. I left the old Brady Taylor in Lincoln, Nebraska. The one who fucked up and got his family killed. The new Brady wasn't going to fuck up anything. The new Brady was a machine. A machine with no human emotion. I threw myself into baseball and never looked back. I only stayed in Tampa for two months before they moved me up to Tucson, and after a month there they moved me up to Vegas. I rose through the ranks quicker than anyone in Hawks history, and by the anniversary of their deaths, I was playing in my first MLB game.

"Sawyer's been acting strangely today," Murphy says. "Is he okay?"

"Wow, you must think he's really screwed up to be asking about him over me."

She touches my hand. "I know today must have been horrible for you. I also think that one of these days, you'll tell me exactly why. But I've never seen Sawyer act that way. He just seems … lost."

I shrug. "Maybe he's not the perfect pretty boy everyone assumes he is."

"He is kind of pretty," Murphy teases.

I roll my eyes. "It's always the fucking shortstops. They are the pretty boys."

"Yeah, but the pitchers and catchers – they have all the muscles." She gives me a wink.

"Are you hitting on me, Murphy?"

She laughs. "You wish." Then her face turns serious. "Hey, speaking of hitting on people, are you still seeing Rylee?"

"Yeah, why?"

"I don't know. The two of you seemed pretty into each other. I was just wondering if that's a good idea."

"Why the hell wouldn't it be a good idea?"

"I just don't want you getting hurt, that's all."

"No chance, Murphy. Did you forget who you are talking to here? Why the concern? And why the change of heart after you practically threw us together at the restaurant?"

She shrugs. "Forget it. It's nothing."

I eye her skeptically. It's never nothing with the future Mrs. Kessler. She's deliberate in everything she does.

Caden leans over his fiancée. "Did I tell you they moved up the shithead's trial?"

"Finally," I say. "When is it?"

Caden smiles and raises a drink. "It wrapped up yesterday."

"What? Really?" I look to Murphy. "You didn't say anything when you came to Tampa a few weeks ago."

She shakes her head. "I didn't know until after I left. Until the prosecutor's office called me last week to bring me in as a witness."

"Well? What happened?"

Murphy smiles. "Guilty on all counts. It only took the jury an hour to deliberate."

"How long did he get?"

"Sentencing is next week," Caden says. "But the prosecutor is going to recommend the maximum, so he'll be going away for at least three or four years. Stupid fucker should have pled no contest. At least they might have gone easier on him. But he denied everything and even tried to blame it all on Murphy's old roommates. They all eventually turned against him and testified for the prosecution. It was a beautiful sight to see, man."

I raise my glass. "To justice for our girl."

The three of us toast and then Murphy tells me that women showed up in court wearing *Murphy Strong* t-shirts. Even after all these months.

It makes me think of Rylee and the wristband she wore that weekend.

Then I think of Rylee and the Ferris wheel. And what happened after the Ferris wheel, and then the zoo, and the fishing on the pier, and the paddle boarding in the bay, and the dinners we've shared, and all the fun we've had in the past few weeks since she said yes.

I look down into my drink realizing what this means.

It means I miss her.

Fuck.

~ ~ ~

"I have to talk to you," Nat says, pulling me into her dorm room at Schramm Hall.

"Well, hello to you too," I say, leaning down to kiss her on top of her head.

She walks over to her bed and sits down. She wrings her hands together and looks at the floor.

I sit next to her and grab one of her hands. I've never seen her like this. "What is it, Natalie?" I suspect it may have something to do with her father. He never wanted her to follow me to the University of Nebraska. It's a long way from SoCal. And even if he does make good on his promise to open an office here, that will take some time — time where he can't check up on his oldest daughter whenever he wants.

She looks up at me and a large tear catches on her eyelash before dripping down onto her cheek. I wipe it with my finger. "Whatever it is, we'll get through it. Are you failing one of your classes?"

She belts out an agonizing laugh before turning away. "I wish."

I get on my knees in front of her and force her to look at me. I cup her face in my hands. "Nat, you're scaring me."

She reaches behind her and picks up something off her desk. She hands me a small white stick. "I — I don't know how this happened. I'm s-so sorry, b-babe."

I take the pregnancy test into my hand. The one that clearly reads 'pregnant.' It's not one of those tests with a line that has you guessing if it's dark enough to be positive. This one shouts the result out to you loud and clear.

"Are you sure?" I ask. "Sometimes these things can be wrong. Maybe it's defective. We're always so careful."

She reaches behind her again and gets a small brown bag. She turns it upside down and we watch as six other pregnancy tests tumble onto her comforter.

"I took seven of them. I had to drink a ton of water. They say to do it in the morning because your pee is more concentrated. But even after three bottles *of water, they're all still positive. I'm not just a little pregnant, Brady — I'm super pregnant."*

"How could we not have known? I mean, yeah, you've always been irregular, but don't things happen like your boobs get bigger and stuff?"

She shrugs. "I guess, but maybe not."

"Maybe they are all wrong," I say. "Maybe you ate something yesterday that affected the tests. You know, like poppy seeds or something."

"I made an appointment at the campus medical center. Will you go with me?"

"Of course I will, Nat. We're in this together."

More tears fall down her cheeks. "What if ... What will we do?"

"We'll get married. We'll walk right down to city hall and tie the knot. We're over eighteen. Nobody has to know until after. Your dad can't stop you." I touch her flat stomach. "Then we'll have a baby and he'll look so fucking cute in tiny baseball caps."

For the first time since I walked through the door, she smiles. "What if it's a girl?"

I laugh. "Girls can wear baseball caps, too."

"Do you really think we could do it?" she asks. "We're only freshmen. Where would we live, what would we do?"

"I think the university has married housing. And what do you mean, what would we do? We'd have a family. I'm going to the big leagues, Nat, and you are going right along with me. We've always known we would get married. What's the difference if we do it now or later?"

She stares at me with puffy red eyes. "You're not mad at me?"

I sit on the bed and pick her up into my lap. "I could never be mad at you, Rylee. I love you."

I jolt awake and reach over to get the stress ball on my nightstand. Then I throw it into the mirror on the wall, shattering the glass into a hundred pieces.

Chapter Nineteen

As the wheels of the plane touch down, I'm still staring at the small picture in my hand. The one that has a crease worn into it from being in my wallet all these years.

It was just a dream, I tell myself as my finger traces the outline of Natalie's face.

Then why do I feel so damn guilty?

Maybe I should end things with Rylee. Nothing is worth a few good romps in the hay. Not even if Ry is different from the others. Not even if she's the only woman who has ever come close to being in the same ballpark as Nat.

But therein lies the problem. These feelings I'm having, whatever they are – they can't lead anywhere and I know it.

I put the picture away as we taxi up to the gate.

I have two more weeks down here. Two more weeks of spending my mornings with Rylee. Two weeks of looking forward to whatever time she'll give me after work. Two weeks of touching her, smelling her, laughing with her.

Two weeks can be a long fucking time. And right now, it seems like forever.

I need to end it with her.

I get off the plane and bypass the luggage carousel. I was only gone for two days so I just have my carry-on. As the escalator takes me down toward the exit, I notice a familiar face. I see Rylee standing there, wearing a black hat like one a limo driver wears. I wonder what she's doing here wearing that silly hat and a huge smile. Then, just as I'm stepping off the escalator, she flashes a sign that reads 'Scott Eastwood.'

I laugh. I laugh harder than I've laughed, well, since the last time I was with Rylee.

It's only two more weeks, I think, justifying my sudden change of heart.

"What are you doing here?" I ask when we stop laughing and I can finally speak again.

"I drove you here Wednesday night, remember? You told me your itinerary."

"Oh, well, you didn't have to pick me up. I could have taken a cab. Or called Lenny."

She shrugs. "It's Friday. We always hang out on Friday. That is unless you don't want to."

"That depends. What did you have in mind?"

She takes something out of her back pocket and hands it to me. It's two tickets to a concert.

I recognize the name of the band. I should, I've been backstage at a few of their concerts. "You like White Poison?" I ask.

She shrugs. "I've heard them on the radio. I guess they're okay."

"If you think they are just okay, why did you buy tickets?"

"I didn't buy them. One of the guys gave them to me."

I furrow my brow. "A player?"

She nods. "Lorenzo Santos."

"Why didn't he go himself?"

"Something about it being his sister's birthday and she's not a fan."

"Oh, well we should go. They're pretty good. I know Adam Stuart."

"Who?"

"The lead singer for the band."

We reach her car and she takes the hat off. "Of course you do," she says, rolling her eyes.

I grab the hat and put it back on her head. "You should wear this later tonight. It looks sexy on you."

She blushes. She's so darn cute when her cheeks and neck pink up like this. I can't help it when I lean down and pin her to the side of her car as I kiss her. I don't know if it's the crappy few days I've had with the funeral or what, but kissing Rylee just makes me feel … better somehow.

She doesn't seem to mind that we're in a public place. But the parking garage is somewhat dark and there aren't many people around, so she deepens the kiss. She presses herself into me, teasing me with what we both know will happen later tonight. Later, when we'll go back to my hotel room and devour each other like we have numerous times in the past few weeks.

"Well, hello to you too," she jokes when we break apart.

I grab the keys from her and then walk around the car to let her in the passenger side.

"Do we have time to grab a bite first?" I ask.

"A quick one. Maybe a sandwich somewhere."

"What is it with you and sandwiches?"

She shrugs. "They're quick, easy, cheap, and the possibilities are endless."

I laugh a little too boisterously.

"What?" she asks.

"I think you just described most of my sexual conquests."

I see her look of annoyance out of the corner of my eye and I realize she might not find my joke funny.

"Not you, Ry. I said *most.*"

"Whatever. Listen, I'm a big girl, Brady. I know what this is."

I reach over and put my hand on her thigh. "I'm sorry. I shouldn't have said that. You are nothing like them, least of all easy and cheap. But if that night in the bathroom is any indication, you're sure as hell quick."

We share another laugh and I realize just how good it feels to laugh with her. Sure, I laugh with the guys. I laugh with Murphy even. But I can't remember ever laughing with any of the others. Not like this. Laughing with Rylee makes me feel … alive.

We stop at a sub shop along the way.

"Alex saw a picture of us at the fair," she says as we eat. "Someone took a photo of us sitting on the bench while we were eating."

"Was he mad?"

She sighs. "He seemed jealous, that's for sure. I think I've been in denial."

"I told you that man wants you, Ry. But I have to ask, other than the no fraternization thing, why don't you want to go out with the guy?"

"He sleeps with all the interns," she says. "But you never heard that from me."

"Really? Isn't the guy like thirty-five?"

"Thirty-seven, actually. And the interns are usually in their early twenties."

"He's taking advantage, Ry. That's not right. You should say something."

"Maybe they have an arrangement," she says, elbowing me. "And I'm not about to say anything and lose my job. They are consenting adults, Brady and it's none of my business. But he creeps me out. And since you've been around, he's been kind of territorial."

"Territorial?" Alarm bells go off in my head. "What the fuck does that mean? Has he made a move on you?"

"Calm down, Brady. He just asks a lot of questions about me and my personal life. And about you."

"And what do you tell him?"

"That you are my patient. Nothing more."

"And the picture? How did you explain that?"

"I told him you were getting impatient and anxious about your recovery and that I needed to think outside the box. I said the fair games were therapy and it helped to do something different. It wasn't a lie."

I smirk and lean in close. "I suppose you left out the part where I gave my fingers a good workout later that night by pinching your nipples and stroking your clit."

She flushes and squirms in her seat. "Uh, yeah, I left that part out."

"I need another good workout," I whisper in her ear.

"We might be able to arrange that, if you behave yourself tonight."

"Behave myself? What, no touching at the concert? Come on, Ry. It'll be dark."

She laughs. "I'm not talking about that. I'm talking about you knowing the lead singer. You are not allowed to use that fact or your celebrity status to get us anything. No backstage passes. No

167

private parties. We're just two normal people going to a concert, okay?"

I blow out a breath. "Fine." I tug on my Nascar hat. "It's a good thing I'm wearing this instead of a Hawks one, maybe it'll provide camouflage."

"That and your clean shave," she says, reaching over to run a finger along my jaw.

"Oh, you like that? I thought I should shave for the funeral."

"I do, but it's a lot different than your usual scruff."

"Scruff? I work hard to keep it that way I'll have you know."

"I'll bet. And it works for you. Obviously," she says rolling her eyes. "But it was nice to kiss you back at the parking garage. No scruff-burn."

I look her up and down, my eyes falling to her lap. "No scruff-burn *anywhere*," I say.

Her face pinks up again when my eyes meet hers. "Actually, that's one place I don't mind it. It kind of enhances the whole feeling."

My pants get tight at the thought of going down on her. "Well, damn – I'm never shaving again."

She giggles as she checks the time. "Come on, we'd better go."

"In a minute," I say. "You can't tell me what you just told me and then expect me to walk out of here without a hard-on."

~ ~ ~

It's been a while since I've been to a concert. Especially a concert where I'm not in some VIP section with an all-access pass. It's kind of refreshing to just be one of the crowd. For five years now, I haven't been treated like a normal person. Not until Rylee forced me to be. And being normal is so much better than I remember. It's freeing. It's cathartic.

We make our way to the seats printed on the tickets. They aren't near the stage but are close enough to see without squinting. We're in the first row in the stands behind all the floor seats. There is a railing in front of us and we're a few feet above the people sitting on the floor. All in all, they are decent seats and provide an unobstructed view.

The opening band is a local band I remember seeing at a bar last spring. But the real fun starts when Adam and the rest of White Poison come on stage. The pyrotechnics are a sight.

If the crowd wasn't excited before, it is now. The people on the floor are getting shoved around in what is becoming a mosh pit.

"I'm glad we aren't down there," Rylee says, pointing to the sea of people.

I see some guys putting arms around their dates, trying to protect them from the mayhem. And suddenly, I have the urge to pull Rylee against me. So I do.

"I don't know," I say, stepping behind her and caging her to the railing in front of us. I lean down and let my breath tickle her ear. "It looks kind of fun."

She cranes her neck and looks back at me with raised eyebrows. I know what she's wondering. Brady Taylor doesn't do PDA. When I'm out with a girl, there's no touching. There never has been. So why am I breaking my rules with her? The Ferris wheel. The parking garage. Here. I convince myself that none of those count because they were all in dark places.

I kiss her temple. "Turn around, you're missing the show."

I spend the next thirty minutes torturing myself by lightly grinding into her from behind. She doesn't turn and look at me again, and we share no words the entire time, but she does push herself into me, making me crazier than I already am.

One of my hands is on her hip and the other wraps around and grips her stomach, firmly pressing her to me. She reaches up and threads her fingers with mine.

Finally, I break our silence and lean down, putting my face next to her ear. "Let's get out of here, Ry."

She turns around in my arms, looking surprised. "But the concert is only half over. Don't you want to stay and see your friend sing?"

"Fuck the concert and fuck Adam Stuart," I say. "Because all I want to do right now is fuck *you*, Rylee."

She looks up at me with a seductive grin. "Well, what are we waiting for?"

I laugh and take her hand, blazing a trail through the crowd until we reach the other side of the tunnel where the bathrooms and concession stands are. Few people are out here since the concert is still in full swing.

Rylee tugs on my hand, pulling me to a stop in front of a booth. "What size are you?" she asks.

I look over at the concert t-shirts. "Adam will send me fifty if that's what you want."

She admonishes me with her stare. "That's no fun. This is all about the experience, Brady. If we buy a t-shirt here, you'll always remember this day."

My heart pounds in my chest as I have a *déjà vu* moment. My eyes briefly close as my memories go back to when I was eighteen. "You don't have to do that, Ry."

"Extra-large?" she asks.

I pull out my wallet since it looks like she's not going to back down.

"No." She brushes my hand away when I try to give her some cash. "This is my treat."

She pays the guy and hands me a shirt. As we walk away, I realize she didn't get one of her own.

"Why didn't *you* get one?"

"I don't wear a lot of t-shirts. Maybe I'll just borrow yours once in a while."

I don't tell her that it won't be possible. I don't remind her that I'm leaving in two weeks and we most likely won't see each other until spring.

I throw the shirt over my shoulder and grab her hand. "Maybe you can borrow it tonight. Because the thought of you wearing this shirt with nothing under it, just made me hard again."

She laughs. "Brady, is there anything that doesn't make you hard?"

"Not when it comes to you," I tell her.

My driving is on the verge of reckless as I race us back to my hotel. She teases me with light touches to my thigh all the way home. I park in the lot instead of driving up to the valet stand. Rylee gets the key card I gave her out of her wallet. She knows the drill. She goes into the hotel a few minutes before I do. Her going in first is less likely to cause a stir or foster a connection between us should any lurking fans notice me.

As I watch her walk away from the car, I realize she's the only woman I've ever given a key card to.

Convenience, I tell myself. It's nothing more than that.

After she's inside, I look around to find the t-shirt, but I can't see it in the darkness. I'll find it later.

When I enter the lobby, I breathe a sigh of relief that Rylee entered first. A group of fans rushes over to me before the front door has a chance to swing shut.

"Brady!" one squeals. "Can I get a picture with you?"

"An autograph?" another asks, holding out a pen.

I oblige them all, taking a few minutes to heed their requests.

When I finally make it up to my suite, I walk in with a smile on my face. Rylee appears in the doorway to my bedroom wearing nothing but the concert t-shirt she just bought me.

"Why do you look so happy?" she asks.

"You mean other than the fact that a beautiful half-naked woman is standing in my bedroom?"

She laughs. "Yeah, other than that."

I stride over to her and pick her up, swinging her around. "I signed an autograph downstairs."

"Okaaaaaay," she says, looking confused.

"Ry, I signed it with my left hand. And I didn't drop the pen."

"That's great! See, I told you it would happen. I'm so happy for you."

I put her down. "Well, it's not a jar of pickles."

"Baby steps," she says. "This is a very good thing, Brady. And you have every right to be happy. Progress is progress, no matter how you look at it. You are going to make a full recovery. I know it."

Rylee has always been my biggest cheerleader when it comes to my recovery. I still have such a long way to go. What will I do when I'm back in New York? Will my physical therapist there push me as hard as Rylee has? Will he believe in me the way she does?

She grabs my hand and pulls me over to the bed. She leaves me standing at the end of it while she crawls seductively onto the middle of the bed, letting the shirt ride up just enough so I can see what's *not* underneath.

Damn. I realize just how much I like her wearing my shirt. I think back to earlier when she said she'd just borrow it once in a while. I don't tell her that I want nothing more than for her to borrow my shirt. Or anything else she wants to borrow. And more than once in a while. I want her to borrow it and return it. And borrow it again.

Suddenly it hits me like a ton of fucking bricks falling off the Empire State Building.

I want this woman lying on the bed wearing my shirt. I want her for more than tonight. For more than these few months. I don't want her to be my *Tampa* girl. I want her to be my *only* girl.

But I push the thought aside. Because no matter how much I want her. I know better. I can never have her. I can never have anyone.

Not anymore.

"Are you just going to stare at me, or are you going to join me?" she asks, teasing me by pulling the shirt up even higher.

I can see her soft tuft of curls. Her flat belly. The undercurve of one of her breasts. Hell, I can smell how much she wants me.

I kick off my shoes and crawl onto the bed, working my way up her body starting at her bare feet. I kiss her ankles. I lick the inside of her knees. I knead her thighs. By the time I reach her sex, she's already writhing beneath me.

I push a finger inside her. "Ry, you are so wet."

"Well, what do you expect? This whole night has been one big production of foreplay."

I push a second finger in and press my thumb on her clit. She whimpers in pleasure. "Oh, God."

"You'll be shouting out *my* name in two minutes," I tell her.

"Two? You're awfully confident, aren't you?"

I pull out my phone and set the stopwatch.

She looks at what I'm doing. "You're kidding, right?"

I put down the phone next to me and press my mouth to her opening. I work my tongue inside her, fucking her with it as I give her a taste of what's to follow. I replace my tongue with my fingers when I move it to her clit, sucking on it as I feel the little nub grow harder. Her moans become louder and I smile knowing she's close. I double my efforts and work my pinky finger back to the pucker of her ass. I slip the tip of it in, pushing her over the edge as she pulsates around each finger I have inside her.

As she recovers from her orgasm, I pick up my phone and turn it around, showing it to her. "Ninety-four seconds," I say, smugly.

"Give me that thing." She takes it from me. "Now take off your clothes."

I laugh. "You think you can beat my time?"

She watches my every move as I strip, my erection springing proudly from my boxer briefs as I lower them to the floor. When I'm completely naked, she peels off the t-shirt she's wearing, revealing her gorgeous body. Her breasts are perfectly proportioned to her petite, trim figure. Her nipples are stiff and puckered. Her face is flushed and her hair is messy from her orgasm. I've never seen such an incredible sight. My dick throbs almost painfully.

"Oh, I know I can," she says arrogantly.

I dive onto the bed and turn around, my head on the pillow and my hands laced behind my neck. "Give it your best shot."

She hits the start button on my phone's stopwatch and smiles deviously. She gets on all fours next to me, her bottom inches from my face. She takes my dick into her hands and strokes me steadily. Then when she leans over to take me into her mouth, I get an all-access view of her wet pussy.

Holy shit. I can't help it when my hand travels up and my fingers find their way inside her again. She moans around my cock, probably still sensitive from her orgasm. The vibrations from her noises drive me insane. Her hand works beneath me to massage my balls and I feel them tighten with my impending release.

She works her mouth faster, up and down, up and down, stopping momentarily to suck on the head before continuing on. I feel a finger traveling across my perineum and when she carefully plunges it into my ass, it sends me over the top. "Jesus, Rylee!" I shout, my powerful orgasm flooding her mouth as she works every last drop out of me.

She sits back on her haunches and picks up my phone with a brilliant smile on her face. She shows it to me. "Eighty-nine seconds," she says. "I win."

I laugh and pull her on top of me. "I'd say we both won at this game."

She laughs with me as she runs a finger across my jawline.

Damn I love this.

I kiss her finger when it traces my lips. "Let me rest for a few minutes and then we'll go for the record."

"You should know I'm very competitive," she says. "We may be at this for a while."

"Challenge accepted, Rylee Kennedy."

"Game on, BrayTay."

"If you keep impersonating Lenny, I guarantee you'll never beat the record."

I watch her bounce up and down on my chest as we share another laugh, and for a moment, I feel something I haven't felt in what seems like forever.

I feel happy.

Samantha Christy

Chapter Twenty

"Did you have a good weekend?" Matt asks, after we go over this week's strength and conditioning plan.

I smile as I think back to Friday night. Never did I think after going to the funeral that I would come back to have one of the best nights I can remember.

Matt laughs and holds out a hand to stop me from saying anything. "Forget I asked. I can see by the look on your face it must have been epic."

He breaks my balls this morning with all the squats and leg presses he has me do. But that's one of the reasons I like working out here instead of the hotel gym. And I can say one thing for sure, after following his plan for the past six weeks, my legs and core have never been stronger.

He sends me over to the complex pool to do laps before my appointment with Rylee. Matt and Rylee both agree that swimming is very therapeutic for my shoulder. Not pitching day in and day out makes my shoulder tighten up. Swimming helps keep it strong and loose. It's something I've come to enjoy and plan to continue doing at the gym back home.

My arms and legs guide me through the water and the laps tick away as my mind wanders. I can't help but think of Friday and the shirt Rylee wore in my bedroom. When she left, the shirt lay in a crumpled heap by the bed. When I picked it up to add it to my laundry, I realized how much it smelled like her. I remember sitting on my bed, looking at the shirt. I remember putting it to my nose and burying my face in it. Then I held it up, studied it, and looked over at my closet, where another such shirt lay on the shelf.

I couldn't bring myself to put Rylee's shirt in the closet. Not when another one was in there that meant so much to me.

But I also couldn't bring myself to throw it in the laundry.

That night was beyond any expectation I ever had of being with a woman. We broke all kinds of records. We laughed so hard that we cried. I'd never felt so much like myself and not like the celebrity ball player I'd become.

And when it was over, and she got up to leave, I almost asked her to stay the night. It was on the tip of my tongue. Like it was only natural for me to ask it. But I didn't. Staying the night is not what we do. Staying the night leads to feelings and expectations that I'm not allowed to have.

Still, I wonder if she'd have stayed.

She's never asked to stay. She's never hung around long enough for it to be a possibility. She's the only one who hasn't. All the girls ask to stay eventually. But not Rylee. And it makes me wonder if it's because she has someone to go home to. And the thought of it has me seeing red.

I finish my swim and head over to the PT building when I hear Ry's voice. I walk to the side of the building where the employees park their cars and I see Rylee talking to Alex. Well, talking is not exactly what I'd call it. It's more like she's yelling at him.

"Alex, stop it!"

She has to pull her arm out of his grip and I go ballistic. I run over to him and push him against Rylee's car. "What the fuck is going on here?"

Alex looks at my hands that are holding him captive. "You mind getting your hands off me, Taylor?"

"Only if you don't mind telling me why your hands were on Rylee."

He shrugs my hands off him and I take a step back.

"I was only helping her out of her car," he says smugly.

"That's not what it looked like from where I was standing."

"Are you stalking her now?" he asks. "It's not enough that you see her every day and go to the fair with her? I'd say *you're* the one breaking the rules, not me."

"You need to back off, Alex. Rylee isn't one of your interns. She's not interested in you. So if I were you, I wouldn't try to help her out of her car again if you get my meaning."

"Don't you have somewhere to be, Taylor? As in New York? Or, maybe you don't. It's not like you'll ever play for the Hawks again. Maybe you *will* end up here. Maybe being a single-A player is all you'll amount to anymore. But hey, I hear Little League needs coaches – there's always that."

I lunge forward, fire running through my veins, but Rylee steps between Alex and me. "Brady, don't. Please. You don't want to risk re-injuring your arm."

No matter how mad I am, I realize she's right, and I reluctantly let her drag me away to the front of the building. I also realize that Alex has just voiced every fear I've thought but have been unable to say.

"Don't listen to him," Rylee says. "He isn't your PT."

I stop walking. "How many times has he touched you, Ry?"

"He hasn't ever. He doesn't do that. This was just a fluke."

"Rylee." I pin her to the wall with my stare.

"It's fine. I'm fine," she says. "I can handle myself. I can handle him."

"He's your boss. You shouldn't have to handle him. That's sexual harassment."

"Well, the hope is I won't have to deal with him forever. I'm trying to get a transfer, remember?"

"I understand that," I say. "But even if you leave, what about the next person? What if there is ever an intern who *doesn't* consent but he takes what he wants anyway?"

She looks at the ground. "I know. I've thought of that. It makes me a horrible person to put my career above doing what's right."

I lift her chin so she has to look at me. "You are anything but a horrible person, Ry. Just promise me if he ever does anything like that again, you'll do something about it."

She nods unconvincingly. "Okay."

We walk into the back room and get started. I can't help staring at Alex when he comes out of the office. I can't stop seeing his hands on Rylee like that and her trying to rip herself out of his grip. I can't stop feeling like I want to protect her from him and anyone else who might touch her. I can feel my jaw tightening and my temples throbbing.

Rylee must notice it, too.

"So, what have you decided about the modeling job?" she asks.

I shrug. "I guess I'll do it. But it's really just a favor for Murphy. That woman could sell ice to an Eskimo. She's very hard to turn down. Kind of like some other girl I know."

Rylee smiles. "I'm glad you decided to do it. It helps to keep busy. Even though I'm confident you'll make a full recovery, these things can be slow."

I look down at my left hand that still tingles and burns. "Don't I know it."

"Do you know who your PT will be back home? I'll send him or her your progress notes so they can pick up where we leave off. Your elbow is almost fully healed. Maybe by next week when you leave it will be."

"I'll find out who it is and let you know."

We look at each other and I know we're both thinking the same thing. It's the first time we've ever talked about me leaving and going back to New York.

It's the first time I've ever not wanted to leave.

Chapter Twenty-one

I roll to Rylee's side, both of us drenched in sweat and laughing. I've never known sex to be so funny, but somehow it always turns out that way with us.

I'm glad she's laughing because earlier, I wasn't sure she was even having fun. At dinner, she seemed disconnected. Or maybe distracted. There are so many reasons why she could have been, not the least of which is that this is our last Friday night together.

She cuddles up next to me and puts her head on my chest. "I'm going to miss this," she says, her finger curling in my chest hair. "I mean, I know you're leaving and I'm not a fool. It's just ... well, I'm going to miss this."

Part of me wants to pull her on top of me and hold onto her for dear life. To tell her that I'll miss this too, and maybe we don't need it to end. Maybe there's spring training. Maybe there could be even more.

I don't tell her any of that, however, because I'm not capable of more. More died along with Natalie and Keeton. But if there ever were to be more, I know for a fact it would be with Rylee.

I give her a kiss on the top of her head. "We've had fun, haven't we?"

"I suppose I should thank you," she says. "These past few months have been great. And I'm not just talking about the sex. I've actually been more productive at work. More focused. I think having this outlet has been good for me."

"You've been good for me, too, Ry. I'm not sure I could have had such a good outlook on things if it weren't for you." I stare down at her and our eyes lock together. "We're good for each other."

"I guess we are," she says with a sad smile.

Then she gets off the bed and walks towards the bathroom. I want to pull her back. I want to tell her she doesn't have to go. The words are begging to come out of me. "Ry …"

She turns around and I try to gauge if I see hope in her eyes. "Yeah?"

"You're not leaving yet, are you?" I remove the sheet and flash her with my nakedness.

She looks at my body and then at the clock on my nightstand that reads 9:00PM. "I don't turn into a pumpkin until ten o'clock," she says. "I just have to pee."

While she's in the bathroom, I dispose of the condom and make sure there is another handy. Then I go out to the mini-bar and grab a few bottles of water. When I return to the room, I stop dead in my tracks when I see Rylee. She's sitting on the edge of the bed looking all mussed up and sexy.

And she's wearing my goddamned Bumbershoot t-shirt.

I walk to my closet and find a plain white t-shirt. I hand it to her, hoping she doesn't see how my heart is practically beating out of my chest. "Would you mind putting this one on instead?"

She looks up at me and guilt washes over her face. "I'm so sorry," she says, removing the t-shirt and taking the one I offered her. "I should have asked."

She walks over and places it back in the closet. Then I go over and re-fold it and put it in its proper spot.

"Is that …?" She nods to the t-shirt on the shelf.

"It's nothing. Don't worry about it."

She was going to ask if it's my lucky shirt. Then she was going to ask why. That right there is why I don't do personal questions.

She scoots back on the bed. "I'm sorry. I just killed the mood, didn't I? I just … sometimes I don't know how to act around you. Like I swear just a few minutes ago you were going to ask me to stay."

"And if I did, what would you have said?"

She shrugs. "I would have said I want to, but I can't."

I nod. "We're two peas in a pod then, aren't we?"

She laughs, but it's not a fun laugh. It's a pained one. "Only I get the feeling my reason for not staying and your reason for not wanting me to stay are quite different ones."

I look over to the closet where the Bumbershoot t-shirt sits on a shelf. Then I look back at Rylee. We stare at each other. This is the closest we've come to crossing the line into personal conversation. This is the closest we've come to admitting whatever feelings there might be between us.

My heart is pounding. My head is cloudy. Maybe I don't know what I'm doing, but sometimes, you just have to jump off the cliff to feel the exhilaration. "Rylee, I think you should —"

Her phone rings on the nightstand, and we both look over at it. She reaches for it to see who's calling.

"I have to take this," she says, jumping off the bed and walking quickly into the other room. "Hannah?" I hear her say as she walks out the door.

I think you should stay anyway, I was going to say. I was going to tell her that despite my reasons, despite her reasons, she should stay the night. I sit on the bed and run my hands through my hair wondering what is happening to me.

Rylee comes running back into the room, frantically searching around for her pants on the floor. "I have to go," she says, tears rolling down her face.

I spring off the bed and go to her, putting my hands on her arms to calm her. "Ry, what is it? Who was on the phone? Who is Hannah?"

For a split second I think maybe her mother has passed away.

She brushes my hands away and pulls on her jeans. She doesn't bother to take off my t-shirt, she just throws her jacket on over it, leaving her blouse in a puddle on the floor.

"What's happening?" I ask again, more forcefully.

"Stryker's hurt. She's taking him to the hospital. I have to go there. Now."

"Stryker? Your boyfriend?"

She pulls her purse over her shoulder and stops to look at me in surprise. "Boyfriend? No. Stryker, my son."

"Your *what?*" I fall back against the bed.

"Brady, I h-have to go to the hospital, I'm s-sorry."

Mascara is running down her face and I see that her hands are shaking.

Fuck.

"Well, you can't drive yourself. You'll have an accident. I'll drive you."

I quickly throw on some clothes and join her in the living room as she's waiting impatiently by the front door. I take her keys from her knowing she's in no condition to drive.

"Can you tell me what happened?" I ask as we get into the elevator.

She closes her eyes. "He loves those little iced cookies, the ones I keep in the jar on the kitchen counter. He knows he only gets one every night. But he's precocious and sometimes he tries to sneak more, so I have to put them up in the cabinet where he can't see them. B-but, I f-forgot to put them away tonight before I left. It's my fault. Hannah said he came out of his room after she put him to bed and he must have climbed up on the counter to get one. She heard the crash in the kitchen and when she went in … " She covers her mouth in horror. "Oh, God … when she went in, he was lying on the floor – dazed."

"Jeez, Ry, I'm sorry."

I know only too well that she's going to blame herself if anything happens.

I'm still reeling. *Rylee has a fucking kid?* Everything starts to make sense all at once. The way she's always having to *move things around* so she can go out with me. The way she knows all the animals at the zoo and the aquarium. The way she's always home by ten.

"How old is he?" I ask.

"He's only three. Oh, my God, Brady. What if he's really hurt? What if he …"

I don't hear anything she says after *"He's only three."* I lean over like I've been punched in the gut. I put my hands on my knees and try not to hyperventilate. Because Rylee's the one who is losing it here, I can't afford to lose my shit as well. I do my best to pull myself together, but I feel like I've just been hit by a truck.

The elevator doors open and she runs ahead of me. I can't get my feet to move. She turns around. "Are you coming?"

When I don't answer – when I *can't* answer, she gets pissed.

She holds out her open hand. "If you can't act like an adult long enough to get over the fact that you've been sleeping with a single mother, then hand me my goddamned keys and I'll drive myself."

"It's not that," I say, finally walking out after her.

"Can we not do this now, Brady? Stryker is hurt. *He's* my top priority, not the fact you're thinking I deceived you. Which I didn't."

"It's not that either." We reach her car and as we get in, I look in the back seat. No child seat. "Why don't you have a booster seat in the back?"

"I always put it in Hannah's car when she watches him. He likes to go to the park and the playground."

If only it had been in here and I had seen it that very first time I rode in her car. If I had seen it, we wouldn't be doing this. And if we weren't doing this, Rylee would have been home and she would have put the cookie jar away.

If only I hadn't walked out of our apartment thinking only of myself.

I shake off my thoughts of that horrible day.

"Which hospital?" I ask.

She gives me the directions as I speed through the nighttime traffic to get there. As I do, my stomach turns and bile rises in my throat thinking of the other time I raced through traffic to get to the hospital.

I drop Rylee at the emergency room entrance.

"You don't have to stay," she says, jumping out of the passenger seat. "You can leave my keys at the desk."

I watch her run into the hospital. I know exactly how she feels. I know exactly what kind of pain she's in for if …

I pound on the steering wheel, wanting so badly to stay for her. Wanting so badly to leave for me.

I find a parking spot and sit for a minute, contemplating my options. She gave me an out. She doesn't expect me to stay. I can walk away right now.

But despite the voices in my head screaming at me to leave, I find myself walking into the waiting room of the emergency department. I look around and find a seat in the corner, pulling my baseball hat down low so nobody will recognize me. I sit here and people-watch as the minutes on the clock above my head tick away.

A lady comes in through the doors, frantically trying to find her husband who was brought in by ambulance. "He's dead, isn't he?" she screams, as a nurse takes her into the back. I listen to her pathetic pleas to God in her weak and broken voice as she disappears down the hallway.

It doesn't work, I think to myself. Pleading with God doesn't work.

I put my forearms on my knees. Then I lower my head and close my eyes, succumbing to the memories that I know will devastate me.

Dripping wet from the many bottles of champagne that were poured over us in the locker room after our momentous victory, my coach pulls me aside, looking as somber as I've ever seen him. Oh, shit, did we lose after all? Was there some kind of technicality that disqualified us?

"Son, you need to head back to Lincoln right now," he says. "There's been an accident."

"Accident?"

He nods sadly. "Natalie and Keeton are at Lincoln Memorial."

"What? No, Natalie is here at the game."

"I'm sorry, son. She never made it here."

"A car accident?"

"I don't have any details, Brady." He motions for one of the assistant coaches. "Dan will drive you as soon as you get changed."

Nat and Keet are in the hospital? The gravity sinks in and I feel a wave of nausea. I run over to Dan. "I don't need to change, let's go now."

In the car, I call Natalie's phone, hoping she'll answer. Car accidents happen all the time. Maybe they took them to the hospital as a precaution. She doesn't answer. I try her sister, Katie, next since Natalie was supposed to drop Keeton off with her before she came to the game. No answer.

I hesitate as my finger hovers over her father's name on my contacts screen. Was he in town this weekend? I can't remember. I tap on his name, wondering if it's the right thing to do. If he doesn't already know about the accident, I have no details to tell him. If he's not in town, knowing him, he'll jump on the next plane just so he can try to micromanage the doctors and nurses should Natalie or Keet need special care. But my call rolls to voicemail.

I start the process over again, first calling Natalie, then Katie, then Dennis. Someone has to answer eventually. I'm about to give up and try to call the hospital directly when Katie answers her phone.

"Brady, hold on." I hear her talking to someone who yells at her before the voices go silent and a door shuts in the background. I could swear it was Dennis's voice I heard. "Are you on your way?"

"Yes. What happened? And why hasn't anyone been answering the phone? Was that your dad? Why was he yelling at you?"

"He ... he thought it best not to bother you during the game. He knows how much the game meant to you."

"Wait, hold on a damn second. He told you not to bother me during the game? Just how long have they been in the hospital?"

"About five hours."

"Five hours?" I shout into the phone. "Why didn't you call me? Why didn't someone get me out of the game? Hell, that was before the game even started. What the fuck happened, Katie?"

I can hear her crying. Shit.

"Katie?"

"J-just get here as f-fast as you c-can, okay?"

"Katie, what the hell is going on?"

The line goes dead. I check the time to see we're still about twenty minutes out. "Drive faster, Dan."

When we reach Lincoln Memorial, he drops me at the emergency entrance and I run in and tell them who I am. A nurse buzzes me through to the back and puts me in a room where she tells me to wait for a doctor. I pace around the room as I wonder where Katie and Dennis are. Where my family is.

A short and stocky man with a white coat walks through the door. "I'm Dr. Lathem," he says. "I was the doctor on call when your wife and son were brought in." He gestures to a chair. "Why don't we take a seat."

I don't want to take a fucking seat. Taking a seat is what they tell you to do when they have bad news. Taking a seat is how they keep you from falling down when they deliver it.

In the end, though, I do take a seat, because I double over when I listen to what the doctor has to tell me. I sit in the fiery pit of hell as he describes in detail what happened to my wife and child. I lose the contents of my stomach when he tells me my son is gone and my wife is critical.

A nurse rushes in with a glass of water for me as someone starts cleaning up the mess I made. Dr. Lathem asks if I have any questions. I have a million, but I can't put two words together to ask them. I just need to get to Natalie.

The nurse takes my arm, telling me she's going to bring me up to Natalie's room in the ICU. She goes over some of the things that the doctor told me on the way up.

"Do you understand what he told you?" she asks. "Your wife may be aware, but she's unable to move or speak due to the damage to her brain stem. It's called locked-in syndrome. You can talk to her and if she's awake, she can communicate with you with eye movements. Blinking and such."

"Oh my God," I say, doubling over in the elevator. Our life. Our perfect life with the three of us — gone in an instant. All because of me and my stupidity.

I can't even think about Keeton right now. I'm compartmentalizing this. I can only deal with one thing at a time. Natalie is alive. I have to focus on that. I have to be strong for her.

When I get to her room, Katie and Dennis come outside before I reach the door. I'm trying to plow past them, but Dennis stops me.

"Get your fucking hands off me," I tell him. "You've kept me from her long enough. What the hell were you thinking, not calling me earlier? I could have been here hours ago, you bastard. You robbed me of this time and I'll never forgive you."

Katie steps between us. "What's done is done," she says. "It wouldn't have mattered, Keeton was …" She chokes up and tears roll out of her blood-red eyes. "He w-was gone when they brought him in."

"It does matter!" I yell. "I could have been with Natalie. She needs me more than she needs anybody." I look at her dad with fire in my eyes. "More than she needs you."

I put my hand on the door, but Katie covers it with hers. "Wait. We haven't told her about Keeton. She needs all her strength to fight this."

My forehead falls to the wall as reality sinks in. My son is dead. My wife is dying.

My world is over.

"You two stay out here," I say, before walking through the door.

There are all kinds of machines hooked up to Natalie. Despite that, she looks perfect except for the bandage around her neck and some cushions holding her head in place. Tears cloud my vision as I walk over to her and take her hand.

Her hand is limp and heavy in mine. I squeeze it hoping she can feel it. The nurse in the corner of the room coughs and Natalie's eyes open. When she sees me standing over her, tears fall down the sides of her face. I wipe them. And then I wipe my own.

"I'm here, babe."

Her nurse comes over and explains what I've been told. She says I can ask Natalie questions and she knows to blink once for yes and twice for no.

"Are you in pain?" I ask.

I watch her eyelids close once, then again, and I breathe a sigh of relief.

I lean down and place a kiss on her forehead. Her eyes. Her lips. "I love you so much, Natalie."

She blinks her eyes three times. She's telling me she loves me.

I ask her a few more questions but then she starts batting her eyelids like crazy and looking to the door. I don't have to ask what she's trying to say. I know she's asking about Keeton.

She might hate me for lying to her. She might never forgive me. But there is nothing I can do for him. She's my priority now. And even if it kills me, I have to be strong. "Keeton is fine," I lie. "He's waiting for his mommy to get better so she can hold him and sing to him. They won't let him in here because he's too young. He wanted me to give you a kiss for him."

My words break up and my voice cracks and I wonder if she can see through all the lies I just told. More tears stream down the sides of her face. She blinks her eyes three times again and then they close. Then alarms go off in the room and the nurse rushes over, pushing me away from Natalie as she presses a button and calls "Code Blue" before more people come swarming in the room.

Someone pulls me out of the room as I fight to get back in. "No!" I yell. "No!" I try to push and claw my way through everyone to see her again. I have to be with her. It can't happen like this. This is not how our story is supposed to end.

"Brady!" someone yells, shaking my shoulders.

I look up and see Rylee, worry etched into her face as she pulls me from my nightmare.

I look around the room and remember where I am. Soaked with sweat, I hop up from my chair and run outside just in time to vomit into the bushes.

I hear footsteps behind me, then a gentle arm on my back. "Brady, are you okay?"

I shake my head and wipe my mouth with my t-shirt. "Isn't that what I should be asking you? How is he?"

"He's going to be fine, thank God. They did a CT scan to rule out any bleeding in the brain. They said he has a mild concussion and will stay overnight for observation. They are putting a cot in his room so I can stay with him."

I look at what she's holding in her hands. Two stuffed toys – a stingray and a tiger. She follows my gaze. "Hannah grabbed them on their way out. She knows they are his favorites. I'm watching them while they move him to his room."

"Good. That's good news." It's all I can manage to say as I stare at the stuffed animals thinking about another three-year-old boy who loved them.

"I'm sorry I didn't tell you about Stryker," she says.

"No need to be sorry." I shrug. "It's my fault. My rules."

She puts a hand on my arm. She nods back at the hospital. "What just happened in there? It's like you were in a trance or something."

"I'm fine. I just need to get out of here. I can't be here. I ... I can't do this. Do you need anything?"

She shakes her head sadly. "Hannah is going back to my place to get me a change of clothes. But thanks for asking."

She looks at me like the broken man that I am. She feels sorry for me. She feels sorry for things she doesn't even know about me. This is why I don't tell anyone. They ask too many questions and shed too many tears. I don't need their sympathy.

I back away slowly, looking into her green eyes. The green eyes I thought could maybe heal me. I was stupid to think such a thing. Nothing can heal what is broken beyond repair.

"Good luck with everything," I say. "I'm glad your boy is okay."

She cocks her head to the side, studying me.

"Goodbye, Rylee," I say, slowly backing up into the darkness.

I think I see a tear escape the corner of her eye. "Goodbye, Brady."

I walk down the sidewalk, away from her. Away from my pain. When I reach the corner, I turn around to see her sliding down the wall, head in her hands as her body shakes with sobs.

Yeah, it fucking hurts, I think, feeling my own heart being squeezed like it's in a vise.

But it could be worse.

Part Two

Rylee

Chapter Twenty-two

Four months later ...

He's everywhere.

On posters pinned behind glass on subway platforms. At bus stops. I even saw him on the top of a cab the other day. I can't get away from his chiseled face; his hard body that I've felt with my own hands.

Even here, at work – especially here at work – likenesses of him are plastered everywhere.

"You're going to see him sooner or later, Rylee," Murphy says, catching me staring at a cutout of Brady by the front desk at my new place of employment. "They got back from spring training yesterday."

I nod. I know only too well. I follow their schedule more than I'd like to admit. I follow it even though I'm no longer employed by the Nighthawks.

I follow it because I'm a stupid girl.

And no matter how much I tried. No matter how many times I convinced myself I wouldn't let it happen, it did anyway. I went and fell in love with Brady Taylor. The most ineligible bachelor to ever walk the earth.

I'm no different than all the other girls he's had in all the other cities. I'm sure most of them are in love with him too. I suppose that just makes me a groupie. But even all these months later, I know what we had was different. And after some long talks with Murphy, I know she thinks so too.

That's not to say I'm not mad at him for walking away and not looking back. But I have no right to be. I knew what we were doing and I knew it was going to end. And even though Murphy told me his behavior has nothing to do with me and everything to do with something he lost in the past, it still hurts.

Mason Lawrence, my new boss and part-owner of the gym I now work for, walks by and nods at the life-sized Brady. "Do you think I can round the two of you up for one more shoot?" he asks Murphy.

"I'm not sure," she says. "Their season starts in ten days. I can get you their schedule and see if we can work something out."

"That would be great, Murphy. Thanks." He turns to me. "How are things going, Rylee? Are you getting into the swing of things?"

"Oh, yes. I love it here. Thank you so much for the opportunity."

"Any friend of Murphy and Brady's is a friend of mine. And I've heard nothing but good things about you from our clients."

I freeze at his mention of Brady. "Uh, you haven't—"

He holds up his hand to stop me. "No, I haven't told Brady you're on my staff. Murphy gave me strict instructions." He shakes his head before walking away. "You girls and your silly games."

"Game? It's not a game," I tell Murphy after Mason leaves the room. "I just didn't want Brady to think I followed him here."

"He's not going to think that, Rylee. You said you told him multiple times that you wanted to move back to New York."

I rub my temples. "He's going to think I'm stalking him."

She laughs. "I'm willing to bet that will be the furthest thought from his mind when he sees you."

"How do you know?"

"Because he still talks about you," she says. "You have no idea how upset he was that you weren't in Tampa when he got there in February for spring training."

"What?" I look at her in surprise. "You never told me that."

She shrugs. "I didn't want to rub salt in the wound. But now you're here and he's back so who knows what will happen."

I furrow my brow. "Nothing is going to happen, Murphy. I promised myself that even if he wants to see me, I won't do it. I can't let myself go through that again. It's taken me a long time to get over him."

"The best things in life are worth fighting for," she says.

"I have the best things in life. I have Stryker. And I'm back here where I can see my mom anytime I want."

She stares me down.

"Not every woman needs a man to be happy," I say.

"Of course they don't. But, Rylee, he's changed. I've told you before that he was different with you."

I shake my head. "It doesn't matter. It's been four months. *Four.* If he wanted something more he would have told me by now."

"He's scared. He's been through a lot and I think the thought of loving someone terrifies him. Just do me a favor and don't rule anything out just yet. Talk to him. See for yourself how he's changed."

"Does he know you and I talk?"

"No. I almost told him once. Last fall, I sensed he was getting closer to you than he'd ever gotten with anyone I'd seen him with. You and I kept in touch after my visit to Tampa so I knew about Stryker before he did. And with the losses he's suffered, well, I just didn't want him getting hurt."

"Losses? As in plural? Murphy, what happened to him?"

She shakes her head. "It's not my story to tell. And it took him a long time to finally open up to Caden and me. But I feel in my heart that you might be the one to heal him. And oddly enough, I think Stryker can too."

"Stryker?" I look at her sideways.

"Hey, I have to run," she says, not bothering to elaborate. "We still on for Thursday night? I've got some great apartments lined up for you to see."

"Of course. Thank you. I've asked the sitter to stay longer so I'm yours for the evening."

"We'll grab a bite and then find you a new home." She heads down the hall to her office.

"Sounds good. Wait," I say. "How is he? You said the season starts soon. Is he ... better?"

Murphy shakes her head. "He's not pitching yet if that's what you mean. Not hitting either."

My heart sinks. I was hoping he'd be fully recovered by now. I hate that I can't keep up with his progress anymore.

Gregory, the front desk supervisor, tells me my next client is ready so I head back to the designated PT room. I've only been here for two weeks, but I love it here. I only work on gym patrons which means a lot of high-end clients. I've already worked on a few off-season pro athletes, two former Olympians and one movie star.

It was almost a miracle, my landing this job, and I have Murphy to thank for it. She knew I was hoping to get back to New

York so when she found out about the opening, she hooked me up with the owners. It was a hard decision, knowing I could run into Brady from time to time. But then again, had I taken the transfer the Nighthawks offered me a few months ago, I would have seen him a lot more frequently.

That wasn't the only reason I turned down the transfer, however. It would have required traveling with the team, something I couldn't do with Stryker. And a more desirable job with the Hawks in New York required more experience than I had.

I took some time off between jobs. What happened with Alex back in January pushed me over the edge. Between that and missing my mom, I gave my notice and was back in New York six weeks ago. My timing was deliberate. I didn't want to see Brady when the team went to Tampa for spring training. I wasn't about to let myself be his *Tampa girl* again. I knew if I had stayed, there was a good chance of it happening.

But I was also without a job. A stupid move on my part, hence the miracle when Murphy brought me in to meet with Mason just a few weeks after my move here. So I've been back in town for over six weeks, and now that I have a steady job again, I'm ready to move out of the hotel Stryker and I have been staying in and get a more permanent place to live.

"Mr. Stone," I say, seeing my client waiting for me next to the training table. "Nice to see you again."

"Call me Chad, Rylee."

"Okay, Chad. How's the knee today?"

"Better after our last visit. Can you remind me again never to do my own stunts?"

I laugh. "I would, but somehow I think when it comes time for the next movie, you'll forget everything I said." I pat the training table. "Hop on up. Let's get started."

Chapter Twenty-three

"You picked a good time to come," Barbara tells me on our way to my mom's room. "She's lucid this morning."

I look at her in surprise. "Really? Oh, I wish I had Stryker with me."

We get to her room and I peek through the doorway. Mom's face lights up and her arms open wide, inviting me into them. "My darling girl," she says.

I try not to cry as I embrace her. The times she is aware of who I am are few and far between these days. I'm lucky to have this piece of her a few times a month.

"Mom. I've missed you."

"How long has it been since you've seen me?" she asks.

"I was here the day before yesterday."

She gives me a sad nod. "You visit me a lot, don't you?"

"I try to, Mom. And now that I'm living in New York again, we can have our visits in person."

"Why didn't you bring that boy with you?"

"Stryker? I wish I would have, but I have to go to work right after I leave."

"Not that boy, the other one you always talk about. What was his name, Brody?"

I scold myself for being such a jibber-jabber when I visit her. Sometimes I run off at the mouth just to have something to talk about. And I forget on the days when she's lucid that she might remember things we've discussed.

"It's Brady, Mom. He's just a friend. Someone I spent some time with last year."

She studies me like she used to when I was a child. "You like this boy."

"He's not a boy. He's a man. And yes, I like him. But he doesn't like me back so I can't see him anymore. Do you mind if we talk about something else?"

She rubs a motherly hand down my arm. "Of course, sweetheart. Why don't you tell me about my grandson?"

I spend the next half hour showing her pictures of Stryker on my phone as I go over everything that she's missed in his life.

When it's time to go, I don't want to leave. I don't know when I'm going to have her back again. She could be lucid for days at a time, or just hours.

I give her a long hug before I leave.

"You're a good daughter," she tells me. "Don't ever think you have failed me in any way. I couldn't be more proud of you. Never forget that, even when I can't tell you."

"Thanks, Mom," I say through my tears. "I really needed to hear you say that."

On my way out, I ask Barbara to call me if Mom's still lucid tonight. I'll bring Stryker by if she is. I want him to know his grandmother. He's been to see her before, but never when we could all bond as a family. And if there is one thing I truly desire for my son, it's a family.

~ ~ ~

"You're doing much better today, Mrs. Patterson," I tell her as I help her out of the pool. "You've made a lot of progress."

I hand her a towel and make sure she gets to the locker room without slipping. Then I go back to the pool and dive in.

I always schedule Mrs. Patterson right before my lunch break. She likes to get her therapy in the pool and I like to stay afterwards for a workout.

I've always loved swimming, ever since I was a kid. But growing up in the north didn't always lend itself to the sport. As a child, I begged my parents to put a pool in our backyard, but they insisted it was a frivolous expense for something that would only be used a few months out of the year.

That's when I started going to the Y to swim. And that's where I saw a young disabled girl getting physical therapy in the pool. I didn't know what it was at the time, so I asked her caretaker. I was intrigued. I befriended the girl and even participated in some of her therapy sessions as a helper. That's when I knew I wanted to be a physical therapist. I was only thirteen.

After thirty laps, my legs are burning and I take a break, holding onto the side of the pool.

"Ry?"

I look up and my heart skips a beat.

Hell, my heart *stops*. And I have to will it to start beating again.

Brady is standing at the edge of the pool looking utterly surprised to see me. He has a towel draped over his shoulder and nothing but his swim trunks on. I stare at him shamelessly, like I've stared at the cutout by the front desk. Only this time, it's the real thing.

I turn around and push off the wall, gliding under the water to the other side of the pool. I need a minute to compose myself. To figure out if what just happened was real or only a figment of my imagination. To conjure up the strength to have a conversation with the man I've tried so hard to forget.

When I reach the other side, I look back, but I don't see him. I sigh, thinking I'm losing it. But then he pops up out of the water right next to me.

"Rylee, what are you doing here?"

I climb out of the pool and go in search of my towel.

He follows me. "You can't just ignore me, Ry," he says, his loud words echoing off the walls.

I wring out my hair and dry my face before I whisper, "Not here, Brady. There are too many people around. Dry off and come back to my office."

"Your office?" His eyes dart around the aquatics room and then over to the glass that separates us from the main gym. "You *work* here?"

He thinks about his statement for a second and then looks pissed. But I don't think he's pissed at *me*. He's realizing he has friends – good friends – who work here who have kept this information from him. And suddenly, I feel guilty that I've put them in this position.

"Give me ten minutes and then come back to the PT room. My office is back there."

I walk away, leaving him staring after me.

"She works here?" I hear him say to no one as I turn the corner into the ladies' locker room.

I quickly rinse off and towel-dry my hair before putting my clothes on. I have just enough time to put on some mascara and a touch of lipstick before heading back to my office.

I knew this day would come. I was just hoping I had more time. More time to think about what I would say to him. More time to get him out of my head.

More time to stop loving him.

When I reach the PT room, he's already there. Unlike me, he didn't bother to change. His hair is still dripping water down his back and onto his chest. I follow one such drop until it gets absorbed by his swim trunks.

"You couldn't have changed first?" I ask, forcing myself to look away.

He smirks. "I haven't finished my workout yet." He takes a few steps towards me. He reaches out his arms as if he's going to touch me, but then stops. "What happened to you, Rylee? You disappeared into thin air. And then you show up here."

I walk back into my office and sit at my desk, needing a barrier between us. "I could say the same thing about you. You never even showed up for your last two therapy appointments. What happened that night?"

He closes his eyes and shakes his head. I want to pry, but I keep remembering what Murphy said about him losing someone. Maybe he *actually* lost someone, as in they died, not just a bad breakup. Maybe being at the hospital triggered some bad memories for him. I remember how pale he looked when I found him shaking in the waiting room that night.

"I needed to get back to New York," he says. "And I never hid from you. You could have called. I wasn't the one who changed my number."

"How do you know I changed my number?"

"Because I tried calling you in January."

My eyes snap to his. "You did?"

"Why did you change your number, Ry?"

"It's a long story," I say.

He walks forward and leans on my desk. "Was it because of me? Tell me."

I shake my head. "No. A lot happened after you left. I had to change it because—"

"Shit," he says, slapping a hand on my desk. "It was that slime-ball, Alex, wasn't it? Matt told me he was fired for sexual misconduct in the workplace. He also told me that you quit shortly after. What did he do to you, Rylee?"

"It's fine. I'm fine. He just got out of control. He became obsessed with me which is why I changed my number. And then when he found out I changed it, he got mad, saying he was my boss and had to have my number. When I wouldn't give it to him, he ... he forced himself on me."

Brady's hands ball into fists and his face turns red.

"I'm okay. He didn't do anything. Matt walked in on us before he had the chance, and then I called the higher-ups and told them everything. He was removed from his office that same day."

I see someone walk into the PT room. "Listen, Brady, I have a client now."

"We're not finished with this conversation, Ry," he says, walking backwards and then stopping in my doorway. "We're not even close."

Before he walks away, he stands there and stares at me. He studies every curve of my face. He traces my arms with his eyes. And by the time his gaze meets mine again, my heart is pounding. And when he finally turns to leave, I feel ... bereft.

"I'll be right there, Mr. Harold," I yell from my office.

Then I take a minute to control my racing heart. To calm my shaking hands. To ward off the crazy thoughts that are invading my head.

Samantha Christy

Chapter Twenty-four

"Can we go straight from here?" Murphy asks, as we finish up our lunch together in the gym café. "I can't wait for you to see what I have lined up. Thanks for letting me help you find a new place."

"Are you kidding? I owe you big time for doing it. I've been so busy trying out nannies and looking at preschools, not to mention the time I'm spending with my mom, that I haven't even been able to think about it. You are a life saver. And, yes, we can leave from here. I should be done with my last client at five thirty."

I pick up my trash and throw it in the garbage can. But before I leave, I can't help it. I have to ask.

"Murphy, have you talked to Brady? Did he say anything to you?"

She laughs. "I was wondering when you were going to bring that up. And yes, I got an earful last night. He reamed me out for not telling him you and I were friends."

Guilt consumes me. "I'm so sorry to have put you in that position. I never should have asked you to keep your mouth shut. It was unfair of me."

"I wouldn't have done it if I didn't think it was the best thing for both of you. But at least now he knows you didn't change your number because of him."

"Is that really what he thought? I had no idea he was going to try to call me, especially after six weeks of radio silence."

"He was going to invite you to my wedding in January."

"What?"

She smiles and nods. "It's true. He ran the idea past me, and at the time, you were still in Tampa and we hadn't become good friends yet. I told him to go for it. But truth be told, I couldn't believe he was even considering bringing a woman to a wedding. I mean, this was Brady Taylor we were talking about. But that was just the first of many changes I've seen in him since he came back last fall."

Murphy was the second person I called when I decided to move back to New York. My mother was the first. Murphy and I had gotten along well during her visit to Tampa. We kept in touch afterward and she told me if I ever needed anything to call her. Being a single mother with a parent in a memory care facility does not lend itself to friendships and most of the friends I made growing up and in PT school had fallen away.

I stand here looking stunned about the fact that he wanted to take me to Murphy's wedding.

"Don't look so surprised, Rylee. The man was completely taken with you. Still is, if his behavior last night tells me anything. I told you, he's changed."

I look at my watch and realize I'm late for my one o'clock. "I have to go, Murphy. I'll see you tonight."

Walking back to the PT room, I wonder what she means by that. He's changed. He's changed how? He's not an arrogant spendthrift? He's not bedding everyone in sight? He's not running away from hospitals?

As I contemplate the possible answers to my questions, I come to a halt when I see none other than Brady Taylor himself sitting on one of my training tables. I look around for Jeannie Nolan, my one o'clock.

"Brady, I have a client. You can't be here."

"I know you have a client. I'm it."

"You are not my client, Brady. Not anymore." I walk back to my office to check my schedule on the computer and shake my head when I see Brady's name pop up in this time slot.

"What? How?"

"I ran into Ms. Nolan at the front desk when I was trying to make an appointment with you. She agreed to switch her appointment to a later date."

"She agreed?" I stare him down.

"Well, after I said I'd pay for it."

I snort at him. *Yeah, still an arrogant spendthrift.*

"Brady, you can't go bribing my clients so you can talk to me."

"I didn't do it so I can talk to you. I really do need a physical therapist."

He holds out his left arm and my eyes find a new pink scar. Not the scar from his broken elbow. My eyes snap to his. "You had the nerve transposition surgery?"

He nods. "Some smarty-pants PT told me it was my best shot."

"When did you do it?" I ask.

"Right before training camp," he says. "I felt my progression had halted. I wasn't getting any better. It was do or die time. And, well … I knew you'd be there to help in my recovery. Or so I thought."

"So why come here now? You have team PTs you can work with."

"I'm allowed to work with any PT I choose, even those outside of the organization. I know you. You will push me harder than anyone."

"But you'll travel with the team, won't you?"

"Yes, whenever I can. But I'll work with you when I'm home. You're going to get me back, Rylee, I know it."

I know he means get him back in the game, but I think of how else that statement could be interpreted.

"How long have you worked at the gym?" he asks, oblivious to how his double entendre has affected me.

"A little over two weeks."

"But you quit your job more than six weeks ago. Did you leave before spring training because of Alex or because of me?"

I shrug. "To be honest, a little of both. I needed some time off after … everything. I was beginning to fear for my safety being in Tampa. Alex knew where I lived. And I had been away from my mom for too long. And yes, there was the thought of having to see you."

"How is your mom?" he asks. "I know dealing with Alzheimer's can be difficult."

I furrow my brow. I'm positive I never spoke of her.

"I walked in on you one time when you were Skyping your mom. I didn't want to say anything because we weren't talking about personal stuff."

"But we are now?"

He looks to the floor. "Depends on what stuff, I guess."

"Meaning we can talk about my stuff, but not yours."

I start to walk away but he pulls my arm, tugging me back to him. "Meaning we can talk about lots of stuff, but not *all* the stuff. Some things I just don't talk about, Ry."

I look at the clock. "If we don't get started, you'll have wasted a lot of money for nothing. Let's do your evaluation."

He watches me meticulously as I measure his wrist flexion and extension and his grip. He silently follows my direction when I put his arm, wrist and fingers through their paces. I'm reeling on the inside, knowing he's already stronger than he was last fall. If anyone can overcome this, he can.

"You've done a lot of work today. I'd like to ice your arm before you leave."

"What, no manual therapy?" He winks at me.

"I'm not sure that's a good idea."

I can sense that he's getting ready to argue, but then he backs down.

"Fine, ice me up. We'll work up to the other stuff."

I type my notes into my laptop while he sits with ice on his arm.

"I tried to get you a transfer, you know. I'm sorry I couldn't make it happen."

"You did?" I look up, surprised.

"That day when I saw you Skyping your mom, I called the team owner and put in a good word for you."

"So that's why I got the job offer."

He looks confused. "You got an offer to come back to New York and didn't take it?"

"They offered me a staff PT position, but it would require traveling with the team during the season. I couldn't do it. Not with Stryker. But thank you for trying."

"How is he – your son?"

I can't help smiling. "He's great. He recovered quickly and is just like any other precocious three-year-old."

Brady's eyes close and he winces.

I touch his arm. "Are you in pain? Is the ice too cold?"

"It's fine," he says.

My next appointment comes in the room. "I'll be right with you, Kathy."

"Can we talk some more?" Brady asks. "After work maybe?"

"Sorry. Murphy's taking me apartment hunting."

"You don't have a place yet? Where have you been staying all this time?"

"In a hotel. I know, it's awful, Stryker and I sharing a room. I put all my stuff in storage. But I've been so busy, I haven't had a chance. Murphy has been great. She's lined up all the places for me to see."

"Yeah, she's pretty great, isn't she? I'm glad you two have become friends."

He studies me as I unwrap his ice pack.

"I guess I'll see you next time," I say.

"Ry." He looks over at my next client to see that she's keeping herself busy with her phone. "I'm sorry for how I left. I had my reasons. Reasons that had nothing to do with you. I just wanted you to know that."

I shake my head. "You don't owe me any explanations," I say. "I knew what we were doing was a short-term thing. If I allowed myself to think anything else, it was my own fault."

He steps closer. "Are you saying you wanted it to be something else?"

I look up at him but don't answer.

He sighs and brushes a stray hair behind my ear. "It's okay, Rylee. I wanted it to be something else, too."

He walks away, leaving me incapable of … anything.

I hold a finger out to Kathy, letting her know I'll be just another minute. Then I go into my office, close my door and just breathe.

Chapter Twenty-five

I walk out to the front desk to meet Murphy. "Ready?" I ask.

She pulls a folder out of her bag. "I'm ready. We're seeing three places today."

"Want to grab a sandwich from that deli on the corner first?" I ask.

"Ugh – sandwiches? What is it with you and sandwiches?" a deep male voice asks.

Murphy and I spin around to see that Brady has snuck up behind us. "What are you doing here?" I ask.

"If you think I'm going to let the two of you go apartment hunting without protection, you're crazy."

"I'm not taking her to the slums," Murphy says defensively.

"Still, are you sure you know what buildings are safe? I mean, you're from Iowa, Murphy, and Rylee grew up outside the city."

"We know enough," I say. "Plus, I told her I wouldn't live in one without security."

"They all have doormen and twenty-four-hour security," Murphy says. "So you can see we're far ahead of you."

"I'm coming anyway," he says, walking to the front door to open it for us.

I stare at him and wonder why he's doing this. He walked away. Four months ago he walked away from me at the hospital and never looked back. Why is he interested in being around me now? Does he think he has to protect me from guys like Alex? Or does this have anything to do with what he said earlier?

"Want me to get rid of him?" Murphy asks in a whisper.

I shake my head. "No, it's fine."

"Maybe he can intimidate the managers into giving you a better deal," she says.

I laugh. "I wouldn't doubt it."

Murphy and I talk on the way to the deli with Brady walking behind us. After we order our dinner, he asks, "So, the sandwiches?"

I shrug. "Stryker likes them, so they are pretty much a staple in my house. I've had to get creative to make sure he's getting enough nutrition, but it's fun. I make a mean chicken salad avocado hoagie."

Brady looks like he swallowed a bug. He must not like avocado. Or chicken salad.

"Uh, where is the little tyke?" he asks, running a hand nervously through his hair.

Murphy gives him a sympathetic look.

"I asked my sitter to stay late today. Believe me, you would not want him tagging along. We'd get nothing done but chasing him around the apartment buildings."

"Oh, okay."

I don't miss the relief that pours out of him and I wonder if that's the whole issue. Maybe my having a child is a deal breaker. The certified bachelor of baseball doesn't want a girlfriend with a kid. I guess I can't blame him. I mean, even if he has changed like Murphy said, it's still a lot to take on. Not that I want him to take anything on. I might have at one point. But I'm over that. I'm over him.

Aren't I?

As Murphy and Brady talk about scheduling another photo shoot for the gym, I appraise him and wonder what it would be like to be with him. I can't even imagine it. He has a girl in every city. *Every* city. How would one reconcile that? Even if he did want to be with me, I'm not sure I could do it knowing there are twenty-something other girls out there who had sex with him on a regular basis? That's just gross. And wrong.

And entirely hypocritical of me to think considering I was one of those girls.

I let my forehead fall to the table.

"What is it?" Murphy asks.

"Nothing. Don't mind me. I'm just tired, I guess."

"Well then, let's finish up and find you a new place. We won't keep you any longer than necessary. I'm sure you want to get home to that gorgeous kid."

Brady looks at Murphy. "You've met him?"

"I have. He's absolutely precious." She puts her hand on Brady's arm in a motherly manner. Then she balls up her wrapper and stands up. "Come on, let's go."

The first apartment we see is awful. Even in a secure building, it doesn't look safe. No way is the fire escape up to code. Brady threatens to call a building inspector if I even think twice about signing a lease.

The second one turns out to be in a not-so-desirable school district. But it's not Murphy's fault. I didn't make that a requirement.

The third one, where we are now, is perfect. In fact, it's better than perfect. It has everything I asked for and more. Two bedrooms, two bathrooms, a designer kitchen, even an office that I can make into a playroom. And it has a balcony, something I never thought I'd be able to get in my price range.

"How did you even find this, Murphy? It's a gem. What's the catch?"

"It is pretty sweet," Brady says, taking another look at the balcony. "There must be something wrong with it." He turns to the manager. "Did someone die here or something? Is it haunted?" he jokes. "Why is it so cheap?"

"Really?" the manager asks. "I was thinking it was going for a bit too much." He looks at his paperwork and quotes us the rent.

My eyes bug out. Even at my generous salary, it's three times what I can afford.

"What are you talking about?" Murphy asks the guy. "I called your assistant earlier this week and she said it was a third that price. Are you bait-and-switching me?"

The manager flushes. "Wait – *you're* the one who talked to Trisha?" He rummages through his folder. "Oh, my. I'm very sorry. I was supposed to show you 3B not 16F."

My heart sinks as I glance around once more. "Is 3B anything like this one?"

He shrugs. "If you call a smaller apartment without top-of-the-line appliances and a balcony 'like this one,' then—yes."

"Let's just leave," Murphy says. "This is ridiculous." She eyes the manager as if she thinks he did this deliberately.

"No. Let's see it. I really like the building. It's the perfect location for me. It's close to work, it's in a great school district, and Stryker will love the indoor playground we saw downstairs."

"You might as well give it a look as long as we're here. What do you have to lose?" Brady says.

We take the elevator down to the third floor as I mourn the place I was already envisioning Stryker growing up in.

I'm apprehensive as we enter apartment 3B. I know anything I see will be a letdown after the one on the sixteenth floor. We tour the apartment in silence, looking at the two modest-sized bedrooms, the one bathroom, and the nothing-special kitchen.

"Look over here," the manager says. "There is this alcove off the dining area. Maybe you could make this into a play area for your child. And I can check my records, this unit might be on the list for upgraded appliances. Did you see the bathroom? I know there is only one, but it's rather large and has both a tub and a shower – that's hard to find in this price range."

The manager looks genuinely sorry to have shown me the wrong apartment.

"Do you like it?" Brady asks, pulling me aside.

"I guess." I look around again. "I mean, if I hadn't seen the other one, I'd probably be excited about it. He's right about that alcove – it's more space than I thought I'd get."

Brady walks over to the manager and points to his folder. "Why don't you go check your records and see about those appliances? Then maybe look to make sure you were exactly right on the rent. Ms. Kennedy would be the perfect tenant. You want her here. Keep that in mind before you come back and tell us your final offer."

"Final offer?" he says. "This is an apartment, not a negotiation to buy a car."

Brady stares the guy down. "Everything is a negotiation." He puts his arm around the manager and walks him out of the apartment. "Do you like baseball?" I hear him say before the door shuts.

Murphy laughs. "I told you he might be good to have around."

We take one more long look at the place, and this time, I try to picture us here. I picture Stryker sitting at the bar watching me cook pancakes. I picture snuggling him in my bed on lazy Saturday mornings. I picture bringing Mom here for Sunday dinners.

"I think I like it," I tell Murphy. "In fact, I think I love it."

"I'm glad to hear you say that," Brady says, coming back in and joining us in the living room. "Because not only will you have new stainless steel appliances, but the guy came down by two hundred dollars a month on your rent. And you can move in on Saturday."

I stare at him incredulously. "What did you do?"

"Nothing much. I just promised him tickets to a few games and a shitload of signed crap."

"Brady," I admonish him.

Murphy puts a hand on my shoulder. "It really isn't a big deal, Rylee. Caden gives that kind of stuff away all the time."

"Okay, well, I guess I should thank you then," I tell Brady. I walk over and jab him in the ribs. "Thank you."

He jabs me back. "You're very welcome."

I smile. I smile big as I twirl around looking at my new home. I'm finally back where I belong.

Chapter Twenty-six

I stare at my list of appointments, knowing Brady is my next one, and my heart races. I'm taken back to last fall. I was like a schoolgirl with a crush on the senior quarterback. Every time he came in for therapy, I hoped I didn't screw something up because I was so darn smitten. Every time he left, I fantasized about my hands on him. And when that fantasy became a reality, I was sure I could handle it. I was positive I wouldn't be like one of his other girls who follow him around like a puppy dog lapping at his feet.

On the outside, I think I did a good job tamping down my feelings, but on the inside – I was barking up a storm. It was the first time I'd felt a connection with a man since being with Denny. But I'm not stupid. I know how that turned out, so connection or not, I wasn't going to let myself fall for Brady. Until I did.

My father's words echo in my head. *You can't help who you fall in love with.*

I hear a noise and look up from my desk to see Brady standing in my doorway. God, he looks good. His hair is perfectly messy in the most put together way. His t-shirt shows off his biceps and is just tight enough to tease with what's underneath. His jeans are faded and worn and look soft to the touch. His looks should come with a warning sign, because they are dangerous.

He raises a smug brow as if he knows exactly what I'm thinking. I clear my throat and grab my laptop, not making more eye contact as I pass him on my way to the main room.

"How did your arm feel last night?"

"Fucking great," he says, looking at it as he rolls his arm from side to side. "Sore as hell, but that's how I like it. I was right to come back to you. Calvin never works me like you do. You know how far to push me."

"You've still got a ways to go, Brady. You're only two months post-op on the nerve transposition. While you're making good progress, you can't expect to be pitching until at least the three-month mark."

He smiles. "See, that's why I need you. Calvin would always say three to six months. He's not nearly as optimistic as you are. Hell, he would even say we can't be sure the surgery even worked yet."

"The surgery worked," I tell him. "You are ahead of where you were last fall. If the surgery had failed, you'd have stayed the same or even regressed."

"You're good for me, Ry."

I search his eyes and try to gauge the meaning of that statement.

I start him off slowly, with hand grips of various tensions and rubber band exercises. Then I move him up to shoulder and elbow motions that involve the wrist and fingers. By the end of our session, I have him throwing a small rubber ball into a net that bounces it back out. He keeps trying to impress me with how strong his throws are, and I have to chase more than a few balls around the room when they bounce back powerfully, almost hitting us.

"Are you back working with a pitching coach yet?" I ask.

"I never stopped. Since I came back to New York last fall, I've been working with him on my form and my motion. He won't let me throw yet until I get more of my grip back."

"Good. Like I told you before, it might happen slowly, but then someday you'll realize you can do something you couldn't before."

He laughs. "Do you know how many jars of pickles I have in my apartment?"

"Huh?" I furrow my brow.

"Last year you said that someday I would do something completely normal without realizing it, like opening a jar of pickles. So I went out and bought some."

"You mean to tell me you sit around your apartment trying to open jars of pickles?"

He shakes his head. "No. I sit around my apartment squeezing stress balls and hand grips and *occasionally* trying to open a jar of pickles. But after I try one and fail, I throw it away because I have to make sure I haven't just loosened it for the next attempt."

I can't help it when I laugh out loud thinking of his trashcan full of unopened pickle jars. "So, do you limit yourself to pickles, or do you try relish as well?"

We both fall into fits of laughter as we start listing all the different kinds of pickles we can think of.

Laughing with Brady brings on waves of nostalgia. I miss this. I miss him.

When the room falls silent again, he says, "You worked my ass off today. Did I earn a massage?"

I bite the inside of my cheek as I contemplate it.

"Come on, Ry. I'm a paying client. Treat me like one."

I roll my eyes and motion to the training table. "Fine. Get on up." I reach into a cabinet and throw him a hand towel. "But cover up. I don't want to see … anything."

He smiles and lies down on the table, balling up the towel in his lap as I asked.

I try to keep my fingers from shaking as I work them behind his neck, around his shoulders and up into the base of his skull. I know just how he likes his massages. I know how he likes to be touched. I know how he likes to be touched *everywhere.*

I close my eyes and pretend I'm working on another patient. Anyone but him. I try to think of Mrs. Patterson – but her flesh is old and wrinkled and thin, not anything like his smooth and toned skin.

A hand reaches up to grab one of mine. "Ry, it's okay. It's just me. Just us."

My eyes open to find him stretching his neck to look at me.

"Sorry," I say, pulling my hands away. "Was I hurting you?"

He doesn't release my hand, but puts it back on his neck. "No, you weren't hurting me. But you're so tense. Maybe *you* need a massage."

I feel heat flush my face at the thought of his hands on me.

"Please don't say things like that, Brady."

"I'm only saying what we're both thinking." He lets me go and sits up.

I shake my head. "It doesn't matter what we're thinking." I point my finger between us. "This is not happening again."

"Why?" he asks. "Why can't it happen again?"

I back away and lean against the other table. "Oh, the reasons are endless. One: I want to be your *New York girl* about as much as I want a hole in the head. Two: your season is starting and you have about thirty other girls ready and willing to service you. And three: you ran away last time without so much as a word. Maybe that was fine when I was in Tampa and you were here in New York, but I live here now, Brady. And some of your friends are my friends. Need I go on?"

He jumps off the table and approaches me. He gets close enough that I can feel his breath on my face. "I don't give a shit about those other girls, Ry. The only woman I give a shit about is you."

I put my hand on his chest and shove him away. "I don't know anything about you, Brady." I laugh sorrowfully. "Well, that's not true. I know plenty about your reputation. How could I ever trust you knowing your track record? Knowing how easily you could walk away from someone you claim to have wanted more with?"

"Maybe that's *why* I walked away, Ry. Did you ever think of that?"

I have thought of that. But when he never came back; when months went by without a text or a call, I knew that couldn't be the reason.

There is a knock on the door to the PT room. "I have to go. I have another client. I'll see you next week."

He walks towards the door. "See you soon," he says.

I watch him stroll down the hallway, disgusted with myself that I'll be counting down the hours.

~ ~ ~

"Where is that handsome boy, Brody?" Mom asks for the third time.

I spoon soup into her mouth. "Mom, you are thinking of Denny. He doesn't come around anymore. We broke up, remember?"

I laugh inwardly, wondering how many times I say *remember?* to her when I'm visiting. Dozens? Hundreds?

"Broke up? But he was here just the other day."

"That wasn't the other day, Mom. That was four years ago. I brought Denny to see you a few times. He's Stryker's father."

"Who is Stryker?"

I sigh getting out my phone to show her pictures. "He's your grandson. He's three years old now. He'll turn four this summer."

She looks at me in confusion. "My, you must have been just a baby yourself when you had him."

"I was twenty-three, Mom. I'm twenty-seven now."

She looks around her room. The room I helped decorate when Dad and I moved her here almost five years ago. Five years ago, when I had just started PT school and he couldn't look after her full-time. Five years ago, when both our hearts broke as we drove home without her.

"Where am I?" she asks. "Is this a hospital? Am I hurt?"

"This is a memory care facility. You live here now. You have Alzheimer's, Mom."

"You're being silly," she says. "Why isn't Brody with you?"

"His name is Brady, Mom. And you've never met him. Why do you keep asking about him?"

Barbara comes in to take her tray. "She asks about this Brody person all the time. She has for months now. Is he someone significant in your life?"

I shake my head and look at the floor. I guess I did talk about him a lot when I Skyped her last fall. When she was not lucid, and when I couldn't be here in person to watch television, or help her with her food, it was sometimes hard to find things to talk about with her.

It's hard dealing with her sometimes when she's so confused. She doesn't even know who I am on the really bad days, but most of the time, she thinks I'm still twenty-two years old. She thinks dad is still alive which is both a blessing and a curse. She sometimes thinks Stryker is my brother, her child, but most times she doesn't remember him at all.

I put my head in my hands thinking about Barbara's question. *Is he significant to me?*

"Yes. No. I don't know."

She puts a calming hand on my shoulder. "It's okay, dear. The best relationships are sometimes the most complicated ones." She nods to my mother. "Talk to her about it. It can be good therapy just to get it all off your chest."

I nod. "Thanks, Barbara."

She takes the dinner tray and leaves the room, closing the door behind her.

I take my mom's hand. "I'm a fool, Mom. I'm a fool to love a man who can't love me back."

"I'm sure Denny loves you dear. I saw him kiss you the other day when you didn't think I was looking."

I ignore her comment. "He's a baseball player. A celebrity. He's rich and famous and women throw themselves at him. *He* throws himself at women. Can anyone really change after being that way?"

"Right. He plays baseball. What team is he on again?" she asks.

"The Nighthawks."

"No, that's not the one. It was the Mets, wasn't it?"

"Not Denny, Mom. Brady."

"Brady? Who's Brady?"

I shake my head. "Never mind." I stand up and give her a kiss. "I have to go now. Stryker is waiting for me. We're moving into our new place tomorrow. We can start doing Sunday night dinners again, would you like that?"

"I'll make my famous lasagna," she says proudly.

"That sounds great, Mom. That's exactly what we'll make."

"And will Brody be joining us?"

"No, Mom. Brody, Brady and Denny all have other plans. It will be just you, me and your grandson."

"My grandson?"

"Yes. Stryker. My son." I point to a picture mounted on her wall of Stryker when he was just two years old.

"My, he's handsome. That Brody must be quite a looker."

"He's not Brody's, uh, Brady's ... Ugh! I have to go, Mom. I'll see you soon."

I put a reminder in my phone to go grocery shopping for her recipe after I get settled in tomorrow. I can't wait to get out of that hotel room and get back to normal.

I laugh at my thought. *Normal.* My life has been anything but normal from the day she was diagnosed. From the time I got the horrible phone call about my father. From the moment I found out I was having a baby with a man who dumped me.

From the second I laid eyes on Brady Taylor.

Chapter Twenty-seven

I run my hand along the beautiful hand-made 'Welcome' sign Murphy brought me to hang outside my new front door. It's engraved with my last name. I smile thinking I'm finally getting settled into adulthood. Yeah, I guess technically I've been an adult for a while, but I've never had a place of my own that I thought I might live in more than temporarily.

When Dad died, I sold the house and took the proceeds to pay Mom's expenses. The best memory care facility on the East Coast does not come cheaply. Between that and school, I couldn't afford much else so I got an inexpensive third-floor walk-up with a friend from PT school. Then once Stryker came along, I moved into a small one-bedroom until I graduated. From there I did a short internship in the city and then went to Tampa with the Nighthawks organization. I've bounced around from place to place over the past four years and am looking forward to putting down some roots.

"It's perfect," I tell Murphy as she pops her head out the door to see me admiring it.

"I'm glad you like it." She looks at her watch. "The guys should be here any minute with your furniture. You picked a good day to move. One week later and Caden and Sawyer would have been on the road and unable to help."

Sawyer, Caden, and Caden's brother-in-law, Kyle, rented a moving truck to empty out my storage unit outside the city. Murphy and I have been putting away everything else we moved over from the hotel. I left a few toys behind since Stryker and the sitter aren't coming over until all the heavy lifting is done. I didn't want him underfoot.

"Are you dreading it?" I ask her. "Caden leaving?"

She nods. "This is our second season together and even though we're married now, I'm not sure it will get any easier. But we've found out that it's true what they say about absence making the heart grow fonder. Sometimes I'll fly out and join him for a weekend. And I do get to see him every day when they aren't traveling. We make it work because we have to. We have no other choice."

"I envy you guys, you know."

She laughs. "I'm pretty sure you could have your own uber-hot baseball star if you wanted one."

I shake my head. "I'm not so sure about that. And even if that were true, I'm not sure I'd want it. He has a girl in every city, Murphy."

She puts her hand on my arm. "I know he did. I'm not so sure he does anymore. But I guess time will tell, won't it? Oh, look, here they are now."

Caden and someone I don't know, presumably Kyle, come off the elevator with a mattress. I direct them to the master bedroom in the back. They put it against the wall and Caden introduces us.

"Kyle Stone, meet Rylee Kennedy," he says.

Kyle shakes my hand. "I hear you are in the medical profession as well, a physical therapist?"

"That's right I am."

"And Brady tells me your father is the famous orthopedic surgeon, Gerald Kennedy, is that true?"

I'm wondering how that conversation even came about. Are Kyle and Brady friends?

"Yes. He died four years ago."

"I know. I'm very sorry for your loss. He gave a guest lecture in one of my medical school classes about eight years ago. Almost turned me to ortho instead of emergency medicine."

I laugh. "Yeah, that sounds like him. He was very passionate about his profession."

"Well, it's nice to meet you, Rylee. I should introduce you to my wife, Lexi."

"Oh, my gosh, yes!" Murphy squeals. "And they have two adorable little girls, the oldest is about Stryker's age. You could have play dates."

"That would be wonderful. I'd love that."

"I didn't really think of it until now," Murphy says. "But I have a lot of friends with kids who I could introduce you to."

"I'd be grateful," I tell her.

"Head's up!" Sawyer yells as I see him come in the front door holding one end of my couch.

I watch as it comes through the door so I can see who's holding the other end. I thought it was just the three of them helping.

When I see Brady, my heart pounds. I'm aware that Murphy is watching me, so I try to play it cool like I don't care who just walked into my apartment.

"Well?" Brady says as they are standing there waiting for my direction. "Where do you want it?"

"Uh, sorry." I inwardly roll my eyes at myself. "Over along the far wall just under the window."

Brady nods his approval. "That's exactly where I would have put it."

I watch as he works meticulously to center it perfectly. Then he comes over. "How's that?"

"It's great. Thank you. What are you doing here?"

"I happened to be in the area and saw these guys struggling with the moving truck."

Sawyer swats him on the back of the head. "You just *happened* to be in the area. Right. And I was not struggling with the truck – it was as expertly parked as one could get."

Brady shrugs him off and holds up his left arm. "And moving shit is good physical therapy, don't you think? I have to try like hell not to drop any of your stuff. You might kick my ass if I break some fru-fru heirloom vase."

"I don't have fru-fru *anything*," I tell him.

"Oh, good. So that box I dropped off the back of the truck, you're okay with that?"

"What?" I squeal, running to the door.

"Just kidding, Ry." He winks at me as he walks by to go get another load.

"Did you know about this?" I ask Murphy.

"No," she says, laughing. "But you must admit, the man has shown up and been helpful lately."

"Hmmm. I guess."

Kyle and Caden bring in my bed frame and box spring. Kyle grabs a tool box off the counter. "I'll put your frame together if you tell me where you want it."

I head to my bedroom with Kyle and we discuss the various places that would be good for my bed. I settle for the far wall since he pointed out the outlet for my television is on the wall by the door.

When I get back to the living room, Brady comes in carrying a box. "Where does this go?"

I read the side. "Stryker's room. First door on the right."

Brady doesn't move.

I point down the hallway. "It's that one."

He just stares at the door down the hall.

Caden comes over and takes the box from him. "I've got this one. You can head down for another one."

Brady walks back out my front door without a word and I wonder what in the world just happened.

When he comes back up a few minutes later with a box that belongs in *my* room, he has no problem traipsing down the hallway to put it there.

As the apartment gets filled with my stuff and I realize their job is almost done, I order out for several boxes of pizza. When they arrive, I pull out the case of cold beer I'd put in my new refrigerator when I got here this morning.

I tell everyone to leave the boxes and come enjoy dinner. It's been a long day and I just want to organize things by myself tomorrow. Kyle has a beer with us but then goes home to his wife. Sawyer eats and leaves shortly after. So, awkwardly, Murphy, Caden, Brady and I are left sitting around my living room like we're on a double date or something.

I'm grateful when my doorbell rings. I smile knowing who's behind it. I hop up and walk to the door, thanking my new nanny, Helen, for bringing my son over. I've been trying out nannies for a month now, even before I went back to work. I'd gone through

239

three before finding Helen. She's perfect. She's a grandmother who became a widow last year and was looking for something to keep her busy. She sometimes takes Stryker over to play with her grandkids. I hired her through an agency that does thorough background checks so I feel confident he is in good hands.

I hug my son and thank Helen, quickly slipping her a key so she can let herself in Monday morning while I'm getting ready.

"There was a police down there. He let us in," Stryker says.

"That was the doorman, sweetie. He wears a uniform, so he kind of looks like a policeman."

"Oh." He looks around the room. "Who are all these people, Mommy?" He sees all the boxes. "Is this our new house?"

"Yes, this is our new house. I'll show you your room as soon as you say hello to everyone." I take his hand and walk him over to the living room. "Stryker, you remember Mr. Caden and Ms. Murphy, don't you?"

"Hi, Stryker," Murphy says.

I don't miss that she's eyeing Brady warily the entire time.

"Hey, slugger." Caden picks up Stryker and spins him around to pleasured giggles.

My own smile fades when I watch Brady. He's staring at my son, looking like he's in physical pain. Maybe he's stricken by how much Stryker looks like me. Everyone always tells me he is my carbon copy. His hair is my exact shade of brown and his eyes mirror my green ones. He even has my nose. I'm more than a little grateful for the resemblance. I didn't need to be looking at a mirror-image of my ex-boyfriend who didn't want anything to do with either of us.

Maybe reality is setting in and Stryker being here in the flesh is reminding Brady that I'm a single mom. A single mom he doesn't want to mess with. Or even mess around with.

"Mommy, who's that man?" Stryker asks from Caden's arms.

"This is Mr. Brady. He plays baseball just like Mr. Caden."

Stryker's eyes light up. "You like baseball?"

Brady doesn't answer.

"Brady?" I touch his arm.

He looks down at my hand and then back at my son. "Uh, sorry. Yeah, I like baseball," he says with as much emotion as a turnip.

"Will you play with me sometime? With me and Mr. Caden? He likes baseball too. He got me a hat. Can I show it to him, Mommy? Can I show him my new hat?"

"I … I, uh, …" Brady looks at Caden and Murphy with eyes as distant as I've ever seen.

Murphy takes Stryker from Caden's arms. "Come on, little man, let's you, me and Mommy go see your new bedroom."

"Okay. I'll show him my hat later. And can I have pizza, too?"

"Yes, sweetie, you can have pizza," I say as we walk towards his new room.

I look back, confused when I see Brady doubled over and Caden putting a hand on his back.

Stryker squeals when he sees his race car bed. He missed it while sleeping at the hotel. He opens the lids of some of the boxes and gets out toys, littering his room. As I watch him put his mark on our new home, something hits me like a ton of bricks – Brady didn't once come in Stryker's room. Caden or Murphy would take boxes or bags from him if they had Stryker's name on them. Brady seemed terrified of Stryker just now. Not in an *I-don't-want-kids* kind of way. More like an *I've-seen-a-ghost* kind of way. And then there's the way he reacted at the hospital last fall.

Oh my God.

I turn to Murphy with tears in my eyes. "Did he lose a son?"

She looks down at Stryker to see him happily playing. Then she gives me an affirming nod.

I think back to all the autographs I've seen him sign at the request of kids. He never seemed to have a problem with that. I look at my son and have a horrible thought.

"How old was he?"

She nods to Stryker and my hand comes up to muffle my cry.

"What's wrong, Mommy?" my sweet boy asks, dropping his toy to see if I'm okay.

"Nothing, baby." I force a smile. "I'm just so happy you like your new room."

When he goes back to playing, Murphy whispers, "I couldn't not tell you anymore. There was no way I could explain what just happened out there. But please, Rylee, he placed his trust in me. He doesn't ever tell anyone. Please don't tell him I said anything."

"You didn't," I assure her. "I guessed it. All you did was nod." I run a hand through my hair. "But what do I do? What do I say?"

We hear a door close. "I'm not sure you need to worry about that tonight. I'm willing to bet he just left."

Caden walks down the hall and joins us in Stryker's room. "Brady had to leave. He had a thing. He told me to tell you he'd see you later." Caden looks between Murphy and me. I don't doubt he sees my teary eyes. "You told her?" he asks Murphy.

"She figured it out," Murphy says. "Don't worry, she won't say anything."

"Yeah. Don't," he says. "He won't talk about it. He won't talk about *them*. It took him three years to say anything to me."

"Wait. *Them?*" I ask, wide-eyed.

"I thought you said she knew," he says to Murphy.

"About the kid, yeah," she says.

Caden leans back against the wall. "It was more than just his kid, Rylee. It was his wife. He lost both of them."

Tears stream down my cheeks for the second time tonight as I can only imagine the horror of what he must have gone through. I want to ask them how, but they've told me more than they had the right to already.

Everything I know about Brady Taylor makes sense now. The way he doesn't want attachments. A different girl in every city. The way he carries on like a certified bachelor, an arrogant baseball player who rules the world. But there is nothing further from the truth. He's hiding his pain. He's trying to prevent himself from ever feeling that kind of pain again.

My head hangs low. Any fantasy I ever had about ending up with the man I accidentally fell in love with has just been trampled. He could never be with a woman like me. A woman who represents everything he lost, right down to his three-year-old son.

And he knows it. It's why he left me at the hospital.

It's why he walked out of here tonight.

My back hits the wall and I slide to the ground knowing I've just lost him for the second time.

For the *last* time.

Chapter Twenty-eight

"Read me a book, Nana?" Stryker begs, holding out his favorite Dr. Seuss title to my mom.

My mother looks around my living room. "Who's Nana, little fella?"

"You are, Mom." I pick up Stryker and sit him next to her on the couch. "You're his grandmother. He calls you Nana."

"I have a grandson?" She lights up and gives him a hug. "My, he's a handsome one, isn't he?"

"I'll let you two read while I check on dinner."

I peek in the oven to make sure the cheese isn't getting too brown. Then I use the bathroom and wash up. I look in the mirror, wondering not for the first time, if I will someday end up like my mom. I've done the research so I know early-onset Alzheimer's can be inherited. There is a blood test I can get to see if I have the gene that will predispose me to it. I'm afraid to have the test. I'm afraid of having to put Stryker through this. And the worst is yet to come.

She's pleasant for the most part. Not combative like some Alzheimer's patients can get. It's why they let me take her on outings from time to time. But I know the day will come when I'll be a complete stranger to her. The day will come when every single memory she had will disappear never to return. I'm grateful that I decided to move back. I don't want to miss out on what could be some of her last good days.

"Mommy, Mommy, the baseball man is here!" Stryker yells at me as he runs down the hallway.

"Who?" I grab his hand and he pulls me to the living room.

"The baseball man." He points to the front door and I see Brady walking in carrying a gift bag.

So many things go through my mind all at once. Why is he here after what happened yesterday? What is he going to think of my mother? How am I supposed to act around him with Stryker here?

Brady pastes on what I know must be a painful smile when he looks at my son. But he does it. I can tell he's trying hard not to react like he did yesterday.

"It's so nice of you to join us for dinner, Gerald," my mother says.

I look at Brady in horror. *Oh, God.*

"Mom, this is Brady Taylor. It's not Dad."

She looks at him and touches his hair. "Nonsense. Come, put down your things. I made lasagna, your favorite."

Brady looks like a deer in headlights. "I, uh … I brought you a housewarming gift. I'm sorry I had to leave yesterday. I had forgotten about a thing I had to do."

He holds the pretty bag out to me.

"He brought you a present, Mommy!" Stryker squeals.

"Thank you," I say, taking the bag from him. I look from Brady to Stryker. "Would you like to come in?"

Mom pulls Brady's arm, forcing him into the living room. "Of course he's coming in. Your father never turns down my lasagna."

"Can you come with me to the kitchen, Brady, while they finish their book?"

He nods.

"Wait, Mommy – your present."

I put it down on the table. "You watch it for me and I'll open it in a minute."

Brady follows me into the kitchen and I lean against the counter. "I'm so sorry. She's confused."

"You don't need to explain, Ry. I'm no stranger to Alzheimer's. My granddad had it. Growing up, we spent every Sunday afternoon going to the home to keep him company."

I study his face while he talks and something dawns on me. "You know, you do look a bit like my father. He was in his thirties when they first met. But they didn't marry until a decade later."

"Are you telling me your dad was a Scott Eastwood lookalike, too?"

I laugh. "He was a good-looking man."

Brady reaches out and touches a lock of my hair. "I suspect he was, to have such a beautiful daughter."

I feel heat cross my face. "Thank you for whatever is in the bag. You obviously don't have to stay. I'll make up an excuse."

"I'll leave if you want, but she was pretty insistent. Sometimes it's just easier to go along."

I narrow my eyes at him. "You'd stay for dinner?"

He walks over and starts opening kitchen cabinets. He pulls out two wine glasses. "I happen to love lasagna," he says. "And my gift will pair well with it."

I peek out of the kitchen and look at my son, knowing just how hard this will be for Brady if he stays. "You are welcome to stay, but please don't feel obligated. I know it could be difficult."

I catch myself before I say anything else that could betray our friends.

"You know, because of my mom. She can be a handful."

Brady puts the wine glasses on the bar and laughs. "I know how to handle women, Rylee."

I shake my head and roll my eyes. "I don't doubt that you do. I'll just set an extra place then."

I take another place setting and put it as far away from Stryker's seat as I can. I don't want to make this more difficult than it already is.

"Gerald, did you know we had such a feisty grandson?"

"He does look like a fine boy," Brady says.

"Mommy, can you open the baseball man's present now?"

"Sure, sweetie, can you help me?"

Stryker gets excited as his hands dive into the bag. I help him pull out a bottle of wine. Then he pulls out a large decorative candle. Then he shouts as he pulls out the third item.

"Cars!"

I look at the ten-pack of Hot Wheels cars and then glance at Brady.

He shrugs. "I didn't know what he'd like."

I give him a heartfelt smile. "They're perfect. Thank you." I turn to my son. "Say thank you, Stryker."

"Thank you, baseball man!" he shouts as I tear the package open for him.

A minute later, the timer goes off and I get up to pull dinner out of the oven. Brady follows me into the kitchen, leaving Stryker and my mom on the couch where he is showing her each tiny car.

"Thank you for my gifts as well. This *will* go nicely with dinner." I hand the bottle of wine to Brady. "The corkscrew is in the drawer by the sink."

Brady pours our wine and I get drinks for Stryker and Mom while the lasagna sets. I get the salad from the fridge and the bread from the oven.

I can't help but stop and smile as I look at my surroundings. This is everything I want for my son. Sunday family dinners. I just wish it was by choice and not something my mother forced us into.

"Dinner's ready," I announce. "Can you put the salad out, Brady? Then you can take the seat at the head of the table."

I dish everyone a generous portion and give Brady a double serving. Mom doesn't fail to notice. "My girl, you'll give your poor father a soft middle if he eats that much."

"Not with the way he works out, Mom."

"Nonsense. The man has no time for exercise with his schedule. Doctors are very busy, aren't they, dear?"

She looks at Brady, expecting him to respond.

"Yes, uh …" He looks at me for help.

"Georgia," I tell him, realizing I failed to properly introduce them.

"Yes, Georgia, doctors are very busy. As are baseball players."

"I suppose they are," she says. "Maybe that's why that boy never visits our daughter anymore."

Brady raises his brow at me but I ignore him.

"Go ahead Rylee, tell your father about the handsome boy who never visits with you. What team does he play on again?"

Brady smirks. "Is it the Nighthawks?" he asks, thinking she must be talking about him.

"No, no, that's not it. What team is it, dear?" I don't answer. "Oh, yes, the Mets. Tell your father about the handsome boy from the Mets who is courting you."

Brady's smirk falls into a frown. "Yes, Rylee, tell us about the boy from the Mets."

"Stryker, do you want a piece of bread?" I hold out the bread basket to him.

He shakes his head with a mouthful of lasagna.

"Bread, anyone?"

I pass it across the table to Brady and he takes it, removing a piece without ever losing eye contact with me. It's killing him in the worst way not knowing who we're talking about. I have to keep myself from laughing, yet I'm not about to discuss Stryker's father here at the table. For all intents and purposes, he doesn't have one. Denny gave up all rights to him at birth. His name doesn't even appear on Stryker's birth certificate.

My mother picks at her food and then asks to be excused to lie down on the couch. The three of us are left to finish our meal together. I try to steer the conversation away from my son to make Brady more comfortable, but Stryker is three and he requires a lot of attention.

I encourage Stryker to eat quickly and then I allow him to leave the table to play with his new cars while Brady and I finish our wine.

Brady motions to the living room. "He's quite a boy."

"He's my whole life. He and my mom."

"So, the Mets player?"

"You know how there are some things *you* don't talk about? Well, Stryker's father is the one thing *I* don't talk about."

His jaw goes slack. "Stryker's father is a ball player?"

I stare him down until he holds up his hands in surrender. "Alright. Fair enough."

I can see the wheels turning in his head. "Just leave it alone, Brady. Please."

He eyes me over the rim of his wine glass. When he puts it down, I give him a refill.

"We're doing a photo shoot at the gym this week," he says. "You should come."

"We'll see. I might be busy with a client."

"Are you afraid to see me with my shirt off?" he teases.

"Why would you have your shirt off? Aren't you trying to sell clothing?"

He laughs. "Yes, we are, but sex sells, Ry. Surely you've seen the posters they did from the last shoot. Murphy will have more clothes on than I will, but they'll have her looking pretty damn good, too. Some of those workout clothes for chicks barely cover anything."

I roll my eyes. I've seen some of the so-called workout clothes around the gym. More like pick-up clothes. Of course, they have a full range of clothing in the new line, so some of the outfits are actually functional.

"What do you do in the photo shoot? I mean, how does it go? I *have* seen some of the pictures of you guys, they seem pretty racy."

He smiles at me. "You're not jealous that Murphy gets to touch me and you don't, are you?"

"Don't flatter yourself. Besides, I get to touch you three times a week now."

He smiles bigger. "That you do. And I look forward to every session."

"So what time did you say that photo shoot was?"

He tries not to laugh. I know I'm a petulant fool. And I'm not jealous of Murphy. Okay, maybe I'm a little jealous of her.

"Ten o'clock on Friday."

I frown. I know I'll have a client then.

"Nana's sleepy," Stryker says, walking back into the dining room.

We get up to see she's fallen asleep on the couch. "I should go," Brady says. "Thank you for a nice dinner."

"I'll walk you out." I turn to my son. "I'll be back in two minutes, baby."

He holds up two fingers.

"That's right," I say, reaching down to kiss them.

I prop the door open and walk Brady to the elevator. "I hope that wasn't too terrible," I say.

"Not at all. In fact, maybe we could do it again sometime."

I furrow my brow. "You want to come to Sunday dinner again?"

"Sunday, Tuesday, Friday, any time really."

I think about what he's saying. I'm just not sure I'm ready for that. I'm not sure *he's* ready for that. "I don't know."

The elevator doors open and I realize at this moment that he pressed the wrong button. As he steps on, I tell him what he's done. "Brady, it's going up, not down."

"Yeah, I know. I have to go *up* to get to 16F."

The door closes before I can question him, but I don't miss the devious smile he flashes me.

Chapter Twenty-nine

Apartment 16F?

That was the one the manager showed me before this one. What the heck? I race back to my apartment and call Murphy.

"Why did Brady just leave my apartment and go upstairs to the sixteenth floor?"

"Well, hello to you, too, Rylee. And Brady was at your apartment?"

"Long story. Why did he go to sixteen, Murphy?"

"Have you asked him?"

"No. I have my mom and Stryker here so I couldn't follow him up."

"Did you want to follow him?"

I stomp my foot. Hard. "You ask too many questions."

She laughs into the phone. "I could say the same thing about you."

"So you don't know?"

"Listen, if you want to go ask him yourself, I can be over there in half an hour. I'll watch Stryker and your mom."

I look at my mom who's still sleeping on the couch. Then I look at my watch. It's just after seven. "Can you make it forty-five minutes? That way I can run my mom back to her place first."

"See you then."

"Thanks, Murphy."

"Anytime. I mean it."

I wake up Mom, and Stryker and I take her home to the memory care center. We make it back just in time to meet Murphy in the lobby. I don't even walk them back to my apartment, I give Murphy my key and stay in the elevator.

"I'll put him to bed if you're not home in an hour," Murphy says with a wink.

"Ha-ha. I'll be back in fifteen minutes."

"Want to bet?" she asks as the doors close.

I press sixteen with a shaky finger. *Why is he here?*

I knock on his door twice before he answers. "Are you stalking me?" I ask before he even gets the door fully open.

"I was hoping you'd come up," he says, opening the door to let me in. "I didn't know it would take you an hour though. I almost left."

I look around the place. There are a few boxes stacked by the kitchen but nothing else. "What are you doing here?"

"I live here."

"You *live* here? It doesn't look like *anyone* lives here."

"Well, I will live here as soon as the movers bring all my stuff next week."

I narrow my eyes at him. "Why?"

"Because I thought it was a nice place. Don't you think it's a nice place?"

"Well, yes. But I happen to know what your current address is, Brady. It's on your records. And I'm pretty sure this one pales in comparison to your current place."

He shakes his head and laughs. "It really does. But here's the thing – One: I don't need all that space; and two: this apartment is less than half of what I pay for the other one. Someone once told me to quit spending so much money and save for the future." He looks at his arm. "Because you never know what could happen."

I lean back against the wall. "I'm not worried about your future in baseball. You'll make it back. I'd bet my job on it."

"I'm just glad one of us has confidence in me."

I pick up a takeout menu on the bar, wad it up and throw it at him. "You are one of the most confident people I know, Brady Taylor, so don't give me that crap."

He throws the paper back at me. I smooth it out and look at it. "Was this going to be your dinner?"

"I was moving some personal stuff over that I didn't want the movers to touch and I thought I'd check out the restaurant next door. Turns out I got upgraded to your mom's famous lasagna. Far better than Mama Choo's if you ask me."

I look over the menu. "I don't know, it looks kind of good."

"Then maybe we should check it out together," he says.

"Why are you really here, Brady? In this building. In *my* building?"

"I thought we could, you know … date … or something."

"Or something?" I give him a look. "No."

I turn around to leave but he grabs my arm. "That's not what I meant, Ry. I meant we should date. Period. No *or something*. We should date. You and I should date."

I lean back against the wall. "Define date."

"Go out to dinner. Maybe the movies. I hear bowling is fun."

"You leave in a week, Brady. Your season is starting in case you've forgotten."

"I'll be home half of every week, Rylee. I'm not leaving for the entire season."

There are so many things I want to say to him I just don't know where to begin. I sigh and try to think of how to tactfully say what I need to say.

"I know what you're thinking. I'm the guy with a chick in every city. I've changed. I'm not like that anymore."

"So everyone keeps telling me."

He raises a brow. "Everyone?"

"Murphy. Caden. My boss. Even Sawyer pulled me aside yesterday and told me what a nice guy you are."

"No shit?"

I nod. "But what does that mean? Have you called all thirty of them and told them not to expect you to bed them when you're in town?"

"It's twenty-seven," he says. "And I can't. I don't have their phone numbers."

I look at him in confusion. "Then how do you meet up with them?"

He shrugs. "They always find me after the games."

"Wow," I say, shaking my head. "You sure have them trained well, don't you?"

"Damn it, Rylee. I know I sound like a misogynist pig, and maybe I was, but I swear I've left all that behind."

"Why have you left it behind, Brady?"

He paces over to the balcony door, runs a hand through his hair as he looks out, and then walks back to me. "Do you need me to spell it out for you?"

"I guess I do. I'm not that bright."

He runs a finger down the side of my face. "You're wrong. You're brilliant," he says. He puts his hands in his pockets and leans against the wall next to me. "I've never been good with words or feelings. Not in a long time anyway. But you're different, Rylee. You're intelligent and fun and despite being pint-sized, you're strong, both physically and mentally. You call me on my shit. And you're just so … normal – but don't take that the wrong way."

I try not to smile. "Is that all?"

"No. You're damn sexy, too. And one of the most beautiful women I've ever seen."

My heart soars and falls at the same time. I know exactly why he didn't say *the* most beautiful. And the fact that he didn't makes me like him even more.

"But, Brady, there's one other thing you failed to mention. Before anything else I'm a mom. And I'm also a daughter who is solely responsible for her mother."

He nods and takes a deep breath. "I know and I understand they are your priorities. I'm not asking you to marry me, Ry. I'm not even asking to be your number one. I can be your number three. I'm perfectly fine with that."

I almost tell him that I can be his number three, too. But I don't. He still doesn't know what I know. And I still don't know if he really has changed like everyone claims.

"I don't like to share," I tell him.

He turns suddenly and cages me to the wall. "I don't like to share, either."

"But how can I be sure?"

He knows what I'm asking without me having to say it.

"Do you want Caden and Sawyer to keep tabs on me when we're away?"

I stare at him and realize he's being totally serious.

Samantha Christy

"No … Yes … No. That would be silly and juvenile. But, Brady, I really do mean it when I say I don't share. It's a deal breaker for me. I can put up with a lot, maybe even more than most, but cheating is the one thing I can't forgive."

"I can live with that."

"Can you? Because I promise you there will be no second chances. I won't make that mistake again."

He gives me a sad smile. "Stryker's dad?"

I look out the window.

He takes my hand in his. "We'll have a trial run."

"A trial run. At dating?"

"Yeah, what do you say – two months? And if you don't trust me after that, I'll leave you alone. Hell, I'll break my lease and move out."

"Two months? You're willing to go two months without sex? Without sex with *anyone*? Including me?"

"What?" He gives me crazy eyes. "I didn't say *that*, Ry."

I stare him down.

"Shit, really?" he says.

"If it's going to be too hard for you," I say, ducking under his arm.

He pulls me back to him. "What's two more months when I've already gone four?"

My jaw slackens as I look up at him. "You mean to tell me you haven't had sex since we—"

"Nope. Not once."

"You haven't dated at all?"

"Not exactly. I tried. Hell, I tried hard. After I got back from Tampa I took out lots of girls. But I couldn't bring myself to invite them into my bed. It felt wrong."

He laughs at my expression. "Don't look so surprised. People change, you know."

"What happens after two months?" I ask.

"After two months I can tell everyone you're my girl."

"And Stryker?" I ask apprehensively. "What about him?"

His eyes close briefly. "You're a package deal, I get that. I … I'd like to hang out with the both of you sometimes, but I might need to work up to that, Ry. I'm not great with kids as you clearly saw tonight. You might have to be patient with me."

I stand and look in wonderment at a man who lost his whole world and is willing to fight his demons to try again. Still, I'm not a big enough fool to think this could end in a happily-ever-after. Few relationships do. But he looks sincere. And I might be willing to risk my heart for a chance.

"Two months," I say, pointing a finger at his chest. "And no sex. So don't even try."

He pushes me against the wall and leans down so his lips are inches from mine.

I've dreamed about his lips so many times. I've longed for them. I didn't dare try out any others for fear of nothing measuring up.

"How about kissing?" he asks, his hot breath dancing across my lips. "Is kissing allowed?"

He's so close I can't speak. He assumes consent in my silence and his lips touch mine. They touch mine gently, like a whisper, and then harder, like a scream. He devours my mouth like he's never done before. His hands hold my face to his as he tells me more with his kisses than he did with his words. His kisses seduce me. They almost convince me. They nearly destroy me.

Breathless and languid, I slowly peel myself away from him. I need to be smart about this. He needs to earn his way back into my life.

"I have to go now," I say. They are the five hardest words I've ever spoken.

"I know you do." He walks me to the door. "I'll see you at the gym. And around the building."

I think about what it will be like to have him living so close to me. And then I have a thought when I remember something the building manager said.

"What about your cars?" I ask. "They only allow one per unit here."

"Sold two of them back in January," he says, kissing me on the head as I leave. "I even got rid of the bike."

I smile.

Maybe he has changed.

"Be safe," he says as he walks me down the hall. "Don't talk to any strangers on the way home."

I laugh as I step into the elevator.

"Mark your calendar," he says.

"Mark it for what?"

"Sixty days from today. I don't care where the hell we are or what we're doing – that's the day."

I pink up when I realize he's scheduling a date for sex.

"God you're sexy when you blush."

It's the last thing he says to me before the doors close.

And before I even say hello to Murphy, I walk to my calendar on the wall and circle June 1st.

Then I get my phone out and Google the Hawks' schedule.

Chapter Thirty

I don't know if I'm happy or mad that my ten o'clock appointment got rescheduled. The odds of that being purely a coincidence are very low. It reeks of Brady.

He's been giving me some space this week. The only times I've seen him were at his three appointments and then again last night, when I ran into him bringing a few more boxes to his new place. But every time I saw him, he mentioned the photo shoot. He wanted to make sure I was going to be there.

I contemplate skipping the shoot altogether in protest, but after fifteen minutes of brooding in my office, the pull to see what's happening on the other side of the gym is strong. I walk into the reception area and then back to the part of the gym they've cordoned off for the shoot. They've erected screens around it so gym patrons can't see in, and bright lights are reflecting off the ceiling above.

I approach the entrance to the area and Mason, who appears to be standing guard, waves me by.

"If you stand over in that corner, you'll be out of the way," he says, ushering me past some other people.

I didn't really want to be one of the few who are witnessing the shoot, but now I feel obligated to stay, seeing how I'd have to walk by everyone to leave.

I see Brady standing off to the side as Griffin, one of the other owners of the gym, who is also a big-time photographer, poses Murphy for some photos in front of a weight machine.

Brady sees me and walks over. "Glad you could stop by."

I eye him skeptically. "It's not like I had a choice or anything."

"You always have a choice, Ry." He winks at me.

I have a hard time not staring at his chest. He's wearing nothing but athletic shorts and he's been sprayed with some kind of oily mixture that makes him look like he's been working out. There is a fine sheen across his body, and his muscles – oh, my gosh – they are more glorious than I remembered.

He catches me staring. "They have me pump iron before every set of pictures, it helps my muscles look bigger for a few minutes."

"Because they aren't big enough as it is?" I ask, clearly swooning over his half-nakedness.

He snickers. "I'm glad you approve."

"Are you done? Did I miss it?"

"No, I did my single shots first and now Murphy's doing hers. When she's done, he will shoot us together."

I stare at Murphy, who's been made up to look even more beautiful than she already is. It looks like they had her get a spray tan as she's absolutely glowing. She's completely in her element. I know she wanted to be a model before her face got damaged. But with makeup, you can barely see her scar and if you can, it makes her look edgy.

An attractive woman comes up to me. "Are you Rylee?"

"I am."

"I'm Skylar Pearce, Griffin's wife. Murphy tells me you have a three-year-old son. I wanted to introduce myself and let you know I have two kids myself and would love to get together sometime."

"It's really nice to meet you, Skylar. I would love that. Are you the restaurant manager Murphy told me about?"

"Yes. I manage my parents' place, Mitchells NYC. You should come in if you get a chance. We have a great kids menu."

"I'll do that. Thank you."

She hands me her card. "I have to get to work, but I wanted to stop by and see the excitement and meet you. Call me and we'll set something up."

"She seems nice," I say to Brady after she walks away.

"Yeah, she does. I don't know her all that well, but she's right – we need to take you to Mitchell's. It's really good there."

"Are you asking me out on a date, Brady?"

"I don't know. Is that allowed?" He leans down and whispers in my ear. "I know we said no sex. But there was kissing. Really. Good. Kissing. I'd like to have some more kissing and that usually comes after a date. So how about it?"

He's standing next to me half-naked whispering to me about kissing. I feel myself go weak in the knees.

"Don't you leave tomorrow?"

"Yeah, but we'll be home Thursday. So how about *next* Saturday? Do you think you could find a sitter?" He shrugs uncomfortably. "Or you could bring Stryker."

I appreciate the fact that he's trying to include my son. But I know how hard it is for him. Maybe easing him into things would be better. "I think I could arrange a sitter."

"Brady, we're ready for you," Griffin's assistant calls out.

"Fifty-five days, Ry. Don't think I'm not counting."

I laugh as he walks across the room. He doesn't need to know I'm counting, too.

Brady drops to the floor and does a few dozen push-ups and then someone hands him some barbells, helping him maintain the grip with his left hand as he pumps a few rounds. I know it kills him to need help with his grip, but he doesn't let his disappointment show. And, whoa – what his muscles look like when he's done.

Now I realize what he's been doing all week. He kissed me senseless on Sunday and left me wanting more. Then he tantalizes me all week with his fleeting glances and deliberate touches during his appointments. And he brings me here, knowing I'll see him all buffed up and looking like freaking Tarzan. He wants me to want him. He wants me to squirm during our time apart. He wants me to daydream about how I'm seeing him now.

Griffin positions Murphy on a weight bench and he has Brady standing over her helping her with a free weight. They do various poses, moving an arm this way or a leg that way until Griffin is happy with the photo. Then he has Murphy sit up on the bench and Brady sit behind her as Murphy looks back at him like she's in love with him.

Griffin snaps a bunch of shots and then puts down his camera. "Brady, show me some emotion. You see how Murphy is looking at you? You two are the hottest couple at the gym. You are who everyone wants to be. Let's bring the fantasy out for the camera. Look at her like you want her. Like you can't live without her. Like you want to rip off her clothes and devour her."

Brady raises his eyebrows at Griffin. "Dude, she's my best friend's girl."

"It's called acting, bro," Griffin says. "Caden knows it as well as everyone here in this room. Sex sells. She's sexy. You're sexy.

The two of you together are off the charts. Dig deep and do what you need to do to make it happen."

Brady's eyes find mine. He stares at me long and hard. The rest of the world melts away as I read what he's telling me with only his heated gaze. We share one incredible moment. An indescribable connection. And suddenly, I can't wait for it to be next Saturday.

"Exactly!" Griffin shouts. "Just like that."

Brady pulls his eyes away from me and looks at Murphy the same way he was just looking at me. Griffin was right, they are hot. I watch them make love to each other with their stares. It's almost hard not to get jealous as I watch the two of them.

Twenty minutes later, when they're done, Murphy pulls me off to the side. "Holy shit, girl. Whatever you are doing to that man, keep doing it."

"I'm not doing anything, Murphy."

"Are you kidding? The way he looked at you. The way you looked at him. I felt like I was watching a fully-dressed porn show. You rose the temperature in the room by ten degrees." She laughs.

"But he was looking at you the same way," I say.

She shakes her head. "No, he wasn't. He may have been looking at me, Rylee, but all he was seeing was you."

I look over her shoulder at him. He lifts his chin at me on his way out. "I have something for you," he says. "But I'm going to hit the shower first."

I check my watch. "I have a client in ten. Unless you rescheduled that one, too."

He gives me an innocent smile. "I'll be quick."

I retreat to my office and sit in my chair, wondering, not for the first time this week, if it can really work between us. There are so many reasons why it can't. Why it shouldn't. He leaves tomorrow. He leaves for the start of the season. To the first of many cities and to the first of many girls.

There is a knock on my door and I look up to see a wet-haired Brady, dressed in jeans and a t-shirt.

"Hi," is all I can say.

"Hi, yourself." He walks in and sits in the chair in front of my desk. He holds out a key to me.

"What's that?"

"It's a key to my new place."

"A *what?*" I stand up so forcefully, my chair falls over. "If you think—"

"Will you shut up for two seconds, Ry, and let me finish?"

I put my hands on my hips and stare at him.

"The movers are coming tomorrow. It's the only day I could schedule them. I'm not comfortable giving them a key. I know it's a lot to ask, but do you think you could, I don't know, supervise them for me? The building manager at my old place is going to handle things on that end, but I don't know anyone well enough in the new building. It would mean a lot to me. I have some pretty nice things, Rylee. Things I'd like to make sure are treated with respect."

I close my eyes and breathe a sigh of relief. Then I hold my hand out. "Sure. I can do that. Do they know where everything goes?"

"They can put things wherever you think they should go."

"Me? I can't make those decisions."

"Whatever you tell them will be fine with me, and if I don't like something, I'll just move it. It's not a big deal."

"Okay, if you're sure."

"I'm sure," he says, getting up to leave. Before he goes out the door he turns around. "I'm going to miss you, Ry. I just wanted you to know that. I've gotten used to seeing your face every day."

"I suppose I'll miss you too," I say. Then I look down at the key in my hand. "But just so you know, you'll be getting this back as soon as you return from Arizona."

He smiles big. "So, you know where I'm going, do you?"

I shrug. "I'm a Hawks fan, of course I do."

He laughs as he walks away.

I sink back down into my chair and look at the key, turning it over and over in my hand.

Chapter Thirty-one

"Mommy will be back in a little bit, baby. Chloe is going to play games with you. Be good, okay?"

Stryker runs over and hugs my legs. "Bye, Mommy." He looks skeptically at Chloe until she sits in the middle of the floor and dumps out a box of toy cars. As soon as she starts making car noises, he runs over and joins her.

I smile hoping I've found my new night sitter. I met Chloe and her mom in the laundry room earlier this week. Chloe is sixteen and she and her single mom live in 3D just down the hall. Today is a good day to try her out since I'll be in the building and can pop down and check on them from time to time.

I ride up to sixteen, looking at the key Brady gave me. Today is the first day of the season. They've probably already arrived in Arizona and I can't help but wonder if there wasn't a girl waiting for him at the airport. He said they always find him. He has no way to call them to tell them he can't see them. He has to do it face-to-face. He'll have to do it twenty-six more times after today.

What if one of those twenty-seven doesn't take no for an answer? What if they go to his hotel room and strip naked? Will he be able to turn them down? What if he decides I'm not enough for him, or rather, that Stryker and I are *too* much for him?

I shake off the notion. He has seven weeks to prove himself. There are a lot of cities and a lot of girls between now and then. There's a lot of time for both of us to figure out what we do or don't want.

I put the key in the door and turn it, feeling both like an intruder and like I'm coming home. After all, this is the apartment I wanted. The apartment of my dreams. And the man *of* my dreams is going to be living here.

I walk through his place picturing Brady in each room. He told me nothing about how he wants it. There are three bedrooms. One is obviously the master, but the other two could be anything. Does he have an office? A guest room? I don't even know what furniture to expect, so how can I make decisions on what goes where?

There are a few boxes in each room. I wonder if the contents of the boxes would give me a clue as to what belongs in each room. If I look, however, I'll be invading the privacy of the most private person I've ever known. I decide not to open them. He said he'd either live with how I arranged things, or he'd change it. It'll be his own fault if I mess it up.

I run my hand across the granite countertop in the master bathroom. It's smooth and sleek and much nicer than my marble one. I look into the large shower and think of him naked and wet, rivulets of water streaming off his broad shoulders. His shower is big enough for two. It has a bench on one end and my mind goes wild thinking of all the things that could happen there.

The doorbell rings and I leave my fantasy in the master bathroom as I let the movers in.

"Mrs. Taylor?" a large man with a clipboard asks.

I flush. "Uh, no. I'm Rylee. I'm just here to help organize his things."

"Can you walk me through and label each room for me?"

I shake my head. "Not really. I mean, I can tell you which is the master, but as far as the other two rooms, I don't even know what's supposed to go in them."

He gruffs in displeasure. "I was told there would be someone here who knows everything. We have three televisions to hang on the walls, one of them is seventy inches."

My eyes go wide. "Oh, no. I can't make those decisions. What if I'm wrong?"

He looks through his notes. "Ma'am, I've got strict instructions. Maybe you'd like to reschedule."

"No, we can't do that, you have all his furniture. He'd have no place to go. We have to do it today."

"Then can we do the walk-through, please?"

"Can you at least tell me what kind of furniture goes in the other two rooms?"

"One had a desk and some shelves, so I'd guess it was his study. The other was a workout room."

"Follow me," I say, leading him down the hallway. I look at the two extra bedrooms, trying to figure out which should serve what purpose. One of the rooms has a better view and is closer to the living room. The other is smaller and across from the second bathroom.

"I think this one should be the weight room," I say, motioning to the smaller room. "I think he'd rather have a nice view out of his office."

"And where do you want the television?"

"He had a television in his weight room?"

The guy shrugs. "Working out is boring, ma'am – lots of people watch TV."

"I thought everyone listened to music," I muse aloud. "It's what I do."

He stares at me, waiting for my answer.

"I'm not sure. Can we move the stuff in and then decide? I don't even know what he has."

"I'm sorry, ma'am, but do you even know Mr. Taylor?"

I laugh. "I do. Well, I kind of do. I'm not sure anybody really knows him."

For the next two hours, I direct four movers as they bring in furniture, boxes, electronics, and housewares. I cringe as they drill holes into his freshly-painted walls to attach mounting brackets for his televisions. If I'm wrong about the placement, he will have to patch the walls.

Before they leave, I sign the delivery order stating nothing was damaged and then I hand one of them the envelope on the counter that presumably has their payment or a tip.

Then I walk through his living room, hoping I've put everything where he wanted. I sit on his L-shaped couch that I oriented towards the large TV. I can see myself here, my head resting against Brady's shoulder as we watch a movie.

My eyes go over to the many boxes stacked in the corner that are meticulously labeled with specific contents, and I get an idea. I'm not going to unpack for him, but if I could find the box with his bed sheets and towels, I could at least set those things up for him. I'm sure he'll be exhausted from traveling when he returns on Thursday. Even though he's not playing yet, he does practice with the team every day, and flying across the country is tiring. He'll probably appreciate having a made bed to come home to.

I walk back into the master bedroom and see a box lying on its side, the contents of which are spilled across the floor. "Oh, shoot!"

This wasn't one of the boxes the movers brought, it was one Brady carried over himself. An important one. And the movers must have bumped it on their way out. I close my eyes, hoping nothing is broken.

I fall to my knees and set the small box upright, then I load it back up again. "Please, please, please let nothing be broken."

I pick up an old baseball and look at the signature. *Babe Ruth.* "Oh, my gosh." It's lying next to a glass case that has a Babe Ruth trading card inside. I pick the case up and examine it for cracks. It seems to be intact so I place the ball back inside it, next to the card.

I eye another baseball a few feet away. I reach over and grab it, reading the stitched inscription. *'Brady Taylor – first home run – June 14, 2003.'* Upon further inspection of the ball, it's stamped with *'Cooperstown Dreams Park.'*

Growing up in New York, and working for a baseball team, I know exactly what this ball represents. Cooperstown is a week-long tournament for twelve-year-old baseball players. Young players dream of playing there. Older players often reminisce about the once-in-a-lifetime experience; and you can bet many, if not most, MLB players have played at Cooperstown.

I look around but don't find another case. I wonder if it's because he likes to hold this one. Maybe he throws it up and catches it, over and over, thinking back on the time he only dreamed of playing professional ball.

I smile thinking of a young Brady. Then I frown, wondering how many times he's thought about his own son who will never be able to throw a ball. He'll never go to Cooperstown. He'll never get to see his father pitch in a major league game.

My hand comes up to cover my gasp when I see a picture lying on the floor. It's a small framed picture of a woman and a boy. One you might have on a desk or a bedside table. She is young and beautiful with long dirty-blonde hair. The boy is adorable. He has the same color hair as his mother, only he has a strong cowlick over his right brow. They are both laughing.

I feel a hot tear roll down my cheek. Although the boy doesn't look like Stryker, they are the same age. They have that same sparkle in their eyes. They are full of life and love and possibility.

All of a sudden it hits me. How can Brady even stand to be around me? Around Stryker? Every time he looks at us, he must see them.

I carefully put the picture back in the box. Then I pick up a baseball glove, noting how old and worn it is and I wonder if maybe it was his Little League glove. I turn it over to see his name burned into the leather. My hand fits perfectly inside the weathered glove and somehow it makes me feel closer to him.

I pack the glove alongside the other relics and then I pick up one of the shirts on the floor. I hold it up and read it. 'Bumbershoot 2009.' I think this is the shirt I put on at his hotel last fall. The one he asked me to take off. It too is old and weathered. I wonder if this is the shirt he wears when he pitches. I calculate the year and think that it must have something to do with his wife – the woman who's name I don't know, but who's face is now ingrained in my memory.

I fold it carefully and tuck it inside the box hoping he won't notice the contents have been displaced.

I pick up the last thing that fell out of the box, another shirt. I have to hold back more tears. It's the shirt I bought him at the White Poison concert. I peek back inside the box at all the other things he holds dear and wonder how this little old shirt won itself such a place of pride.

I bring it up to my nose and smell it, hoping it smells like him. It doesn't. It doesn't smell like anything. I wonder if he's even worn it or washed it since coming home last fall. I fold it up and put it in the box and then I close the lid, running my hand over the top of it before I go in search of what I came back here for.

Twenty minutes later, I've got his bed made and his bathroom set up with towels. I contemplate laundering his sheets. They smell like him. In the end, I don't do it. But I do lie down on them and pull his pillow close to me and think about the future.

A future I long for so desperately for my son and me. A future that might not be possible because of what sits in the box in the corner.

Chapter Thirty-two

I stare at the super-large screen that takes up an entire wall in Murphy and Caden's theater room as I'm given a tour of their apartment. "We get to watch the game on *this?*"

She laughs. "You'll almost be able to see the color of their eyes."

"I'm surprised Brady doesn't have a theater room," I say.

"Oh, he did. You should have seen his old place. It was probably twice the size of his new one. It was a penthouse apartment. He got rid of a lot of stuff last week."

"Why would he give that up?" I ask. "Do you think he's starting to get scared about never playing again?"

"I don't think so. Caden says Brady is very optimistic. I just think he finally realized how careless he was being with his money." She looks at me with raised brows. "Somebody must have gotten through to him."

"He sold two of his cars, you know. And his motorcycle."

"I know. I didn't think he'd ever get rid of that death trap. He took me for a ride once." She shakes her head at the memory. "I never went again. The man was as reckless with his bike as he was with his money."

I look around the theater room and see a lot of Caden's old jerseys displayed. Murphy explains about all the hats hanging on the back wall. Then we walk into the living room and she opens a large box in the corner and Stryker's eyes go wide with all the toys he sees.

"For a couple who doesn't have kids, you sure have a lot of toys."

"We know a lot of people with kids. And you never know when we might have our own."

"Are you ...? Sorry, that's too personal."

"It's fine, Rylee. Caden and I both want kids. We're not trying, per say, but we're doing nothing to prevent it either."

"You guys will make great parents, I'm sure."

"Thanks, I think so too."

The doorbell rings and Murphy excuses herself.

I explore the toy box with Stryker for a minute before I hear little feet trample over towards us. Several girls and a boy pile into the room and head right for the toys. The grown-ups follow behind.

"Rylee, you've met Skylar Pearce, and this is my sister-in-law, Lexi Stone."

I stand up and greet both of them.

"That's my Aaron over there and his sister, Gracie," Skylar says.

"And those two are mine," Lexi says. "Ellie is my oldest and Beth is my baby."

"That's Stryker over there. He's three," I say.

Skylar laughs at the way he and Aaron are both trying on baseball caps from the toy box. "It's always the baseball stuff

Aaron goes for. It drives Griffin crazy. He's gotten him a dozen toy cameras. Real ones even, and all Aaron wants to do is play sports. I think those two will get along fine."

"I met Kyle," I tell Lexi. "He was kind enough to help me move in last weekend."

"He said you were very nice," she says. "But he didn't tell me how beautiful you are."

"That's very sweet of you. Sounds like you have yourself a good husband."

"He's a *great* husband. Better than a lot of other ones out there," Lexi says with a sad smile.

Murphy puts a hand on her arm and it makes me wonder if Lexi has had experience with any of the so-called *other ones.*

I know everyone has a story. I wonder what hers is. On the surface, it seems like some people live charmed lives. I thought that about Brady when I first met him. Boy was I wrong. And even though Caden and Murphy's story ended fabulously, it took a lot for them to get where they are. Murphy's aspiring career was ruined and her reputation almost tarnished after what she went through.

While I used to think everyone else had better luck than I do, now I know my life has been a virtual walk in the park compared to some.

I hope I will get to know these ladies enough to find out *their* stories.

"Are you guys ready to watch the game?" Murphy asks.

"I'll make the popcorn," Lexi says.

I walk into the kitchen. "I'll get the snacks and juice boxes for the kids."

Skylar opens a cabinet and finds some glasses. "I'll pour the wine. Rylee, are you a wine drinker?"

I point to a bag I brought with me and she walks over to pull two bottles out of it.

"I knew we were going to get along great," she says, laughing.

The doorbell rings again and in walks a young girl.

"Everyone, this is Alicia. She's going to keep the kids busy so we can watch the game. Alicia, there are snacks on the counter and a selection of movies by the living room TV. We'll be in the theater room if you need us."

Murphy messes with the electronics on the side wall until the game comes on the large screen. I'm excited to see the game. I really do like baseball. There were a lot of years that I thought my dad wished I was a boy because he took me to so many Saturday games growing up. He even put me on a baseball team when I was five. I played until I was eleven, when the boys started teasing me about getting boobs.

My eyes are glued to the screen when they show the visitors' dugout. I hope to catch a glimpse of Brady in his uniform, but the camera moves too fast. Caden gets a close-up when he walks out to go behind the plate. I look over to see Murphy watching the screen intently.

"It never gets old," she says. "I can't believe that gorgeous man is mine."

"He is gorgeous," Skylar says.

"Yeah," I agree. "Totally."

"Eeeew. You are talking about my brother," Lexi broods.

"Your brother who is gorgeous," I say.

"I have sex with that man," Murphy teases her. "Lots and lots of sex."

Lexi throws a piece of popcorn at Murphy. "I do not need to hear that."

We eat and drink and talk as we're watching the game. Then during the seventh-inning-stretch, I finally get my close-up of Brady as the announcers discuss his injury.

"He's traveling with the team now, so we can assume they believe he's recovering," one of them says.

"I've never seen a six-month recovery from a simple elbow break," the other announcer replies.

"Obviously there is more to it than that. We've all seen bone breaks that end careers. But the rumor is he's having nerve issues as well."

They go on discussing what may or may not happen in Brady Taylor's future, and the whole time, they are either showing old game footage, the video of the hit that broke his elbow, or Brady talking with his teammates in the dugout.

I can't peel my eyes away from the screen. When they show him laughing, I reel over how roguishly handsome he is.

"Now, there's another gorgeous one," Skylar says. "He might even give Caden competition in the looks department. It's a shame about his arm. Think he'll ever play again?"

"He'll play again," I announce to the room.

Murphy smiles and Lexi and Skylar question me with their eyes.

"I'm his physical therapist," I explain.

"Wait," Lexi says. "You aren't the physical therapist from Tampa, are you?"

I narrow my eyes at her.

"I overheard my brother and Brady talking a few months ago about a girl from Tampa. Brady seemed very, um, enamored … which is decidedly uncharacteristic of him. Were they talking about *you?*"

"It's her," Murphy says with a smile.

"Oh, my gosh!" Lexi squeals. "Someone is finally going to tame the beast."

I about spit out my sip of wine thinking of Brady and the comment he made about his 'beast.'

"I'm not so sure about that," I say.

"I am," Murphy says. "He's moved into her building. He stopped sleeping around. The man is looking to settle down I tell you."

I give Murphy a scolding look. "Nobody is looking to settle down," I say. "We're not even officially dating. Not for seven more weeks anyway."

"What happens in seven weeks?" Skylar asks.

I roll my eyes thinking about our silly deal. "He wanted me to give him two months to prove himself to me."

"Prove himself?" Skylar asks.

"Brady is ... was ... kind of slutty," I explain. "And there are a lot of girls in the cities they travel to who would like him to remain that way."

"My bets are on Brady," Lexi says.

"Mine too," Murphy says. "Do you know that he's rooming with Caden?"

"What?" My eyes snap to hers. "Why? I thought they all got their own room."

"I guess he's trying to prove something to you."

I shrug sadly. "Or maybe he thinks he'll give in to temptation if he has his own room."

"Let's give him the benefit of the doubt until he proves otherwise, okay?" she says.

I nod. "Caden doesn't mind having a roommate?"

"No, not at all. Unless he snores. He doesn't snore, does he?"

"Don't know," I say before taking a sip of wine. "I never slept with him."

Murphy stares me down skeptically.

I roll my eyes. "I never *fell asleep* with him."

"Well, when you do start dating, have him bring you to Mitchell's," Skylar says.

"He's bringing me there next Saturday," I tell her.

"And yet you're not dating," Lexi says smiling.

"Semantics," Murphy says.

"Can we talk about something else?" I plead.

Lexi looks back at the screen and squeals. We all look to see what happened, and on the replay, they show Sawyer Mills stealing home.

"Well, since the most eligible bachelor on the Nighthawks is about to be taken, looks like that slot has just been filled by number fifty-five." She nods to his picture plastered up on the screen.

"From what I hear, the guy is as bad as Brady," I say.

"And yet Brady has been tamed," Lexi says. She sees my unappreciative stare and holds up her hands. "Fine, fine, no more talk about the former playboy of baseball."

"Wow, he's super-fast," Skylar says, watching another replay.

"They call him *Speed Limit*," Murphy says.

"Why?"

"He's fast and his number is fifty-five," Murphy explains. "Sawyer hates it when they call him that."

"I think it's a great nickname," I say.

"Since when has the speed limit been fifty-five?" Skylar asks.

Murphy laughs. "I know, right? But I think his grandfather called him that when he got assigned the number."

"I guess it is kind of catchy," she says. "What's his story?"

Everyone looks to Murphy who seems to know more about the players than anyone.

She shrugs. "Beats me. All I know is that management hates him man-whoring around. He has no shame. Sleeps with just about anyone in a short skirt. But never more than once. He'd better watch himself or he'll turn up in a ditch somewhere after he's pissed off one too many boyfriends or husbands."

"What do you mean never more than once?" Skylar asks.

"He never takes a girl out more than one time," Murphy tells her.

"He must be seriously messed up," Skylar says.

"You never know what drives people to do what they do," I say.

Murphy gives me a knowing look. "Yeah, you never know. Don't go judging a book by its cover."

"You're absolutely right," Skylar says. "I was quite a slut myself back in the day, so I have no right to judge anyone."

I raise my brow at her.

"Long story," she says. "But if you really want to know, go buy the book my sister wrote about it."

"That's right," I say. "Murphy told me your sister is a famous romance author."

Lexi laughs. "Don't let Baylor hear you call her famous. She hates that. And I'm her assistant. I'll get you the book and any others you want to read."

"That sounds wonderful," I say. "I could use a good book."

"Let's do a real girls' night," Murphy says. "I haven't been out with your sisters in forever, Skylar. And Lexi's sisters-in-law could come too. No boys, no kids."

"That sounds heavenly," Lexi says. "I'll set it up."

We watch the rest of the game and hang out drinking wine until some of the kids start getting cranky.

It isn't until I get home that I realize I missed a text.

Brady: Heading to bed now. Alone, by the way. It's been a long day. Sweet dreams, Ry.

It's the first time he's texted me since we were in Tampa.

I smile. But I don't text him back. My mother taught me long ago never to text a man after you've been drinking. And now I understand why. There are so many things I want to say – but shouldn't.

Chapter Thirty-three

I've resisted the urge to use his key again. I wanted to so badly. I wanted to sneak up and lie on his bed to smell his scent. I've thought of excuses for going. Maybe I left lights on. Did I close the balcony door tightly enough? Anything that would give me a reason to visit 16F one more time while he was away.

But I never went up. And now it's Thursday. He's coming home. I wonder if he's going to like the way I arranged his furniture. I wonder how long it will take for him to invite me up.

I wonder how long my willpower will hold out before I cave and accept his invitation.

I never responded to his nightly texts telling me he was in bed alone. I didn't know what to say and I didn't think it was appropriate that we start having conversations while we were in bed.

"Mommy is crazy," I tell Stryker as we eat grilled cheese sandwiches and apple slices. I whirl my finger in a circle around my ear and he mimics me.

"What is it about him?" I ask no one. "He's so wrong for me. I'm so wrong for him."

There's a knock on my door. I'm not expecting anyone so I look through the peep hole.

It's *him.*

My heart thunders as I look down at my t-shirt, yoga pants and bare feet. I pull my hair from the ponytail and give it a fluff before I open the door casually like I don't care who's behind it.

Brady doesn't say a word. He just lets his eyes wander over my face. Then my shirt, my legs and finally my feet. "You are a sight," he says.

I snicker. "Well, if you're going to show up unannounced, you get what you get."

"That's not what I meant, Ry. You're beautiful. I missed you."

I smile, not wanting to reveal just how much I've missed him too. "How do you like the apartment? Did I mess anything up?"

He nods to his large duffle bag on the floor of the hallway. "I haven't been up yet. I'm sure I'll love it."

"You haven't seen it yet?"

"I wanted to come by and thank you first."

I walk over to the counter and pick something up. "Of course. You wanted to come get your key. Here it is," I say holding it out to him.

Stryker comes up behind me. "Hello, baseball man."

"His name is Brady, Stryker. Not *baseball man.*"

Brady laughs. "It's okay. I kind of like the sound of *baseball man.*" He reaches down into a side pocket of his bag and pulls out a stuffed animal snake. He hands it to Stryker. "Here you go, champ ... uh" —he runs his hand through his hair and bites his lower lip. Hard— "Stryker. Here you go, Stryker."

"It's a rattlesnake, Mommy. See the tail?"

"Say thank you, Stryker."

"Thank you, baseball man."

"You're welcome," Brady says.

Stryker goes to play with his new toy on the couch.

I try to hand Brady the key a second time.

"Keep it," he says.

"I'm not keeping your key, Brady."

"Don't you think it's important for someone else to have a key to your place? You know, for emergencies?"

"Yes. He's called the super."

"Just put it in your junk drawer and forget about it if you need to, but I'd really like you to keep it."

I put it on the table. "For emergencies only," I say. "Do you want something to eat? I could make you a grilled cheese sandwich."

Brady smirks at my mention of a sandwich. Then he eyes Stryker on the couch. He shakes his head. "No, I'm good, but thanks for asking. I should probably go check out the new pad and get some sleep."

I nod to his arm. "How are you? How's the hand?"

"I wore through another stress ball this week. But it's basically the same."

"Are you coming in for an appointment tomorrow?"

"Ten o'clock. I'll go right to practice from there. Are you going to the game tomorrow night?"

I shake my head. "There are only so many nights I can get a babysitter. I'll watch it on TV though."

"Are we still on for Saturday? Do you have a sitter?"

"I found a great one." I nod to the door at the end of the hall. "She lives right down there. Dinner at Mitchell's, right?"

"I'm looking forward to it," he says, picking up his bag and slinging it over his shoulder. "I have one more question, Rylee."

"What is it?"

"How come you didn't answer my texts?"

I step outside into the hallway so my son doesn't hear me. "I guess I didn't know what to say. *Thank you for keeping your dick in your pants'* just didn't seem right, but I didn't know what was."

He laughs. "Ry, you never have to thank me for keeping my dick in my pants when I'm away. It's a given. And I know if I don't, you go away. It's not going to happen."

"I guess we'll see, won't we?"

He checks his watch. "Six weeks and three days." He leans close. "I dreamed about what I'm going to do to you on that day."

I look up at him and see the heat in his eyes. He drops his bag on the floor. "I'm going to kiss you, Rylee Kennedy."

My tongue comes out to wet my lips just before his mouth claims mine. My body falls against the wall of the hallway as he kisses me. His hands wander around to my neck, then down my arms and finally, he grabs each of my hands in his.

He pulls away, leaving me wanting more. This kiss was just a teaser. A glimpse of what's yet to come.

"Mmmm," he mumbles. "You taste just like grilled cheese. Kind of makes me want one now."

Then he backs up and walks away. But I call out after him. "Brady?"

"Yeah?"

"I put your sheets on your bed and hung your towels in the bathroom. Whoever labeled your boxes did a very good job and I found them easily. I, uh, didn't go through any other boxes. I just thought you might be tired when you got home."

He smiles and walks back to me, kissing me once more. "Thank you. That was very considerate. I knew you were the right person for the job. Maybe you could come help me unpack my kitchen this weekend. On Sunday before your mom comes to dinner and we leave again?"

I'm impressed that he remembered my mom comes to dinner on Sundays. And it takes me all of two seconds to cave into this man and say yes. "I'm not going anywhere near your bedroom, Taylor."

"I'm okay with that. Besides, just knowing you've already been there is good enough for me." He studies me for a second. "Did you lie down on my bed, Ry? Tell me the truth."

I shrug innocently. "I might have just for a second. It was a long afternoon."

"You have no idea how happy I am to hear you say that. Now I can fantasize about you on my bed and know you've been there."

I feel heat come up my face. He laughs as he walks away. "You don't expect me to refrain from *all* sex, do you?" he jokes, holding out his left hand. "I'm willing to bet my PT would call that some damn fine therapy. Gives the hand a hell of a workout."

I'm sure I've turned three shades of red when he spins around and gives me a wink before getting on the elevator.

I take a second to collect myself before going back through my door. I almost can't wait for bedtime. And when I finally crawl under the covers and my hand wanders beneath my panties, I look up at the ceiling, wondering if Brady is thinking about me at this exact moment. And wondering if he's doing what I am.

Chapter Thirty-four

For weeks he's been courting me. With his words. With his looks. With his kisses.

He texts me every night after his away games. Sometimes he even calls. Sometimes we talk on the phone for hours. Sometimes we just listen to each other breathe, having run out of things to say, but not wanting to hang up.

Two more weeks until June 1st and I can hardly stand it. I long for his hands to be on me. But he's been the perfect gentleman, never pushing me to give more than what we'd agreed upon.

He came for Sunday dinner again and my mother is completely enamored with him. Of course it could be because she thinks he's my dad.

And he's trying with Stryker, too. No matter how much I know it hurts, he's trying. He brings my son a stuffed animal representative of each city he visits. He's still standoffish with him, however. Understandably so. But we're a package deal. And no matter how much Brady and I get along, this will never work if he can't fully accept my son.

My phone pings and I smile. Eleven o'clock. Just like always.

Brady: Did you catch the game?

Me: I saw the highlights. It looked good.

Brady: It was. God, Ry, you have no idea how much I want to be out there.

Me: I know you do. It will happen. You're getting stronger every day.

Brady: You tell me that all the time. But it's been almost three months and I still can't throw a baseball better than my grandmother.

Me: That's not true, Brady. You are throwing well. And once your grip comes back, you'll be throwing better than before. Every single time I measure your hand, you improve. Every millimeter of progress you make is one step closer to your goal. Someone once told me that the best things in life are worth fighting for. You need to keep fighting and you'll get what you want.

Brady: Are we still talking about baseball, Ry?

I reread my text and realize what I said. And I wonder if he thinks *I'm* worth fighting for.

Me: So you get back tomorrow, right?

Brady: Way to deflect the question. Yes, tomorrow. Is it okay if I come by for a minute and drop off Stryker's animal?

Me: What is it this time?

Me: Wait. Let me guess. You are in San Diego … um, a seal?

Brady: Guess again.

Me: A sea lion?

Brady: Nothing from the water, but you're close on the name.

Me: I give up.

Brady: A mountain lion.

Me: Really?

Brady: Yeah, San Diego is close to the desert. It was either that or a bobcat.

I look at the shelf where Stryker keeps all the stuffed animals Brady gives him. He gets so excited when he knows Brady is coming home. We often play guessing games on what kind of animal he's going to bring. It's been fun for Stryker. And surprisingly educational.

Me: Remind me never to go walking at night
if I go there.

Brady: I'll go with you if you do. I'll always
protect you, Rylee.

I know he will. I feel it. But the question is, can he ever feel
the same about Stryker?

Brady: Are you still there?

Me: Yes.

Brady: I know you must be tired. I just
wanted to say hi. I miss you, Ry.

Me: I suppose I miss you too.

Brady: You suppose? Come on, throw a guy a
bone.

Me: Okay, fine. I miss you.

Brady: How much?

Me: Now you're pushing your luck.

Brady: See you tomorrow night, Ry.

Me: See you then.

I put the phone down and think about how much I miss him. I miss the way he kisses me until he knows I can't stand it and then he does something mundane like picks up a magazine or turns on the television like he didn't just wreck me. I miss the way he follows my every move with his gorgeous brown eyes when he comes for physical therapy. I miss the way he holds my hand when he takes me to the movies.

I miss everything about him.

And I realize I also *love* everything about him. Or at least the man he's proven himself to be.

I just wonder if he's capable of loving me. Of loving *anyone*.

~ ~ ~

There's a knock on my door. I check the time. It's just after nine o'clock. He said he would stop by, but I figured he was too tired when he didn't show up at the usual time.

I check the peep hole to make sure it's him and I see a … mountain lion?

I laugh and open the door. Before he even says hello, he sweeps me into his arms and plants a kiss on me. But he releases me almost as hastily. "Oh, shit," he whispers, looking past me into my apartment. "Is the little guy around?"

I shake my head. "He's been asleep for an hour."

A devious smile comes up Brady's face. He picks up his duffle bag and drops it inside my door then he lifts me into his arms and carries me to the couch.

"How light of a sleeper is he?" he asks.

"A freight train couldn't wake him."

He laughs. Then he looks into my eyes. Deep into my eyes. I swear he's telling me all the things he's afraid to say out loud. And I'm saying them right back to him.

"God, you're beautiful," he says, leaning down to give me a proper kiss hello.

His kisses start out light and feathery. He explores my face with his lips. He tickles my eyelids with them. He traces a path down my jaw. He tastes the lobes of my ears.

I take his head into my hands and pull him towards my lips. I need to taste him. I need to feel the connection that I long for when he's away. I force his lips onto mine. I kiss him long and hard.

My hands wander across his biceps, along his back, even down to the seat of his pants. His hands never leave my face, my shoulders, my arms.

When I can't stand it any longer, I grab one of his hands and put it on my breast. "Touch me," I say, breathlessly.

He pulls back. "Are you sure?"

I haven't felt his touch on my body for far too long. I crave it. I need it. I grab his other hand and pull both of them to my chest. "Touch me," I say again.

His eyes close as he feels me beneath his hands. I'm wearing a t-shirt and yoga pants. I didn't bother with a bra so I know he can feel every part of me.

"Jesus, Ry. You're incredible."

"Put your hands under my shirt."

He obliges without question, lifting my top to get a full view of what he's touching. He stares first, before putting his hands back on me. He traces every inch of my creamy flesh with his eyes, causing my nipples to pucker.

He sees my reaction and reaches out to roll my nipples between his fingers. My head falls back against the couch at the sensation. And without thinking, I grab his shoulders and pull his head to my chest.

He takes me into his mouth, giving equal attention to both my breasts. The one he's not tasting, he's fondling. He licks and sucks and laves me until I'm squirming beneath him. My hand goes in search of his lap, needing more.

When I find what I'm looking for – when I find his manhood straining beneath his jeans, he stops me, removing my hand. "No, Ry. That's not why I'm here."

I question him with my eyes.

"We still have two more weeks," he says.

My head falls forward in frustration. "What if I tell you we should change the rules?"

For a second, I see hunger in his eyes. For a second, he wants to change the rules, too. But then he pulls my shirt back down. "We're not changing the rules. You're not ready."

"I am," I tell him.

He shakes his head. "Do you trust me, Ry?"

I study him. "I *think* I do."

"That's not good enough."

He jumps up off the couch and holds his hand out to help me up. "Do you have a sitter this week?"

"Chloe can come on Tuesday if that's okay."

"Tuesday is perfect. I'll pick you up at ten o'clock. I'm sorry it has to be so late."

"I get it, Brady. You have to be at the games. It's okay. But Chloe can only stay until eleven thirty."

He leans down to kiss me. "That's not nearly enough time with you, but I'll take anything I can get."

"Thank you," I say.

"For what?"

I shrug. "For understanding *my* schedule. For bringing presents for Stryker. For being patient even when I can't be."

He grabs his duffle bag and opens the door. "You're worth it, Ry. You're worth waiting for. You're worth *fighting* for."

I watch him walk down the hall before I retreat into my apartment. I lean against the wall wondering how this man could be so perfect.

Then again, however, maybe he's not. How can a man go from being the playboy of baseball to being the ideal man in just a few months?

My father once told me a leopard never changes his spots.

But perhaps Brady never really had spots. Maybe his spots were camouflage, hiding who he truly is.

I go to bed and dream of my leopard, thinking that maybe I can be the one to break down the walls he's built up around his heart. Hoping he has room left in that heart for two more people. Praying he can find his way to love me the way I love him.

Chapter Thirty-five

"This has been one of the most fun nights I've ever had," I tell Murphy as the eight of us leave the dance club.

"I'm glad we could do it," she says. "It's been far too long since we've all gotten together. Someone is always pregnant or traveling or working. All the stars had to align to set this one up."

"I need a drink," Skylar's sister, Piper, says.

The oldest Mitchell sister, Baylor, stops and reprimands her. "Are you kidding, Pipes? Mason will have my head if I send you home drunk."

"Not a drink-drink, Baylor. Water. I need water," Piper says.

"Oh." Baylor laughs at her youngest sister.

"Let's go in here," Mallory says, pointing to a tavern. "We can sober up with coffee and water before heading home."

"Good idea," Charlie says, opening the door to let us all file in.

We get settled into a large corner booth and order a round of non-alcoholic drinks.

Lexi points to the television that is showing highlights of the game. "I can't believe you missed a game for girls' night," she says to Murphy.

"It's not like I've never missed a game, Lexi. I miss a lot of the games when I'm working. What do you think DVRs are for?"

"Do you really watch all of them?" I ask.

She shakes her head. "Caden thinks I do, but no. I mostly fast-forward to the good parts. I pick out one highlight, something they might not cover on the news, and I tell him about it. It makes him feel important."

"What is it about men and their need to be the center of the universe?" Mallory says.

"But your man actually *is* the center of the universe," Skylar says to Mallory. "I mean, *the* Thad Stone?" She fans herself melodramatically.

Mallory's husband is one of the movie stars I've worked on at the gym. He goes by his real name, Chad, when he's not acting. I can't believe he's actually an A-list star. He's so normal and down-to-earth.

"Not to sound too fan-girl or anything," I say. "But what's it like being married to one of the world's hottest actors?"

"Probably the same as it is dating the world's most eligible baseball player," she says with a wink.

I roll my eyes. Sometimes I forget the truth of that statement. But only sometimes. Other times my stomach is in knots knowing that thousands of women want him. They want what I have. Well, what I kind of have.

"How do you handle it, Mallory? There are so many women. And Chad has to kiss them and stuff. I can't imagine."

She gives me a sympathetic smile. She knows what I'm asking. "It was hard at first. I didn't trust the girls who threw themselves at him. I didn't even trust some of the actresses he got paired with. But once I knew he loved me, it got easier. Because no matter how much I don't trust the women, I trust Chad."

"But how did you know you could trust him?"

"I just did." She puts her hand on top of mine. "You'll know when you know."

"Look!" Lexi says, pointing to the TV. "They won. That's fifteen in a row. They are setting up for a press conference."

It's late and the tavern is relatively quiet. Murphy asks the bartender if he could turn up the volume on the television.

We all watch as the manager of the Nighthawks talks about the winning streak. Then Cole Crawford talks about being the most winning pitcher on the team right now. My eyes fall to the table. I know that must kill Brady.

Murphy touches my arm in empathy.

Cole gets asked about Brady and he waves someone up to the mic. "Why not let him speak for himself?" he asks, surrendering his chair to Brady.

Brady sits down confidently, looking uber-handsome in his all-too-clean jersey.

"How's the arm?" a reporter asks.

He holds it up. "Getting stronger every day."

"Any idea when you'll be off the DL?"

"Soon," he says.

My eyes are glued to the TV as he gets asked some more technical questions about his injury which he answers very diplomatically.

"Rumor has it, you've met a special lady and you're off the market, Brady," another reporter asks. "Care to comment on that?"

All eyes at the table turn to me. My heart races and my palms become sweaty.

"I don't ever like to talk about my personal life, haven't you learned that by now?"

Another reporter starts asking a question, but Brady cuts him off. "But in this case, I'm happy to confirm that the rumors are true. I do indeed have a girlfriend." He pretends to look at his non-existent watch. "Well, as of midnight tonight, I will."

"Midnight? Why midnight?" the reporter asks.

"Nothing. Next question," Brady says.

"What's the lucky girl's name?"

"I meant next question about baseball," he says. "Anyone? Okay, I guess I'm done. Jason, you want to talk?" He hands the mic over to the team owner.

I'm left with my chin in my lap. "Did he just …?"

"Yup," Murphy says.

"Oh, my God."

Several of my friends squeal in delight.

"What happens at midnight?" Baylor asks.

"At midnight, it becomes June 1st," I tell her, still reeling over his declaration. "I gave him until then to prove to me he was done with other women. He said that would be the day he called me his girlfriend. I just didn't think he would tell the whole world."

"But he didn't say your name," Baylor says.

Murphy shakes her head. "Doesn't matter. Everyone knows he's taken now and that was his intention. Talk about grand gestures, Rylee. That man just put himself out there. The most private guy I know just gave up a very personal detail."

I stare at the TV as the news anchor glosses over the story of the winning streak in favor of Brady's uncharacteristic declaration. "There you have it, New York," he says. "And if I were a betting man, I'd bet the quest to find out who this girl is will pale the quest to find out who shot J.R. back in the eighties."

I drop my forehead and bang it on the table.

"What's wrong?" Lexi says. "This is a good thing, isn't it?"

"Maybe," I say looking up at her. "Or maybe Brady has just made me enemy number one."

Mallory, Murphy and Piper all try to comfort me, being that they have been in my position in one way or another.

"They'll get over it soon enough," Mallory says. "In two months, this will be old news."

"Just remember who your friends are," Piper says. "You can trust every woman at this table, but you can't trust anyone else. People will try to break you up. Crazy women from his past may become jealous and try to sabotage your relationship. Don't go jumping to conclusions and believe them."

"You say that as if you speak from experience," I say.

"Sadly, I do. Even after I trusted Mason, I still almost let someone rip us apart."

"I don't know if I can do this," I say, tearing up at the gravity of my situation.

"Do you love him?" Murphy asks.

I stare at her. How could she possibly know?

"Do you?" she prods again.

I close my eyes and nod.

"I knew it," she says. "And he loves you too. I'm just as sure of that, Rylee."

"But … Stryker." I look at her with sad eyes.

"Brady will come around," she whispers to me. "Healing has a funny way of happening slowly and then all at once."

Murphy stands up and puts money on the table. "Come on, you're going to need your sleep. After all, at midnight you transform into a girlfriend."

Suddenly I'm excited and terrified all at once. He's talked about tomorrow so much I fear it will be a huge letdown when it actually happens. I fear *I'll* be a letdown. He's put me on a pedestal these past six months. How can I live up to that?

Maybe that's not the problem. Maybe the problem is that I can never measure up to a ghost who was his first love. To the woman in the picture who will always be perfect in his eyes. And to the son who can never be replaced.

Chapter Thirty-six

I've been plucked, waxed, shaved, and perfumed in all the right places. I've changed my clothes three times. I've had a glass of wine to calm my nerves.

Still, I pace around the apartment until he arrives. I take a deep breath when he knocks on the door fifteen minutes early. I open it to see he's still got his duffle bag.

"Sorry," he says. "I know I'm early. I still have to hit the shower, but I wanted to bring Stryker his animal before he went to bed."

I want to jump into his arms but my son is in the room behind me. And we don't hug or kiss in front of Stryker. I don't want to give him hopes of having a man in our lives until I'm sure about who that man will be.

Stryker runs over to stand next to me. He looks up at Brady. "Did you bring one?"

"Of course I did," Brady replies, handing a stuffed eagle to my son.

I laugh. "You were right, Stryker." I turn to Brady and explain, "We research every city you visit and guess which animal you'll bring home."

"Sounds like a lot of fun," he says. "I have something for you, too. But you have to come upstairs to see it."

I smile at the seductive look on his face. "I'll bet you do," I say.

Suddenly, my son surges forward and latches onto Brady's leg. "Thank you, baseball man. I love it."

It's the first time Stryker has shown affection for him.

Brady stiffens and I try not to notice the intense pain that crosses his face when he leans down to ruffle Stryker's hair. "You're welcome, sport."

"Baby, why don't you go add him to your collection? Chloe will be here in a minute and you can show her."

Stryker traipses off happily as Brady's gaze follows.

"How about you go shower and I'll be up in about fifteen minutes?" I ask.

"Sounds good," he says, his eyes coming back to meet mine. Then he looks at me as if he's seeing me for the first time tonight. "Holy crap, you look amazing, Ry."

I wonder if he gets so nervous about seeing my son that he doesn't even really see *me* sometimes.

"Thank you. Is there anything I can bring when I come up?"

"Just yourself. There is nothing else I need."

He grabs his bag and I smile knowing what's in store.

Chloe arrives and I assure her I'll be home by eleven thirty as it's a school night for her. I brush my teeth again and do one last check of my makeup before leaving.

308

When I arrive at 16F, Brady opens the door wearing a white linen shirt, a black tie and tan dress pants. His hair is just slightly damp and he smells heavenly.

"Wow," I say.

"You didn't think I could clean up, too?"

He traces the heart neckline of my little black dress, his fingers tantalizing me, his hands making promises of what's to come.

He pulls me through the door and I look around the room to see it decorated with candles and flowers. There is champagne chilling in an ice bucket and canapés on the bar.

"You did all this in fifteen minutes?" I ask.

He laughs. "I had a little help. I had the caterer come early and set things up."

"We're eating in?"

"Rylee, I've waited two months for this day. Hell, I've waited *six* months for this day. I'm not going to drag it out any longer by having to sit through dinner at some stuffy restaurant."

He grabs my hand and pulls me to him. "Now, am I going to get a proper hello from my girlfriend, or what?"

I smile at my new designation. But then his lips find mine and I lose all sense of who I am, who he is and where we are. He feels divine as his hard body presses against my soft one. His mouth explores my mouth and his tongue tangles with my tongue as we taste each other. He moans into me. I sigh into him. We kiss until we're breathless. We kiss beyond that, needing each other more than we need air.

Our lips finally part and he presses his forehead to mine. "Now that was worth waiting for."

We walk over to the bar and he pops the cork on the champagne. I eye the label on the bottle, impressed that he's not trying to impress me.

He sees me peeking at it. "You expected Cristal?" he asks with a smirk.

I shrug. "Old habits die hard."

He hands me a glass. "All of my old habits are dead, sweetheart, you can be sure of that."

Sweetheart.

It's the first time he's ever used a term of endearment for me.

"I saw the press conference. I can't believe you said what you did."

"What, that I'll be off the disabled list soon?"

I roll my eyes and he laughs.

"I know what you meant, Ry. I told you I was going to tell the world about us."

"Well, I suppose I should thank you for not saying my name."

"People will find out soon enough."

"Women everywhere will hate me," I say.

"They'll move on as soon as they know I'm serious."

"Are you? ... Serious?"

He pulls me to him and wraps his arms around me. "As a heart attack."

I put my glass on the bar. "What am I supposed to say when people find out?"

"Say whatever the hell you want, Rylee. Admit it. Deny it. You do what you're comfortable with and I'll back you up."

A timer goes off in the kitchen. "Dinner is ready," he says.

"But we haven't even tasted the canapés," I say, nodding to them on the bar.

He quickly pops two of them into his mouth. "Sorry," he says after he's swallowed them. "I might just be a little eager to get to dessert."

I raise a seductive brow at him. "What's for dessert?"

He belts out a throaty laugh. "You are."

My stomach flutters. "I was hoping you'd say that."

We go to the kitchen and I help him carry the pasta dish, bread basket and salad to the table. Then he brings our champagne over and makes a toast. "To tonight. To us. To … possibilities."

I touch my glass to his and take a drink wondering what all the possibilities are. Hoping beyond hope that those possibilities include my son.

"Aren't you hungry?" Brady asks a few minutes later, seeing me push food around on my plate.

I take a bite to show him I'm eating. "It's really good."

"What's wrong?"

I shrug and glance back towards his bedroom.

"You aren't nervous, are you?" he asks.

I push more food around my plate.

"Rylee, we've been together plenty of times."

"But that was just sex. It didn't have a label on it. Now that we're—now that I'm …"

"My girlfriend? You can say it, Ry. You're my girlfriend."

"Now that I'm your *girlfriend*, there are certain expectations."

He gives me crazy eyes. "There are no such expectations. And if there ever were, you've exceeded them, believe me." He puts down his fork and lays a hand on my arm. "It's okay. We're good."

I nod my head. Then I steel myself up to ask him something that's been on my mind for two months. "What did they say when you told them?"

"The reporters?"

"No, the women. The girls in each city. What did they say? You've told, what, eight of them by now?"

"Nine."

"Nine?" I ask, surprised. I know they've only been to eight cities in the past seven weeks.

"One of them looked me up last month when she was visiting New York. Cornered me outside the stadium one day after practice."

"Really? Why didn't you say anything?"

"I didn't want to worry you. I was still trying to make a good impression and I didn't want you thinking you had to worry about things when I'm home. I know you worry enough when I'm away."

"What did you say to her? To them?"

"I tell them all the same thing. That I'm done playing around. That it's not going to happen anymore."

My heart soars to hear him say the words. "And how did they take it?"

He shrugs. "Some better than others. Let's just say I was right not to give any of them my number. And it's a good thing they all live in other cities."

"Oh, Brady. Do you think any of them will stalk you?"

For a second, his face pales and it looks like he might be sick, and that has me more than a little worried.

"I've gotten a few letters that were delivered to the Hawks' offices, but nothing too alarming. Nothing you need to worry about. The security in this building is second to none."

"Will you tell me if there is ever anything to worry about?"

He laces his fingers with mine. "If there is ever anything to worry about, you'll be the first to know. I won't let anything happen to you."

"I'm not worried about *me*, Brady. Fans can be crazy. I see the news. Just be careful, okay?"

"You too," he says. "I want you to be careful as well. It's why I didn't give the reporters your name. If you see or hear anything unusual, if someone follows you, if they even take your picture, I want to know about it."

"People are going to take my picture. Surely you realize that."

He shakes his head in disgust. "I know, and I'm sorry. I guess I put you in a position, didn't I?"

"It's fine. Part of me is glad you said it publicly. Maybe some of them will leave you alone."

"Sweetheart?"

I look at him and smile.

"Can we stop talking about this shit? It's not exactly how I imagined us spending our first official date."

"How did you imagine it?" I ask.

He pushes his plate away and then lifts me out of my chair and onto the table. "Something along the lines of this," he says, right before kissing me.

I taste the pasta. The champagne. Him. I feel the heat growing between us. His hands wander from my face around to my back where he strokes me up and down before moving his hands around to my front. He squeezes my breasts through my clothing.

"I've waited so long, Ry." He steps back. "I love this dress and all, but I'd really rather see it on my bedroom floor."

He holds his hand out to me and helps me off the table. Then he picks me up and carries me back to his room, placing me on the bed. He stands back to look at me. He looks at me as if he's never seen a woman on his bed before.

"Do you trust me, Ry?"

I nod.

"I need to hear you say it."

"I trust you."

A brilliant smile comes up his face as he loosens his tie. He pulls it over his head and then starts to unbutton his shirt. I lunge forward and brush his hands away.

"I'll do it," I say.

I carefully unbutton each one purely by feel since I'm looking up at his face the entire time. The lower I get, the more heated his stare becomes. When I reach the last shirt button, I lower my gaze and continue on to his pants. I lower his fly and let his pants fall to the ground as he removes his shirt.

His erection is peeking out of the waistband of his boxer briefs, begging to be released. I pull them down and he kicks them off leaving him standing gloriously naked in front of me.

I take him in my hand and look up at him. "Are you saying this is all mine?"

He laughs, pushing me back onto the bed. He climbs on top of me. "Every single inch of me is yours, sweetheart."

He flips me over and slowly unzips my dress, caressing my back, my butt, my thighs as he removes it. He leaves me on my stomach, unclasping my bra before he reaches around to play with my breasts. I lift my behind for him when he moves his hands to my panties.

He kisses the dimples on my lower back. He slips a hand between my legs and runs a finger along my sex. I moan and bury my head in his pillow, enveloping myself in his scent.

"God, Rylee," he says, feeling how wet I am. He slips a finger inside me. Then another. His thumb finds my clit and in seconds, he has me on the verge of pure euphoria.

I flip over. I need to feel him. See him.

I grab his length in my hands and feel every silken inch of him. He groans when I quicken my movements. Then he removes his hands from me and reaches into his nightstand for a condom.

"It's been so long," he says, rolling it on. "I will take my time with you later, but right now I need to bury myself inside you."

"Yes," I say arching my back as he climbs on top of me.

I watch his face as he slips inside me. His eyes close until he hits the end of me. He stops and stills, letting my body get used to him. When he looks at me again, he makes love to me not only with his body, but with his eyes.

This is unlike any other time we've been together. He's slow. Tender. Deliberate. It's like he's trying to savor every second. Trying to record every movement.

I've never known sex to be anything like this. I never imagined it could be. I find it hard not to let a tear slip out of the corner of my eye. He kisses it away. Then he whispers in my ear.

"You feel so good. I've dreamed about this for months. Touching you. Kissing you. Putting my fingers inside you. Tasting you. You're mine, Rylee Kennedy."

His words and his thrusts have my insides coiling. My belly burns and my thighs tighten as he moves to the right, hitting the place inside me that sends me over the cliff of pleasure. I hear myself cry out his name. Then I hear him utter mine over and over into my hair.

He collapses on top of me, keeping the brunt of his weight on his elbows and I smile realizing he can do that now. He catches his breath and rolls to the side.

"You want to know what I hate?" he asks.

"I'm not sure lying in bed naked with me is the time to tell me," I joke.

He reaches over and runs a hand across my breasts and down to my belly, resting it over my heart tattoo. "I love every inch of you, Ry. That's not what I meant."

"Okay, what do you hate?"

"I hate the signs women hold up at the games. The '*I love you*' signs and the '*Brady is my hero*' signs. Promise me you'll never hold up signs like that."

I giggle. "So while we were making love, you were thinking about other women holding up '*I love you*' signs at your games?"

"Hell, no. I was thinking about how much I want you to come to my games. I was thinking about how I'd love to finally be able to look into the stands and see someone I care about."

I rise up on an elbow. "I promise never to hold up an '*I love you*' sign."

I want to tell him. I want to tell him that even though I'll never hold up that sign, it's how I feel. But I don't. I don't because I know he won't say it back.

"Why the long face?" he asks. "You know we're just getting started, don't you? We have a lot of lost time to make up for."

And with that, he climbs down my body, making me laugh as he acts like a starving animal that hasn't just eaten. But then he shuts me up when his mouth lands on me. When he takes me over the cliff once again. When he makes me fall even deeper for him.

Chapter Thirty-seven

Brady comes out of my bathroom and slips under the covers, pulling me over to lie on his chest.

For the past two weeks, he's snuck into my bedroom every night he's been home.

Well, snuck is not exactly the right word when I invited him. He comes over after my son goes to bed and leaves before Stryker wakes up. Needless to say, we've both been sleep deprived. We've discussed more than once that as soon as he's back playing, he won't be able to do it. It's a bittersweet thought.

How have I gotten used to sleeping with a man in my bed in just a few short weeks?

"You'll be playing soon," I tell him. "And despite how much I want that to happen, I will hate for this to end."

"Who says I'll be playing soon?" he asks, holding up his hand. "The damn thing is practically useless."

"Listen to me, Brady. Listen to your doctors. We all think it's only a matter of time. Be patient." I put my hand on his chest and balance my chin on it as I look up at him. "You are going to make the biggest comeback in Hawks history."

"God, I love how optimistic you are."

'God, I love you, *Rylee,'* is what I want him to say. I think he does. I can feel it. We spend every minute together that we can. Will he ever say it? *Can* he say it? I realize it's only been a few weeks since we've officially been together, but it's been the most intense few weeks of my life.

He kisses me on the tip of my nose. "Who says this has to end when I start playing again?"

"We do," I say. "We've talked about this. You're burning the candle at both ends. We'll figure something out. Maybe I can find a sitter who can stay the night and we could sleep at your place once in a while."

"Once in a while isn't good enough," he says. "I want you every night."

"That's not possible."

"It is if you live with me."

I sit up, stunned. I scoot back and sit against the headboard and pull the sheet up to cover me. "You have got to be kidding."

He shrugs. "What?"

"One: we've only been a couple for two weeks—"

"That's not how I see it," he says, interrupting me. "We were together last fall. And we started dating more than two months ago, Ry, and you know it."

"And two," I say, "There's my son. Brady, he doesn't even know we're together."

He shifts around uncomfortably. "So, we'll tell him. He likes me, doesn't he?"

"Only because you bring him animals."

"We'll put him in the office, or I'll get rid of the weight room. Hell, we can move and get a bigger place."

"Wait. No. We are not discussing this. It's ridiculous."

He pulls me to him. "It's not ridiculous, Rylee. You know how I feel about you."

I pull away and get off the bed. I wrap a robe around my naked body. "Actually, I don't. You've never told me."

"Well, you've never told me, either, Ry."

"You want to hear me say I love you?" I say, trying not to cry. "Fine. I love you. Now you say it."

He looks at me, panic-stricken, as if he's lost the ability to speak – or maybe just the ability to speak those three little words.

I hear Stryker call out and I run into the other room. "Hush, baby. Were you having a nightmare?"

He whimpers in my arms for a few minutes while I tell him a story. I tell him a story we made up about the animals Brady brings him. I rub his back and speak to him softly until he falls asleep.

When I go back to my room, Brady is sitting up in bed.

"Are you ready for that?" I ask, pointing to Stryker's room. "Nightmares. Bed-wetting. Preschool. Babysitters. Illnesses. Birthday parties. Boo-boos. Are you ready to take it all on?"

He looks horrified.

"See that look on your face? That's why we can't move in together. I need my son to *more* than like you, Brady. I need him to love you. But more importantly, I need you to love him. I'm not about to bring a man into his life who won't be there permanently. Do you want to be there permanently?"

It hurts me to say these things to him. I know exactly why he can't love Stryker. I've known it for months. Yet I still let myself fall for him knowing he could never be who Stryker needs him to be.

He looks at the door to the hallway and then down at his hands. "I … I don't know."

I feel like the worst kind of bitch knowing what happened but being so selfish that I'm giving him ultimatums. "And that's why you need to leave, Brady. That's why this won't work."

Tears stream down my face as I hand him his clothes.

"You're kidding, right?" he says. "You're ending this because I asked you to move in?"

I shake my head. "I'm ending this because I should have known better from the beginning."

"Rylee, please."

"I'm sorry, Brady. I have to do what's best for my son."

He dresses in silence, the whole time pleading with me with his eyes.

"Change your mind, Rylee. We can make this work."

"I just don't see how."

My eyes sting and my throat burns as I watch him walk out my bedroom door and then my front door. He looks back before closing it. And he looks as broken as I feel.

I run back into my room and collapse onto my bed, pulling my pillow to my face so Stryker doesn't hear my sobs.

I cry until my stomach hurts and I have nothing left but hiccups.

My phone pings and I wonder who would be texting me after midnight. I check it.

Brady: Open the door, Rylee. I need to talk to you. Please let me back in.

I dry my eyes and walk to the front door. When I open it, I see a man who's been crying. I pull him inside. I lead him back to my bedroom in case Stryker gets up again.

He has something in his hands.

I sit down on the bed and pull my robe tightly around me. "What did you want to say?"

He sits on the bed and hands me a picture frame. It's the picture from the box that day.

"I was married once," he says with a shaky voice. "And I had a son. But they're gone now. They're dead."

My hand covers my heart as it breaks for him. "Oh, Brady. I'm so sorry." More tears spill out of my eyes. I know how hard this must be for him. I'm glad he's finally telling me but at the same time I feel terrible that I pushed him into it.

He studies my face. "Did you know?"

"Your reaction at the hospital last fall. I suspected you lost someone."

He nods. "It's why you've been so understanding."

I laugh sadly. "I just kicked you out. I'm anything but understanding. I'm a selfish bitch."

"No, you're not, Rylee. Everything you said was exactly what you should have said. Your son *should* be your priority. You shouldn't settle for someone who won't make him a priority, too."

He takes the picture back from me and looks at his boy. His eyes close and a tear rolls out. "Keeton was only three when he died. The same age as Stryker. I ... I want to love your son. I think maybe I could love him, but I need time. I need you to give me time, Rylee. And I hope that you will. Because" —he looks at the picture again and then back at me— "because I love you. And as crazy as it sounds, I tried really hard not to. I feel like I'm trading my old family for a new one. And that makes me a bastard. I'm a bastard because if I love you, I'm betraying her. And if I love your boy ... I'm replacing Keeton."

I move over on the bed so our legs are touching. "Brady, you're allowed to love again. You could never replace them. And I would never ask you to."

"It's more than that. What if I love you … love *him*, and then …" He puts his head in his hands. "What if I fail you like I did them? What if something happens to you, too?"

I put a hand on his back and rub it around gently to try and comfort him.

"They are gone because of me. Because I was a self-centered asshole who didn't even think about them when they needed me the most."

"Did you leave them?" I ask.

"No. God, no. I would never have."

I take the picture from him and run my finger over their faces. "What was her name?"

He looks at me like he's not sure he wants to say it. Like he's scared to open up to me. Like maybe he thinks I *will* replace her if he lets me in.

"It's okay, you don't have to talk about it."

I hand the picture back to him and get up off the bed. I need a drink of water. All the tears I've cried have dehydrated me. But Brady takes it the wrong way.

"Rylee, wait."

I walk to my bedside table and pick up my water bottle. I take a drink and then climb back on the bed, settling myself against the headboard. Letting him know I'm ready to listen if he's ready to talk.

He looks relieved. He thought I was going to throw him out again. He takes his shoes off and scoots up the bed. He reaches over me and turns the light off. Then he pulls me to him, spooning himself behind me. He breathes into my hair. He rubs a hand along my arm over and over and over. He finally stills. He's so still I wonder if he's fallen asleep.

"Her name was Natalie," he says softly. "But I called her Nat."

I don't say anything. What is there to say?

"We met in high school. She followed me to Nebraska when I got a baseball scholarship there. We knew we were going to be together since we were sixteen. When she got pregnant our freshman year in college, I wasn't even mad. It was always in the plans to have kids, it just happened sooner than was ideal. But we made it work. We lived in student housing. She only went to school part time after Keeton came. She was born to be a mom."

I grab his hand to let him know I'm listening.

"My junior year I became somewhat of a celebrity on campus. I broke all kinds of records and got a lot of media exposure. But with that came unwanted attention."

He takes in a deep breath and I can feel him tense up behind me.

"There were a few break-ins at our apartment. Someone stole a family picture once and then some of my clothes another time."

"That must have been awful," I say.

"It wasn't such a big deal for me," he says. Then he pauses. He pauses for a whole minute or more. "But I had them to think about so I convinced the athletic department to put a security system in our apartment."

His breathing becomes erratic and I'm worried he might hyperventilate. I hold his hand tightly and his grip around me becomes almost unbearably strong, like he's trying to hold onto them.

"I forgot to set it," he says, his voice cracking with desperation. "I always set it. I never left without doing it. But that day … It was the last game of the College World Series. It was my glory game." His voice is thick with emotion and shaky with fear. "We all left at the same time. She was going to run some errands and then come home before dropping Keeton at her sister's so she could drive up for the game. I never knew she didn't make it there."

He buries his head into my hair and I can feel a hot tear roll onto my neck. "Nobody even told me until after the game. After we'd won. If her father just would have called me earlier I would have had hours with her, not minutes. By the time I got to the hospital, Keeton …"

I turn around and embrace him as he breaks down and cries. "Shhh," I murmur into his hair. I let him hold me as tightly as he needs to as he relives his nightmare.

"It was the same person all along," he says. "One crazy woman broke in all three times. She'd tried once after we got the alarm, but the alarm scared her away. But that day—I forgot. My mind was on the game and I just walked out the door without thinking about it. And she got in. That day of all days, she got in. She went through our stuff. And when Nat and Keeton walked in on her …"

He moans out a cry of pure devastation.

"Oh, Brady. I'm so sorry."

He shakes uncontrollably in my arms, sobbing into my shoulder.

"She never intended to hurt them. It said so in her suicide note when they found her body later that night. She said she just wanted my stuff. She said Natalie scared her and the gun just went off. It went right though Nat's neck. And …" —his body stiffens and he can barely get out the words— "And when it happened, Nat's body went limp and she dropped Keeton. He fell against the corner of the counter and struck his head. They said he died instantly."

My sobs mix with his. The horror of not only losing a child, but the love of your life, is unimaginable. He lived through hell.

"I got to say goodbye to her. She couldn't talk to me because of her injuries, but she could hear me. And I lied to her. I told her Keeton was alive and waiting for her. But the truth was … he was dead and waiting for her. I knew it the minute I saw her. I knew she was dying, too. And two things battled in my mind in those last minutes. I wanted her with me. But I wanted her with him."

He cries out. "Goddammit! First I let that crazy bitch in my house and then I practically prayed for my wife to die. I killed them, Rylee. They are dead because of me."

He sobs into me. He cries harder than I've ever heard any man – any *person* – cry. I've never been in the presence of so much pain. I comfort him the only way I know how, with my hands. I work my hands around his neck and massage him. His sobs become weaker and his breathing evens out. I think he falls asleep from exhaustion.

I lie here and hold him. I think of a young family that never had a chance to grow. I think of a young man who had to endure more than any person should have to endure. I think of the man lying next to me who I love with all my heart. And I know I will give him as long as it takes to heal his heart. Because he's worth fighting for.

Hours later, he stirs in my arms. "Their funeral was the same day I got drafted by the Hawks. I walked out of the reception and never looked back. I took one small picture, the framed photo, a few of my old baseball mementoes, and a shirt. I left the rest of the details to her parents. They packed up our apartment. Put it all in storage. I couldn't do it. I just ran away. I guess I've been running ever since."

"I'm so sorry, Brady. I can't even imagine your pain. But thank you for telling me. Thank you for trusting me."

Light starts to shine through my curtains and he pulls away. "I should go," he says.

"No. Wait." I reach over to my nightstand and pull out my photo book from the drawer. I open it and show him a picture. "This is a picture of my dad. We were very close. He had me late in life and I was his only child. And then when Mom got sick, well, all we had was each other. And, Brady, I know it's no comparison to what you lost, so please don't think I'm trying to measure my loss with yours, but I'm not sure you've ever gotten closure. You left almost immediately. You never had time to grieve them properly. When my dad died, I was devastated. I felt so alone. It took me more than a month to get myself to go through our house and his things. But packing up his things was exactly what I needed to start healing. Every shirt had a memory. Every trinket had a story. And as hard as it was to go through his belongings, it was what I needed to move on with my life. I think you need closure, too."

He studies my face. He lifts his hand and cups my cheek. He traces my jaw with his finger.

"Would you go with me?" he asks. "Would you go with me if I go back to Nebraska?"

Tears sting the backs of my eyes as I nod my head over and over. "Just say when."

The light is bright through my window now, and he gets off the bed looking guilty that he kept me up so late. I stand up and grab his hand. "Come on, I'll go make us some coffee."

"But …" He nods in the direction of Stryker's room.

"We're not going to parade around naked or anything, Brady. But I think it's time he gets used to having you around."

He smiles. "Thank you, Ry. I promise I'm going to try with him. I'm going to try hard."

"I know you are. And I promise I'm going to be patient."

He pulls me into his arms. "I love you, Rylee Kennedy."

I wrap my arms around him. "I've waited my whole life to hear someone say that." I look up at him. "I'm so glad it's you."

Chapter Thirty-eight

The fasten-seatbelt light is turned off and the flight attendant brings us some bottled water. Brady stares out the window, lost in thought, as I look around the cabin seeing how the other half lives.

I've never flown first class before. I've never wanted to. It seems a waste of money just for extra leg room and free drinks. But now was not the time to fight with him about it. We're flying into his past. And he's bringing me along with him. He's trusting me enough to let me in.

The last week has been full of ups and downs. Brady has been around the apartment more often when Stryker is awake, but I can tell he's struggling. And he has a sadness about him I've not seen before. Ripping the Band-Aid off his past has opened up old wounds that need time to heal.

Brady grabs my hand. "Talk to me. Tell me something to keep my mind off where we're going."

I nod and I take a drink of my water. "His name was Denny Sharp."

He raises his eyebrows. "Stryker's dad?"

"Yes. He played for the Mets. I met him through my father. Dad took me to a benefit once after my mom got sick and wasn't able to attend."

"I've never heard of him," he says.

"He only played for two years. He played right field and didn't have a great batting average. He was arrogant and charming and frivolous with his money."

"Just like me." He squeezes my hand.

I laugh. "Well, there were some similarities. But I was young and naïve. He swept me off my feet and made me feel like I was the only woman in the world. The problem was, he was making several other girls feel the exact same way."

"Shit," he says. "No wonder you weren't jumping at the chance to be with me."

"It wasn't until I got pregnant that I found out about the others. I found out because he told me. He said he never wanted to be tied down. He wanted nothing more to do with me, which quite frankly was perfectly fine by me. I wasn't about to stay with a man who was cheating on me. I thought about going after him for child support. I was a poor grad student, after all. But if he were paying support, he'd still be in my life. We'd be connected for eighteen years. He might even want to see the baby at some point. And that wasn't okay with me. If he could so easily turn away from me, from us, he didn't deserve to be in our lives. So my father hired a lawyer and Denny signed away his parental rights as soon as he legally could after Stryker was born."

"I'm sorry you've had to go through it all alone," Brady says.

"It's okay. Stryker is the light of my life. If I had to do it all over again, I'd still do it. I can't imagine not being his mom."

"You've done a fine job raising him. He's a great kid."

"Thanks."

"So whatever happened to Denny Sharp?"

I shrug. "The last I heard he was selling used cars over in Jersey."

Brady laughs. "Serves him right. Thank you for telling me."

We make some small talk over the next few hours, but mostly Brady just holds my hand and stares out the window. And I mostly stare at Brady.

I'll admit at first, I did think he was a Denny. And I was right. He was. Fast balls. Fast cars. Fast women. It could have been his motto. And I think part of the reason I agreed to sleep with him last year was to prove to myself that I could be with Brady and not fall for him. And I didn't at first. I fought my feelings with everything I had. But when we were together, life was carefree. Fun. Easy. It was everything I'd never had being a single mom.

As the wheels of our plane touch down in Lincoln, Nebraska, I know today will be anything but easy. Today may be one of the most difficult days of his life.

We rent a car and drive straight to the storage facility Natalie's parents have been renting for almost six years. Brady makes them out to be villains, especially her father, because he robbed him of those last few hours with her. But I have to believe they knew this day would come. Why else would they have kept the stuff from his apartment all this time?

Brady shows his ID to the man in the front office who then gives him a key. We follow the man's directions, walking back to storage unit thirty-eight. Brady holds onto my hand for dear life, his steps becoming slower the closer we get.

We stop in front of the unit and he looks at it for several minutes before putting his key into the lock. The unit is much bigger than I anticipated and when he pulls the large door open, I see that they must have put everything from his apartment in here.

Along the back wall, there is a couch, a dining table with chairs piled on top, and a couple of beds. There are larger boxes lining one side of the unit and smaller boxes lining the other.

Brady walks around, appraising the boxes, running his hand along the tops of them as if he doesn't know where to start. He stops when he sees a box labeled 'photo albums.' He freezes.

I grab a chair from on top of the table and set it down next to him. Then I squeeze his arm. "I'll be outside."

He nods and then sits down in the chair. And before I turn the corner, his painful sobs echo down the hallway.

I wait out by the car for almost an hour trying not to think of the agony he must be going through. I stand here the whole time hoping I'm not wrong about him needing this.

He comes walking out with two boxes. I open the trunk for him and he places them inside. He looks down at me with red-rimmed eyes. "I want to go on campus for a bit, is that okay?"

"Of course. Anything you need. Our flight back isn't for three more hours."

He drives us onto the University of Nebraska campus and finds a place to park by the baseball stadium. He pops the trunk and gets something out. A small baseball glove. He holds it as we walk the perimeter of the stadium, peeking through anywhere there is a break in the fence.

We come to an opening where we can see the team practicing. He pulls me inside. "Do you mind if we sit and watch for a minute?"

"Not at all."

I can see so many emotions cross his face as he watches the team practice. And the whole time, he rubs on the glove like it's a bottle with a genie inside.

After thirty minutes of complete silence, he turns to me. "Do you think Stryker would want this?" he says, holding up the glove.

Tears collect in my eyes. "I think Stryker would love to have it, baseball man."

He nods and smiles weakly.

Then I notice something written on the wall of the stadium. "This is called Hawks Field?" I ask.

He laughs. "It is. Pretty apropos, huh?"

When we get up to walk out, someone comes over to Brady. "Well, I'll be. Brady Taylor, nice to see you. What are you doing in our neck of the woods?"

Brady holds his hand out. "Hi, Coach Brown. Good to see you too. I'm just here for the day. This is my girlfriend, Rylee."

"Good to meet you, Rylee." He shakes his head back and forth like he can't believe what he's seeing. "You've done well for yourself, Brady. I was sorry to hear about your injury. How's that coming along?"

Brady holds up his left arm. "It's getting better every day. I'll be back in the game soon."

Several of the players are coming up behind their coach. I back away and let them talk to Brady. I watch as Brady signs several Nebraska ball caps for them and answers their questions about the big leagues. He's in his element talking about baseball. I see the gleam in his eyes return. I smile knowing that maybe all of this is part of his healing.

"Come on," he says, grabbing my hand after he says goodbye to his coach and the players. "I'm taking you on a tour of campus and then we're going to eat at my favorite lunch place."

He walks me past a building called Oldfather Hall, talking about the classes he had there. Then he takes me to the student union, pointing out all the changes they've made since he'd been here. A few blocks beyond that is downtown Lincoln where he takes me to a place called The Old Spaghetti Factory.

"Athletes love this place because it's all-you-can-eat," he says as we walk in.

The hostess tries to seat us in the far corner, but Brady refuses. "We'd like to sit over there if that's okay," he says, pointing to the opposite wall.

I look at the corner table wondering if that was where he used to sit with Natalie. Or perhaps he would bring Keeton here.

When our meals arrive, Brady laughs at my voracious appetite. "Natalie was the same way," he says. "She was small like you, but she could eat her weight in spaghetti."

I smile, thinking this is the first time he's ever shared a happy memory.

"Does that bother you?" he asks. "Me talking about her?"

I shake my head. "No. It doesn't. She was an important part of your life and you talking about her keeps her memory alive."

"It's her shirt I wear under my jersey," he says. "Well, it's mine, but we got it together a long time ago when we were still in high school."

"Your lucky shirt," I say. Then I cover my mouth. "Oh, Brady. That was the shirt I put on that night at your hotel, wasn't it?"

He nods.

"I'm so sorry. I never should have—"

"You didn't know, Rylee. It's fine." He sighs deeply. "A long time ago when we first met, you asked me why I chose number three for my jersey number?"

"I remember."

"Natalie's and Keeton's birthdays were both on the third day of the month. Nat's in November and Keeton's in March. And we got married on the third day of the month as well."

"What a lovely way to honor them, both then and now. Don't ever change it."

He grabs my hand across the table and kisses it, but he doesn't say another word about them for the duration of our lunch. He tells me about playing baseball for the Cornhuskers.

On our way back to the car, we're stopped by a few groups of students for more autographs. I caught some of them taking pictures of Brady and I walking together hand in hand. I'm sure it won't be long before those get posted on the internet. It's happened a few times before, and my name even got published last week. Brady doesn't seem bothered by any of it, other than he talks about keeping me safe, so I try not to let it bother me either.

After he calls his former in-laws to make arrangements for Goodwill to pick up anything in the storage unit they don't want to keep, we're back on the plane by three thirty.

"Murphy said she'd hold dinner for us since I have to go there anyway and pick up Stryker. Are you okay with that?"

He looks at the glove that he's still holding. "Yeah. That's fine."

"Maybe you should buy Stryker his own glove and keep that one in a special place," I say.

He shakes his head. "I'd rather give it to him if it's all the same to you." He turns to me and holds my eyes with his. "Would you mind if I taught him how to play ball? He's almost four, isn't he? He should start now."

I can't help my smile. I was hoping he would ask. "I would love that. And so will he."

Brady shrugs. "Maybe it'll help us, you know ... bond or something."

"I think that's a fine idea."

He puts the glove on his tray table and stares at it.

"Will you tell me about Keeton?"

He closes his eyes for a second and I'm not sure he's going to talk.

"I knew he was a carbon copy of Natalie the instant he was born. They had the same hair. The same eyes. The same smile. He was going to play ball, that's for sure. When he was a baby, he loved to roll baseballs across the floor. When he started walking, you'd be hard pressed not to see him carrying a ball. And when I gave him this glove for his third birthday, he took it to bed with him. He was always swinging a bat or throwing a ball. He broke more than a few things around the house, but we never punished him for it. He was just taking after me."

Those last few words were hard for him to choke out and he turns away and gazes out the window.

"Thank you," I say. "I want you to feel comfortable talking about him—about them—whenever you want to."

He nods. "I brought all the photo albums back with me. I'll show them to you someday."

"I would like that."

He grabs my hand and turns back to me with misty eyes. "Thank you, Rylee. If it weren't for you, I'm not sure I would have done this."

"You're welcome. I'm glad I could help."

He runs his finger across my knuckles. "You did. You helped more than you'll ever know."

He motions for the flight attendant. "We'll take those drinks now."

"Right away," she says, rushing to bring us the champagne we refused earlier.

He raises his glass to me. "To the future."

"To the future," I say, tapping my glass to his.

~ ~ ~

It's almost nine o'clock when we get to Caden and Murphy's. It smells divine when we walk through the door.

"Hey, you two," Murphy says. "I hope Mexican is okay. Caden requested it. He just got home himself. Stryker crashed on our bed about an hour ago. He had tacos earlier."

"I can't thank you enough for watching him," I tell her. "I know it was a long day."

"Are you kidding? That child is an angel. I'll watch him any time."

Caden comes down the hallway, hair still wet from a shower. He pours everyone a glass of wine. "We missed you at the games," he says, patting Brady on the shoulder.

Brady flew home early from Minneapolis, missing yesterday's and today's games so we could head out to Lincoln at the crack of dawn this morning. Being on the disabled list, he's not required to be at all the games, but he likes to go anyway.

"Thanks," Brady says. "I had shit to take care of."

"And did you take care of it?" Caden asks.

Brady nods and looks at me. "Yeah. Yeah, I did."

The guys talk baseball while I help Murphy put the finishing touches on the meal. Then she calls everyone to the kitchen. "Caden, can you and Brady take the platters over to the table please? Here, Rylee, you bring the wine. I'll get the rest. And can someone open the salsa?"

Caden is still filling Brady in on the game when Brady picks up the jar of salsa and opens it effortlessly.

"Oh, my God!" I say, my jaw slack as I stare at him.

"What?" he asks.

I nod to the jar of salsa.

When he realizes what he just did, he says, "Holy shit!" He looks at me. "Holy shit!"

"Murphy, do you have any more salsa?" he asks.

"You don't like that one?" she says.

I'm tearing through Murphy's pantry before she even realizes what's going on. I come out with another jar and hand it to Brady. He opens it with a huge smile on his face.

"Well, it's not pickles, but I'll take it," he says. "I'll fucking take it." Then he picks me up and spins me around.

I'm laughing and crying at the same time while Murphy and Caden are looking at us like we're crazy.

"I'm back!" he yells at the ceiling.

"You're back," I say. "I never doubted it for a second."

He stops spinning and kisses me. Right here in Murphy's kitchen with the two of them watching, he kisses me with as much passion as he's ever kissed me before.

He pulls his lips away, but he's still holding me. "Marry me," he says.

My eyes go wide. I'm not sure I heard him correctly. "Uh ..."

"Come on, Ry. Marry me."

I wriggle out of his arms. I look over at Murphy and watch as she grabs Caden's arm and pulls him out of the room.

"What the hell is happening here?" I hear Caden ask his wife on their way out.

"Brady, you're talking crazy. We can't get married."

"Why the hell not?"

"We haven't been dating long enough."

And you pretty much just buried your wife and child today, I want to scream.

"We've been over this before, Ry."

"Yes. We have. And I love you, Brady. But before I commit my life to you, before I commit Stryker's life to you, I have to be one hundred percent sure. And you should be, too."

"So the answer is no?" he says.

"I'm not giving you an answer," I say. "I'm not giving you an answer until I'm ready."

"I'm not giving up, you know," he says. "Not until I get the answer I want. And I can be very persuasive."

I smile, knowing just how true that is.

"Is it safe to come back in?" Murphy asks.

"Yes, come on in," I say.

Caden and Murphy just stand there and stare at us when they enter the kitchen.

"We're not engaged," I say. "Brady was just excited over his hand."

"Yet," Brady says. "We're not engaged *yet* is what Rylee meant to say."

Murphy gives Caden a knowing smile. "Okay, come on, let's eat. And you can tell us what's so great about opening a jar of salsa."

Brady tells them about the pickle jars and his grip.

"So how long do you think before he can pitch in a game?" Caden asks me.

I shrug. "I'm not a coach, guys, don't look at me. But if I were betting on it, I'd say a few weeks to a month."

"I'm betting on a few weeks," Brady says. "I've always beaten the odds when it comes to baseball." Then he looks over at me. "You did it. You got me back."

"I guess we make a good team, don't we?" I say.

He puts his left hand on mine and traces his thumb across my ring finger. "That's exactly what I'm counting on."

Chapter Thirty-nine

The past few weeks have been tough on Brady. He's pitching again. But he's not pitching particularly well. He was so looking forward to being out on the mound again, but now it's almost like he dreads it. He's lost his confidence.

I think he expected to jump right back in where he left off and be at the top of his game. When that didn't happen immediately, it messed him up. The team is giving him some latitude because they know it takes time, but even after only a few weeks, he tells me he can feel his manager's confidence waning as well.

It kills me to see him like this. I go to as many games as I can. I take Stryker with me a lot. He loves to watch baseball. He wears the glove Brady gave him. Keeton's glove. Someday we'll tell him where it came from.

Brady always looks up at me when he's walking to the mound. Sometimes he looks at me between pitches, especially when he seems to be getting frustrated. I just wish there was something I could do to calm him down. He's always telling me that when he thinks too much about pitching, it messes him up.

The past few weeks have been tough on me, too. Since he's back playing, I haven't gotten to see him much. Especially since he's done with physical therapy. While it's true that players get some sort of PT on a daily basis, they don't go outside the organization for that day-to-day stuff.

It's plain and simple. I miss him.

Today is Saturday and Stryker and I are getting our Hawks shirts on. Murphy and Lexi are coming by shortly and we're going to the first game of their double-header together.

Stryker already has his baseball glove on. "I'm gonna play baseball like Bwady," he says.

He stopped calling Brady 'baseball man' when Brady started spending more time with him. Ever since we got back from Lincoln, Brady has made it a point to eat with us—both of us—whenever he can. And he's gotten creative about it, even coming for breakfast when he's in town since he knows Stryker will be in bed by the time he stops by after his games. Sometimes he spends the night and then gets dressed before Stryker wakes up, pretending he's just shown up for breakfast. I love those nights. Nights when I can lie in his arms and dream about the possibility of a future with him.

He asked me to marry him. *Marry him.* I couldn't believe it. I still can't. And Brady hasn't let me forget. He brings it up almost every time we're together. "Marry me yet?" he says. And I give him my standard answer. "Not yet."

I get down on my knees in front of my son. "Do you like Brady?" I ask. "He wants to spend more time with us, would that be okay?"

He nods emphatically. "Bwady helps me play baseball."

"Yes, he does, doesn't he?"

I know Stryker understands the basic concept of a daddy, but he never asks me about it. I guess because he has a nanny and isn't in a daycare setting, he's not seeing men pick their kids up and then questioning me about it. Occasionally when we read books that talk about fathers, he will ask a question or two, but sometimes I think he believes kids either have a mommy or a daddy, but not both.

The doorbell rings and I let Lexi and Murphy in. They both high-five Stryker and then he tells them a knock-knock joke.

His joke is silly and juvenile and it makes us all laugh. It also gives me an idea. "We need to stop at the corner market along the way," I announce.

I put my Hawks ball cap on and give Stryker his and we go on our way.

When we get to the stadium and find our seats next to the first-base dugout, I pull out the thick black marker and the poster boards I bought and get started on my project. I hope Brady doesn't get mad. But in my defense, he only said he didn't want me holding up *'I love you'* signs.

Brady looks up at me when he heads to the mound. I give him a thumbs-up and Stryker yells, "Go Bwady!"

Brady winks at Stryker and then looks over at Caden, who's his catcher. The first two batters fly out to center field. The third batter hits a ground ball and gets thrown out at first. The fans go crazy. But Brady isn't happy. All three batters got a piece of him. He's not going to be happy until he strikes out every last player on the team.

When the Hawks are up and Caden comes up to bat, Murphy grabs my elbow. She still gets nervous every time he steps up to hit. We all yell and scream when he hits a double.

Sawyer comes up next. He gets a few strikes on him and then hits a good dinger over the head of the second-baseman to bring

Caden home. It's so much fun to watch Sawyer on base. He steals more bases than anyone in the league and everyone knows it. It's a game between him and the pitcher—will the pitcher throw him out or will Sawyer add another stolen base to his impeccable record? Luckily, Sawyer wins that game most of the time. In fact, we're all on our feet cheering when the next pitch gets past the catcher and Sawyer steals home.

Brady doesn't get to hit because the next few guys get out and he's pretty far down in the lineup. Hitting is not Brady's strong suit. Whereas Caden is one of the best batters on the team, Brady is considered average. They didn't hire him because of his hitting ability. And that's the problem. They won't keep him because of his hitting ability either. If Brady doesn't prove himself on the mound, there will be no reason for him to play.

The second inning is more of the same. Brady gets the ball over the plate well enough, but balls are being hit to the outfield and the other team scores a run. I can tell how frustrated he is when he goes back into the dugout.

When he comes out to pitch the third inning, I decide it's time to hold up the sign. I turn around and apologize to the fans behind me and then I hold up the large white poster board over my head. It reads: KNOCK KNOCK.

As usual, he glances over at me on his way from the dugout. He looks confused, however, when he sees me holding the sign. He looks away and then the batter comes up to the plate. He throws a strike, but then throws four balls and walks the batter.

I hold up the sign again, hoping he'll look over. He does. I stare him down until he mouths the words, "Who's there?"

I smile and change the poster to a new one. This one says: EUROPE.

The second batter comes up and the first pitch is a strike. Then Brady throws three balls. He's frustrated. Caden calls time and approaches the mound. Brady looks over at me and I hold up the EUROPE sign again. I stare him down until he acquiesces.

"Europe who?" he mouths, reluctantly.

I switch to the last sign and hold it high over my head. It reads: NO – YOU'RE A POO.

He reads it and then shakes his head. I can't see his eyes under the bill of his hat, but I'd guess he's rolling them at me right now. Brady and Caden share a few words and then Caden walks back behind the plate. Brady glances over at me and the left side of his mouth turns upward into a half smile.

Then he throws two strikes in a row and the umpire calls the batter out.

The third batter gets two fastballs right up the middle and then a curve ball on the inside. He never stood a chance.

Brady tips his hat at me before walking back into the dugout.

He doesn't look at me much for the rest of the game, but when he does, he's laughing. And he has the best game he's had since he came back.

Hours later, when he comes to my apartment after the second game, he picks me up and carries me back to my bed. He lays me down and crawls on top of me, hovering over me. "What made you do that?" he asks.

"I guess it was a combination of things. You mentioning the signs and then Stryker told a joke earlier today."

"I never said anything to you? Maybe talked in my sleep?"

"About what?" I ask.

He laughs. "You know I hate those girls who hold up the stupid '*I love you*' signs, but I've often thought I'd like it better if they held up a sign with a joke on it."

"Really?"

"It's like you read my mind, Ry. And it worked."

"It wasn't the sign, Brady. It was all you. You just needed to stop thinking about pitching for a minute."

"I did, you know. I kept thinking about that stupid joke every time I looked at you." He leans down to kiss me. "God, I love how much you get me. Marry me yet?"

"Not yet," I say, smiling.

Chapter Forty

Boston is a beautiful city. I love it here. I have wonderful memories of taking the train here with Mom and Dad when I was younger. So when Murphy asked me if I wanted to come for the weekend, I could hardly refuse. The Nighthawks are ending a three-day series with the Red Sox today and she thought we could all have a much-needed night out after the game.

And I must say the thought of spending an entire night with Brady and not having to worry about Stryker walking in, makes me oh so happy.

Stryker is staying with Lexi for the night. He loves her two girls, Beth, and her older sister, Ellie, who is deaf. And although my son just turned four, he's already picking up some basic sign language just by being around them. I've learned a few words myself so I can communicate with Ellie whenever I see her.

Murphy and I check in to the hotel, leaving our bags in the guys' rooms, and then we head over to the stadium. "Can you please stop at a market or convenience store along the way?" I ask the cab driver.

"Picking up supplies?" Murphy asks, laughing.

She knows the drill. Every time I go to a game, I come prepared with signs and a joke. The good news is, I haven't had to use them every time. But it's kind of become our thing. And sometimes I think Brady gets upset if I don't have one for him when he's pitching well.

Stryker helps me with the jokes. And just like a four-year-old, most of them are centered around human waste or bodily noises. I think he and Helen must Google knock-knock jokes when I'm at work, because for as young as he is, he's got some good ones.

"Nice one," Murphy says, as she watches me make the signs. "You know, Caden and Brady are very different out there. Caden won't ever look up at me, not after he finds me in the stands right before the game. But Brady is always looking at you."

"Caden looks at you when he hits a home run," I say. "And maybe Brady looking at me is not such a good thing. Maybe that's what's messing up his game."

"I don't think so," she says. "He's always looked up into the stands. He told me once that it gives him energy. While Caden might not like to think about the forty-thousand pairs of eyes watching him, for Brady, I think it drives him to succeed."

"God, I hope he succeeds," I say. "I can't imagine how heartbroken he would be if he didn't."

"He will," she says. "He is. His pitching is great. It's his head that needs work. Caden tells me he's an ace in practice. He says Brady pitches just like before, maybe better. But in the games, he sometimes freezes."

"Do you think he's afraid of getting hit by another ball?"

Murphy reaches up and touches the scar under her eye. "Could be. I was terrified for a long time after I was hit, even if there was a net between me and the field. I imagine it's worse for him being down there in the direct line of fire knowing what kind of damage can be done. But he'll get over it," she says. "He'll get over it because he has to."

Our guys take the field and look over to find us. Murphy blows Caden a kiss. We both give a thumbs-up to them. And I might say a silent prayer.

After the first two innings, I fear I might need today's sign. He's frustrated. But at least when he gets up to bat, he gets a single and drives in a run. Maybe that will help his confidence.

Halfway through the third inning, however, when he walks another batter, I know it's time. I wait for him to look up at me and then I hold up the sign.

KNOCK KNOCK

I think I see the corners of his mouth turn up in a repressed smile. "Who's there?" he mouths.

Then he turns back to face his batter. This is the dance we do with the signs. He never gets the full joke at once. He likes to think about it; anticipate it. He says it helps him keep his head out of the game. It works. He strikes out the batter. And the third one fouls out to the right fielder.

In fact, I don't need to give him the next part of the joke for three more innings. Maybe he could even go the whole game without it, but let's face it, as juvenile as it is, I know he wants to see it.

A PILE-UP

I see him mouth the words, "A pile-up who?" Then he shakes his head and laughs. He doesn't even need me to hold up the sign that reads: EWWWWWW! But I do anyway.

Murphy puts a hand on my arm. "You're a godsend, I hope you know that."

"They are just stupid kid jokes, Murphy."

"I'm not talking about the jokes. Even as he's working his way through his slump, he's still happier than I've ever seen him. That's all you, Rylee. I do hope you marry him one day."

I look down and watch them run off the field. "Yeah, I hope so too."

During the seventh-inning stretch, the ever-popular '*Sweet Caroline*' song gets played and I see Caden peeking out of the dugout to mouth the words to Murphy. The song, even though it's played only at Red Sox games, has a lot of personal meaning to them.

In the end, the Nighthawks squeeze out a narrow win.

"Come on," Murphy says. "Let's go meet the guys as they come out. We'll be their groupies."

The plan was to meet them back at the hotel before our night out, but how can I argue with her when she looks so excited about it. I shove my signs into a trashcan and we make our way to the visitors' clubhouse.

There is a good crowd waiting where the guys will come out, probably because we're not too far from New York and the fans can travel easily.

I'm eager to see Brady. I know he will be in a good mood tonight. I can't wait to spend the entire night with him.

Murphy and I hang back, but some of the fans are getting close to the barricades they use to separate the crowd from the players. As I see Brady and a few others come out the door, a security guard grabs a woman's arm when she tries to slip through.

"You have to stay behind these, Miss," he says.

"But I'm Brady Taylor's girlfriend," she says.

Murphy and I both look at the girl and then at each other. "Shit," I say. "We should have gone back to the hotel."

She gives me a sympathetic look.

"I don't care if you're the Queen Mother," the security guard says. "Everyone stays behind the line."

"Brady!" the girl yells.

Brady's eyes snap over to her. He sighs and shakes his head. He doesn't know Murphy and I are here waiting so he goes over to the woman. "Shauna," he says, acknowledging her.

She tries to throw her arms around him, but he pushes her off and pulls her to the side.

I scoot closer and camouflage myself behind someone else so I can try to hear what they are saying.

"What are you doing, Shauna? I told you on Thursday I can't see you anymore."

Murphy nudges my elbow. And then Caden spots us and comes over to greet us. Murphy puts her finger to her lips to shush him before he speaks. She wants to hear Brady's conversation as much as I do.

"That's nonsense," Shauna says, putting her hand on his chest provocatively. "Come on, Brady. You know you can't resist me."

Brady looks around and spots Caden, then his eyes widen when he sees me standing just a few feet away. He looks like he's not sure what he wants to do so I shake my head at him, letting him know not to acknowledge me.

He removes her hand from him. "It's over Shauna."

"It's not, Brady. I know where you're staying. I'll just come there. You'll change your mind."

"If you come to my hotel, I'll have security escort you out."

Shauna laughs. "No, you won't."

"I will," he says. "Please don't push me. You knew the score. We had some fun and now we're done. I have to go now." He turns to the security guard. "Will you make sure nobody follows me, please?"

Shauna pouts, and then sure enough as he walks away in the other direction, the guard has to hold her back as she tries to go after him. "Let it go, Miss," he says. "You don't want to be that girl, do you? Don't beg for it."

"What the fuck do *you* know?" she bites at him.

"Come on," Caden says, urging Murphy and me to follow him. "We'll meet him at the hotel." He pulls his phone out and texts Brady.

"Is it always like that?" I ask him. "Do they all act like she did?"

He shrugs. "Some of them do. He was stupid and reckless before you, Rylee. But don't hold it against him. You know how he is now, but his past may follow him around for a while. He's had to make good on more than one threat to have hotel security throw a girl out."

My jaw drops. "Oh, my God, really?"

"Some people don't take no for an answer," he says. "Even though they all knew what they were getting into, you have to know some of them thought they'd be able to get more out of him. Not all women are as classy as you are, Rylee."

"Yeah, I'm real classy. Last fall, I was one of them." I look back at the woman as we walk away. "That could have been me."

"That would never have been you," Murphy says. "Brady came crawling back to you, not the other way around. He loves you. That's a miracle, don't you know that?"

I nod. "I know. I just wish he could love Stryker."

Murphy locks elbows with me. "He will. Give him time."

When we get back to the hotel, Brady is already there signing autographs out front with a few other players. I look around and, luckily, Shauna isn't anywhere to be seen. He smiles when he sees me, and he excuses himself to come over. "I'm sorry about what happened. I tried to let her down the first night. I didn't want you to see that."

"It's okay. Let's just forget about it and not let her ruin our night together."

He takes my hand. "Do we really have to go out? Can't we just hole up in our hotel room?"

"You're going out," Sawyer says, stepping up next to us. "You have to introduce Rylee to our place, man."

"Your place?" I raise my eyebrows.

"It's a bar some of us go to whenever we come to Boston. They have live music, a mechanical bull, pool tables, even a bowling alley."

"A mechanical bull?" I ask warily, looking at Brady's left arm.

He laughs. "Don't worry, sweetheart, our contracts prevent us from doing anything that could cause us to get injured."

"That didn't keep Cole from riding it last year," Sawyer says.

"Cole was a stupid son-of-a-bitch," Brady says, laughing. "Got thrown off. Landed right on his pitching arm. He thought he sprained it. Hid it from the coaches for days while icing it every chance he got. He was lucky. And you can bet he'll never do anything that idiotic again."

"Pool sounds fun," I say.

Brady gives me a cocky smile. "Oh, you play, do you?"

"I've played once or twice."

I don't tell him I was an ace back in college.

"Care to make a wager?" he asks, suggestively.

"And, my cue to leave. See you over there," Sawyer says, slipping away.

"I don't know, what did you have in mind?" I ask.

He thinks on it for a beat. Then he smiles big. "However many balls the loser leaves on the table is how many orgasms they owe the other person."

I blush, looking around to make sure nobody heard. "I'm not sure that's a penalty, Brady."

He pulls me close. "See, this is why I love you. We always think alike."

"Deal," I say.

He grabs my hand and pulls me behind him. "Let's go," he announces to the group.

Twenty minutes later, we arrive at the massive club and are ushered into a VIP area where a private waitress stands at the ready to take care of our every need.

A few of the other guys on the team show up. Sawyer. Cole. Spencer. But Murphy and I are the only women. And you can believe we are getting dirty looks from half the females in the place.

"You'll get used to it," Murphy says. "Just ignore them. Don't make eye contact and you'll never have to know how much they hate you."

"Why would they hate us?"

"We are living their fantasy, Rylee."

I look around at the five uber-handsome players at our table. Four of whom don't hold a candle to Brady in my opinion. "Yeah, I guess we are."

For an hour, we drink, talk, and bowl. Brady hasn't even mentioned playing pool yet. I imagine he intends to get me liquored up so he has a better chance of winning. It's fine by me. If he wins, I still win.

My favorite song gets played by the cover band. I grab Brady's hand. "Come on, dance with me."

"I need to go find a chick to dance with," Sawyer says.

"No! You don't!" the rest of the table yells collectively.

"Come on guys, I'm not that bad," he says.

"Except that you are," Cole tells him. "Can you keep your dick in your pants for one night, bro?"

"But I want to dance to Rylee's favorite song," he pouts.

Murphy stands up. "I'll dance with you."

Sawyer looks at Caden who gives him a nod. "She's all yours. For the dance, anyway."

The four of us head to the dance floor on the other side of the club. The song is fast, but Brady pulls me to him and dances with me oh, so slowly. It's the first time we've danced together. His hands find every place on me that's not indecent – and a few that are.

"You feel so good," he whispers in my ear. It's not the first time he's said those words to me. He says them often, but only when we're making love.

I think that was his intention. He's working me up into a frenzy right here on the dance floor.

I get lost in the music. I get lost in him. I never want the song to end. I want this moment to last forever.

Someone taps my shoulder, pulling me from the trance he's put me in.

"Can I cut in?" a woman asks.

I turn around to see it's the same woman from the game.

"Shauna, leave us alone," Brady says.

She looks me up and down, appraising me like gum on the bottom of her shoe. "This is what you left me for? Boy, you sure traded down, didn't you?"

"Don't be a bitch," Brady says, pulling me to the other side of the dance floor.

"Ignore her," he says. "If she continues to bother us, we'll go sit down. Or we'll leave."

He wraps me in his arms again, but this time it's different. He's protecting me instead of enticing me. A few minutes later, when Shauna hasn't followed us, he finally relaxes.

"What the fuck is wrong with my cousin?" a deep male voice with a heavy Boston accent says behind us.

Brady spins us around and puts me behind him. I don't miss that he looks over to see where Sawyer is, but he is on the other side of a very large crowd.

Brady holds his hands up, showing the guy he doesn't want a fight. "If you're talking about Shauna, there is nothing wrong with her. I'm just not interested anymore and she doesn't seem to want to accept that."

Another guy walks up beside the first one. "The way Shauna tells it, you dropped her like shit in the john."

"That's not the way it was," Brady says. "We went out when I was in town. It was fun while it lasted, but I never gave her false hope. She knew I wasn't in it for the long haul."

One of the guys points to me. "Oh, but you are with the bitch behind you?"

"You don't want to do this, man," Brady says, taking a defensive stance.

I start to freak out. What if Brady fights the guy and re-injures his hand? I look across the bar, hoping one of the other guys sees what's going on. Then I breathe a sigh of relief when Sawyer comes up next to us.

"Is there a problem here?" he asks.

Murphy motions to me that she's going to get the other guys. I nod and will her to hurry.

"You brought reinforcements, tough guy?" one of them says to Brady. "Come on, let's see what you got." The guy pokes Sawyer in the chest.

"I'm not going to fight you," Sawyer says to him.

"Oh, so you're a pussy," the guy says, pushing Sawyer with his hand. "Why don't you just hide behind the dickhead, too, like the other stupid bitch?"

I look over and see Shauna at the bar, watching us with a smile on her face. I wonder how Brady could have been such a poor judge of character. Then again, I don't think character was at the top of his priority list.

"Leave him alone. Your beef is with me," Brady says.

A third guy comes up behind me, pushes me out of the way and grabs Brady's arm. At the same time, one of the other two guys grabs his other arm and they hold him captive as the first guy starts punching Sawyer.

Sawyer takes a punch in the jaw and then spits blood on the floor. But he doesn't raise his hand to the guy.

"Your friend here is just getting a demonstration of what we're going to do to you in about ten seconds."

A crowd is gathering around us as people start to realize what's going on.

Brady is trying to break free, but the two men holding him are as big as he is. I shout to the bartender to get security over and then I watch Sawyer get punched in the gut two times. He doubles over and then stands back up.

Why isn't he hitting the guy back? He's just standing there getting beaten up. Nobody is holding his hands, yet he's just standing there.

"Sawyer, do something!" I scream.

"Yeah, do something, Sawyer," the guy mimics me in a high voice before punching him again.

Sawyer's face is stoic. He looks like he wants to rip the guy's head off, but he just stands there. His jaw is tight and his temple is pounding. Sweat beads on his forehead and rolls down the side of his face.

Then all hell breaks loose as Caden, Cole and Spencer tackle the three guys. Brady is finally free and he participates in holding them down. But Sawyer is just standing there, watching it all happen, frozen.

Security comes over and breaks things up, having enough witnesses to justify throwing the three guys and Shauna out of the club.

We head back up to the VIP section and I ask the bartender for a bag of ice along the way. Then I put it to Sawyer's jaw when we get up there.

"I guess we should call it a night," Cole says.

"Fuck that," Sawyer tells him. "I'm not letting those douchebags ruin this for everyone."

"What happened, man?" Brady asks him. "Why did you just stand there and let him hit you?"

Sawyer looks at Brady, but he doesn't answer him. It's almost like he can't.

"Give him a break, guys. He's hurt." I shoo them all away and lower my voice. I can tell he's traumatized. But I'm not sure it's because of the blows he took. "It's okay, Sawyer. Whatever it is, it's okay."

He nods his head over and over. And I wonder what's going on. I've never seen a man just stand there and get beaten up like that. Whatever it is, it runs deep. I look over at Brady, wondering if

Sawyer doesn't also have skeletons in his closet or demons in his past.

"Do you want me to look at your abs?" I ask when everyone starts to crowd around us again. "I have medical training."

He shakes his head. "Not unless you want to be impressed by perfection," he jokes. "I'm fine. Thanks for the ice, Rylee, but what I really need is a shot of tequila."

"Shots for everyone!" Cole yells, motioning for the waitress to bring us some.

"Way to preserve your throwing arm," Spencer says, toasting Sawyer when we all have our shots.

Sawyer lifts his chin at him. I'm sure he'd like everyone to think that's what just happened, but I know better. And when Sawyer looks over at me, he knows I know it.

An hour and four shots later, we've all but forgotten the altercation. Brady has done everything in his power to turn the evening around and make it a good one. And by the time I've lost two games of pool, I'm putty in his hands.

On our way home, before we walk into the hotel, he stops me. "Knock knock," he says.

I laugh. "Who's there?"

"Five," he says, holding up five fingers.

"Five who?" I ask with a knowing grin.

"Five times you'll be screaming my name tonight, that's who."

I look at him sideways. "But you won. That means I have to give *you* five orgasms."

"That's right, Ry. You have to give me five of your orgasms. Did I not make that perfectly clear earlier?"

I giggle, looking at the time. "It's going to be a long night, Taylor."

"It's going to be the *best* night," he says. "I've been looking forward to breaking our record for eight months now. And believe me, this hand is ready to break records."

He fists and releases his left hand and I smile knowing he's not just talking about sex. He's back in the game. And he's going to be better than ever.

Chapter Forty-one

The best part of playing a series in Boston is that the guys don't have much of a travel day. We're back in New York and picking up Stryker by noon.

I expected Brady to go home and sleep. We did keep each other up very late last night. But he goes to Lexi's with me to pick up my son.

"You don't have any plans today, do you?" he asks in the cab on the way home.

"Just dinner with my mom. I'll pick her up at five."

"Good."

"Why? What do you have in mind?"

"Hey, sport," he says to Stryker. "How about we go play baseball on a real baseball field today?"

Stryker's eyes light up and he claps. "Can I bwing my glove and wear my hat?"

"Of course you can. You need both of those to be a baseball player. Do you think your mom will want to come, too?"

"Mommy, will you play baseball with us? Girls can play, too. Right, Bwady?"

I laugh. "Gee, thanks. I'd love to go."

"We'll stop for a bite to eat and then drop our stuff off and grab his glove."

I reach behind Stryker and touch Brady's shoulder. "Thank you."

He nods.

Two hours later, we're walking through Central Park with a bag full of baseball gear. We come to the baseball fields and Stryker gets very excited. He's seen these fields before and always makes us stop and watch the kids play.

Brady opens the gate.

"Can just anyone use these fields?" I ask.

"No. You have to have a permit and pay a small fee."

"You *planned* this?" I ask.

"Yeah. A few weeks ago."

I can't help my smile. Other than bringing my son the stuffed animals, this is the first thing Brady has done that is just for Stryker. And he planned it weeks ago.

Brady puts his bag down and pulls a few things out. He puts a Hawks hat on my head. "You're the fielder," he says. "I'll get him set up with the tee and he'll hit them out to you."

Brady pulls a large rubber tee out of his bag and puts a ball on it. Then he pulls out a small bat and a pint-sized Nighthawks batting helmet that looks just like the one he wears when he plays. He puts it on Stryker's head and Stryker squeals in delight.

"I look just like Bwady!"

I realize how much effort Brady had to put in to this afternoon and it brings tears to my eyes. I wonder how hard this is for him. I wonder if he's looking at Stryker wishing he were Keeton.

"Okay, sport. You stand just like this. Put your back leg here and bend your knees a little. Now hold the bat up like this."

Stryker swings and misses.

I see Sawyer Mills walking onto the field. "You're teaching him to hit like a girl," he says, winking over at me. "Why don't you let a real ball player show him how it's done?"

"What are you doing here?" Brady asks.

"I heard you talking about it yesterday and I thought I'd come make sure you teach the kid right."

Brady puts Stryker back in position. "Don't take your eye off the ball."

This time, he hits the ball and it dribbles towards the pitcher's mound.

"I did it, Mommy! I did it!"

"Good hit, baby."

"What are you waiting for, sport? Run around the bases," Brady says.

He doesn't need to show Stryker where the bases are. Stryker's been to enough games that he knows exactly what to do. He takes off running, Sawyer right behind him, urging him on as they laugh the entire time. Brady and I both walk slowly towards the ball, giving Stryker extra time to get his home run.

Brady looks at me and touches the bill of my hat. "Have I ever told you how much I like you wearing my hat?"

"No, you haven't. How much do you like it?" I ask seductively. "Are we talking just a little, or really really a lot?" I tease.

He looks over at Stryker to see that he's rounding second, oblivious to what we're doing. Brady pulls me to him and kisses me. It's a quick, but passionate kiss.

"I like it that much," he says, running his thumb down my cheek.

We break apart and watch Stryker cross home plate. We cheer loudly and run over to give him high-fives.

Stryker hugs my leg and then hugs Brady's. He looks up at him. "Are you my daddy?"

My jaw drops and I watch Brady's spine stiffen. I get down on my knees. "Why did you ask that?"

"Mommies kiss daddies," he says.

I look at Brady. He seems to be recovering from the shock of Stryker's words. He picks up the ball and sets it back on the tee, walking over to Sawyer so I can have a moment with my son.

"Yes, mommies do kiss daddies. But sometimes mommies kiss people who aren't daddies, too."

"So, he's not my daddy?"

"No, baby. He's not. But he is very special to me. I hope he's special to you, too."

"If I ask him, will he be my daddy? Ms. Helen says kids have daddies, but some don't, like me. I want a daddy. Can Bwady be my daddy?"

I see Brady trying to look busy, but I know he can hear what we're saying. I'm wondering just how uncomfortable this conversation is making him. Even though he's asked me to marry him, we've never talked about him being Stryker's father.

"I'm not married, Stryker. Maybe someday if I get married, you will get a daddy."

"Can you marry Bwady?" he asks.

Brady snickers. "Yeah, Rylee, can you marry Bwady?" He winks at me.

"Not yet," I say.

"Can I throw the ball with you and then hit another home run?" Stryker asks Brady.

"Yeah, sport, we can do that. And you can hit as many home runs as you want," Brady says, walking over to him. He picks Stryker up and swings him around before putting him back on his feet. Then he tickles him under his arms.

Stryker falls into a fit of giggles.

Sawyer and I stand behind the pitcher's mound watching Brady and my son toss a ball back and forth.

"Thanks for coming," I say.

"I couldn't let your kid learn from anyone but the best," he says with a nudge to my ribs.

"And yet you're standing back here with me."

He gives me a knowing look. "It's not that hard to see this really isn't about baseball, is it?" He nods to Brady and Stryker.

"Thanks for that, too," I tell him, happy that he's letting Brady and Stryker have this moment.

"I know you don't know me very well, and I'm sure you think the same about me as everyone else, but I hope you'll give me the benefit of the doubt when I tell you I'm a nice guy."

"I'm not judging you, Sawyer."

"Well then you might be the only one."

"People have reasons for what they do," I say, staring at Brady.

Sawyer nods. "Yeah, they do, don't they? He told me about Natalie and Keeton a few weeks ago, you know."

I look at him in surprise. "Really?"

"Yeah. And I'll bet my right arm you had something to do with it." He studies me. "You're good for him."

"He's good for me. For us. Maybe someday you'll find someone who's good for you."

He laughs. "Not likely."

"Why not, Sawyer? What are you afraid of?"

He raises an accusing brow. "Are you and Murphy the baseball whisperers or something? Do you guys just go around trying to fix everyone's shit?"

"No. I guess we want everyone to be as happy as we are, that's all."

"Happiness is an illusion," he says. "Just because you love someone doesn't mean you're happy. And it sure as shit doesn't mean *they're* happy."

I look at him, wondering not for the first time, what his story is.

"It's not an illusion if you're with the right person, Sawyer. Maybe we could find someone nice for you to go out with."

"Sure," he says. "I'll take anyone out once."

I scold him with my eyes. "Maybe we could find someone you'd like to take out more than once."

"Again – not likely."

"How come you never take a woman out more than one time?" I ask.

He ignores my question and nods to Brady and Stryker. "Your son seems to be taking to him."

I smile. "He does."

I stand back and watch the two of them bond, trying my best to stave off the tears.

Two hours and one tired kid later, we make our way out of the park, Sawyer going off in one direction and the three of us in another. Even as exhausted as Stryker is, he's got a permanent smile on his face. I think Brady and Sawyer just gave him the best day of his life. He wouldn't let Brady put all the baseballs back in his bag, he's still holding one. I wonder if he'll ever give it up.

"You've created a monster," I tell Brady.

"The best kind of monster," he says. "Nothing is better than a kid who loves baseball."

When we exit the park, I see a police car down the street, pulling my attention to the flashing lights momentarily. When I look back at Stryker, he's not at my side. My eyes dart around and then I scream as I watch my son run after his baseball right out into the busy street.

"Stryker!" I scream, running after him, not even thinking about how I'm most likely going to get hit by a car.

Everything happens so quickly. I get pushed down to the ground and then I hear car horns and screeching tires. I get up and scream his name again, running out into the traffic that has now come to a stop. I'm terrified at what I'm going to see when I come around the cars. Visions of my son's bloody body flash through my head. I'm crazy with fear and the world goes in slow motion as I run across the street.

I fall to my knees as I see Brady's large body wrapped around Stryker. Brady's arm is bleeding with numerous scrapes down one side. He's holding onto Stryker for dear life. When I make it to them, Brady releases him but looks over every inch of his body, just like I do.

"Is he okay?" I ask frantically, as I check Stryker's head and then each arm and leg.

"He's fine," Brady chokes out, a tear running down his cheek as he watches Stryker pick up the ball he was after like what just happened is no big deal.

He picks Stryker up and walks us both back to the sidewalk where he finds a bench to sit down on.

I pull my son onto my lap and squeeze him tightly. "Thank God."

Then I talk to him sternly. "Stryker, you can't run out in the street like that. You can't chase a ball. We can replace a baseball, we can't replace *you*."

As soon as I say it, I realize how those words might affect Brady and I glance at him to see if he noticed.

"Your mom is right, sport. You can't ever do that again. She would be lost without you. I would be lost without you." He puts his arm around us. "Both of you."

Stryker starts crying. I think we've scared him. "It's okay, baby. You're okay. We're not going to let anything happen to you."

Brady runs his hand down Stryker's back, helping me soothe him as onlookers ask if we're okay.

I remember the scrapes on Brady's arm—his pitching arm—and reach my hand out. "Oh, Brady, your arm."

He shakes his head. "Don't worry about it. It's fine."

"But—"

"But nothing," he says. "My arm's okay, Rylee. And even if it wasn't, I'd still do what I did. I'd do anything for you. *Both* of you."

"Thank you," I say, lacing my fingers with his.

"How do I apply for the job?" he asks.

I look at him like maybe he hit his head on the pavement. "What job?"

He nods at Stryker. "The one that puts my name on his birth certificate."

My eyes snap to his. "You'd ... really?"

"Really," he says. "I want him. I want you. I want this."

"I love you," I tell him.

"I love you, too."

"Mommy?" Stryker says.

"Yeah, baby?"

"Are you gonna tell Nana I got a home run?"

I laugh, thinking how quickly children can move on from one thing to the next. "No. I'm not going to tell her, but *you* can."

"Good. I can show her my lucky ball," he says, still holding onto it.

I shake my head at his *lucky* ball thinking how much worse this could have turned out.

"Can Bwady come eat with Nana?"

I look over and raise my eyebrows.

"Yes, I'd love to eat with Nana, sport. Family dinners are the best, aren't they?" He stands up and holds his arms out to Stryker who happily hops up to be carried home.

Brady throws his baseball bag over his shoulder and takes my hand in his. I notice a few people snapping pictures of us and wonder what they must think, the playboy of baseball walking down the street with a child in his arms. But I don't care about the attention we're getting. I'm half tempted to ask one of them to send me a picture so I can see for myself what we look like as a family. The family I've always dreamed of.

Chapter Forty-two

I know Brady thinks he's ready. He says he's ready. But there is a small part of me that isn't sure. And I'm only getting married once in this lifetime, so I'm going to be darn sure I pick the right man.

A few weeks ago, when Stryker ran out into the road, I knew that was a turning point for Brady. I've seen him heal so much since then. I've seen him try to be a father to my son. And every time I see them together, I fall in love with Brady even more.

Still, I'm waiting. For what, I don't know. A sign maybe. Something to tell me this is it—*he* is it.

Stryker puts on his Hawks hat and hands me mine. Then we head out to the game. I grab the poster boards. And on them, the joke I haven't needed to use. I carry them with me anyway. Maybe that's *my* superstition. But he doesn't need them. He hasn't for weeks. He's back in the game. He's back in spades.

We meet Murphy and Lexi and the four of us go to the game together. This is a big game for Brady. This is the team he was facing last year when he broke his arm. He feels like he has a score to settle. I just hope it doesn't mess with his head. Maybe it's a good idea that I brought the posters after all.

The Hawks are winning 3-0 after six innings. As our guys take the field, Murphy grabs my hand and squeezes. "You know what's going on, don't you?"

Of course I know what's going on. Everyone in this stadium knows what's going on but nobody is talking about it. Brady is pitching a perfect game. Not one batter has made it to first base. Not with a hit, not on an error, not because of a walk. He has three more innings to go to be in the history books. Nine more batters. A lot can happen. The odds are not in his favor.

I stare Murphy down, refusing to talk about it.

"Et tu, Brute?" she says, giggling.

"Don't you dare mess with the mojo or I'll have to hurt you."

"Seriously, Murphy. What's wrong with you?" Lexi says.

Brady and Caden knock their gloves together and then go to their respective places, Caden behind the plate and Brady on the mound. As always, he looks up at me on the way. I smile and Stryker yells, "Go Bwady!"

It's a tough inning. The first batter is really putting Brady through his paces. The batter has fouled off seven balls. I can tell Brady is getting frustrated. He throws two wild pitches and then Caden calls time and walks up to the mound. Brady shakes his head at him and Caden puts a hand on his shoulder.

I reach down and grab the poster board. I wait to see if he looks up at me. When he does I hold it up.

KNOCK KNOCK

He doesn't smile. He's stoic and focused. He turns back to Caden and they have another word before Caden walks back behind the plate.

Brady throws a strike, finally getting the guy out. He tips his hat at me.

The next batter hits a fly ball to right field and you can hear the collective sighs from the entire stadium when the outfielder catches it. I'd hate to be the fielder who drops the ball in a game like this. He'd never hear the end of it from Brady.

Brady takes a deep breath and then looks up at me and mouths, "Who's there?"

I hold up the next poster.

INEDA

He turns back and gets his sign from Caden. He throws two strikes and then two balls. Then he strikes the guy out with his curveball, never needing my third poster.

He looks up anyway before he leaves the field. "Ineda who?" he mouths.

I hold up the last one.

I NEEDA POO

He shakes his head, laughing as he jogs off the field.

It's the first time he's ever asked for the joke when he didn't need it. It's how I know I won't ever have to bring the large white poster boards again.

Caden and Sawyer both get a run, bringing the score up to 5-0 as they head into the top of the eighth. Two innings left. It's beginning to seem like a real possibility. It's closer than most pitchers ever get to having a perfect game.

I'm so nervous I can hardly stand it. I'm lucky Lexi and Murphy are here with me. Lexi takes Stryker to the bathroom when he asks to go and Murphy gets him a soft pretzel when he's hungry. No way am I missing a second of this game.

Brady takes the field, knocks his glove to Caden's and looks up at me. Then he puts his glove under his arm and unbuttons the first three buttons of his jersey, flashing just the top part of his shirt underneath. But it's enough to show me. It's enough to bring tears to my eyes.

It's enough to make me know that this is the sign I've been waiting for.

Because the shirt underneath his jersey is no longer the one he's always worn since he was eighteen. The shirt under his jersey is the one I bought him last fall. It's his White Poison shirt. The one he kept in the box. The one he kept alongside everything else he holds dear.

I know what a monumental step this is for him. He's letting go of the past. He's showing me that I'm his future.

Tears blur my vision as I make a split-second decision and pull the thick black marker from my purse. Murphy and Lexi can't hide their excitement as they watch me draw in the words on the backs of the poster boards.

But then Brady has a phenomenal inning. He strikes out all three batters. He doesn't look up at me once. I'm not sure if that makes me happy or sad.

The Hawks don't score any more runs in the bottom of the eighth. So as long as the other team doesn't score five runs, we'll win. But he still has three batters to face. And when Brady takes the field, everyone gets on their feet. The stadium is as loud as I've ever heard it. Everyone wants to witness history in the making.

Brady looks up at me. He's nervous. I hold up the first poster.

KNOCK KNOCK

He cocks his head to the side. He knows I never bring two jokes. But he doesn't ask me who's there.

He throws a pitch to the first batter and the ball gets fouled into the right-field stands.

Then he throws two balls.

He steps off the mound and back on. Then he steps off again. He's trying to find his balance, his mojo. He takes his hat off and wipes his brow. Then he looks up at me. "Who's there?" he mouths.

I hold up the second sign.

MARY

He throws a fastball right down the middle and the batter hits a line drive to left field. The fielder runs in on it and scoops it up, quickly and powerfully throwing it to the first baseman who stretches into a split to catch the ball.

The first-base umpire calls the batter out and the stadium erupts in cheers.

I have to will my heart to re-start.

Batter number two comes up. Brady takes a deep breath. The first pitch is a strike. But the second pitch is the scariest thing I've ever seen. The batter makes solid contact, sending the ball hurdling at one hundred miles an hour right at Brady's head. Brady barely has time to put his glove up and catch it.

But he does. He catches it for the second out.

And as the crowd goes wild, he doubles over, putting his hands on his knees.

Caden calls time and runs out to Brady. I can tell he's trying to calm him down. I can't imagine what that must have been like for him, considering what happened the last time a ball was hit to him like that.

As Caden returns to the plate, Brady looks up at me. "Mary who?" he mouths.

I hold up the third sign.

MARRY ME

I think his jaw drops open. I believe I see him grasp the front of his jersey over his heart and nod his head. But I can't be sure. I can't see him very well through all the tears in my eyes.

Everyone is on their feet as the last batter comes to the plate—the one man who stands between Brady and ultimate glory.

I pick up Stryker so he can see the game over the tops of the heads in front of us. Murphy grabs my free hand and holds it tight.

Brady throws a strike and I scream. Well, I try to. It's now that I realize I've lost my voice.

The next pitch is a ball. Brady steps off the mound and takes a breath.

He looks up at me and we lock eyes. Then he looks at Stryker. Then he throws strike number two.

My heart is beating so fast I think I will faint. Lexi takes Stryker from me and Murphy and I cling to each other. One more strike. That's all he needs to have the game of his life.

He throws his fastball and the batter gets a piece of it, sending it flying high up in the air. Caden throws his mask off and runs over near the third base dugout. He dives for the ball, but it's just out of his reach.

Collective moans echo throughout the stands.

I've never wanted a foul ball to be caught more in my life. I've never wanted a foul ball to be called a third strike more than I do at this very moment. But you can't get out on a foul ball. Not unless it's caught.

And I wonder who made up that stupid rule.

Brady shakes off a sign from Caden. Then another. Then he nods. I've never seen him more focused than he is right now.

He winds up for the pitch. It's going to be his breaking ball—I know it. I watch the ball travel out of his hand to the plate. Then

I watch the bat swing and miss the ball. Then I watch as Caden catches the ball in his glove and the umpire calls the batter out.

Ear-splitting screams bounce around the stadium. All of Brady's teammates run to the mound, throwing off their gloves before they tackle him. Other players pour out of the dugout and join the fielders. Caden and Sawyer put Brady on their shoulders and carry him off the field. They carry him as he points over to me.

Crying, I hug Lexi. I hug Murphy. I hug my son.

Stryker's too young to understand what he just witnessed. Odds are, this will never happen to Brady again.

"You realize we both got engaged at a Hawks game," Murphy says.

"Does that make us sisters or something?" I joke with a hoarse voice.

"Close enough," she says.

I see Brady double back, he comes over to where we're sitting and I walk down the few rows to meet him. He puts his hands through the net and pulls me to him, our lips meeting through a hole in the netting. He kisses me while the world watches. But I don't care. Nothing matters more than this moment.

"You did it," I whisper.

"We did it," he says. "Everything I do from this day forward is because we're a *we.*" He looks over at my son. "All of us."

"Come here, sport!" he yells up to Stryker.

Stryker comes down the few stairs to where I'm standing. "You won! You won!" he squeals, jumping up and down.

"Yes, we did." He lifts up the net. "Want to come into the clubhouse with me?"

"Can I, Mommy?"

I nod my head, not having words as my eyes mist up once again.

Stryker slips under the net and Brady hoists him up onto his shoulders. "Don't worry," he says to me. "I'll keep him safe."

"I know you will."

He starts to walk away but then he turns back. "Don't throw away the signs. We're keeping them."

I smile when I watch him carefully step over the foul line as he walks Stryker to the pitcher's mound. He stands there with my son on his shoulders, slowly turning around and absorbing every last ounce of this momentous occasion.

Murphy, Lexi and I make our way out of the stands and to the boisterous waiting area where I promptly get bombarded by reporters.

"Are you Brady Taylor's fiancée?" one asks.

"Who is the boy?" asks another.

"How did you manage to snag the hottest bachelor in baseball?" a third one says.

I ignore their questions as we try to move away from them.

Some of the women waiting alongside us give me dirty looks and talk to each other about me.

Then two security guards walk up. "I'm Drew," one of them says. "Brady thought you might need a little extra help today." He escorts us to the front of the gathering crowd and past the barrier. Then the two guards stand with us until the guys come out of the clubhouse twenty minutes later.

As soon as Brady is through the door, he hoists Stryker up on his shoulders again. The reporters forget about me and go after Brady. He's got security around him, so I'm not worried about them. I get out my phone and snap some pictures.

"Who's the boy?" someone shouts.

Brady looks over at me and smiles. "He's my son."

I didn't think I had any more happy tears to cry. I was wrong.

Murphy grabs onto me. "You have yourself quite a man there, I hope you know that."

"I do," I say nodding. "I do know that."

Brady sends Stryker over to me so he can sign autographs and pose for pictures. Then he walks over and pulls me into his arms. "Come on, let's go home."

"And where exactly is that?" I ask, wondering whose apartment we're going to.

He picks up Stryker in one arm and holds my hand with the other. "It's wherever the two of you are."

~ ~ ~

It takes longer than usual to get an excited Stryker to fall asleep. I read to him. Brady reads to him. Then Brady tells him a story about a boy and his guardian angel.

"It was Keeton, wasn't it?" I ask Brady as we crawl into bed.

"What was?"

"The guardian angel in your story. It was Keeton."

He nods.

"I love you," I tell him.

"No more than I love you."

He proves it to me with his kisses, his loving caress. He takes his slow time with me. He moves his lips across every inch of my neck. His tongue blazes a path down to my breasts. I moan breathily when he takes a nipple into his mouth.

My hands travel across his strong, broad back. I can feel his muscles contract as he moves. I trace the ripples and ridges with my fingers. I reach down to take him into my hands. His steely erection throbs under my grip as I stroke him.

He moves a hand to my sex, inserting his fingers, making me arch my back into him. He traces his thumb across my clit. He whispers sweet nothings to me as we work each other to the edge of ecstasy.

"I can't wait another minute," he says. "I have to be inside you."

"Yes," I cry.

As he enters me, we lock eyes and I wonder how this even happened. How did this man wrap himself so completely around our lives that I have no choice but to love him? How did he fight his demons and overcome such loss so that he could love again? How did he take this ordinary girl with an ordinary life and turn us into an extraordinary family?

With every thrust, he says my name. With every breath, he declares his love for me.

And when we come, he watches me. I watch him. And for a moment, we are one. One person. One entity. One perfect being.

He nuzzles his head into my neck as we chase our recovery. Then he spoons himself behind me. "Hello, fiancée," he whispers.

I smile for the millionth time today. "I think I like the sound of that," I say with my raspy voice.

"Don't get too used to it, sweetheart," he says. "You won't be one for long."

"You want to get married soon?"

"As soon as possible."

I think about it. "I'd like that, too, while there's a better chance of my mom being lucid."

"We'll record it for her and show it to her later if she isn't."

I turn around in his arms. "When did you become this perfect man, Brady? You think of everything. You say the right things. You take care of us so well."

He climbs on top of me. "It happened when I met you," he says. "Don't you know, Rylee—you're everything to me. My Holy Grail. My jackpot. My perfect game."

His lips crash down on mine and he shows me just how much he means those words. "I never want to spend another night without you. Move in with me."

"Will tomorrow be too soon?" I ask.

He props himself on his elbows. "What changed your mind? Why did you finally say yes?"

"I always knew I would," I tell him. "I knew I would from the moment you asked me. But it all happened so fast. I just had to be sure."

"And you're sure now?"

I nod. "I've never been more sure of anything."

He cups my face with his hands. "I meant what I said about Stryker being my son. I want that. Will you let me adopt him?"

A tear rolls out of the side of my eye and he wipes it away with his thumb.

"Yes," I say. "He's going to be so happy to have a daddy."

He laughs. "Let's not forget to remind him of that when I take away his car keys after he fails chemistry in high school."

"Car keys? But we live in the city."

"We do now, but someday I'd like to have a house. A big house with a white fence and a basketball hoop. We'll have a batting cage out back for Stryker."

"And a pool," I say. "I've always wanted a pool."

"You got it," he says, leaning down to kiss me again. "You can have anything you want, future Mrs. Taylor."

He settles in behind me pulling my back to his front, yawning after his big day.

"I still can't believe you did it today," I tell him. "You accomplished what most pitchers will only ever dream of. Kids all over the world will want to grow up to be like you. Books will be written about what you did." I squeeze his hand. "What were you thinking when you struck out that last batter?"

"I was thinking what a lucky man I am. And I was thinking I never thought I'd feel that way again. I was thinking none of it would have mattered if you and Stryker weren't with me, Ry. And even if that last batter had stepped up to the plate and hit a home run, I promise you, I would still have been a winner."

Epilogue

Brady

Eighteen years later …

I sit in our house, the one with the white fence, the basketball hoop, the batting cage, and the pool—I sit here doing something I haven't done in twenty-four years.

It's not that I wouldn't have done it after Rylee and I got married. I probably would have, but just like Ry, she planned something extra special every year on this day knowing it might hold bad memories for me.

But today, every eye in our house is glued to the television. Reporters and cameramen mingle with our family and friends, all of them giving space to the six of us who are so anxiously watching the screen.

Stryker is sitting next to me, wearing his University of Florida hat for maybe the last time. From this day forward, he'll wear a different hat. One that will shape his future.

383

"I think you're more nervous than I am, Dad," he says, putting his hand on my leg to stop it from shaking.

I nod my head, trying to hold back the tears of pride that I feel for this incredible young man.

His three younger sisters sit on the floor in front of us, all holding hands as we wait impatiently.

Rylee comes out of the kitchen, laughing. "You guys are a sight," she says, coming to stand next to me.

I pull her down onto the couch and grab her hand. "What if Arizona takes him? I don't want him to go there. Or Washington. Anywhere else but those two."

Everyone knows I despise both of the teams we lost the World Series to when I was playing. I look down at the ring I got from the one we did win. I wonder if Stryker will wear such a ring someday.

Then I look at my wife. She's still one of the two most beautiful women I've ever seen. She gave me three gorgeous daughters. And when our third girl was born, Rylee insisted on naming her Tara. By chance, our first two daughters were named Nina and Ana. When Rylee realized it, she said she wanted to honor the first woman I loved by spelling out Nat's name with the first letters of our daughters' names.

She never ever lets me forget the two I lost. And I love her for it more than she will ever know.

And as much as I want Stryker to follow in my footsteps professionally, the one thing I truly wish for him is that he find a woman like his mother. If he can do that, it's better than winning the World Series; more rewarding than pitching a perfect game.

"Oh, come on," Rylee says. "You know you want the Hawks to take him. You want it so badly you can taste it."

"Shhhh," Ana says. "They are starting up again."

The MLB commissioner takes the podium. "For the third selection of the MLB draft, the Arizona Diamondbacks select the center fielder from James Madison High School, Nelson Menendez."

I breathe a sigh of relief.

"Dad. It's fine," Stryker says. "If Washington picks me, I'll ask to be traded."

Then I watch as he shakes his head and mouths *'No I won't'* to his sisters as they laugh.

Rylee squeezes my hand. I lean over and whisper to her. "I've waited my whole life for this moment."

"I know you have."

A few minutes later, when the commissioner takes the stage again to announce the first pick for the Hawks, I get up, needing to pace behind the couch because I have too much nervous energy. Rylee's right, I want this so badly. I want his story to be the same as mine, but also different. I've done everything I can to protect him all these years. And now he's going out into the world.

Rylee comes up behind me, putting her arms around me. "He'll be okay, Brady. He'll be okay wherever he goes. He's just like his father. He's strong, resilient, loving. He's *you*."

"He's *us*," I say, pulling her around to kiss her forehead.

"For the fourth selection of the MLB draft, the New York Nighthawks pick the right-handed pitcher from the University of Florida, Stryker Taylor."

Sawyer's book is the next in the series

Stealing Sawyer

Acknowledgements

Benching Brady was both fun and heart-wrenching for me to write. While I love writing about bad boys who become good guys, his journey was painful. Brady had so many redeeming qualities. I'm glad Rylee could finally get him back in the game – in every sense.

I couldn't have written this book without the help of physical therapist extraordinaire, Adam Schoenberg, and athletic trainer, Dylan Wiedeman. I appreciate you both answering my endless questions about Brady's injury and recovery.

Many thanks to baseball coach and former MLB player, Talmadge "T" Nunnari, and minor-league player, Spencer Herrmann, who helped me with the many baseball details.

None of this would be possible without my beta readers, Joelle Yates, Laura Conley and Tammy Dixon. You keep me honest, you help fix my mistakes, and you make my books quality reads.

Much appreciation to my hard-working editors, Ann Peters and Jeannie Hinkle, who work tirelessly to make sure my indie novels can rival traditionally-published ones.

And lastly, thank you to my Sweethearts. The daily love and encouragement from my private reader group on Facebook keeps me motivated.

About the author

Samantha Christy's passion for writing started long before her first novel was published. Graduating from the University of Nebraska with a degree in Criminal Justice, she held the title of Computer Systems Analyst for The Supreme Court of Wisconsin and several major universities around the United States. Raised mainly in Indianapolis, she holds the Midwest and its homegrown values dear to her heart and upon the birth of her third child devoted herself to raising her family full time. While it took time to get from there to here, writing has remained her utmost passion and being a stay-at-home mom facilitated her ability to follow that dream. When she is not writing, she keeps busy cruising to every Caribbean island where ships sail. Samantha Christy currently resides in St. Augustine, Florida with her husband and four children.

You can reach Samantha Christy at any of these wonderful places:

Website: www.samanthachristy.com

Facebook: https://www.facebook.com/SamanthaChristyAuthor

Twitter: @SamLoves2Write

E-mail: samanthachristy@comcast.net

Printed in Great Britain
by Amazon

17275056R00230